Paranormal and Loving it!

Allyson Lindt, Sofia Grey, Sotia Lazu

This book is a work of fiction.

While reference might be made to actual historical events or existing locations, the names, characters, places and incidents are either the product of the author's imagination or are used fictitiously, and any resemblance to actual persons, living or dead, business establishments, events, or locales is entirely coincidental.

Manufactured in the United States of America
Acelette Press

Table of Contents

Dreaming of a Wolf, A Snowdonia

Wolves Novella by Sofia Grey

Alun was Olivia's first, and he was supposed to be her forever. After a tragic accident steals him away, Olivia wonders how she can ever be whole again.

When he starts talking to her in her dreams, she has to ask herself: is she going mad with grief, or is there still a chance for their forever?

Chapter One

Alun was my first, and I thought he would be my forever. Then he was taken from me.
This is our story.

It just seemed so fucking unfair. It should have been pouring down, with heavy grey clouds, and an arctic wind swirling dead leaves around our ankles. We should have huddled under umbrellas, our tears obscured by rain. Instead, there was brilliant sunshine. Birds sang, children played in a nearby park, and lovers held hands and kissed by the pond.

Everything carried on as normal.

The vicar rumbled on, switching to Welsh and producing even more tears from Alun's family. A small girl toddled forward, and peered into the hole that had been torn in the ground. She held a crumpled bunch of flowers, and tossed them on top of his coffin, before running back to her mother—one of Alun's sisters.

The sun continued to beat down, but I tugged my coat closer around me. Even on this absurdly hot autumn day, I was frozen. I didn't think I'd ever be warm again.

Alun was only twenty-one. We shouldn't be putting his remains in the ground. He should be standing here now, chattering about obscure bands he'd seen in the pub, whistling out of key, and tangling his fingers with mine. Kissing me. Reminding me, in his seductive, lilting voice, how I'd marry him one day. How he'd keep asking until I gave in.

I'd only been to one funeral before this, for my grandfather, and that was a few years ago. I'd been an awkward, gangly teenager, subdued by the grief that surrounded me. I'd barely known my dad's father, and so I'd kept quiet and stared at the ground a lot.

Now I wondered if everyone in the village had turned out for this. How well Alun had been loved. There must have been thirty from our combined group of University friends, and many faces I recognized from family gatherings. His family all shared his brilliant blue eyes, an unearthly shade that almost glowed at night. I'd wondered if our children, one day, would share those eyes too.

Standing beside me, Tom wrapped an arm around my shoulders and turned my head into his chest. "It's okay," he whispered. "Let it go."

I'd been crying silently, and the tears continued to fall, slow and steady, blotted by his shirt.

Somebody stroked a gentle circle on my back. Probably Luce, Tom's girlfriend.

"You *are* coming to the pub with us?" Yes, it was Luce. She and Tom had welcomed me into their circle with open arms, even though the only thing we had in common was Alun. They'd grown up with him in this picture postcard village in deepest Snowdonia.

His voice rang in my head. His laugh as he tried to coax me to wrap my Manchester tongue around the complicated Welsh syllables. "It's not Tanygrisiau, it's Tan-na-*grish*-eye."

I'd never hear that voice again, unless he visited my dreams. In the shock and numbness that followed the news about his death, I'd stopped dreaming. Completely. For most of the last four years, since we first kissed on that long ago summer holiday, I'd dreamed of him almost every night. We'd have long, playful conversations and kiss and make love. God. The dreams had been so real.

When I'd told him about them, he flashed me a smug grin, those gorgeous blue eyes twinkling, and told me, "We're a bit psychic in my family. How d'you know they're not real?"

I'd scoffed, of course. Even though it was odd how things I swore we only talked about in dreams, he somehow remembered too.

With a start, I realized the crowd had thinned, and just a handful of us stood beside the grave.

Alun's mum came and hugged me. "I can't face going to the pub, so we're going home instead. Do come and see me before you leave."

I nodded, unable to find the words to reply. I wasn't sure I could face the wake either.

****

In the end, I just wanted to be by myself. I'd given my apologies, taken a cab back to the nearest town with a mainline rail station, and caught the first train that went anywhere near Manchester.

Many hours later, I arrived home, to the place I grew up. Since finishing at University, I'd moved all my stuff back here, but it'd only been intended as a temporary stop. Alun and I were looking for somewhere together.

I pressed my fists into my temples. We *had been* looking. This was going to take some getting used to.

3

It was Mum's turn to hug me. My parents had offered to accompany me, but it was something I needed to do on my own. All I wanted to do now was sleep, and hope to dream of him again.

Chapter Two

I squeezed my eyes tight shut, and focused on Alun. If I held him in my thoughts when I fell asleep, I might dream of him. Instead, I dived into a memory of the day we met.

Tansy's parents had rented a cottage in St Ives, a bustling and colorful seaside town in Cornwall. At the last minute, they'd been unable to go. It didn't take much for Tansy, my then-best friend, to persuade me. With my High School exams behind me, and a fine art degree course at St Andrews beckoning, I was happy to take a two-week holiday with my school friends. Jools came too, and Brigitte—a stunning blonde Swede—and we vowed to make this a holiday to remember.

The drive from Manchester, in peak summer traffic, was tedious. We were tired, frazzled, and grumpy after spending six hours crammed into Tansy's small car. Jools and I were dispatched to find food, while the others made up the beds and unpacked. We were just a few minutes' walk from the sea, and that was where we headed, when we found a café about to close for the day, right on the waterfront.

Standing out front, a striped apron tied around

his slim waist, was the most delicious guy I'd ever seen. Shaggy light brown hair fell to his collar in messy abandon, and white teeth gleamed in a friendly smile, but it was his eyes that drew me.

I studied art, and knew more than a little about painting, but I couldn't come up with a color to adequately describe his eyes. Cerulean blue perhaps? The shade of the Aegean Sea on a postcard of Greece? Darker than sapphire, bluer than lapis lazuli, they twinkled at us both as we stared at this vision of godliness.

"We're just closing, but I could get you a takeout." His voice had an equally delicious lilting Welsh accent. I clutched Jools's arm. He could have been reciting a shopping list; I still would have hung on every word.

He grinned, and ran a hand through his hair, the multiple string bracelets on his wrist shifting as he did. "Or maybe you're in need of a drink. I'll be finished here in ten minutes, if you don't mind waiting, and then we could go to the pub. We can sit outside, and watch the sun go down over the sea."

"Food," muttered Jools, and I shook myself into action.

I longed to say *pub*, but Tansy and Brigitte were waiting for us. "A takeout?" My voice came out croaky, and I probably sounded stupid, but he continued to smile as though we were the nicest things he'd seen all day. The idea of sitting somewhere and watching the sunset with him was too tempting for words. "Our friends are waiting, you see."

"Maybe the pub later?"

I shoved my hands in my pockets, and tried to look nonchalant. "Maybe."

His smile grew wider. Wiping his hands on his apron first, he pointed to a grey stone building farther along the waterfront. "The Old King. Meet me there in an hour? Are you here on holiday?"

My brain was slow to process his words, and I scrambled to reply. "Yes, we're renting a cottage. There're four of us."

"I'll bring some friends too." Was that a dimple that flashed in his cheek?

"Pinch me now," I whispered to Jools. "I must be dreaming."

I must have been louder than I thought, for he snorted with laughter. "I think you must be hungry. Let me get you fish and chips now, and then we can have dessert in the pub."

I knew that once he clapped eyes on Brigitte, he'd forget me, and so I basked in his attention while I had it. Jools and I perched at the counter inside, while he sweet-talked the chef into cooking for us, fixed us tall glasses of iced coffee, and found us some chocolate chip cookies to nibble while we waited.

It was only as we left, laden with hot food, that I realized we hadn't swapped names.

****

The insistent buzzing of my phone dragged me out of my memories, and back to the new Alun-less reality. With a huge measure of reluctance, I answered.

It was Luce, and from the slurring in her voice, she was very drunk. "Why didn't you stay, Livvy?"

I fumbled for the right words, and tripped over them. "I couldn't face it." Like a wounded animal, I'd sought refuge in a safe place. "I'm sorry."

"He loved you so much, Livvy. So much." I heard a muffled sob, and my heart ached even more. "You were his Mate and he was lucky to find you." The raw grief in her voice threatened what remained of my composure.

"His soulmate, you mean? I always thought that."

"His *what*?" Luce paused, and then muttered something under her breath.

"Sorry, didn't quite catch that."

"Oh, shit. You didn't know." The words rattled out of her, rapid and shaky. "I thought… Fuck. Forget I said that. His soulmate, yeah."

"What did you mean, Luce?"

I heard a muffled rustling sound, and then Tom spoke. "Hey. Don't pay any attention to Luce. She's talking rubbish. I'm taking her home now." His tone softened. "Don't be a stranger, Livvy. Come back and see us soon."

I made a non-committal noise, and hung up to stare blankly at the ceiling again. Luce was a lawyer. Being clear on details could have been her mantra, so what had she been talking about? What didn't I know about Alun that maybe he should have told me?

Chapter Three

I lay on my side in bed, facing Alun, knees bent, our hands linked between us. He was cooking up some mischief, I was sure. The devilish glint in his eyes was usually a precursor to some wild idea. Driving twenty miles in the darkness of very early morning to watch the sun rising from a particular hill top. Throwing clothes and toiletries into a backpack for an impromptu weekend hike. Kite flying on a windy beach.

I'd never been so impulsive before I met him, or as bold.

He squeezed my fingers. *Here we go.* "You *are* going to marry me, aren't you, Olivia Tanner?"

He asked me every time we got together, and I couldn't help giggling. "You know I am, but not yet. We graduate first, figure out where we're going to live, and *then* we get married." I rubbed my knees against his, and watched a smile spread across his face. "What's the rush?"

"You're my Mate, *Cariad.*" The Welsh endearment sounded beautiful the way it rolled from his tongue. "I'm impatient to share my life with you."

I blinked, and he was gone. My heart skittered,

and I took a rapid breath. *Had I been asleep?*

Cautious, I stretched out one hand to where he'd been lying. The sheets were cold. He'd looked real. Felt as alive as he always had. *You're my Mate.* I'd never heard him call me that before.

I buried my face in the pillow, and clung to it with both hands. The conversation with Luce must have been playing on my mind. I'd have to call her later. Fears assaulted me. What was I going to do without him? How would I fill my days? He was meshed into my life so tightly. I couldn't just untangle him and move on, even if I wanted to.

For the first time in my adult life, I had no direction, and it terrified me. Everything had been planned out—with Alun. He didn't want to live too far from Wales, and so we'd been looking at Bristol for jobs. I had another interview lined up next week—or was it this week? I'd have to reschedule. I was in no fit state to sit an interview.

****

A week later, I perched on a hard chair in my doctor's examining room. "I can't sleep." I stared at the sunshine pouring through the window, and remembered the funeral. "I just lie there and stare at the ceiling. I don't think I've slept properly since..." I swallowed. "Since two weeks ago."

My doctor had known me since childhood. He sat back in his chair, and steepled his fingers together. "I'm not prescribing sleeping pills. Not just yet, anyway. Have you tried warm milk at bedtime? Chamomile tea? A little yoga in the evening?"

"Yes, yes, and yes." It felt as though my eyes were filled with grit; they were so tired.

"It's only been two weeks." His voice was

sympathetic. "It must have been a huge shock."

I wrapped my arms around myself. It was still too painful to think about.

He carried on. "Any nightmares?"

"No." You needed to be able to sleep, to have nightmares.

"I can give you a referral, if you'd like to talk to someone."

I didn't want to talk. I just wanted to sleep. If I slept, I might be able to dream of Alun.

****

Hot breath flashed over my neck, and a familiar hand closed around my breast. I knew with a pang that it was a dream, but I'd make the most of every second, just to be with him again.

"*Cariad*," he murmured, his voice vibrating against my skin. His thumb brushed my aching nipple, and I moaned, aroused just from that brief touch.

"Let me turn around," I mumbled. "Want to kiss you."

"Nope. Stay there." He slid his hand across my stomach, skirted my hipbone, and squeezed my butt. "You have the most gorgeous ass I've ever seen."

We were in bed, but I couldn't be sure *where*. When he nipped my ear and then licked away the sting, I realized I didn't care.

"I have to be inside you. I've missed you, baby." He nudged my thigh and bent my leg at the knee, gaining access to my pussy. "Jesus, you're so fuckin' wet already." Sometimes he teased me, but not tonight. He nuzzled my neck, and I arched my back, leaning into his caress. I was hungry too. His cock bumped my ass, and I tried to touch him, but he wouldn't let me.

My breasts yearned for his touch, and I wanted his mouth on mine. "Alun," I whispered.

In reply, he sank two fingers inside me, and I forgot how to speak. I think I cried out. I couldn't be sure. He groaned, and held me tighter, one hand pumping in me, the other holding my hip. Caging me.

"Now," I murmured.

"Now." He surged forward. His cock filled me in one deep, swift thrust. Holding my leg up, he kept me in position, and slowly pulled back, before gliding in again. I moaned, every nerve ending alight.

We'd stopped using condoms a while ago, when I went on the pill, but I still wasn't used to the feeling of heat from his naked dick. Pleasure radiated through me.

"Livs," he whispered, "you feel so good, baby." He continued to torture me, slowly pushing in, only to retreat, pause, and then ease back in on another slow glide. It was torment of the most delicious kind. "Touch yourself, *Cariad*."

I obeyed, my fingers grazing my clit, and making my insides clench even tighter.

"Oh, fuck." He groaned, and then shifted position a little. Thrusting deep, he finally sped up.

I rubbed my clit in time to his rhythm, and in moments, I balanced on a knife-edge. My stomach tightened, and every cell seemed to hold its breath, waiting for Alun.

"Now," he said, and sank his teeth into the tender flesh of my shoulder.

"Alun," I cried, and opened my eyes.

Sunlight flooded the room. I was alone in bed.

Chapter Four

Tom rang me, but I let it drop to voicemail. I sat at Mum's kitchen table, a mug of cold coffee and an untouched bowl of cereal in front of me. I'd slept a little, and finally dreamed of Alun, only to wake far too soon.

My phone jangled again, and when I continued to ignore it, it beeped with a message from Tom.

Livvy. The public inquiry starts in 2 weeks, in London. Will you come with us?

I shrank away from the prospect of sitting through a public investigation into the tragedy, but Mum had read the screen over my shoulder. "It might be a good idea. It could start to give you some closure."

"I don't want closure. I just want him back."

She hugged me from behind. "I know, love. But until you accept it, you can't begin to grieve properly."

I considered it. "But it doesn't feel as though he's dead." I pressed my hand to my heart. "Not in here. I dreamed about him last night, and it felt real." My neck stung a little, as though he'd really bitten me, and I could swear I ached between my legs.

"We'll come with you to London. You know

that."

"Yeah, thanks." I felt exhausted just thinking about it. "I'm going back to bed for a bit."

I hadn't bothered dressing, and so I slid between the covers and buried my face in the pillow. Taking a deep breath, I paused, and then sniffed the soft white fabric. It smelled faintly of Alun, the distinctive pine forest fragrance he carried on his skin. He joked about spending his childhood running wild in the Snowdonia mountains, and how it was part of his DNA.

I had to be going crazy. He hadn't been here, to Mum's, for months.

"Alun," I whispered, "why did you go and leave me?"

With my eyes tightly shut, and his fragrance in my nostrils, I pretended I felt his hands squeezing the tension out of my shoulders.

"I didn't, baby. I'm still here." His voice filled my mind. This wouldn't be the first time I'd had an imaginary conversation with him.

"I wish you were. I don't want to carry on without you."

"I *am* still here. You don't shake me off that easily."

Tears welled, but I wouldn't let them fall. "I keep thinking about everything we were going to do. All the places we planned to go."

He chuckled in my head. "Which first, eh? India or South America?"

It was an old debate, and I felt a smile emerge, unbidden. "Neither. It's New York first, or Venice."

"Or New Zealand."

I felt myself drifting in that almost-asleep space, and I welcomed it. Alun's hands continued to soothe me, and I relaxed. "Why not Australia?"

"I've got a friend in New Zealand. We grew up

14

together, but he lives in Wellington now."

Sleep beckoned, deep and dark and all consuming. "I don't want you to be gone when I wake up."

He pressed a hot kiss to my nape. "I'm not going anywhere without you, *Cariad*."

****

Sunlight filtered through green leaves in a dense canopy above me. I lay on soft, springy grass, staring up at patches of blue between the treetops. Water splashed nearby, and birds called and chirruped all around. It was the definition of tranquility, and I stayed there a moment longer, absorbing all the different sensations. My dreams were getting more lifelike every day.

I knew Alun was here, and I smiled. "Where are we?"

"Swallow Falls. Have you been here before?"

That was the water I could hear. "No." I sat up and looked around, finding him right away. He leaned against a nearby tree, bare chested and barefoot, hands in the pockets of his jeans, and a huge grin on his face.

"Let me show you." He held out a hand, and pulled me up, tugging me into his arms. "I used to come here when I was a kid."

I slid my arms around his neck and inhaled his scent, holding it deep in my lungs. So familiar. So good. "Why are you only half dressed?" His chest was warm, as it always was, and I buried my nose in the base of his throat.

"There was something else I wanted to show you, but it can wait," he said. "Come and see the falls."

With our fingers tangled together, he led me along a narrow path, to emerge from the trees onto a grassy ledge. The sound of the water had grown louder with every step, and now it rushed and roared, making speech impossible.

Alun stood behind me, arms wrapped around my waist, his chin resting on my shoulder, as I gazed down. It was breathtaking. Far below, the waterfall raged in a torrent, pouring over rocks and boulders, filling and re-filling pools, and then smashing into the river at the bottom. Droplets of water vapor hung in the air in little rainbows.

"It's beautiful," I shouted, and felt his chuckle against my skin.

"So are you." He kissed my neck. "I used to come here with Sasha and Tammy. We were little hell raisers."

"Who?" He didn't reply, and so I wriggled free and turned to face him. "I said, who are Sasha and Tammy?"

I spoke into thin air, the sudden silence making my heart judder. I was in bed again. When I rubbed my eyes, my face was damp. As though I'd just been standing near a waterfall.

Chapter Five

The crowds in London were terrifying. I was swept along with Tom and Luce, as we struggled to make our way into the hotel they were using for the public inquiry into the accident. I'd never been claustrophobic before, but it was now a distinct possibility. I'd persuaded Mum and Dad to stay home, and I wished I'd stayed there too.

Cameras flashed, video recorders hummed, and journalists darted through the crowd, talking to people, and searching for stories. Meanwhile, a body of official-looking people sat at a table, facing the crowd. A man in the center stood and fiddled with his tie, waiting for the audience to quiet.

Someone jostled me from behind, and I missed the guy's opening words. This was worse than being in the mosh pit at a rock concert. The acoustics were terrible, and even when I tried to concentrate, I could only make out half of what the investigators said. After twenty minutes of being barged into, and having my feet trodden on a dozen times, I pushed my way to the exit. I'd meet the others later.

Why had I come today?

When I'd dreamed of Alun last night, he'd urged me to come to London. We'd been standing at the top of a mountain, so high it felt as though I could touch the ravens that surfed through the air above us. Another of his favorite places, he'd said.

Perhaps my brain was cycling through all the places he'd said he loved, as it tried to accustom me to the idea that he was gone.

When I reached the end of the list, would I stop dreaming about him?

I shoved *that* thought away, and wandered down the streets. The weather was foul, a typical wet November, but it suited my mood. Settled inside a warm café, and nursing a mug of hot chocolate, I sent Luce a text to tell her where to find me.

The newspapers all carried the story of the rail inquiry. I wouldn't be able to escape it today.

I didn't even know why Alun had been on that particular underground train. He'd been in Brighton for a guys' weekend, drinking and partying with some of his friends, in advance of one of them getting married. We'd spoken on the phone, and he'd texted me. On that particular Sunday, he should have been catching a train to Manchester to meet me, not crossing London on the Tube.

Phil, the distraught groom-to-be, said Alun had left Brighton before the others, because he had an errand to run. London was an hour away by train, and Alun should have changed there for a connection to Manchester. Instead of waiting at Euston station though, he'd been miles away in East London. Why?

The last text I had was as he'd left Brighton. He said he was too old for all-night parties, and was going to sleep on the journey home. There was no mention of any errand.

Tom and Luce arrived, and sank into the free

seats at my table. Luce was pale, her face tight and drawn, and Tom's hands shook. "Fuck this," he muttered. "I need a real drink. Let's find a pub."

Half an hour later, with cheap Tequila shots lined up, I asked about the initial findings from the official inquiry.

"They've no idea." Tom gazed into space, his eyes unfocused. "They know one train managed to drive into the back of another, but they've no explanation why it burst into flames. They're electric fucking trains. It's not like they're carrying gallons of diesel, or anything flammable."

"They think it was a suicide bomber," whispered Luce.

I gulped down my shot, and reached for the next. Tequila was our preferred option for getting drunk quickly, and I wanted to blot everything out as fast as humanly possible.

Nobody said anything, and we all knocked back another shot. It was weird, but in some ways, I felt closer to Alun here than I had at home. Was that because he'd died here?

The liquor seared the back of my throat, and I gulped another shot.

Tom had arranged hotel rooms for us, and we headed there in a taxi. I'd never ride the underground again. Oblivion beckoned, but I remembered a question I'd meant to ask earlier.

"Who're Sasha and Tammy?" I wasn't slurring too badly.

Tom frowned at me. "They're friends of Alun. Distant relatives, I think."

"Were they at the funeral?"

"Yeah." Luce had passed out already, and was safely tucked into Tom's side. He stroked her hair, and then glanced back at me. "Didn't you meet them?"

I thought about it. "No."

"Why d'you ask?"

"Alun mentioned them."

"Yeah? He was close to Sasha when they were little, but I don't know him that well."

The cab sped around a corner, and I gripped the seat to avoid sliding into the sleeping Luce. I thought back to my dream. Had Alun mentioned them to me some time, and I'd only just remembered them? "He said they were hell-raisers."

Tom grunted, a brief smile flashing over his face. "They were. My mum told me tales of what they got up to." He stared out the window at the night flashing by, and I followed his gaze. Alun felt closer than ever, and I wondered where we were. Was this near the crash site? No. That had been on the way out of the city.

I leaned across, and touched Tom's arm. His attention snapped to me.

"Where are we?" I asked.

He looked outside again. "Near Covent Garden. Our hotel is just a few streets away."

Alun had never mentioned going here. In all our conversations about London, I didn't recall it ever being mentioned. I rubbed my gritty eyes, frustrated. Not content to dream about him, and to hold long conversations in my head with him, I now imagined my dead lover was close by.

The Tequila had to be to blame. Either that, or I was going mad.

Chapter Six

The Tequila had been a mistake. I awoke to a pounding head, and a taste like old socks in my mouth. Exhaustion swamped me. I wanted nothing more than to pull the covers over my head and never move again, but then I heard Alun's voice.

"Livs." I lifted weary lids to see him sitting cross-legged on the bed next to me, fully dressed, and with a familiar teasing grin on his face. "At last. I've been waiting for you."

"You have?"

"We don't have long, and I need to show you something."

I hid a yawn. "Okay."

"Come on, sleepy." He held out a hand, and wriggled his fingers. His smile was irresistible, making me remember our first date and how entranced I'd been. The pub in Cornwall. We'd drunk local beer, and watched the sun setting over the harbor, with Alun claiming a place next to me.

My mind jumped back to Alun watching me, his head cocked slightly to one side. "You coming?"

"Of course." I clasped his hand, and just like

that, we were somewhere else. Open countryside, soft grass underfoot, and mountains surrounding us. Tilting my head, I looked up to see a brilliant blue sky, the sun blazing down. Like all my dreams with Alun, it could have been real. Birds called, and sheep bleated in the distance.

"Wales?" I asked.

"Snowdonia." He gave my fingers a quick squeeze, before releasing me. He stepped back, shoved both hands into his pockets, and gazed at me, a hint of a smile tugging at his lips. "You trust me, don't you, Livs?"

"Of course."

"And if I asked you to keep something a secret, to tell nobody at all, you'd agree?"

I'd promise you anything, if it would keep you with me. "Yes."

He dragged his T-shirt over his head, and dropped it on the grass. Holding up a hand to stop me from interrupting, he popped the button on his jeans.

I had to smile. "We're going to have hot monkey sex in this field?"

"Later." He slid the zipper down slowly, his eyes molten. "There's something you need to know first."

As always, Alun went commando. I'd never seen him wearing underwear. I watched, amused, as he kicked off his sneakers and then dropped his jeans to the ground and stepped out of them. What was he up to? With Alun, you never knew what to expect.

I didn't expect him to vanish before my eyes.

A shimmer of rainbow sparkles filled the space where he stood, clearing rapidly to show a huge dog in his place. *Holy shit.* I clasped a hand over my mouth, before I screeched. My heart galloped, and I forgot how to breathe.

It's just a dream.

The dog cocked his head slightly to one side. It was unlike any dog I'd seen before, from the brilliant blue eyes, to the ruff of paler fur that ringed its face. If I had to guess, it looked like a wolf. A nervous giggle escaped me. I'd watched too many horror movies.

"Okay, babe." My voice wavered. "Joke over. Where are you?"

The wolf stared at me, its mouth opening into a wide doggy grin. The beast then flopped to the grass, lay on its back, and whined.

What the fuck?

My feet could have been glued to the ground. There was no way, dream or no dream, that I was going to rub its belly. Its teeth were vicious. If it turned on me, I had no chance. I sucked in a rapid breath, and forced myself to move. To take a step back. *Keep watching it. Keep eye contact.* I liked dogs, always had, but this one was scary.

The beast lifted its head, and scrambled to his feet, to dissolve into another rainbow shimmer. What the fuck was next? A bloodthirsty vampire to chase me? I took another step backward, ready to flee. I didn't like this dream, and it was definitely time to wake up.

When I thought my heart was going to leap out of my chest, the shimmering mist cleared to show Alun, wearing nothing but a delectable grin. "Hey, you." He strolled toward me, as though everything were perfectly normal.

I sucked in a jagged breath and pointed at him. "That was you? You just changed into a *dog*?"

"A wolf." He stopped a couple paces from me, a smile playing across his face. "And we call it shifting."

"We?"

"Yeah. There're a few of us." He rubbed the back of his neck, and looked uncomfortable for a

23

second. "I was supposed to wait until we married, but I need you to understand."

The man I'd planned to marry was a werewolf? My heart hammered.

I glanced up at the sun arcing high across the sky. "Is it full moon?" I whispered.

This drew a delighted laugh. Alun covered the distance, caught my hand, and tugged me down to sit on the grass with him. "It doesn't matter about the moon. I'm not a werewolf." He tangled our fingers together, and looked at me expectantly.

"Can you read my mind now?"

"Not as such."

Just a dream. It was getting harder to hold onto that thought. I focused on what he'd just said. "What am I thinking now?"

"Hmm." He leaned forward, and placed his free hand on my chest. "You're thinking about how freaked out you are, and wondering if you're going to turn into a wolf too, since I've bitten you."

Fuck. That hadn't occurred to me. My heart hammered faster. "Am I?" It came out as a squeak.

His brows dipped, and the teasing smile disappeared. "If I said yes, how upset would you be?"

"*What*?" The word escaped on a gasp. Before I went into total panic meltdown, I saw he was trying hard not to smile. I managed a breath with lungs that had forgotten their basic function, and he flopped back onto the grass, pulling me with him.

He shook with laughter, great huge howls producing tears of mirth. I tumbled on top of his very naked body and just stared. The truth sank in. He'd been teasing. "You... You..." I groped for something smart to say, "That wasn't funny."

"Oh, baby, it was fuckin' hilarious." He gently cupped my face in both hands. "I'm sorry." He sounded anything but. "I shouldn't have done that, but I couldn't resist. Showing you my wolf side—it's a once in a lifetime thing, you know."

"No, I don't know." Weak with relief, I felt bizarrely comfortable sprawled on top of him in the soft grass.

"We Mate for life, *Cariad*." His voice softened to a husky growl. "I only get to tell you once."

Someone else had called Alun my *Mate*, but right now I couldn't remember who. Lying so close to him again was more than I could resist. I clung to him, burying my face in the base of his throat, and inhaling his pine-forest fragrance. "Alun, baby, I miss you so much."

"I'll be back soon, with your help, Livs." He encased me in his arms, and held me tight. Even when he was playing the fool, I always felt safe with him.

"I wanted to talk to Sasha. To see how he told Megan, his girlfriend." Alun dropped tiny kisses on my hair. "She didn't take it too well—thought she'd turn into a werewolf."

"Which is where you got the idea of scaring me?"

He chuckled, the vibration rumbling through me. "I think of it more as research."

Now the initial shock had worn off, I knew it was just my mind playing games. People didn't turn into dogs. Or wolves. I yawned and closed my eyes, determined to enjoy this cuddle while he was here. I knew from experience that these dreams, while vividly real, only lasted a short time, and I felt myself tumbling into deeper sleep.

"Livs, baby"—Alun's voice held an urgent ring—"talk to Sasha. He can help."

Chapter Seven

Talk to Sasha. I didn't even *know* Sasha. I'd probably met him briefly at the funeral, but that wasn't enough to seek him out, and even if I did, what the hell would I say to him?

Alun had been so insistent.

Alun was dead.

Every cell in my body screamed that he was still alive.

I wandered aimlessly, while Tom and Luce were out, and found myself in a tiny café close to Covent Garden. Just as I had yesterday, I felt oddly close to Alun here. I didn't know London well, and to my knowledge, he'd not spent much time here either. I pressed my fingers into my forehead, and gazed blindly at the coffee I'd ordered.

Was I going mad?

The newspapers littering the café counter all carried headlines from the inquiry. *Bomb terror on the Tube. Death toll rises, and some victims may never be identified*

The fire that swept through Alun's carriage had been so intense, some of the passengers had been reduced to ash. The usual identification methods had been useless.

I took a sip of almost cold coffee, and forced back a rising tide of nausea. I should be attending the inquiry with Tom and Luce, but if I couldn't even cope with the newspaper headlines, there was no way I could listen to the details.

Wait a minute.

There'd been almost nothing left of Alun or the backpack he'd have been carrying, but jammed underneath a metal briefcase, they'd retrieved the remains of his wallet. His credit card and travel pass, while badly damaged, were clear enough to read.

That, combined with his silence, and his last known position, made us all believe he was on the train, but what if we were wrong?

The breath caught in my lungs. What if it wasn't Alun carrying his wallet? It might have been found by someone. Stolen even. If they'd identified the wrong guy, Alun might still be alive.

Hope flooded through me, washed away quickly by common sense. Alun would have told us if he'd been robbed. He wouldn't have dropped off the face of the earth.

Jesus. I was really grasping at straws.

For the rest of the day, as I walked in slow circles around that part of London, I couldn't get the idea out of my head that it might not have been him on the train. I waited eagerly for Tom and Luce to reappear, and then we all went to another bar. I avoided Tequila this time, though, and stuck with water.

They picked at a bowl of tired looking peanuts, and shared the little they'd learned. Security measures. Eyewitness statements. Other meaningless, useless words floated around in the air. I waited until they ground to a halt, and then leaned forward on our small, sticky table.

They looked at me expectantly, as I groped for the right words. "What if he's still alive?"

After a long, painful moment, Tom and Luce glanced at each other, and then Tom sighed. "Livvy, believe me, I know how you feel. Alun was like a brother to me, and if there were the slightest chance he was still alive, I'd be knocking on doors and demanding answers."

"We saw pictures of the carriage." Tears glistened in Luce's eyes. "Livvy, nobody could survive that."

"How do we know he was on the train?" I rushed on before they could interrupt. "By his credit card. It might have been stolen."

"In that case, where is he?" Tom's words were harsh. He blinked. "Sorry, but we've been over this—me and Luce. He wouldn't just vanish. If his gear was nicked, he'd phone. He'd let us know."

"It's been weeks," added Luce. "If he'd been mugged, even if he'd been hurt, we'd know."

"He wasn't supposed to be on that train, or even on the Tube." Now I'd gotten the idea, I wasn't letting it go. "He was *supposed* to be at Euston Station, but maybe he went somewhere else first."

They exchanged another loaded glance, before Luce touched my hand. "What makes you think this now?"

My dead lover has convinced me he's still alive? No, maybe not.

"I don't know." I adored Luce and Tom, trusted them implicitly, but trying to convince them I'd been talking to Alun in my sleep smacked of crazy. "The evidence, it's just not conclusive, is it?"

"It's circumstantial," murmured Luce, the lawyer. "But it's compelling, since we have nothing else to go on."

"What about Sasha? If I wanted to talk to Sasha, did you say he lives in New Zealand?"

"Yeah." Tom was hesitant, a worried furrow digging into his brow. "What can Sasha add?"

Alun wants me to talk to him. Nope, that pushed me firmly into crazy territory again, so I improvised. "He was talking to Sasha that day."

Tom's frown deepened. "I thought you didn't know who he was."

I made a vague gesture with my hand. "I forgot the name; that's all. So if I wanted to talk to him, do you have his phone number?"

Luce kept darting anxious looks at me, and Tom was clearly worried, but he came up with Sasha's phone number. "They're eleven hours ahead of us at the moment."

I stared at my phone, and shuffled numbers in my head. "So it's early morning for them?"

He nodded.

I deliberated some more, and composed a text.

Hi, this is Olivia. I think we met at Alun's funeral, and I'd really like to talk to you. Please text or call me back. Any time is good. Thank you.

Chapter Eight

We were still in the pub when Sasha replied to my text.

FaceTime in 1 hour?

It gave me time to get back to the hotel, settle my nerves with some chamomile tea, and then get nervous again. I had no idea what I was going to say. Sitting cross legged on my bed, I made the call, and stared at the guy halfway around the world, on my screen.

Young and handsome, he had soft-looking dark hair, and the same brilliant blue eyes as Alun and most of his Welsh friends. Sasha ran a hand through his already rumpled hair, and then hid a yawn.

"Sorry. Late night with Megan and her brothers. I'm sure they're trying to kill me through alcohol poisoning." He flashed me a lopsided smile. "It's good to talk to you, Olivia. How are you doing?"

"I don't think we spoke at the funeral."

"There were a lot of people there."

Alun had trusted this man, if my dreams were to be believed. Then again, Alun also morphed into a wolf in my last dream of him. I stared at his childhood friend, and tried to pull some words together.

"Did you speak to Alun before he... Before the accident?"

He blinked, once, twice, and then a third time, before he replied. "Yes," he said eventually. "I gave him the address of an artist I know. He wanted to commission a piece of work." His mouth twisted. "That was the last time we spoke."

Out of everything I might have considered, I hadn't expected that. "An artist?"

Sasha gave an awkward one-shouldered shrug. "A jeweler. He has a little workshop near Leicester Square in London."

Why would Alun be getting a piece of jewelry commissioned? As though he'd read my mind, Sasha broke into my thoughts. "He wanted a special present for you."

"Oh." Warmth flooded my chest, and tears pricked my eyes. "That's where I am now. In London." I gazed at this man, so similar in appearance to my lover. "I feel closer to Alun here."

"I'll text you the address. Maybe check them out, in case he did order something?"

"Thanks." I didn't want to let him go just yet. Alun had talked about a different conversation. *Yeah, in my imagination.* I pressed on. "Was there anything else significant?"

Sasha's gaze sharpened, his eyes narrowing. "Significant?"

He was thousands of miles away, and I was unlikely to ever speak to him again. If I let a little of my crazy slip out, there wasn't much he could do. I took a rapid breath, my heart already thumping hard. "He told me about a conversation he had with you, when he asked how you told Megan." I studied his face. There was no flicker of recognition, but he stared back at me, alert and watchful. Like a hunting dog that had scented prey. "She thought she would turn into a werewolf."

Sasha was silent for an age. I was on the verge of caving in, and admitting it was all in my overactive imagination, but he finally cleared his throat. "When did he tell you this?"

"Oh my God, you really had that conversation?" I babbled with giddy relief. "I thought I imagined it."

"When did he tell you that, Olivia?"

"This morning. I dreamed about him. Well, I dream about him every night, but this one was different."

Sasha frowned. "Tell me what happened."

He wasn't laughing, or telling me I was insane. That was a good start.

"We went to somewhere in Snowdonia, and he...umm...took off his clothes. Then he turned into a dog in front of me. *A wolf.* And then he turned back, and we talked." My cheeks burned, and I covered my mouth with my free hand. "Crazy, huh?"

"This morning? And he'd never done that before? I mean, you'd never dreamed anything like that before? Ever?"

"Never."

"Fuck." He leaned forward, his face filling the screen on my phone. "I don't know what to think. Is there any chance it wasn't Alun on the train? Any chance at all?"

The tiny spark of hope I'd been nurturing lifted its head and nodded. "That's what I think too. But how is he doing this?"

"We're a bit psychic. It's pretty common for us to share dreams."

"He talks to you in your dreams too?"

"What?" He snorted. "No, I mean with our— uh, partners. But that doesn't matter. He might still be

32

alive, Olivia. We have to find him."

He believed me. "Thank you. I thought I was going mad." The whole psychic dream-thing made no sense, but that wasn't important right now.

I drew in an unsteady breath, and considered the implications. "What can we do? If I go to the police, they'll just laugh."

"You're right." He screwed up his forehead. "When you talked in your dreams, did he give you any indication where he was?"

"No. Should I just ask him?"

"Definitely, although if he's not volunteered the information, he might not know."

This was surreal. I felt overwhelmed. I'd gone from believing Alun gone, to thinking I was losing my mind, and now to something even crazier. If he was still alive though, I'd do whatever it took to find him.

I wiped away the tears that trickled down my cheeks, and found a smile for Sasha. "What can we do?"

He shook his head. "I've no idea. I'm just... Yeah, I'm kinda blown away by this."

"I have to ask. What's the whole werewolf thing about?"

"Huh?" Sasha flashed me a grin that lit up his face. "It's a private joke. I guess he knew you'd get my attention with it."

Something didn't ring quite true, but I pushed it to the back of my mind. I had bigger things to think about.

Chapter Nine

I sent texts to Luce and Tom, asking them to come back to the hotel, and I braced myself to tell them of my conversation with Sasha. I needed help, and they were best placed to provide it.

It sounded too bizarre to ever be plausible.

We sat around the table in my room, and I haltingly relayed the conversation with Sasha. I wrapped my arms around myself, and took a deep breath when I'd finished. They'd think I was mad. I looked up to see tears in Luce's eyes.

"Oh, Livvy." Luce scrambled out of her seat and hugged me tight. "That's fantastic. You might be right."

What? My thoughts scrambled. "You believe me about the dreams?" I looked into Luce's blue eyes—absurdly bright, like Alun's, but with a hint of green. "Don't tell me. You're both a bit psychic too?"

Her laugh sounded choked. "You could say that. But now we have to figure out what to do." She squeezed my hand. "Let's work out some details."

Luce retrieved her laptop, and called up a map of the London Underground. "Right." She pointed to Euston, roughly in the middle. "It's not representative of positions above ground, but it's enough to work with. We know he arrived in Euston on the Brighton train, and we can guess what time that would be."

"Ten-ish in the morning," I added. "And we know he was supposed to arrive in Manchester at three oh-seven, because he asked me to pick him up at the station."

Luce frowned. "How long does it take from London to Manchester on the train? No more than three hours? He'd have two hours to wait in London."

"He told Sasha he was going somewhere near Leicester Square, so he must have planned to get there and back in plenty of time for his train." Tom gazed at the map. "Quickest way from Euston to Leicester Square?"

"Tube." Luce and I spoke together.

"Five minutes on the Underground," she continued. "It's only three stops on the Northern Line. We'll go to the jeweler's first thing tomorrow, to see if they remember him visiting."

"And then somehow"—Tom's voice was somber—"his wallet ended up miles away, in Bethnal Green."

Luce gazed intently at the map, and traced a line with her finger. "Bethnal Green is on the Central Line, which doesn't intersect with either Euston or Leicester Square. But"—she paused, a frown on her face—"it would only take you ten minutes to walk from Leicester Square to Holborn, which *is* on the Central Line."

Tom slung an arm around my shoulder, and gave me a squeeze. "I guess this all seems a bit strange," he said. "You need to ask Alun tonight if he can tell you where he is, what he remembers... That kind of thing."

A bit strange. Yep, that was the understatement of the decade. If I stopped to think about the past day,

I'd go crazy. The changing-into-a-wolf trick. The message to talk with Sasha. The fact that Alun might still be alive, and actually talking to me in my dreams.

No. I could only focus on one thing at a time. Everything else could wait.

When I went to bed, I was eager and excited, and confident that I'd see Alun.

****

I jerked awake to a dimly lit room, my heart racing and palms damp, and I tried to figure what had woken me. *I thought I heard Alun call my name.* I rolled over, and there he was, in bed with me.

"Babe," I mumbled, clinging to my half-asleep state, and closing my eyes again.

"Livs?" Panic threaded his voice, and I forced tired eyelids open. "How...? What...? *Where* am I?" He lay beside me, his breathing uneven, and in the glow from the streetlights outside, I saw a sheen of perspiration on his face.

Of all the strange dreams, this was the weirdest. "In bed with me."

He swallowed hard. "This isn't real."

I knew it was just my brain creating a nightmare, stitching together snippets of horror from the previous day, but it felt real. I rolled closer, and wrapped my arms around him. "It's okay," I whispered. "I'm here."

Was I comforting him, or me? He was clammy, his body tense and unyielding.

"I'm here," I repeated.

I snuggled closer, and pressed my lips against his neck. Long moments later, I felt him sag, the tension leaching out of him. "Something's wrong," he whispered. "I don't know how much longer I can hang on, *Cariad*." I clung tighter, his words terrifying me. "Talk to me, Livs. Help me remember."

My throat was dry, but I whispered to him. "Our first time together. My first time ever." I paused and collected my thoughts. "You wanted to make it special, and so you booked a weekend away for us in the Lake District. I was intimidated by the hotel owner, and we pretended to be married." Why had the woman been so scary? Maybe it was just my being nervous about taking the leap into intimacy. I was eighteen, and quite old to still be a virgin according to my friends, but I wanted to wait for someone special.

"You sent me to take a bath, and you lit candles in the bedroom, only they set off the smoke alarms, and the hotel had to be evacuated. I was soaking wet, and wearing just a bathrobe. I had a fit of the giggles, and couldn't stop laughing while we waited outside. I'm sure the other guests thought I was deranged," I said.

Alun sighed and held me tight. "I fucked up, didn't I?"

"It was memorable."

"I was worried about hurting you."

He'd been so careful. Kissed every inch of my body, and teased me with his deft fingers until I'd come to pieces in his arms. My first real orgasm, and I'd been ready for more. "And I was worried about disappointing you."

"You could never disappoint me, *Cariad*." He nuzzled my shoulder, and scraped his teeth over the skin. "I left my mark on you."

I snorted with amusement. "Is that what you call it? You bit my neck. I'd never had a hickey before."

"I like to think I fucked you senseless first."

He had. I'd been loose-limbed and sated, before he even fitted a condom and entered me. All my nerves had been for nothing. "It was one of the best moments of my life," I said.

I expected to wake up any second and find myself alone, but after a long pause, his hands stilled. There was something important I had to tell him—to ask him—but I couldn't pull it out of my brain. As I clung to him, desperate to keep him with me, he sighed. The next moment, he was gone.

****

The weather was foul in the morning, as we all prepared to go see the jeweler. Even though the rush-hour traffic meant a cab would take forever, there was no way I'd venture underground, and go on the Tube. Luce pointed out gently that Alun probably hadn't been on the train at all, but the idea of being so far below the surface now freaked me out.

We climbed out of the cab, onto a busy side street, filled with small independent shops and studios. The jeweler was sandwiched between a leather shop and a tiny café—no more than a takeaway cart. I hesitated, ignoring the wind that whipped my hair, and the rain it carried.

This place might hold the key to Alun's disappearance. I was scared it might come to nothing.

"Come on." A bell jangled when Tom opened the door, and I followed him inside.

I stood transfixed when I saw the display cabinets.

The specialist study area for my degree—and my favorite art style—was Impressionism. I loved Monet's work in particular, and owned many reproductions of his paintings, but nothing like this. The artist here had recreated some of his famous images in stained glass. Water lilies. Lakes. Sunrises. Light and water spilling together in a multitude of exquisite variations.

The shopkeeper perched on a stool behind a messy counter covered with scraps of wire, pots of ink, and a stack of thick, cream cards. He smiled at us, his twinkling brown eyes set in a lined face. He could have been anywhere between forty and sixty, with close-cropped dark hair, and he looked friendly. "Can I help you?"

I glanced at Luce for support, and she nodded. "I hope so," I replied, stumbling over the words. "I believe my boyfriend may have bought something for me."

The guy raised one eyebrow. "And…?"

"And he's gone missing. We're trying to retrace his last known movements, and a friend thought he'd come here." Luce squeezed my arm in a little gesture of support. I gave her a grateful smile. "His name is Alun Jones. He would have been here on Monday the fifteenth of September, around lunchtime." I thrust my phone at the guy, and showed him the picture of Alun on my home screen. "This is him."

Chapter Ten

The shopkeeper frowned as he stared at my phone. "I remember him. Welsh lad?"

Relief made me dizzy for a second. "Yes."

"I think he ordered a jewelry box. One moment." His fingers flew across the keys of the laptop by his side, and then he smiled. "Your name would be...?"

"Olivia. I'm Olivia Tanner."

"I only finished it a few days ago. I left a voicemail for him to call me back, but I guess he didn't get it." The jeweler turned from the counter, and examined a shelf of items, before selecting a small white box. "This is it." He placed it on the counter. "Let me show you."

He opened the box and extracted the contents— a tissue wrapped item not much bigger than my cellphone. We all leaned forward.

"Oh." The breath caught in my throat. On the palm of his hand sat a tiny, shallow box, with a colored glass top. More of Monet's water lilies, in delicate shades of blue and green. *Olivia* was written in a curling script in one corner. "It's beautiful." My heart stuttered.

We *had* to find him.

Luce cleared her throat. "Well, at least we know he was here. Did he say anything about where he was going? I know it was ages ago, but do you remember anything? Please?"

The guy looked surprised. "Let's see. He was in here for about half an hour, while we looked through all the options and styles. He told me about his beautiful girlfriend, and how he hoped to persuade her to marry him soon." He slid the box onto my hand, and I gazed at it, dumbfounded. "It's yours," he said, "you should take it. It's fully paid for."

He looked back at Luce. "You said he's gone missing?" She nodded. "He said he was going to meet his girlfriend. I don't remember him mentioning anything else. I'm sorry."

We thanked him and headed outside, with the beautiful little box shoved deep inside my coat pocket. Had he planned it for a Christmas present?

Standing on the doorstep, my back to the driving rain, I realized I had no plan for what to do next.

Luce did. "Let's ask the other local shops, in case anyone saw him."

The little café next door was first. We had to wait a few minutes to be served, but as soon as we showed the waitress Alun's picture, she recognized him.

"It's him," she squealed. Her black apron was embroidered with the name Molly. "I was doing the bank-run, the morning takings, and I was mugged halfway up the street."

What?

"I don't understand." Tom sounded as confused as I felt.

The girl's mouth dropped open, and then she snorted with laughter. "No, no, he wasn't the mugger. *God*, no." She held her hands to her cheeks. "It gave me such a fright. No. He chased the thief down the street, while I called the police."

I let out a breath I hadn't realized I was holding. Chasing a mugger. That sounded like something Alun would do. "That's my boyfriend. Did he catch him?" My voice was faint.

"I don't know. I last saw him running up toward Kingsway. You know, the Holborn road," she added.

Holborn again. On the train line to Bethnal Green.

"Alun is missing, and you might be the last person to have seen him." Luce joined in, calm and confident. "Is there anything else you can tell us?"

"We got the takings back. We were so lucky. There was a copper on patrol, who gave chase, and he found the bag snagged on a fence, just outside the old entrance to the tramway. They must have dropped it."

"Where's that?" Luce asked. "The tramway."

The waitress glanced at her colleagues, who'd gathered round. "It's not Newton Street, is it?" She snapped her fingers. "No, it's Parker Street. Right at the end. There's a disused tram tunnel that runs under the Kingsway road. It's not supposed to be accessible, but dossers and druggies hang out there, because it's dry and out of the cold."

I shivered, and closed my fingers around the box in my pocket. An underground tunnel sounded like the last place I wanted to go, but if Alun had gone there, we needed to follow. "Could you take us there, please? Can you spare the time?"

"Sure." She grabbed a jacket, and we set off. "He was ever so brave, your boyfriend. I hope he's okay."

I did too. Every time I thought of last night's dream, I felt cold with dread. Alun had been so different from every other dream, and I couldn't shake the fear that time was running out for him. We *had* to find him.

Molly led us through a maze of busy streets, to a narrow alley between two blocks. Around a corner, the alley narrowed further, and I saw broken metal rails in the remains of a cobbled street, the stones wet and shiny in the rain. The road sloped down to a set of tall wooden gates set in a high fence, surrounded with scrubby grass and weeds growing wild. The paintwork was blistered and peeling, with heavy chains looped through a rusted padlock.

It screamed, *keep out.*

How odd that we were just steps away from a typical London street, and yet at the same time, somewhere so remote.

"This is it." The girl pointed to the gates. "Our takings bag was there."

"You say people go in there?" I heard the disbelief in Tom's voice.

"Yeah. If you push the gates, they open enough to let you through." The girl shoved her hands in her pockets. "This place gives me the creeps. It's supposed to be haunted, even without the druggies. I'd better get back. I hope you find him." She spun on her toe, and hurried away.

I looked at Tom and Luce, and they both nodded. "Do we really think he went down there?" I hated how scared I sounded.

"We're here," said Tom. "We may as well take a look. And then, if we find anything, we can go to the police."

Sure enough, the wooden gates flexed when he shoved one side, and opened enough for a person to slip through. He held it open, and Luce went first, with me second. Just before I squeezed through the gap, I paused. Something glinted in the long grass by Tom's feet.

"Hang on." I bent down and picked up a broken iPhone. The screen was smashed beyond repair, and the back cover cracked, the guts of the phone hanging out.

There was enough of the cover left for me to see the image, though. An obscure Finnish rock band. A band Alun had seen on tour in England. He was the only person I'd ever known with that phone cover.

"This is Alun's phone."

Chapter Eleven

Tom squeezed through the gate, just as the rain intensified. Icy droplets hammered down on us, and Luce ran for cover, dragging me with her. The tramlines sloped even further into a dark tunnel.

I dug my heels in. "I can't." My heart raced. "I can't go down there. I never liked being underground anyway, but since the bombing…"

Luce caught me by the shoulders. "I know you're scared, but you can do this. We're with you. And we're all here to find Alun. The trail leads here, and we might find something."

I swallowed hard, fear pounding a rhythm in my blood. "Does anyone have a light?"

"On our key rings." Tom and Luce both lifted sets of keys, each with a tiny LED light. "And on our phones," Luce added.

The tunnel entrance loomed. I could put it off no longer. I nodded, and we set off, Tom and Luce in front.

The track dropped steeply, and we picked our way across the cobblestones with care. They were dry, but our shoes were wet. It wasn't as dark as I'd feared.

Strips of light leaked in from the ceiling, enough to show cobwebs, graffiti on the stone walls, and piles of garbage strewn along the floor. Empty beer cans and bottles, fast food wrappers, and black plastic bags littered our path.

It smelled of unwashed bodies, and the coppery tang of blood. Unease prickled up and down my spine, and I had to work hard to keep my breathing steady.

Shards of shattered glass sparkled with the broken tips of needles. I took care to step over those.

Up ahead, the tunnel opened out, and I could see more light, flickering like candles. I tugged Luce's sleeve, but she'd seen it too. "I think we've found someone. Let's go talk to them," she murmured.

We had to be crazy. Alun wouldn't be here. What did we think we'd find?

I found his phone.

Every step farther into the abyss made me more anxious. Would the people here be able to help? It had to be worth a try.

Four people shrouded in blankets huddled around a cluster of candles on the ground. They watched us approach but didn't move, and didn't speak. I couldn't tell how old they were, or even if they were all men.

Tom broke the silence. "Hey. I'm sorry to interrupt, but we're looking for a friend of ours. We think he might have come down here. If I show you his picture, would you please take a look?"

I noted the way he phrased his request, as though Alun was a runaway or an addict. These strangers might be more sympathetic to us.

The guy closest to us grunted, and then stood. "It'll cost you."

"Sure. How much?" Tom sounded as though he was ready for that.

"Rich kids like you? Twenty notes each."

Jesus. Sixty quid just to look at a picture? We weren't in a position to bargain, though.

Tom dug into a pocket, and produced his wallet.

"And a bottle of Scotch."

Tom paused. "Don't have that, but I'll throw in an extra ten."

"Deal." The man held out a filthy hand, and Tom counted out the money, before slapping it onto the man's palm.

I held up my phone. "This is our friend." My voice trembled. "He went missing about a month ago."

The guy stared at Alun's smiling face, forever captured on my screen. "I've seen him before. Can't remember where." He smelled disgustingly of mildew and wet earth, overlaid with the sour stink of someone who hadn't seen soap for days, if not weeks. I tried not to grimace when he leaned closer. He was younger than I'd thought, not much older than me, but he looked as though he'd lived rough for some time.

"I might need my memory jogged." He grabbed my wrist, and I squealed. His fingers dug in, the nails scraping my skin. "Your phone will do nicely," he said.

"Let go of her." Tom lunged forward, and the guy twisted my arm sharply and pushed it up my back, turning me around at the same time.

A shockwave of sudden pain flew up to my shoulder, and I whimpered.

"Give me your phones. All of you."

Luce spun on her toe, and I realized we were surrounded. More people appeared from the shadows. Four—no, five more guys.

My heart crashed inside my chest, and I tried hard to shake myself free. "Let go of me, *please.*"

Tom and Luce took positions back to back, and I tried again to reason with the man. "I just want to find

47

my boyfriend. We're asking for your help."

The thug pulled me against his body, and I felt his breath on my neck. I wanted to throw up.

"Trouble, bro?" One of the new arrivals spoke, his voice gruff and heavily accented.

"They're after the pig. Chances are, they're the filth too."

What? I didn't get it.

Tom understood. "We're not the police. And Alun—our friend—he's not, either."

"He brought the fucking pigs down here with him." The man holding me dug his nails in tighter. The stink pouring off him made my stomach churn.

"He was chasing a mugger. The police showed up, because the café he stole from called them." Tom's voice was tight. "Now please let my friend go. We'll walk out of here, and leave you alone."

"Nu huh." He shook his head. "Your pretty little friend is going to wait here with me, while you go and find the nearest bank. Five hundred will see her right. I'll have your phones, and I'm warning you, if you even *think* of calling in the filth, you'll regret it. I'll mark her for life."

My stomach plummeted, and I swayed on my feet. Every instinct told me to run, but he could break my arm easily from this angle. I was also surrounded. It hurt to draw breath into my lungs, and spots danced before my eyes.

Luce made a growling noise, and Tom grabbed her arm. "What guarantee do I have that you won't hurt her?" He snarled the words. Dear God, he wasn't going to leave me here, was he?

"Tom?" My mouth was so dry, I couldn't say anything else.

His gaze searched my face, and then he dug into a pocket and produced his phone. "Luce, your phone as well." She hesitated, and then handed it over.

"We'll be fifteen minutes. No more." Tom held out the two phones, and one of the other men snatched them.

Holy fuck. They were going to leave me. The guy holding me chuckled and curled his free arm around my waist, hugging me to him. Bile rose in my throat. I begged Tom with my gaze, but he didn't say anything. He just took Luce's hand, and then shoved his way through the small circle of men.

Chapter Twelve

They *wouldn't* leave me. Tom had to have a plan.

I hoped he had a plan.

Tears sprang to my eyes, but I refused to acknowledge them. I wouldn't give these bastards the satisfaction of seeing me cry. My chest hurt with the effort of breathing, and my lungs grew tighter with every passing second. The men gathered in front of me, laughing, and jostling each other. Arguing over who would have me first. I blinked my tears back, and stared at the floor. At the cluster of burning candles. Could I kick them over? Create a distraction?

The man holding me squeezed me hard, his hand creeping up toward my chest.

I would *not* let him grope me.

Breathe. And again.

I went wild in his arms. If I dislocated my shoulder, I'd have to deal with it; I'd get free somehow. I wriggled, and tried to jerk out of his grasp. I caught him by surprise. His grip loosened a fraction. I kicked out. My foot swung woefully short of the candles.

"*Bitch.*" He yanked my arm so hard, I thought

he'd drag it out of its socket.

Pain roared across my shoulders in a burning torrent. And then I saw something odd.

Up ahead, where the tunnel curved around to the entrance, was a shimmering, glittering haze. I blinked, and it was gone. Where had I seen that before?

"Feisty," sneered one of the men, as he reached for my face.

"Let *go* of me." I jerked my head back, but he closed his fingers in my hair and tugged hard. My eyes watered, and he laughed.

I was trapped. Pinned like a butterfly to a board. Dear God, would I get out of here? Or would I vanish into the same place Alun had? My teeth chattered with fear, and I braced myself for another touch from the hand on my chest.

A growling noise sounded close by. The man holding my hair paused. "What was that?"

Another growl answered, rising to a roar.

The world went crazy. Two huge dogs charged, jaws snapping, and teeth flashing. The guy hanging onto my hair let go. He stumbled back, and was knocked to the floor. Men scattered, shouting, feet slapping on the cobbles.

My knees gave way, and I dropped to the floor in a heap. Breathless and dizzy, I realized the dogs weren't interested in me. They leapt up at the man who'd held me. He screamed, but the dogs didn't back off. They snatched at his arms, and dragged him to the floor.

They weren't dogs. They were wolves.

I rubbed my eyes, and pushed to my feet to stand there, swaying. Was this a dream? Realization hit me. *The same shimmering light as when Alun morphed into a wolf.*

Luce had mentioned Alun being my *Mate*.

Tom and Luce were *a little bit psychic*.

They had the same bright eyes as these wolves.

In the seconds since the wolves arrived, the men had run away, apart from the one now lying face down, his arms over his head. The larger wolf stood on the man's back, the smaller inches from his terrified face, snarling.

The disgusting thug was whimpering, and begging me to help him.

I hauled in a shaky breath. Swallowed hard. Found my voice. "They're my dogs. You want me to call them back?"

"Get the fuckers off me."

The wolves gazed at me, familiar blue eyes gleaming in the reflected candlelight. This was beyond weird.

The large wolf, a sleek black beast, growled deep in his throat and swiped his paw at the phones lying on the ground, where they'd been dropped.

I forced myself to move. On unsteady feet, I stumbled forward, picked up the phones, and clutched them in my hand. "I want something in return. I need to know what happened to Alun, and I want the cash back. The money you just took from my friend."

The guy opened his fist, and released the notes, and I stooped to pick them up.

"What happened to my boyfriend? He chased a mugger in here. You recognized his face."

The wolves snarled, their teeth close to the man's neck. He whimpered. I felt nothing except a savage anger.

"Tell me what happened," I yelled at the top of my voice, and he went silent. "What did you do to my boyfriend?"

"I didn't do anything."

"Try again." I paused, an icy calm settling over

me. "Or I walk away and leave them here."

"*Okay*. It was Paulie. He screwed up." His voice was high and frightened, and I was glad. I wanted him to be scared. His words poured out in a torrent. "We sent him off to do a job, a simple grab-n-dash, and he fucked up and nearly got caught. Next thing, the cops are pouring down here with your boyfriend. Paulie didn't even have the goods; the stupid fucker dropped 'em."

"And?" I prompted.

"And yeah. Someone jumped your boyfriend. Paulie snatched his backpack, took the wallet, and ran for home, and I went the other way. I haven't seen Paulie since. I found your boy's pack, though. Paulie must have dumped it."

The pieces of the jigsaw puzzle were fitting together in my mind. "You said Paulie was going home. Where was that?"

"He lives near Bethnal Green. Did he get nicked?"

No, he got blown up. I couldn't bring myself to care about him. The wolves growled again, and I shook myself. *Focus, Olivia.* "And Alun? What happened to Alun?"

"Fuck knows. I left him here. He was gone when I came back."

My knees shook, and I sank to a crouch on the dirty floor. "You *left* him here. Was he hurt?"

"He wasn't moving. I thought he was one of the pigs," he whined, as though that would make any difference.

"You're the pig," My vision blurred, and I closed my eyes for a second. Sweet relief made me dizzy. Alun hadn't been on the train at all. A thought struck me. "What did you do with his backpack?"

"Sold it. Guy in the pub."

We needed the police. Not only to arrest this arsehole, but to tell us what happened that day. They had to have found Alun.

With shaking hands, I sifted through the phones for mine, only to find there was no signal. *Duh.* We were underground. "I'm going to call the police," I told the wolves. Would they understand me? The smaller one walked to my side, and nudged my leg.

"What?" The guy sounded panicky. "You can't leave me here. You said you'd let me go."

I took two steps toward the entrance, and then paused. I stared at him over my shoulder. "I lied."

Chapter Thirteen

The soft-furred brown wolf walked by my side, and bumped me when my steps faltered. I checked my phone. Still no signal. We walked farther, rounded the bend in the tunnel, and I stopped. Lying on the floor was a haphazard pile of clothes. I'd swear they weren't there earlier. When I looked at them, I realized they were familiar. Luce's puffer jacket and Tom's fleece. Luce's flat leather boots.

My gut knew, but my brain refused to accept it.

The wolf whined and nudged me, as though urging me to keep moving. I couldn't. Not yet. I crouched down, and looked the beast in the eyes. *"Luce?"*

A shimmer of sparkles later, and my friend reappeared. *Naked*.

Everything I thought I knew about the world was wrong.

Luce took my hands and pulled me to my feet, and then enveloped me in a tight hug. *"Jesus*, Livvy. It nearly killed me, when we had to walk away from you."

It was weird, but I felt completely detached. Dream-like. *"What are you?"* It came out a croak.

She released me, but caught my hands in her own. "You mustn't tell anyone, Livvy. Nobody at all." I frowned, but she carried on. "We're born this way. You don't need to worry about growing fur and claws." An awkward smile played across her face. "You must have a million questions, but they have to wait. Right now, you need to call the police. I'll wait with Tom, in case the others come back."

Psychic dreams. People that morphed into wolves. It was too much to wrap my head around. I chose to ignore the craziness, at least for the moment, and just focus on Alun. Where he might be.

I found my tongue. "What about your clothes?" *Was I really asking this?* "How—*when*—will you…uh…change back?"

"Push them into the shadows for us. When the police arrive, we'll run off, and then come back to get you." She hugged me again, fierce and strong. "We're closer to finding him, Livvy. You have to hang on in there."

****

I'm not sure what I told the police on the phone. I think I babbled about being assaulted and my friends being threatened, and finding evidence of my boyfriend being attacked. Now the initial shock had worn off, my arm and shoulder really hurt, and I couldn't stop shaking. I staggered back to where Tom and Luce held the man down, and then I slumped to the floor and huddled into myself.

Sirens blared, followed by footsteps. Someone called my name. The cavalry had arrived. Luce melted into the shadows, reappearing as herself again, a couple of minutes later. As soon as three uniformed officers hurried in, Tom bolted up the tunnel, returning fully clothed.

I answered the questions as best I could. Tom and Luce chipped in too.

When the thug shouted about being attacked by giant dogs, the three of us just shrugged and looked puzzled. Yes, there had been a couple of strays in here, but in the confusion over the arrival of the police, I'd no idea where they went.

I didn't particularly care about the assault; my sole focus was on finding the report about the original callout. The details about Alun. We ended up at the police station, where we had to tell our story all over again.

My patience snapped. "For God's sake! My boyfriend may be lying in a hospital bed right now, while everyone thinks he's dead. *Please.* Just tell us what happened."

It worked. Half an hour later, a kind-faced female officer escorted us to the nearest hospital. I huddled in the back of the car with Luce, clutching her hands like a lifeline. What if it wasn't him?

The day Alun disappeared, the police had raided the tunnel and arrested a number of people, before someone literally tripped over a young man lying unconscious in the shadows. He carried no ID, had no phone, and looked as though he'd been in a fight.

They'd made the assumption he was there to buy drugs.

He'd suffered a knife wound and a head trauma, and currently lay in a coma. Until he woke up—*if* he woke up—they couldn't identify him.

We walked up endless brightly lit corridors, rode in an elevator, and finally had to wait in a side room, while the police officer talked to the medical staff. Tom paced up and down, his hands shoved into his pockets, his lips a tight line. Luce sat with her arm around my waist. I refused to let anyone examine my shoulder, until we had an answer. I couldn't waste another minute, or have any other delay.

"What are they *doing*?" snarled Tom. "It doesn't take this fucking long to find out which bed he's in." He glanced out of the window at the darkening sky. It was already dusk. "If they don't come back in the next minute, I swear I'm going to look in every room I come to. This is driving me insane."

I knew how he felt. I clung to my composure by the finest of threads. My stomach churned endlessly, and I knew—I just *knew*—I was close to breaking down, and howling. If this wasn't Alun, if it really was some idiot doing a drug deal...

No. I couldn't think like that. He hadn't been on that train. He *couldn't* have been.

A young nurse entered the room and looked at us. "Is Olivia Tanner here?"

"Yes." I pushed to a standing position. "That's me."

She took a step closer, and I tried to interpret her expression. Her eyes were kind, and her smile was sympathetic. I felt, rather than saw, Luce stand up next to me.

"The patient you were asking about is in the HDU," the nurse said.

I knew the letters, but my mind couldn't make sense of them. I stared at her.

"High Dependency Unit," she said. "He seemed to be stabilizing, but his condition deteriorated yesterday."

I heard *deteriorated*, and very little else. "Please," I croaked, my throat as dry as the Sahara, "can you take us there?"

"Of course. Follow me."

My knees felt like jelly, but I knew Tom and

Luce would keep me upright. Another set of endless corridors. Another elevator. And finally, two sets of double doors, and a nursing station. Our nurse spoke rapidly with someone behind the counter, and then beckoned us closer.

"He's in this bay. You can look from the entrance, and see if you recognize him."

Oh God. This was it.

Chapter Fourteen

Four steps.

My feet could have been encased in lead. I was terrified. There were so many possibilities. If it wasn't Alun. If it was Alun, and he was dying. If it was Alun, and he never woke up.

I made deals with whatever deity might be listening. I didn't care if Alun was different. If he was some kind of freaky werewolf. I still loved him anyway. I'd accept him however he was, if he would just come back to me. I'd move anywhere he wanted. I'd marry him, at the absolute earliest opportunity.

The room was larger than I'd expected, with four beds separated by thick white curtains. The low light levels reflected back in the dark windows, and machines beeped and hummed everywhere. The nurse pointed to the second bed. My heart stuttered.

"Alun," I whispered.

He lay motionless, wires connecting him to a bank of monitors. His face, normally tanned and healthy, was pale, and obscured by a ventilator mask.

He was alive.

I remembered Tom and Luce, and turned

around, my eyes filling with tears. Luce clung to Tom, and they both stared at me, matching expressions of hope and fear on their faces. I couldn't speak. Tears blinded me, but they were tears of happiness. Of utter bone-shaking relief. I nodded and smiled, and suddenly we were all hugging. Luce sobbed, Tom wiped his eyes, and I held onto Alun's friends. His amazing, loyal, wonderful friends. God, how I owed them.

We surrounded Alun's bed, and for the first time in way too long, I tangled my fingers through his. Luce pressed a soft kiss to his forehead and stroked his hair, while Tom squeezed his arm.

"Alun, baby." The words stuck in my throat. "I'm here. *We're* here. And we need you to wake up."

"We need to tell his parents," murmured Tom.

I nodded. "Will you? Please?" I couldn't leave Alun's bedside. Not now. Not after finding him again.

****

The night passed in a blur of interviews with the nursing staff and the police, and with phone calls. Tom broke the incredible news to Alun's parents, while I rang mine. I also made a short and emotional call to Sasha. One day, I would have to thank him in person.

It would be good to do that with Alun. Having lost him, and then found him again, I refused to believe he might not recover.

"Comas are tricky," explained the doctor. "Sometimes the brain just needs time to heal. Talk to him, play him music through earbuds, and touch him."

I nodded. I would do all that anyway. No matter how long it took.

****

61

The hospital quickly became my new world. They moved Alun into a private room, since he now had a continuous stream of visitors. Apart from food and bathroom breaks, and sporadic attempts at sleeping, I didn't leave his side.

Night after night, I fell asleep, but he didn't visit my dreams. I clung to the belief that if he did, it would mean he was improving again.

We developed a routine, Luce and Tom and I, and our families. Long games of Scrabble played on the end of his bed, endless hours of listening to his favorite rock bands, and quiet time when I curled up in the chair next to his bed and just held his hand. I talked to him. A lot. Told him I knew about his animal side, and how it didn't matter in the slightest. Over and over, I told him how much I loved him, how I wanted to marry him, how beautiful his gift to me was. How he needed to wake up.

I told Luce I didn't want to know any more about the wolves. I hoped to learn everything from Alun, when he woke up, and she smiled and hugged me. "That's as it should be, Livvy."

My job interviews went on hold. Nothing else mattered right now.

We'd been there two weeks, when I heard a strange noise in the corridor. Singing? Christmas carols? The duty nurse appeared at the doorway. "The local church choir are touring the hospital, collecting donations for the homeless. Would you like them to come in to Alun's room?"

It was Christmas already? The past weeks had all blurred together. I was there with Pam, Alun's mum, and we looked at each other. She nodded and smiled. "He might enjoy it, and I think I would."

They gathered in the doorway, and sang two traditional carols, their voices soaring, as though they carried all our hopes skyward. It was beautiful, and Pam and I both donated generously to their collecting tins. I sat holding Alun's hand, and thought about our original plans for Christmas Day. We'd spent it the previous year at my mum and dad's, and this year we'd planned to spend it with Alun's parents in Tanygrisau. I might well be spending the holiday with them, but here in London instead.

I ran my fingers through Alun's hair, and pressed a kiss onto his cool cheek. "It's nearly Christmas, babe. The present I want most of all is for you to wake up."

I played more Scrabble with Pam, read some stories aloud from the newspaper, and then we talked about leaving for the night. We were staying with some distant relatives on Alun's side, and luckily it was just a short cab-ride away.

Pam yawned. She looked exhausted, and I suggested she go back early and get some sleep.

Alone in the room, I curled up in the chair, and held Alun's hand. I'd stay a little longer, and then head out. Maybe I'd finally see him in my dreams tonight.

Chapter Fifteen

I knew I was dreaming when I looked up to see Alun sitting cross-legged on top of his bed. No longer dressed in a backless hospital gown, he wore jeans and a faded T-shirt, sneakers on his feet.

"Hey." He quirked one eyebrow. "I thought you'd never go to sleep."

"*Alun.*" Raw delight filled me, and I stared at him, hungry for every detail. "Babe, I've missed you so much."

"Come on, then." He held out a hand, and wiggled his fingers. "Shall we go?"

I'd go anywhere with him. I clasped his hand, and blinked. We appeared on a rocky outcrop in the middle of a winter storm. Snow fell steadily, creating a thick carpet for our feet. I never felt the cold, even though I should have been freezing. The sun was completely obscured by clouds, but it had the feeling of early morning.

"Where are we?" I asked.

Smiling, he led me a few steps to a gentle slope, covered entirely in pure, untouched snow. It could have been a blanket, freshly laid for us. I'd never seen so much pristine snow before. "If you look over yonder"—he pointed in the distance—"you'll see Tanygrisiau at the foot of the hill."

"Beautiful." I twirled round and admired the view from every angle, then realized Alun was watching me.

"Yes," he murmured, intensity burning in his eyes. "But it's time for the angels."

"What?" An icy hand clutched at my heart. Was this Alun's way of saying goodbye? Bringing me to his home one last time? "*No.*" I stumbled into his arms. "No, baby. Please, don't go. I don't want to be without you. I only just found you again."

He held me close, and stroked my hair, kissed my eyebrows and cheeks, and then chucked me under the chin. "I heard you singing about Christmas." That was right; the choir had been singing carols. "And yeah, it made me think about angels." I burrowed into his arms. I wasn't letting him go. Not again.

"Come on," he whispered into my hair. "It's time." He moved back, creating a tiny gap between us. I clung to his hand so tightly, our fingers would have to be pried apart with a crowbar. "Are you ready, *Cariad*?"

Fear rushed in. If I died in my dream, would I die in real life too?

Alun cocked his head to one side. "On three." *Huh?* He led me forward, to the start of the brilliant white slopes. "One, two, *three.*"

He leapt, pulling me with him to land on our butts in the snow. All the air rushed out of my lungs, but I heard Alun whoop in delight.

"Snow angels," he shouted. Lying on his back, he flapped his arms, and scissored his legs in the snow. "Let's do a double." He squeezed my hand, where it lay on the snow. "Perfect snow, perfect angels."

I laughed so much, so hard, my stomach hurt. Perfect Alun.

****

I lurked in the not-quite-asleep fog of pre-waking, and smiled at the crazy dream I'd just had. We'd made snow angels and played together like children, as the flakes fell around us, creating fresh fields of white at every turn. Magical, silly, and fun. I'd also been aware that Alun had drawn me into a dream. Was it a sign he was getting better?

A squeeze on my hand dragged me awake. Had the nurse come in? I opened sleep-filled eyes, and lifted my head, only to find the room empty.

I glanced at Alun. I didn't dare to hope.

Our hands rested on the bed, fingers linked. I lifted them to my mouth, and pressed a kiss onto his knuckles. This time, I didn't imagine the squeeze. His fingers moved in my hand.

"Alun?" I leaned over the bed, and stroked his hair. *Please wake up.* He squeezed my hand again, harder, and his eyelids fluttered. "Alun, baby? It's me, Olivia." I could barely speak over the crashing of my heart. I held tightly to his hand, and forced myself to take a deep breath. To speak more clearly. "Are you going to wake up now?"

His nose twitched, and then his lips moved. This was it; he really was waking. Common sense finally kicked in, and I stretched up and hit the red alarm button over his bed.

The world went a little bit crazy. Nurses flooded in, a couple of doctors, and the quiet evening calm was replaced with noise, voices, footsteps, and chaos. And in the middle of it all, Alun opened his eyes and smiled at me.

Dreaming of a Wolf by Sofia Grey

****

The hospital finally agreed Alun would be able to go home on Christmas Eve. He was cranky, and tired of being confined, and had nagged non-stop to be released, but now he had a date, he was focused on getting well.

Luce took me for coffee one afternoon, while Alun was undergoing his physical therapy exercises, and she tried to explain. "It's our animal side. It needs to come out, and he's not allowed to shift here, in the hospital. Can you imagine what would happen?"

In the last two weeks, I'd had very little time alone with Alun, and I looked forward to some privacy with him. I wanted to know everything, and I wanted him to teach me.

We'd talked in my dreams, of course. I knew Alun, his family, and his friends from Snowdonia called themselves *Shifters*. They were born with an animal side to them—a wolf that emerged during puberty. For their mental health, they needed to shift at least every other day, and they preferred to live near wild open spaces. It was a secret way of life that had been around so long, nobody knew where or when it had started. I also knew they Mated for life, and once they found their soulmate, they could communicate in their dreams.

I knew the headlines, but there was so much more I burned to understand.

We'd done a lot more than just talking, and as I sat in the coffee bar with Luce, my cheeks warmed at the memory of my dream from the night before.

He'd followed me into the shower, and taken me from behind. My hands had been pressed to the wall, and he'd pounded into me, one hand on my hip,

67

the other playing with my breast. Water cascaded down, steam rose up, and I moaned with every long, slow glide. I'd already come once, and a second orgasm drew closer. Alun was close too, his thrusts shallow and rapid, and they stoked me to fever pitch.

"I love you, *Cariad*." He sunk his teeth into the base of my neck and my vision splintered. "I promise you, we'll do this for real again soon."

I leaned back against him, while I caught my breath. "I'll hold you to that, Wolf-Boy."

Chapter Sixteen

We were married in Alun's village church, two days after Christmas. The pews were filled to bursting, and people also stood at the back. It was the complete opposite in mood to his funeral, and my cheeks ached from smiling. We celebrated in the pub, and danced all night to a raucous local rock band. I couldn't have been happier.

Waking surprisingly early the day after, my first day as Mrs. Jones, Alun insisted I get up. We had to go somewhere. Tanygrisiau might not have been snowbound, but some of the surrounding roads were blocked, and so I figured we couldn't be going far.

Ignoring my grumbles, he made me dress in warm clothes, and led me to the edge of the forest.

"What are we doing, babe? More snow angels?"

"Maybe later." He turned to face me, and cupped my cheek in his hand. "We had the wedding yesterday, but today it's my wolf's turn. We have a special ceremony, called a Mating Ritual."

"Oh?"

"All the pack attend, and watch us swear our bond." He smiled, mischief dancing in his eyes. "It's a beautiful thing."

Swearing our bond? It sounded harmless, so I let him lead me a little farther, to a sun-dappled glade. The trees were bright with ribbons. I hesitated, surprised at the size of the crowd gathered around the clearing. Many faces I recognized from the wedding and from the village.

"Are they all wolves?" I whispered.

He hugged me. "All these are, yes."

There were so many. Every time I thought I'd figured out something about Alun's wolves, he surprised me again. "So what happens at this ritual?" I kept my voice low.

He led me to the center of the circle, and took both my hands before he replied. "Well"—Alun cleared his throat—"we take off all our clothes, and make love in front of the Pack."

What? My mouth dropped open.

"Then they anoint us with blessed water from the sacred spring, and we howl to the moon. Naked."

I almost fell for it, but then I saw the way he was biting his lip, as though trying not to laugh. I blinked, and my lips twitched in return. "Was any of that true?"

"The howling. But not to the moon."

"You're incorrigible." I couldn't be mad at him for teasing me. I was still too happy at being with him again. "So what *does* happen?"

"We make some oaths, and then celebrate some more."

We stood together in the weak morning sunshine, and I gazed at my lover. *My husband.* I would never tire of his cheeky grin, or the heat in his eyes. Was it possible for a heart to burst with love?

A tall, darkly handsome man approached, and introduced himself as the Pack Alpha, Jake Bledri. He made a little welcoming speech to me, and then asked if we were ready to continue. His deep, calm voice settled my nerves. We both nodded.

"Alun. Do you promise to stand by Olivia's side, and share her life and her home, to protect her against all danger, to be her Mate and her partner, and to love and care for her until the day you die?"

"I promise." Alun stood tall and proud, his voice strong.

Jake nodded, and turned his attention to me. "Olivia, I have the same oath for you. Do you promise to stand by Alun's side, and share his life and his home, to protect him against all danger, to be his Mate and his partner, and to love and care for him until the day you die?"

"I promise." God knows how, but my voice rang out clear and confident, and Jake smiled.

He closed his hands around our clasped ones. "By the authority vested in me as Pack Alpha of the Snowdonia Wolves, Alun and Olivia are now Mated under Pack law. It gives me great pleasure to congratulate you both, and wish you long health, love, and happiness."

"Long health, love, and happiness." The entire Pack repeated the words, and Alun held me close, love shining in his eyes.

I opened my mouth to speak, but he placed a finger over my lips. "Not yet," he whispered, and so I waited. Silence fell over the group, and then Alun's parents stepped forward. Lifting their heads, they howled to the skies. The sound made my spine tingle, and my blood heat. One by one, the others followed suit.

"They're welcoming you to the Pack." Jake smiled at me. "And so am I." He howled, his call quite possibly the most beautiful sound I'd ever heard.

Two adorable little girls held baskets of flowers and walked up to us, staring at me with solemn blue eyes. They carried garlands, woven of velvety petalled blossoms, draped with care around our necks.

"Now," said Alun, clasping his hands around my face. "Now we can celebrate some more."

Every day with Alun was a celebration for me. His waking was the best Christmas present I could have been given. His life, the most precious gift.

This time, he really was my forever.

THE END

Cherry Pop, A Vampire Cherry Novella,

by Sotia Lazu

The significance of things is rarely apparent at the moment they occur. People don't know it's the last time they're making love with a significant other or the last time they're seeing a friend, until long after the moment has come and gone. Lovers grow distant, friends drift apart, and one day you look back and remember that time you dug your nails in his back or that phone call you ended way too soon, and wish you'd known you'd never get another chance for that level of contact. Wish you'd savored it while it lasted, instead of taking it for granted.

I often wish I'd realized the last time I felt the sun caressing my skin.

Or the last time I heard my mother's voice.

Hell, I wish I'd known the last time I heard my heart beat.

Chapter One

"What are you wearing tonight?" Sheena wrinkled her nose at my open closet.

"Something short?" I ducked inside the mess of clothes and fished out a tiny black dress. "Breathing in it can be hard, but it gives me a killer cleavage."

She tapped a manicured nail against her cheek. "It's a little cheap for this crowd. Don't you have something more...upscale?"

I arched an eyebrow at her. "I doubt *this crowd* will be judging me on my clothing, when I'll only be there because they've seen me without it." The guests hadn't seen me naked in person, of course, but it was a party my production company threw, and what said company produced was adult movies. Very adult. I'd been in two of those as an extra, before I signed a contract for my first starring role in *Knotting Cherry Stem*.

I'm Cherry Stem.

Well, it's my stage name.

"I won't even stay at the party that long," I said. Shooting started tomorrow, and I wouldn't show up with bags under my eyes.

"Still. You'll be mingling with celebrities. It's my agently duty to make sure you fit in." She grabbed the dress from my grasp and tossed it on the bed. "Come. I'll take you shopping before we hit the salon. You can pay me back with your first fat paycheck."

I wasn't saying no to that. I looped my arm through hers, and we hit the road.

It didn't take long to find the perfect dress. It was as short as my first option, but covered in sequins the color of champagne, and the way the reflective surfaces caught the light gave me a glow that made me feel like a star.

Sheena waved away my worrying over the five-hundred-buck price tag, and treated me to a light lunch, before taking me to her favorite beauty salon and having all my body hair removed in a rather painful manner.

"Not even a landing strip?" I looked down at my bare pussy. It wasn't ugly, but I was used to a blonde tuft at the top.

"Nope. You must look perfect for the part. Hair's next."

She meant the hair on my head this time, and by the time Jean Paul was done with it, my natural blonde mane was a bright cherry red—with bangs.

"Your drapes match my front-door mat." Sheena laughed.

Once my nails were buffed and polished, and my makeup applied to Sheena's satisfaction, I just had enough time to go back to my place and change. I squeezed inside the dress, and barely managed to slip on a pair of high heels before my cab arrived.

Sheena pretended to sniffle, as she followed me to the curb. "I feel like your fairy godmother." She'd been just that, since she walked in a bakery for a cupcake, and exited with me in tow. I'd come to the city to build a bigger life for myself than San Luis had to offer, but until Sheena discovered me behind a doughnut display, I had no clue how to go about it.

"Have fun, and do everything I would," she said now.

"Don't mind if I do." I hadn't seen any action since my last movie, and that was with a girl. We didn't do much. Just background writhing bodies at a supposed Roman orgy. I really missed sex since I moved to L.A., but men here were too fast for me.

Yeah, yeah, I know how that sounds coming from an aspiring porn star, but movies were different. I wasn't in danger of falling in love with my partner tomorrow—and I was promised it would only be *one* partner—and I knew exactly what to expect from him and when. Smooth talking city guys didn't come with the same guarantee. Plus, I left my quiet town and my loving parents because I wanted to make it in the big city, and making it didn't come with emotional entanglements. I'd have time to fall in love when I established my career.

Preferably in movies that didn't include nudity. Sheena insisted *Knotting Cherry Stem* was my big break, and I believed her, but I hoped to one day make it to Hollywood. That would be so cool.

I slid in the taxi, gave the driver the address of the club where the party was being held, and blew Sheena a kiss. "I'll call you after the shoot tomorrow."

She winked. "Have fun!"

My phone rang as we took off, and I fished it out of my cleavage. *Home* flashed on the screen. Shit. I'd been avoiding my mom the past month, because she kept asking about work and I was running out of lies about photo shoots.

I really did some catalog work after Sheena convinced me to follow her to Los Angeles and took me on as a client. She booked me for a plus-size clothing print ad campaign, and urged me to lose weight so I could find more work. I never considered the adult-movie industry until she suggested my first job, but I didn't regret dipping my toe in that pond.

If only I could tell Mom about my starring role, without giving her a stroke.

The phone stopped ringing, and I stashed it back between my smooshed boobs. I'd deal with it another day. For now, I fantasized about the day people threw parties to celebrate *me*.

The cabbie knew the quickest route to the club, and we were there before I had time to mentally compose my speech for the Oscar I'd one day receive.

What? Dreaming big is the first step to making it big!

The moment the cab stopped, an iron fist gripped my insides and twisted, ripping my confidence to shreds. This was it. My first celebrity party. I was about to rub elbows with starlets and celebs, and I felt like the bastard child. Sheena had assured me nobody was going to judge, but I felt like a fake—red head to red-lacquered toenails.

I paid the driver, and teetered out on shaky legs. I took a deep breath, and focused all my efforts into getting one foot in front of the other. And again. And again. The line to the entrance was half-a-block long, but I followed Sheena's instructions and made a beeline for the bouncer, maintaining eye contact and beaming a smile his way.

"Cherry Stem," I said when I reached him. "I'm on the list."

He scanned the sheets in his hand just long enough for my heart to skip a beat, then nodded and made way for me to enter. "VIP room is in the back and to your left. Enjoy your evening."

I wanted to thank him, but Sheena had insisted I act above everyone who wasn't *someone*, so I returned his nod, and took the plunge into a world I was utterly unprepared for.

The thudding of the music reverberated in my chest, but the way to the VIP room was surprisingly clear of sweaty patrons juggling alcoholic drinks and rubbing against each other. I made my way to the dark purple curtain with little hassle, and gave a second doorman my name.

He pulled the curtain aside, and gave a small bow that lifted my spirit. "Go right in, Ms. Stem."

This time I said thank you before I slinked inside.

The heavy fabric fell back in place behind me, and the music was magically muted, like the curtain was made of steel, not velvet.

I tried not to look stunned, as I took in the plush fabrics, expensive chandeliers, and familiar faces. The place hopped with energy I ached to become a part of. How to go about it, though? Did I smile and approach clusters of people, as if I knew them? Did I head straight for the bar and be mysterious, until someone came to talk to me?

"Don't over think it." The deep male voice made me jump, and I lost my balance for a split second.

A strong arm wrapped around my waist, and pressed me against a rock solid body.

"Easy now," the man said.

I found my footing, and used both hands to loosen his grip, before turning to face him.

Hot!

"I'm Willoughby," he said, "but you may call me your knight in shining armor."

I laughed and took a step back, light headed by the intensity of his dark eyes. His thick lashes and full lipped smile made up for the horrible name. "You startled me," I said.

"Not my intention. I meant to sweep you off your feet, not make you trip over them."

"Close enough, I guess." The familiar heat of a blush crept up my neck, and spread over my cheeks.

He took my hand in his, and pulled me further in. "Come. I have a booth. You can tell me your name, and we can drink to chance meetings."

I shouldn't. I was there to network, and that meant being seen, not hiding away in a booth with a hot stranger.

But he was just the type of guy Sheena would love me to be seen with. Heads bobbed our way, teeth flashed in smiles of recognition, and champagne flutes were raised in salute, while we waded to his booth. He definitely had connections.

He motioned for me to sit, then unbuttoned his immaculate midnight-blue jacket, and slid on the couch, close enough that the length of my thigh touched his.

I should have sat on the outside. It'd be easier to leave, if things went awry, but there was no reason to think about leaving. We were in a room full of people, and despite his apparent disregard for personal space, Willoughby didn't seem threatening in the least.

That was probably what Little Red Riding Hood thought of the wolf, when she first met him.

"So is your name a secret?" He still held my hand, and now he ghosted his thumb over the knuckles, gaze locked on mine.

A shiver ran down my spine, and my nipples tingled as if he'd caressed them. What was this man doing to me?

"Ger—*Cherry*." I still wasn't used to my stage name.

"Nice to meet you, Gercherry." He chuckled,

and brought my hand to his lips for a demure kiss that nonetheless sent my pulse skyrocketing. "Leave this place with me?"

I was lost in his eyes, dark-chocolate brown and full of warmth, but gathered my wits enough to say, "I don't know you, and I just got here." My objections weren't in the right order, but oh well. "Can't we enjoy the party?"

He nodded. "Now or at the end of the evening, you're mine."

Okay, a little corny and over the top. I took in his wide shoulders and long fingers, and decided I could deal with it.

He got us a bottle of champagne, and proceeded to ply me with it, while whispering naughty tidbits about the rest of the guests in my ear. Who slept with whom. Who had extensive cosmetic surgery they denied. Who was an entirely different person than what they pretended to be.

"See the blonde over there? She's supposed to be a patron of the arts, but is actually a cougar on the prowl."

The woman in question was eating him up with her eyes.

"You're horrible." I tapped his arm playfully.

He leaned close and inhaled deeply. "I cannot wait to taste you."

I licked my lips. If we were alone, I'd be in his lap by now, but I was there for a reason. "This party is work for me," I said. "I'm supposed to meet people."

He flicked his tongue over the inside of my wrist. "You don't need to know anyone else. They're all shallow. Pointless. Aspiring actors with no essence."

That stung. I was one step beneath them in the food chain, so what did that say about me? "I still need to make the rounds. Maybe dance a little."

81

In a blur of a movement, he stood and pulled me flush against him. "Then let's dance." His cologne was dark, with a bitter undertone. He smelled like mystery and mayhem, and I wanted him.

What the hell had gotten into me?

He swayed, his palm splayed at the small of my back, pressing me into his movements. The music was barely a hum in the background, and the people around us faded from my thoughts. An overwhelming wave of lust threatened to drown me, if I didn't give in to its flow.

He glided his hand around to my side, and down my thigh. The tips of his fingers playing with the hem of my dress, he looked into my eyes. "My limo is right outside. Let me take you home. Now."

"Yes," I hissed. His choice of phrase gave no indication of whether he meant his place or mine, but I couldn't care less.

We spilled out of the club and into his limo like horny teenagers. The tinted glass separator was up, so he pressed a button and I heard a man say, "Yes, sir?"

"You know where to go."

The engine purred to life, and we took off, but I barely spared a thought to where we were going. Willoughby whispered naughty things in my ear and traced circles on my thigh with his thumb, and my brain was numb with desire.

The city lights flashed by my peripheral vision briefly, before he cupped my chin and brought his lips to mine.

The kiss was hard, more punishing than passionate. I tried to ease my head back so he didn't crush my chin, but he moved his hand to the nape of my neck and held me in place, his grip too strong for me to escape.

He bit my lower lip. "I'm trying to make it good

for you."

I liked it rough from time to time, but not with someone I didn't know. Which I should have thought before I left the club with him. Why *had* I followed him out? This wasn't me. I was always careful. I'd had one-night stands before, but I made sure to text Sheena where I was going and with whom. Maybe it wasn't too late for that.

"Where are we going? I have to let my friend know, so she doesn't worry when I'm not at the party." I managed to bring out my phone.

Willoughby withdrew enough to capture my gaze. "You don't need to text anyone. You'll tell her all about it in the morning." His pupils were dilated. "Let me do what I please with your body. You know you'll enjoy it." He trailed his fingertips higher between my legs, bunching up the hem of my dress on the way.

His voice was compelling, a deep bass that caressed my skin as sensually as his hand did. I giggled. He was right. I didn't need to text Sheena. I'd tell her all about it in the morning.

His hand edged my legs further apart. I giggled some more. Why was I giggling so much? Had to be the champagne.

He kissed me again, and slipped two fingers under my tiny thong. Pushed them inside me. I moaned against his mouth, and he chuckled and kissed a line to the side of my neck.

"So soft," he said. "So pliable. So fragile."

The words were wrong—so *wet* would have made more sense—but the tone was right. Excited and full of promise.

I should touch him too, but his fingers and his lips were stripping me of thought and energy. I just wanted to let him do what he pleased to my body.

"You'll enjoy it," he said.

I'd enjoy anything he gave me.

He bit my neck. The pain was sharp, but a new rush of pleasure made my spine tingle. He sucked and licked, and drove me insane.

Until my professionalism kicked in where my sense of self-preservation hadn't.

Still rolling my hips to meet the thrust of his fingers, I said, "Stop. I can't have a mark tomorrow."

He didn't react. Just kept finger-fucking me, while giving me the mother of all hickeys.

I smacked his shoulder. "Stop, Willoughby. You'll get me in trouble. I have a shoot in the morning."

The rumbling sound of his laugh chilled me to the bone. I tried to pull away, remove his hand.

No use.

His grip on me was unrelenting, his mouth harsh. He shoved another finger in my pussy and began pumping them harder. Faster.

"I said stop." I lifted my hand to swat him away, but lacked the strength to do anything more than let it flop by my side again. Why was I so weak? Had he spiked my drink?

Something warm tickled my right breast, and I looked down to see a trickle of red disappearing inside my cleavage. Blood? "What the fuck, Willoughby?"

He dug his chin into the crook of my neck, and I realized he wasn't just sucking on my flesh. He'd pierced the skin. I hoped he hadn't nicked any major blood vessels.

"What kind of freak are you?" It came out in a shocked whisper instead of the outraged roar I was going for.

I hadn't felt his fangs enter me, but I felt them sliding out. "The worst kind," he said. He slanted his blood-smeared lips over mine, and pushed his tongue inside my mouth. I gagged at the taste of my blood.

He bit me again, more savagely. His fingers never stopped rubbing. Teasing.

He pressed his thumb on my clit, and my body betrayed me, diving toward an orgasm that compounded shame upon the violation. How could I come while someone was assaulting me? Tears reached the corners of my mouth. "Stop. Please. You're hurting me."

I wheezed out a breath. I wanted to yell at him. Curse him. Shove him off me, curl into a ball, and cry until I felt safe and clean again.

I couldn't move a single muscle, or let out a sound other than a choked sob.

My heart thundered in my chest. My ears buzzed, but I could clearly make out its erratic thumping.

Willoughby kept sucking, until my heartbeat slowed.

And slowed.

And stopped.

Chapter Two

Blerg.

What was that smell?

I was surrounded by all that was foul and horrible and long dead.

And the noise... Some horrible scraping, as if someone was emptying the inside of my head with a spoon.

But the smell was the worst.

"Hello?" I croaked, way more loudly than I thought I could. My throat hurt. Had I fallen asleep with my window open? It might account for the smell, if the sewer outside had overfilled again. It would explain the noise too.

I grabbed for my second pillow, but my palm landed on a hard vertical surface. Metal?

What the hell?

I opened my eyes. I was in some kind of...box? Yes. A dark green box, though I didn't know how I could tell the color. There was no light source above or around me, but I made out every speck of dust and patch of chipped paint on the walls, and saw the filth encircling me in disconcertingly great detail.

Now I knew where the stench came from. I was inside a dumpster.

Memories of the previous night resurfaced, switching my focus to the dull throb in my neck and the ache between my legs. The fucker bit me until I passed out of blood loss, and then left me here for dead.

Unless he was coming back to finish the job.

Panic shot pure adrenaline inside my veins. I sat upright, and pushed at the lid, glad I had my strength back.

But it was a little more strength than I was used to yielding.

The cover of the dumpster ripped off the hinges and flew several feet away.

How did I do that?

"Hey, watch out! You almost took my head off. We don't bounce back from that."

I jumped upright. I miraculously still had my shoes on, and one heel pierced a trash bag. I reeled when its soft and slimy contents touched my foot.

A dark haired man approached slowly from my left. He was of medium height, dressed casually, and with both hands in the air. "I mean no harm. Promise. My name's Ted, and—" He squinted. "Holy shit, you're Cherry Stem! I'm a big fan of your work."

A fan? I hadn't even done the movie... Wait! "What time is it? I have to be on site at eight."

The man gave me a rueful smile. "I don't believe you'll make it."

I looked at the starry sky, and took a careful step back. "Why not? The sun isn't even out yet." But I could see perfectly. Weird, but not my main concern. Right now, I had to stall until I figured out whether this guy was friend or foe.

"I'm sorry," he said. "That sounded threatening. Let me help you out of there, and I'll explain."

"Don't come closer." I had no weapon, nothing to keep him at bay, but he did as I asked.

"Cherry, you were turned, and we have to take you inside before the sun comes up."

I recognized the words as English but couldn't follow their meaning.

He went on. "I'm guessing someone attacked you last night? They bit you?"

"How do you know?" Did he see us? But there were only the two of us in the limo. *Wrong.* The three of us. "You're his driver."

"What? No. I've just seen this before. You were bitten by a vampire, Cherry. Turned into one."

The laugh that escaped me hurt my throat. "You're nuts. Just my luck." He was completely useless as a witness. I only hoped his kind of crazy wasn't as dangerous as Willoughby's.

Ted shook his head. "Vampires are real, and you're one of us now. You don't have a heartbeat. Can't you hear that?"

Two crazies in one night? It couldn't be a coincidence. Willoughby was still playing his sick game, and this guy was in on it.

"I mean it," he said. "You can hear me fine, right?"

I nodded.

"Well, I've been whispering all this time. And you can hear the rat too. I bet you can. I can as well."

The rat? I took in my surroundings. We were in an alley, and sure enough, a disgusting rodent was scurrying up the wall farthest from me. "How...?" I didn't know what to ask.

"Your senses are stronger now. You can smell, see, and hear infinitely better than before. You need to regulate them, or you'll be overwhelmed."

"Regulate them?"

"Tone them down. Try not to smell everything. Keep the night vision on, though. You'll need it till we're at a better lit place."

I squeezed the lip of the dumpster and it creaked in my fists.

"And you're stronger too," Ted said.

"Yeah, I got that." I did what he said, and consciously tried not to smell the reeking contents of my temporary grave. It didn't work entirely, but the stench was less pervasive. "Turn around. I need to get out of here."

"Why do I need to turn around?"

My patience was wearing thin. "Short dress, and you haven't paid for a show."

He shrugged and looked the other way. "Whoever killed you—"

"I'm not dead!"

"—must have accidentally bled on you. The VSS will explain everything. They can help you."

I boosted myself out of there with one hand, and used the other to keep my dress in place as much as possible. I landed on my feet, which actually felt gracious. Feline balance, yo!

Ted turned back to me, and took two small steps closer. "Just come with me."

"No. I was already assaulted once tonight. I'll just go home and shower, and get to my shoot before I lose the job." Was I always this shrill, or was it the vampire hearing kicking in again?

"If you go out in the morning, you'll burn to ash. You are a vampire, as am I," he said. He lifted his arms to the side, and I thought he was giving up, before I saw his feet were no longer touching the ground. "If you don't want to go to the VSS, at least stay inside during the day. I'll have to report you to the council though, and they'll come for you, if you don't check in."

"What council?" And what was this VSS he mentioned twice now?

"They'll explain it all. Come, listen to what they have to say, and then choose what to do. If I wanted to hurt you, I'd have done so already." When I didn't budge, he sighed. "Okay, but you better not come at me."

I watched in fascinated horror as his fangs elongated. He lifted his hand to his mouth. "When you smell the blood, your own canines will grow. The hunger may overtake you. Don't freak out."

"No, wait." I didn't want to see blood. Didn't want to smell it. I'd had enough of it. "Take me to them."

He held out his hand, and I took it before I knew I was doing it.

"Will we fly?" I asked. This was too surreal to be actually happening. I was still asleep and dreaming. "I don't wanna fly."

"Nah. I'll drive."

****

The VSS were the Vampire Social Services, and no, I wasn't dreaming. I was undead. A vampire. A creature of the night.

Ted took me to an old rundown building in the outskirts of L.A., and explained my situation to a giant of a security guard, who pointed to the corridor behind him. "You want Fledgling Affairs. Last office to your right. Ask for Abby."

A lovely smiling woman, who seemed only slightly older than my twenty four years, got the door when we knocked.

"Abby?" Ted asked. When she nodded, he said,

"This is Cherry. I found her."

Abby took in my disheveled and filthy state, and her eyes filled with sadness. "I'm so sorry, Cherry. Come in. We'll sort you out."

"Will you report her turning to the council, or should I?" Ted asked her.

"I will. It's protocol. Thank you for bringing her in." Her tone was dismissive.

"Sure." To me, he said, "I'll be seeing you." It was the first I noticed his faint British accent. He left with a small wave, but neither of us waved back.

I only relaxed when the door was closed behind him. I hadn't realized until that moment how unsettled I was, riding in a car with him. Made sense. Last ride I took turned out lethal.

The inside of the building was nothing like the outside. The walls were a warm cream color, and the floor was covered with thick carpets. Pastel colors completed a picture that came directly at odds with everything I imagined a vampire lair to be.

Vampire.

I was a vampire.

For the second time that night, I started crying.

Abby handed me a box of tissues, and pointed at an armchair. "Sit down, dear. Tell me what happened." Her voice was full of compassion, which only made the tears fall faster.

"There must be a mistake," I said. "I can't be a vampire. I just got my big break. This is all just a dream."

"I wish it were, honey." She sat on her haunches, so she was eye-level with me. "What was done to you, other than against regulation, was despicable. To turn someone, we're supposed to first introduce them to our existence, make sure they are a good fit and can manage eternal life, and of course get a permit from the council. We are responsible for those we create, which is why I believe your maker didn't mean to turn you, but to kill you."

I couldn't believe my ears. "And that's not against regulation? You're monsters. You stole my life from me." I needed to lash on someone, and she was there.

Abby didn't even flinch at my outburst. "Our feeding is supposed to only sustain us, not lead to loss of life. There are always those who fail to restrain themselves, I suppose." She sounded too stuffy to be my age.

"How old are you?" I asked.

She seemed taken aback by that. "Four hundred and twenty nine." I was still trying to wrap my mind around that, when she added, "I still remember lying bleeding on the side of the road. We'll find who did this to you, and he will be severely punished. Tell me what you know about him. I have to present your case file to the council so he can be found and prosecuted."

"What council is that?"

"The vampire council. They're our ruling body. You'll meet them after your orientation program."

"Orientation? To vampirocity?"

She cracked a smile. "It's vampirism, but I call it vampiredom."

I felt the corners of my lips tugging upward, and stopped them. "Can we do this tomorrow? I need to be somewhere this morning."

Her smile wilted and fell. "Cherry, you can't. You can't go to the places you used to visit, or speak to your friends and family again. Ever. Everyone who knew you as a human must believe you're dead."

"Can't I just call my parents and tell them I'm leaving the country?" They'd go crazy with worry, if their only child disappeared.

"I'm sorry. It's against—"

"Regulation," I finished for her. "But you know what? I didn't ask for this, and I couldn't give a shit for your regulation. I'm going to walk out of here, and back to my life, and there's nothing you can do to stop me."

"I'm afraid there is," she said. "Protocol in such cases dictates we take out the rogue vampire, and either terminate every human they came to contact with after their turning, or scrub their memories clear."

A shard of ice pierced my still heart and froze me to the core. "You can't do that."

"We can. And we need to, to preserve our kind."

Maybe she wasn't all that likable after all.

"Tell me about the orientation," I said grudgingly.

"Every new fledgling spends six months here, learning everything there is to learn about their new life."

I snorted. "This isn't a life."

"It is an existence, Cherry, and it can be a beautiful one, if you accept you can't change what happened to you, and try to make the most of it." Her voice was soft. Pleading.

"And if I refuse to accept it?"

Her face fell, and her brown pinched. "I really hope you don't, but your choices are limited in that case. You appear to the council, and they decide how to go about finalizing your demise."

So I didn't refuse. I let her lead me to the first underground floor and show me to the sparsely furnished room that was to be my home for a while.

The next couple months gave me a taste of what eternity meant. I was confined to my room, my only contact being Abby, who brought me reheated bags of blood four times a night. It tasted bad, but I needed the boost it gave me. I tried to sleep most of the day, like a good bloodsucker, though adjusting to a nocturnal existence was hard.

The room's tiny television was my window to the outside world, and through it I saw my parents break down under the pain of my loss. The day I saw my mom cry and plead for me to come back, I busted my room's door and fled.

Abby caught up with me halfway up the stairs, and singlehandedly returned me to my room. She proceeded to explain the dangers my parents would face, if I went to them, the least of which was that my hunger would take over, and I would drain them.

"The first part of your stay here is almost done, hon," she said, cupping my cheek with infinite gentleness. "Now we are sure you're no threat to yourself, we can start your education, and get you ready to return to the world."

Chapter Three

The next night, I was taken to the council, whose members repeated what Abby had said time and again. There was no going back.

At least they informed me Willoughby had been caught and would face the final death as punishment for my turning. There was a hoopla I didn't follow, about how I was a semi-public figure, and my turning put us all at risk.

Abby rushed me out of there and back to VSS in her town car. That she had a car made me hopeful. This was ordinary. Maybe I could have an ordinary second life, since my promising first one had been cut short by a soulless monster.

A thought dawned on me as we entered Abby's office. "Have I lost my soul?" I was never a devout Christian, but the possibility of an eternal afterlife in Hell freaked me out more than the reality of a long existence as a creature of the night.

I hadn't heard someone else enter, and the deep laughter that came from behind me caught me unaware and pissed me off. I'd been killed, everything I fought for was laid to waste, and I'd never see my loved ones again. Who the fuck found anything about the situation *amusing?*

I turned and glared at the tall guy leaning against the doorway. Blond hair cascaded down his wide shoulders, and mirth sparked in his blue eyes. There was something regal about the angles of his face. A warrior king. No, a warrior *god*—that was what he looked like. His body was honed to perfection, judging from the pecs stretching his button-down shirt stretched and how his dress slacks hugged his narrow hips. If he weren't laughing at my misery, I might be tempted to be nice, despite hating his kind.

Our kind.

"That's an idiotic lie, perpetuated by books and movies," he said. "Nobody can take your soul from you."

I hadn't worn high heels since my turning, and my feet hurt now. I wanted to go to my room, bemoan my ill fate, and sleep. I arched an eyebrow, hoping my annoyance got across. "Yeah, well, a few weeks ago I thought nobody could turn me into a vampire, either. I'm kind of reconsidering a lot of things."

He laughed again, and I found it less irritating and more arousing. I remembered Willoughby's laugh turning me on too. Maybe it was a vampire thing. The thought slapped some sense into me. There would be no perving over the hot vampire guy. He'd probably sucked his share of victims dry, and was as despicable as the rest of them.

Except Abby, who was nice.

"To put your mind at ease, I can tell you with absolute certainty that your soul remains intact after your turning." He tossed back his hair, and it caught the artificial light. The man could star in his own shampoo commercial. "What gradually grows fainter is your fear of consequences, which is why many of us turn to the dark side."

If he was part of the dark side, I could certainly see the appeal. "And why should I trust anything you say? Who are you, even?"

"He's Constantine," Abby said. "He'll be mentoring you for the rest of your stay."

"I'll teach you everything I know." His smirk would have turned my knees into jelly any other time. After everything I'd been through lately, it just made them the tiniest bit wobbly.

But that could also be blamed on my shoes.

****

"Let's start with the basics. You know you need blood to survive, but you can have human food for the joy of it. The only things lethal to us are sun exposure, staking, decapitation, and complete exsanguination."

I widened my eyes, and Constantine sighed. "That's blood loss," he said. "Religious objects have no effect on us whatsoever, and we definitely do have reflections."

I'd figured that out myself.

My room wasn't big by any stretch of the imagination, but with Constantine standing in its center, it felt suffocating. Dressed in one of many long t-shirts and saggy pairs of shorts the VSS provided, I sat cross legged on my single bed, my back to the wall.

"You can find more details here. Abby says you refused to even glance at them." He tossed me a bunch of perfectly folded sheets of paper.

I looked at them as they lay on the mattress next to me. *An Informed Vampire is a Happy Vampire* read one. *How to Deal with the Hunger*, another. *Be the Right Kind of Sucker*, a third. I didn't bother with the rest.

"Pamphlets? Are you shitting me?"

He shrugged, and the shirt strained more against his forearms. He wasn't bulky, but if I looked from a specific angle, I could see the definition of the sinewy muscles on his stomach.

"The VSS thought it smart to have the information gathered and accessible," he said.

I shook the pamphlets in the air. "These are stupid."

"Some people find them helpful."

The f in 'helpful' sounded more like a v. His accent, like his looks, was Nordic, but his name sounded Italian. If I cared, I'd ask him about it, but I didn't care. He pissed me off.

"Well I don't," I said. "I just find them dumb."

"Then you don't have to read them." He snatched them from my hand, crumbled them in a tight ball, and tossed them in the trashcan at the corner of the room. "What do you think might help you?"

"Turning human again?" I glared.

"Not possible, as you have been told repeatedly."

I harrumphed.

"You have several long years ahead of you. If this defeatist attitude is the one you plan on maintaining, it will not be pleasant for you or anyone near you."

I climbed to my feet on the bed so I could look him in the eye, and planted my palms on my hips. "Before I met Willoughby, I had a future. I was building a career. I was months away from the perfect body." Tummy tuck and boob job for the price of one. "Now I'm fucking dead, and need blood in order to avoid getting deader. I'm sorry I'm not *pleasant*, but I can't exactly be bouncing with joy."

The weirdest thing happened. His eyes, blue

until then, darkened into a dark violet. I was dying—
ha!—to ask if it was a vampire thing, but I had just
delivered a killer speech. I couldn't ruin it.

Constantine lowered his head, but maintained
eye contact, and his irises kept darkening. Was he mind
controlling me?

I lifted my hand and slapped him. Hard.

His eyes widened in shock. He rubbed his
cheek, and when he looked at me again, they were blue
once more. "What on earth was that for?"

"I wanted to see if you were controlling me. If
you were, I wouldn't be able to slap you."

"If I were—" He inhaled and blew out the air
noisily. "If I were controlling you, you wouldn't be
such an annoying little brat now, would you?"

I slapped him again. "This one was 'cause
you're rude."

He had me flat on the bed, before I could relish
my tiny victory. His hands felt like steel around my
wrists, and his knees kept mine wide apart. I was fully
aware of his strength and his advantage over me, but I
didn't feel threatened for a moment.

"Next time you slap me, I will slap you back,"
he whispered against my ear.

I burned, but couldn't tell if it was with desire or
embarrassment. Could I still blush? I could obviously
still get horny, judging by how I settled my hips so his
pelvis pressed into mine.

I remembered Willoughby again, and how he'd
made me come while he killed me. I remembered the
shame I felt, and let my eyes drift shut.

"Look at me."

I'd almost forgotten Constantine was watching
me. "I don't want to."

"Cherry, I can smell your arousal and your fear.
I'm not going to take advantage of you."

I still wouldn't open my eyes. "I'm not afraid of you." He was handsome and mysterious like Willoughby, but I sensed a different kind of darkness in him. Plus he wasn't spouting weird shit about making me his.

"Vampires are extremely sensual beings," he said. "We seek pleasure, and indulge in it. There's no shame in desire. No reason for you to feel bad for reacting to me. I react to you." I could tell. He was hard.

This made me look at him. "Not it either. I was thinking of Willoughby. He was... We were making out when he bit me. I was enjoying it, and I was *dying*." I don't know what made me open up to the complete stranger after Abby tried for so long to make me talk to her.

He slid to the side, and his hair half hid his face. He tucked it behind one ear. "You cannot blame yourself for that. Sexual stimulation accompanied by blood loss practically guarantees an orgasm. It is a physiological reaction. I can explain the mechanics, if you'd like." He sounded completely clinical, but the matter-of-fact tone was what I needed to hear.

"You're not just saying it to make me feel better?"

He rolled on his back, and threw an arm over his eyes. "Why would I? You've been an utter bitch since I met you."

I should be offended, but I smiled, feeling a fraction lighter. "That's true."

He was still for so long, I thought he was asleep. "Hello? Did you doze off?" I whispered.

He moved his arm. "I tend not to sleep half hanging out of bed, and never with an unwilling bedmate."

I searched for a witty comeback, but my

memory bank came up empty.

"Let's get back to our lesson." He sat up, and began undoing the buttons of his shirt.

"Whoa! What are you doing?" Still, I propped myself up on both arms to have a better view. After my semi-solitary confinement, I couldn't be expected not to ogle a perfect—and naked—male specimen.

"I have to show you how to feed, fledgling. I am to feed you." He sounded so stuffy some times.

My gums itched. Other parts of my body reacted way more favorably to the ever widening sliver of pale skin his fingers revealed. "Don't we feed from humans?" I asked.

"Mostly. Feeding from another vampire entails a different level of intimacy, but you have to learn somehow. We can't risk you going feral on a human."

"But on you?"

"I can handle you."

I had no doubt he could. I sort of wanted to see him do it. "Why do you have to be topless for it? Can't you roll up a sleeve?"

He pinned me with his gaze. "This shirt is made of silk. I will not have it stained with blood."

I rolled my eyes. "So high maintenance."

Done with his buttons, he peeled the shirt off, and I barely saved myself the embarrassment of drooling. Literally. My fangs grew by about an inch each. I'd learned the hard way to open my mouth, not to tear my lips to shreds. Now it hid my gaping at the naked expanse of his chest.

"I think I'm hungry." The words sounded weird wrapped around the new topography of my mouth.

The corners of Constantine's lips tugged upward, as he carefully set his shirt aside. "All hungers intensify after your turning. Learning to control them is a major part of your rehabilitation process. You'd know, if you read the pamphlets."

I'd be paying more attention to what he said, if he didn't run his splayed fingers down his sculpted abs. His upper body was perfect. No blemish marked the pale skin, and my gaze kept returning to the golden trail of fine hair that started below his navel and disappeared into his slacks.

I dare anyone—male or female—to see Constantine topless and not wonder what the rest of him looks like. How his body would feel pressing into them.

My hand was already on his shoulder, when I realized I'd reached for him. He remained completely still as I traced the curve of his shoulder down to his bicep.

"You're not cold," I said.

"I've fed." His voice sounded darker. His pitch lower. I looked from my fingers to his eyes. They were the same fierce violet as before.

"You're doing the eye thing again." I ran my tongue over the tips of my fangs. It tickled.

"It seems I'm still hungry too." He studied me, until I averted my gaze. "You want me to make love to you," he said.

I snapped my head back up, eyes wide. I wanted to protest, but my mom raised no liar—and I was so shocked by his bluntness, I couldn't form words if I tried.

"I will, one day. When you can handle it. I will give your body more pleasure than you believe yourself capable of, and I have no doubt you'll return the favor." His voice was so emotionless, he could be talking about the weather. "If I take you now though, I will be a crutch. Something you can focus on, to ignore your new reality. That isn't what you need."

But it was what I wanted. I wanted to wrap my

legs around his hips and sink onto him. Ride him until I forgot everything but his divine body. I wondered if he was a talkative lover. He had to be. His voice, his accent, were made for whispering dirty promises.

And he seemed to love hearing himself speak.

"You can't tell me what I need." Why was I breathless? I didn't have to breathe any longer.

I was still touching him, but he pulled my hand into both of his, and massaged my wrist. "Right now, you need blood. This is one of the most common spots for feeding. It's easy to take a quick bite without getting noticed, but slows you down when you're looking to be sated."

His thumb lit my skin on fire, and I wanted to jump him. Was he made of pure sex? I had to focus on how he annoyed me. Had to stop thinking of his touch as anything but…instructional.

He made his way up my arm, and tapped the inside of my elbow. "The flow here is better, but I still prefer two other veins."

I gulped. What should be a casual touch had me more turned on than I'd ever been.

He pulled me closer, and dipped his face between my neck and shoulder. "This is one of them."

I rolled my head to the side, praying he'd bite me. I don't know where the thought came from. I wasn't into that shit—even less so since I still felt the pain of Willoughby's bite. But Constantine's fangs wouldn't hurt, and if they did, he'd make them hurt *good*. I could tell by the way he grazed the sharp tips over my skin. I pushed out my chest, aching for more contact, but his touch didn't stray from my arm.

"You have to feed." He sounded even huskier than before. "If you amp up your target's desire, they won't feel pain unless you want them to. Can you make me desire you?"

Oh, buddy, this was a challenge I didn't feel up to.

Even at my chubbiest I had my admirers, and I was by no means a blushing virgin, but I'd never been with someone as stunning or as experienced as Constantine. He was out of my league.

Which was why I had nothing to lose.

I stood and began lifting the hem of my shirt, but he shook his head. "If you wish to feed at a public place, you cannot disrobe."

"A public place?"

"Yes. We feed where people swarm. Where bodies press against each other, and inhibitions are low."

I imagined inhibitions around him were always low, but this could be fun. "So I'm at a club, and find someone yummy I want to feed on. Get up. Dance with me."

He narrowed his eyes, but came to me and encircled my waist with his arms. I stood on my tiptoes, and pressed my breasts against him. I swayed from side to side, so he could feel my nipples, pebbled by their contact with the fabric as well as by his proximity.

"I want you," I whispered, only partially in character. "Right here, with everyone watching. I want you to take me. Show me what I've been missing out on." All men like to think they're unique, that they're better than anyone who came before them.

I turned in his embrace and climbed down his body, undulating to the beat of an imaginary song. On my way up, I made sure to touch as much of him as possible. When I faced him again, I staggered at the intensity of his gaze.

I recovered, and nipped the spot under his ear, inhaling his cologne. Swaying my hips, I danced us back to the bed. I lowered my hands down his sides, and dipped my fingertips under his waistband. This was allowed. It was all part of my lesson.

Still looking into his mesmerizing eyes, I pushed him to sit down, and straddled him. He was hard again. Or still. I savored his thick shaft against my core.

"Do you desire me now?" I worried his earlobe with my blunt front teeth.

He gave a curt nod, his cheek caressing mine, and stretched his neck. "Bite me," he said on a breath.

I sang my fangs inside him, feeling the flesh slice open for me. When I pierced the artery, his blood didn't spurt out as I expected. Made sense, since we had no heartbeat.

"You have to suck." His whispered barely carried to me, but I did what he said.

When his blood touched my tongue, I exploded. The rich, thick flavor that suffused my taste buds was nothing like blood tasted before. I didn't know if all vampires tasted so good, or if Constantine's blood was special. Not that it mattered. I kept sucking and gulping, reaching a new level of bliss with every sip. This was the nectar the gods fed on. The warm liquid ran down my throat and revived each and every one of my cells. I felt rejuvenated. Stronger. More alive.

I felt like a perv, for pumping my hips, seeking the friction that would help me funnel all that energy to an orgasm. Coming with Constantine's blood in my mouth would be the zenith of ecstasy.

He didn't move beneath me, but his arms tightened around me. "Stop." The word snapped and crackled in the air.

I clutched at his shoulder. Dug my nails in. Kept drinking. Rode him faster. I wanted to tear our clothes off, and feel his skin on mine. Feel his cock stretching me.

"Stop now." His voice boomed louder than

before, ripping through my fantasy.

I grudgingly halted my feeding, and put some distance between the soaked seat of my shorts and his cock.

"Good girl." He looked pained, despite the approving words. "Lick the wound clean, so it heals."

It took all my inner strength not to dive in again, but I touched my tongue to the holes I'd made and sat back, watching in amazement as they disappeared in front of my eyes.

"Vampire constitution makes for faster healing. Blood helps with even the worst wounds, barring decapitation or staking. Our saliva helps both vampires and humans with small cuts and pierces."

Who cared? I wanted more of what I just experienced.

"How did I do?" I kept my voice as flat as his.

"Good. Solid bite, no chewing, no spilling. You stopped when I told you."

That was all he could comment on? "But did it feel good?"

He led my palm to the tent in his pants. "You know it did."

It was now or never. I leaned in to kiss him, but he cupped the back of my head and laid a chaste kiss on my forehead. *While my hand was on his cock.*

"Why won't you fuck me?" I was glad and a little surprised that I sounded pissed off, rather than whiny.

A smile blossomed slowly on his lips, as though he tasted the words before uttering them. "Because when I do, I will rock your world, and you've had enough of that lately."

Damn the stupid, sexy man and his smartass replies.

Well, I didn't like him anyway. It was just the

bloodlust talking. Yes, he was hot, but he knew it, and cocky jerks rarely made good lovers. He was probably the kind of guy who lay back and let the woman do all the work.

I stared him down, and he laughed. "Retract your claws, kitty." He unceremoniously lifted me off him, stood, and tossed me on the bed. "Second lesson is at sundown tomorrow. I expect you to have full control over your fangs by then."

"Bastard." I lisped the 's,' which only served to piss me off further.

"Sundown." He waved over his shoulder without a look back. "Your door stays unlocked from now on, and you may roam during the night, but I suggest you avoid strolling upstairs during the day."

Chapter Four

After the excitement of the night, I expected to drop dead—in lieu of a better word—at dawn, but it didn't happen. In fact, I barely slept during the day. I don't know how the annoying vampire expected me to know when sundown was without a watch or a window.

After a couple hours of tossing and turning, I put on the standard-issue hotel slippers that came with the uninspired VSS wardrobe, and went to take a look around.

My room was one of seven on the floor. Two of the others had their doors closed, which I guessed meant they were occupied. More unwilling fledglings?

The rest appeared exactly the same as mine. Single bed at a right corner with a desk. One chair. Waste basket. Closet. Tiny restroom with shower.

It was a dormitory, and I was a vampire freshman. I snorted. If lecturers at my old college were like Constantine, I wouldn't have dropped out to work at the bakery.

And Sheena wouldn't have scouted me.

And I would still be alive.

Tears sprung in my eyes. Weird I could still cry

and get aroused, but had no other bodily functions. I'd have to ask Constantine. Maybe I should make a list of questions, for when he came back.

Or I could venture upstairs.

Not a good idea.

There was a door at the top of the stairs. I tried the handle and was glad to see it wasn't locked. I pulled it open, and sizzling pain slapped my face.

I shrieked. I was burning.

I shut the door again, and batted my face, eyes squeezed shut.

"Cherry? Are you all right?" Constantine.

"No. Hurts. Ow."

"I know. I know." His tone was soothing, and a cool, wet *something* touched the place that burned on my forehead. The pain ebbed immediately.

"What was that? What did you do?"

"I told you saliva cures small wounds."

"Ew. You licked my forehead? Couldn't you give me more blood?"

He laughed, and I loved the tiny lines that framed his eyes. Even laughing looked sexy on him.

And talking about sexy, his slacks were replaced by silk pajama bottoms, and they rode *low*. I doubted he had underwear on.

"You live here? How come I never saw you before?" It didn't seem right. He was too...much for this place.

He shook his head. "I thought I'd stay over for a couple nights, until I get you off to a good start."

I couldn't handle him being thoughtful on top of gorgeous. It was a combination I should be avoiding until—

I was no longer on my way to a career. If he broke my heart, I had several eons ahead to mend it. And I could use some tender loving care.

"I can't sleep alone," I said.

"Cherry, I told you making love is a bad idea at this point."

"I know. I just don't want to be alone."

He sighed in resignation, and before I could ask if we were staying at his room or mine, threw me over his shoulder.

I let out an undignified yelp, and he laughed again. It did all sorts of delicious things to my insides.

Why didn't he come mentor me sooner?

He stretched me out on my bed, and pulled the desk chair by the headboard, shuttering my dreams of cuddling with a Viking god. "Aren't you going to lie down?"

"I shall read you to sleep." In the months that followed, I'd come to realize he only broke out 'shall' when something got to him. In retrospect, I like to think that something was me.

I lay there until he brought a paperback of War and Peace from his room, and then I let his deep, cultured voice wrap around me and lull me to sleep.

He was still in the chair when I woke up, arms folded, chin on his chest.

For the first time since my turning, I didn't hate my life.

My unlife.

I could get used to him being around.

For the next couple weeks, I spent every moment Constantine and I were together trying to seduce him.

I feathered my lips over his ear while he taught me how to thrall humans.

"Focus, Cherry. You must pull them into your will. Have them do your bidding," he said.

"Sleep with me," I said.

I nuzzled his neck and worried it with human

110

teeth before I fed, and made a show of licking my lips clean of his blood after.

"You know you can try other veins," he said.

"But then I have no excuse to be on top of you," I replied.

I gave him demanding looks and promising touches.

He gave me exasperated sighs and speeches on patience.

And books. Tons of books.

And he slept on the chair next to me every morning.

Until our first flying lesson.

****

"Are you sure I can do this?" I wasn't exactly afraid of heights, but I'd take any excuse to wrap my body around his and have him return the embrace.

"You can, as long as you believe you can. All you need to do is believe you can defy gravity, and will yourself to fly. Hold on to me and don't let go." He was in yet another button-down shirt. I hadn't seen him wear the same one twice. I wondered how many suitcases he'd lugged to the VSS—and why, since he spent all his waking hours with me.

I threw my arms around his neck, uncaring that I wrinkled the smooth fabric of his shirt.

He didn't seem bothered, as he circled my waist and brought me flush against him. "It may help if you keep your eyes closed at first. Change your perception, to change your reality."

I nodded, and buried my face in his chest, tangling my fingers in his long tresses. "If I survive this, you better put out."

His chest shook with his laughter. "I'm not

111

holding out on you. I'm only being patient for your benefit."

"Yeah, doing it all for me."

"Cherry."

"What?"

"Look at me."

I turned my face to his, petulant frown in place.

"Haven't you heard of delayed gratification?"

"I'm starting to think you're gay."

He laughed. "Look down."

"I don't want to see you hard, if I don't reap the benefits," I said.

"Look down, stubborn woman."

I did, and watched the floor grow distant. "Shit!" I was actually flying. Impossible. The moment the thought crossed my mind, I lost a foot of height. Constantine tightened his grip on me. As he lifted me, I brought my legs up around him.

He was still laughing, when I slanted my lips over his.

If he didn't return the kiss, I'd give up.

His hands slid down my ass, to my thighs, and he clutched me with such fervor, I didn't know how I ever doubted he wanted me. His lips were soft against mine, his tongue demanding. He kneaded my flesh as he bit on my lower lip, and I moaned inside his mouth.

I broke the kiss to meet his eyes. "Can we please stop waiting?"

"Fuck it." Without adjusting his hold on me, he swooped toward the ground and swerved toward my room. We landed on my bed, hands already busy shedding our clothing.

I was on top of him as soon as I lost my panties, but he disentangled me from him and stood. His pants were still in place, though his belt lay on the floor.

"Lie down. Let me look at you."

112

Argh. Another delay. Yet I rolled on my back and stretched my arms over my head and my legs like a ballet dancer's. The position lengthened the body, and made the boobs and ass look perky.

"Stop posing, woman. I want to see you."

It was the least refined I'd heard him speak, and it got me impossibly more wet.

I relaxed, and kept my gaze on his face as he scrutinized every inch of my body, nodding to himself from time to time.

"Are you going to touch me?" I hated sounding meek.

He nodded again. "I didn't want our first time to be here. I wanted to take you out and woo you, before taking you in my own bed. You'd look gorgeous sprawled naked in my blue silk sheets."

I swallowed the knot in my throat. "I'm sorry I ruined it for you." I *so* wasn't. I was only sorry we were still talking.

"You didn't. My nature did."

I looked at him quizzically.

"I am a Viking, Cherry. When I see something I want, I take it. I've denied myself too long with you."

Finally!

He grabbed my ankles and pulled so my legs dangled off the bed. When he knelt between my thighs, I thanked whatever deity was listening.

"Remember when I told you there were two places I prefer to feed on?" He glided his cheek along my inner thigh, and nuzzled my hipbone.

I hummed, barely recalling what he was talking about. My entire body ablaze with anticipation, I spread my legs wider and shuffled closer to the edge of the mattress. I needed him to touch me.

He placed open mouthed kissed down to my groin. "I love the neck. Love how fragile it is. How

113

close to the heart." He teased two fingers along my slit. "Gods, you are so ready for me."

"Mmhmm." I was. I wanted his face or his fingers or his cock to finally alleviate the ache burning in my pussy.

"My favorite feeding spot is far more intimate. Sinister, in some cases. Easier to hide, but needs the donor completely exposed. Like you are now."

I didn't catch on, until he slid his fangs inside my femoral artery at the same time he buried two fingers in my pussy. Despite the lack of pain, panic surged at the memory of the last time I felt the double intrusion. I chased it away. This was Constantine. He wouldn't hurt me, and the proof was in the pulls he took of my blood.

He wasn't gulping it down. He was savoring it, using his tongue to lave my skin as his talented fingers brought me closer to release.

If he just flicked my clit, I'd come, but he took his time drinking me in and drawing out my pleasure.

I decided to take things into my own hands, but the moment I snaked my hand between my legs, he growled. No words. Just a guttural sound that stopped me in my tracks. His meaning was crystal clear. I was his to please or leave wanting.

"Constantine, please."

He withdrew his fingers, and moments later stood before me with his pants undone. His cock was as pale as the rest of him, long, and thick. I licked my lips and held out my arms to him, expecting him to drape his body over mine.

He smirked. "I don't think the bed can take me." Using the vampire speed I had yet to get used to, he lifted me with my back against the wall, and slid inside me.

Fuck.

He impaled his entire length in me in a single stroke, and I groaned in pain as much as pleasure. Not letting me adjust to his girth, he pulled back and thrust again, and I realized why he wanted to avoid the bed.

I wouldn't have survived sex with Constantine as a human. As a vampire, I knew my bruises where his hips met mine would fade by morning, and I relished the force of our coupling. Each time he drove forward, I felt fuller than ever before. When he withdrew, I clenched around him to keep him in place.

I raked my nails down his back, and my fangs elongated at the dizzying smell of his blood. "I need…" Everything he could give me.

He arched his neck and I bit him without further prompting. I wasn't as gentle as he'd been, but even if I wanted to, his plunges jarred me, tearing the edges of my bite mark raw. As I sucked in his blood, a rivulet spilled down my chin, but I couldn't care. As I'd expected, having him inside me while I fed on him sent me hurtling over the edge, in what felt like a never-ending climax. Lights burst behind my eyelids—when had I closed my eyes?—and my mouth was dry. My limbs felt heavy and made of cotton at the same time.

I sagged against him, his body pinning me to the wall the only thing that kept me from collapsing. "Well, that was fun," I gasped out, dusting plaster from my hair.

"Still is." He jerked his hips forward. "I'm not done with you yet." He kept pumping, building up toward his own orgasm, and I got my second wind.

By the time he finally came, I was a blubbering mess of pleasure, and thanking my good fortune I was turned into a vampire and could actually enjoy this experience.

"Next time, I'll have you in my bed," he whispered, as he tucked me in against him. "It's built for us."

It only took him twenty four hours to get a permit that allowed me to spend days and nights outside VSS as long as I was with him. It took us about twenty minutes longer than that to test his bed. In his *mansion*. Where he had a live-in *butler*. His bed was larger than my entire room at VSS, which meant I got to giggle and roll around a lot when he pounced on me.

It proved to be impressively sturdy, as Constantine took his time contorting me into positions I didn't think possible, and making me come repeatedly, until I begged him for some sleep.

As a human, I never knew sex could be this spectacular.

I never knew a lot of things, and true to his word, Constantine proceeded to teach me. He introduced me to the classics, though I never picked up Latin and was a complete failure in Ancient Greek.

He spent an hour every evening sparring with me, showing me mostly defensive moves in case I needed to fight another vampire, but also how to attack and feed from a human without causing lasting damage. I didn't need the latter while I was with him, of course. After we made love, or even while we were all over each other, he'd let me take my fill of his deliciously rich blood.

He taught me what it felt like to be so in love with someone, I lost myself in him.

Most importantly though, he taught me I couldn't trust any man just because he claimed to love me. Even the most adoring boyfriend could be fucking someone else on the side. Oh, say, his bitch of a maker.

On the bed he shared with me.

And then try to pass it off as something vampires do, since eternity is too long for anyone to be monogamous.

Yes, Constantine taught me a lot.
And now I'm on my own.

(so *not*) The End

~*~*~

*If you enjoyed **Cherry Pop,** the story continues in
Cherry Stem (Cherry Vampire Book 1)*

~*~*~

Operation: Winter Cupid, A Cupid

Novella by Allyson Lindt

Josh loves being a cupid—offering comfort to lonely souls and sharing a little holiday joy. Seeing people smile is his favorite part of the job. Ella should just be another assignment, but something about her smile and sad gaze draws him in and holds his attention captive.

Now, with only one week before The Powers That Be pull Josh away from the woman who's stolen his heart, he has to convince her he's not insane when he says he's a cupid, and make sure their future extends beyond a kiss at midnight.

Chapter One

Ella's footsteps echoed off concrete as she skipped down the stairs. Christmas. An entire week away from work. Away from phone calls, and stress, and deadlines. She pushed out of the stairwell and into the main floor of the office building she worked in.

It was true, she was spending the week alone. Her family lived out of state, and she was single—by choice, so it wasn't like she was moping over some guy—but she was looking forward to all the alone time to catch up on her reading. Maybe do an extra deep clean around her apartment.

Normally the self-assurance sated any gnawing dissatisfaction inside. Today, the word *alone* echoed in time with the slap of her boots against tile, taunting her.

"Ella." Ashton's voice landed against her back.

She bit the inside of her cheek, as her stomach fluttered against her will, and she paused in the middle of the hallway. Ashton was so off limits it wasn't funny. Even if she were looking for a relationship, and even though he was gorgeous with his square jaw and six-foot two inches of sculpted yumminess, he was a solid asshole when it came to relationships. In the two years they'd worked together, he'd flirted with her and every other woman in the office, and skipped from one girlfriend to the next without pausing.

And still, she couldn't stop her body from reacting when he was around. Stupid physical attraction.

"Hey." He draped an arm over her shoulders. "I'm so glad I caught up to you."

Her skin tingled at the contact, and she brushed the desire aside. "What's up?" At least that had come out naturally, instead of the swoony thing her head was doing.

"Got any plans over Christmas break?"

Was he asking because he wanted some of her time, or because he was being friendly? Fortunately, the answer was the same either way. "Nothing specific. Catching up on some reading, seeing what else comes along."

He scooted closer, breath hot against her cheek. "Does that mean you could maybe make time for me?"

Once upon a time she'd interpreted this kind of behavior from him as meaning something. Thought he liked her. It hadn't taken her long to figure out he was this forward with most women who didn't slap him for it. That still didn't stop her body from reacting to his touch, though. Bad idea. Stupid, bad idea. But her racing pulse knew what she wanted to say. Her, "Probably," came out more breathlessly than she intended.

"Because Gordon's got me on call for the next seven days. And I'm supposed to meet Stacey's family, and I can't be hauling my phone around."

Ella swallowed a growl as her creeping excitement vanished. "Sonja."

"What?"

"I thought your girlfriend's name was Sonja."

"Oh, yeah." He laughed and stepped away. "Nah. We're over. I met Stacey during one of the user meetings."

"You're dating a focus group participant?" So much for unbiased feedback. Ella's irritation grew.

"Yeah, I guess. So can you cover for me, please? I'll owe you forever."

She swallowed her sigh. It wasn't like she was doing anything else, and being on call didn't necessarily mean working, just the possibility. "Sure."

"You're the best, Ella." He kissed her on the cheek before almost sprinting toward a car waiting for him by the front entrance.

She watched in the fading light as he hopped into the waiting—was that a Mercedes?—by the front doors, and shared a longer, much less chaste kiss with the driver.

Ella shook her head and turned toward the back parking lot. She was such an idiot. But she would have told anyone yes, not just him. Her colleagues had people to spend their holiday with. It would be selfish of her to take that from them.

Her spirits lifted as she stepped into the cool evening. A bite in the air promised snow, and the crisp night filled her lungs with a wonderful scent when she breathed deep. Yeah, being on call wasn't a big deal.

The parking lights dotted the asphalt as she made her way toward her car at the back of the lot, marking each row.

"Excuse me, miss?" For the second time in as many minutes, a male voice interrupted her thoughts. He wasn't talking to her though—she didn't know that voice. She kept walking.

Her short journey stopped when someone stepped in her path. Her breath caught in her throat as she found herself staring into the most gorgeous blue

Operation: Winter Cupid by Allyson Lindt

eyes she'd ever seen.

"I think you dropped a glove." He held something out.

"I—what?" It took focus to draw her attention from his face. Ashton had a kind of bad-boy sexy going on, but this guy was just...wow. Short, dark hair, a build that she wanted to run her fingers over solely to see if he was as firm as he looked, and that smile. It made her insides melt.

He handed her the fingerless glove. "I think you dropped this."

Right. She was probably staring. At least she wasn't drooling. She forced herself to return his friendly expression, and shook her head. "Thanks, but it's not mine." She held up two gloved hands.

"Oh. I was sure..." His eyes never left her face. "Are you all right?"

The nature of the question caught her more off-guard than the sudden change in subject. "I think so." What did she look like to make him asked that? And even if the loneliness pinging in her heart was more than a temporary longing, it wasn't like she was going to unload on this stranger.

"If you're sure." He shoved the glove in his jacket pocket. Brown leather, and the way it hung off his shoulders taunted her. She wanted to step closer, and inhale the heady scent of leather and soap. "There's something sad in your eyes." He pulled his gaze away for the first time since he'd stopped her. "Don't get me wrong. They're beautiful, but it's a shame to see someone as pretty as you looking down."

Heat flooded her cheeks, despite the cold. A random stranger was complimenting her in the middle of an almost deserted parking lot. It was flattering, but a little creepy. Then why didn't she feel more nervous? Her looming alone time must be screwing with her thoughts. "I'm fine. I hope you find the glove's owner."

"Of course." He stepped aside immediately. Relief tinged with disappointment flooded her.

"Have a good night," she said as she passed him. The bizarre conversation didn't stop her from inhaling one last time as her shoulder brushed his.

"Wait." His request halted her. "I know this is going to sound odd."

Because the entire exchange up to this point had been normal? She turned her head and realized his face was closer than she'd expected. Her heart hammered in her chest. All he had to do was tilt in, and they'd be kissing. Or if she rose on her toes... What was wrong with her? She waited for him to continue, not trusting herself to speak.

"There's a little café across the street. They serve sandwiches and such for the next couple of hours."

"I know the place." She stopped there on the way home from work a lot when she didn't feel like cooking for one.

"I'm heading over there for dinner. I know you said nothing's wrong, but if you want to talk... I'll have a table in the back and you're welcome to join me."

Her laugh came out more nervously than she intended. The whole setup should make her skin crawl. Strange man, deserted parking lot, extra friendly. Why was she hesitating to walk away? "Thanks for the offer, but I'm good."

He shrugged. "Have a good night, then."

By the time Ella sank into her car, he was gone. That was odd. She turned the engine and tossed the hatchback into gear. Why was she thinking about taking him up on his offer? No, bad idea. Ashton was proof that the hottest guys tended to know exactly how attractive they were. This stranger probably expected her to pick up the tab or something.

She navigated toward the exit, and turned her car in the opposite direction of the café.

Chapter Two

The restaurant was almost empty, giving Josh a clear view of the door from his seat near the back of the small dining area. Normally with an assignment, right about now he'd be counting seconds until she—or he—appeared in the entrance. Making a wager with himself. Seeing how long it took the person to change their mind and join him.

This woman—Ella, according to her docket—was different. It wasn't just that her full lips made his skin tingle and his blood roar. There was something about the way she held herself that made her difficult to read. And that was as enticing as anything.

Not that he was there to be drawn into a relationship. He pushed the reminder to the forefront of his mind. As a cupid—someone who had died too young, been brought back, and given a second chance at life in exchange for helping people—his job was to cheer up his assignments. Show them the bright side of life, and make sure they left the meeting feeling better.

Except he wasn't even sure this woman needed that. She radiated a confidence that hid most of the sadness in her face. Maybe hid any sorrow at all. Was he supposed to be waiting for someone else right now?

But no. *They*, the people who gave him his jobs, didn't make mistakes like that.

The chime of the front door rolled through the room, and he pushed his attention back to the entrance. Ten minutes. She'd shown up after all. A grin threatened to split his face, and he reined the unexpected joy back in. Approaching strangers in parking lots was bad enough, he didn't need to scare her off with a toothy smile.

The corner of her mouth twitched when she met his gaze across the room, and after exchanging a few words with the hostess, she made her way toward him.

The sway of her hips kicked his pulse up a notch, and the way her tongue trailed over her lips when she licked them nervously heated his blood. She wasn't the first attractive assignment he'd had, but she was the first he couldn't take his eyes off.

He was on his feet and pulling out a chair before she reached the table. "I'm glad you changed your mind." The words were scripted, but a flicker of joy flared inside when he realized how much he meant them.

After a moment's hesitation, she slid into the seat, as if she wasn't sure what to do with a gesture like that. "Me too." She shook her head, as if trying to scatter something loose inside. "I mean, I needed dinner anyway."

Hesitation, uncertainty. He could handle that. Making her feel at ease was part of his training. He took his chair again, while he studied her. All the thoughts in his head vanished when she tucked a strand of blonde behind her ear, and looked up at him through her eyelashes. The flush of pink on her cheeks from the cold, the way her bottom lip caught between her teeth, it wreaked havoc on his thoughts.

He mentally grasped for reason. "Then lucky me that you chose my table. I'm Josh by the way." He extended his hand.

"Ella." She nestled her palm in his, and a new spark of want raced through him. The desire to pull her close, claim those full lips, taste her until neither she nor he could breathe. He tucked most of the reaction away, but his pulse still thrummed under her touch.

She pulled away far too soon for his liking, intertwined her fingers, and rested her hands on the edge of the table. "Don't take this the wrong way, I'm sure you're a really nice guy, but I'm not sure why I'm here. I don't usually do things like this."

He could do this. It was the kind of response he was prepared for. "Like have dinner?"

A tiny laugh floated past her list. Easy and casual, despite her stiff posture. "With strangers. When no one else is really around."

He nodded at the hostess, and the waiter. "You know the place and the staff. Does that help?"

"Apparently. I'm here, right?" She fiddled with her fork, first turning it over, then nudging it closer to the knife, before finally returning it its original position. "What about you? Do you do this a lot?"

The honest answer would be yes, and for some reason, it took all of his willpower not to say exactly that. He knew better. It didn't matter how much he hated deception, the smart response was never going to be, *"Sure. I spend a large part of my life seeking out strangers who need a smile and doing what I can to help them. I love doing it, and it's only fair I offer that in exchange for being brought back to life by some unknown force."* Yeah, that wasn't such a great response.

Besides, he didn't want her to think she fell into the same category as anyone else. The waiter interrupted before he had a chance to think of an honest answer that wouldn't give too much away.

They placed their orders, and her eyes grew wide when he said he'd get the bill.

The moment the waiter was out of earshot, she leaned in, voice low. "I can't let you do that. I appreciate the offer, but I can pay for my own meal."

"I don't question that. But..." How was he going to get her to open up? The answer flowed to his tongue before he could process the words. "When was the last time you let someone do something for you?"

Her lips drew into a thin line, and she sat up straighter. Wow, that was a bad way to phrase that. He hadn't meant to be accusatory. When she spoke, sadness lined her voice. "It's not something that comes up a lot. Or ever, really."

With any new assignment, he was only given very basic information. If there were a tragedy in the person's life for instance, or some other event that could trigger a negative response. But for the most part, knowing too much made the meeting less natural. There had been hardly anything about Ella, though. A few notes about being a top performer at work, that she was single, and living miles from her family.

"It should be." He risked reaching across the table and lightly grasping her fingertips. The same shock as before raced through him, accompanied by an irrational glee when she didn't pull away. "You deserve to be spoiled. Let me do that."

"How do you know that?" she asked. "I might be a raging bitch." She ducked her head. "Sorry."

"I'm good at reading people." He traced his thumb over the back of her knuckles.

This time bitterness slipped into her laugh. "Okay, sure. Then what do you read from me?"

"You're kind, you're generous, and people take

advantage of you too often." That hadn't been in her docket. But none of that was hard to guess after talking to her even for the short amount of time she'd been there. "And something's got you down tonight."

She flipped her fork over a few more times, and a pause stretched between them. Finally she said, "Nothing I can't handle."

There was that sadness again. Heavier this time. More obvious. It dragged up an instinct to protect her and beat back anything that caused her that kind of melancholy. "I'm not saying you can't. But sometimes it helps to talk."

"No, it really doesn't. Especially not to someone I don't know."

"You're not talking to the people you do know, right?" He prodded. "I promise I don't make judgments. I'm offering a sympathetic ear, with no expectations."

She chewed on her bottom lip, gaze finally meeting his. The longing in her eyes stole his breath, and made his chest ache. When she spoke, her voice was low and raw. "It's nothing big, really. I just get a little lonely this time of year. It's not that I need someone to complete me, or anything like that. But sometimes going home to an empty apartment gets to be too much. Even my friends are telling me I need to get la—"

Pink flooded her cheeks and she ducked her head. "Telling me I need to get out more. You know, do... stuff."

His brain latched onto the slip, and taunted him with it. The almost-confession triggered an avalanche of ideas in Josh's head. Images of scooting her back on the hood of his car. Pushing between her legs. Tangling his fingers in that long hair and tugging hard.

It took all of his restraint to keep his voice steady, despite the nagging ache growing below his waist. "I was serious when I said no judgments. I'm here to listen." *And volunteer to help you out if you're interested.* Wrong direction to let his thoughts wander.

First of all, he'd never see her again after tonight. Cupids weren't new best friends, or dates, their job was to help cheer an assignment up. Second, it was one of the very basic rules. This kind of companionship sometimes led to a connection, which was why the cupid guidelines stated very clearly that sleeping with an assignment could cost a person their second chance.

She peeked up at him again. "Why?"

He backpedaled through the mire of lust, searching for root for her question. "Why would I listen?"

She nodded.

"Why wouldn't I?"

Chapter Three

Ella sipped her drink, wincing when the straw gurgled indicating she was out of soda. She'd managed to make the glass last for the last two hours. Every time the waiter offered her a refill, she'd waved him off, telling herself any minute now she'd cut the conversation short with Josh, and they'd go their separate ways.

She was having too much fun though. Talking openly wasn't something she did, and it had been ages since she'd enjoyed a conversation so much. They clicked in a way she hadn't realized existed.

That and she swore every time things crossed the line into heavy innuendo, his pupils dilated, and he leaned in closer. Which was fine with her. Even if she couldn't enjoy more than this meal with him, she was stockpiling a wide array of fantasies to keep her company over the next few nights.

Images of what it would feel like to have those arms pin her down. To feel his mouth on hers, the rough scrape of five o'clock shadow on her skin. Dampness grew between her legs as she let her mind trip over the thoughts.

"I was at a brand new company, right?" He was animated when he spoke. Arms moving, expression shifting with every word. They were swapping horror stories about jobs. "I'd been there less than two months, and didn't know hardly anyone."

She rested her arms on the table, and leaned in. "I have a hard time believing you didn't make friends with everyone your first day there." The teasing rolled into her tone without thought.

"Well it's true." He scooted his chair closer, until his knee brushed hers. "Anyway. Apparently every Christmas they did this gag gift exchange. Everyone pulled a name from the hat, got that person a gag gift, and we all had to open our presents in front of the entire company at the annual party."

His wit was turning her on as much as his body. Such a delicious combination. He continued. "I thought I'd be clever. I thought *gag gift,* and the first thing that came to mind was literal." He paused, searching her face. "As in, a ball gag."

Delicious heat flooded her skin, and she laughed. "You didn't."

"I absolutely did. And I promise you I knew everyone after that night. For the couple of years I was there, every Christmas around party time, people would talk about how 'no one will ever top what Josh did.'"

"I would have died of embarrassment."

"I'd get you something a little more subtle." He winked. "A blindfold maybe."

Wetness pooled between her legs at the suggestion, and her reply came out breathy. "I like the sound of that." Was she really flirting openly with this guy? She couldn't believe her own boldness.

A question popped into her head, not for the first time that night. She almost didn't want to ask, afraid she might actually get an answer this time, but curiosity won out. "You changed the subject every time I've asked you this. Do you do this often? Invite random strangers to dinner just to let them bend your ear?"

She didn't know why she kept pushing the issue. She should accept she was special and leave it at that.

His gaze dropped to the table for a moment before be looked at her again. "Honestly?"

That wasn't what he was supposed to say. He was supposed to come back with a rapid fire, *Yes, you're the only one.* "Yes. Honestly."

"Yes and no."

Not the answer she'd been hoping for, and it definitely didn't clear anything up. Her gut sank with heavy disappointment. "Could you be more specific?"

He drummed his fingers on the table. The first time all night she'd seen him fidget. Ill-ease filled her. What was so difficult to answer about this one question?

His exhale echoed through the empty restaurant. "I'll tell you but you won't believe me."

"Try me." She couldn't keep the edge from her voice.

He reached for her hand, then pulled his away before he made contact. His voice was heavy and tight when he replied. "I don't— " He snapped his jaw shut, and exhaled through his nose. "Twenty years ago I died."

Not what she'd expected. In fact, that instant the night went from strange-but-dreamy to downright bizarre. "As in, before you were ten?"

"No, I was the same age I was now." If he was joking, it didn't show on his face. In fact, the only thing she could read in his eyes was... Hope? Pleading? She wasn't even sure.

"Okay. You're a vampire?" Her good mood had evaporated and tension flooded in to take its place. At least they weren't alone here. This was seriously weirding her out.

"A cupid, actually. I died before my time. I was brought back to life, and until I find the life I was supposed to have, I have a kind of temporary stay on aging, and I spend that time making people happy."

A nervous giggle slipped out. He had to be yanking her chain. This time she had to force the teasing into her question "You're joking, right? I mean, cupid. Really? Shouldn't you at least be an elf, given the time of year?"

He grinned, and leaned back in his chair. "I guess elf would make more sense. I'm completely joking." And there was no way that was sadness tugging down the corners of his eyes. "Sorry, I've got a bad sense of humor sometimes. The truth is, in the parking lot I thought you dropped your glove, and all I meant to do was return it to you. You looked a little sad, I wasn't looking forward to spending the night alone and I was hoping you might keep me company."

Relief flowed through her. That was a simple enough explanation. A teeny voice in the back of her head told her she was missing something. She wasn't paying attention to the right things. She shoved it aside. He was here for the same reason she was. A little bit of company on a night when most people were spending time with their loved ones. "I'm glad you asked."

"Me too." He scooted back, and disappointment flooded her. Of course the night had to end sometime. Had she ruined the moment with her distrust? No, he seemed to be having as much fun as she was.

He stood and offered her a hand. "I think they're waiting on us to close." Heat seared through her when her fingers brushed his, and he tugged her to her feet.

136

"I guess I should get home, and let you do the same." A nagging ache grew in her chest.

He was silent as they walked toward the exit, but never dropped her hand. Had he heard her? What was going through his head? They pushed out into the parking lot. Her hatchback and a battered old Impala were the only two cars left in the front lot.

"You're lucky you get to work up here." His footsteps slowed as they neared the cars.

She matched his pace, not in a hurry to head home to her empty apartment alone. "I guess."

He intertwined his fingers with hers and tugged her toward the edge of the parking lot. Heat and desire seared her senses. This wasn't the same physical response she had to Ashton's meaningless flirting. She swore something flowed between her and Josh.

He gestured to the valley below. "You work up here in the foothills. The view at night has always been one of my favorites."

She stepped up next to him, and followed his sweeping gesture. They were looking down over the valley, and a million lights twinkled back at them. Every color sparkling like Christmas. How had she never noticed that before? Awe swelled inside. "It's gorgeous."

"It's one of my favorite sights." His voice dropped an octave. "But it's never looked as good as right now."

She turned to ask him what he meant. Her question died in her throat when she realized he was staring at her, not the view.

He brushed a strand of hair from her cheek. "I know, this is only for tonight, and we'll probably never see each other again, but I really enjoyed getting to know you."

Something in his voice stopped her from asking

137

how he could be certain this was it for them. There was no reason they couldn't exchange numbers. He obviously had some reason to be near her office, and he was more familiar with the valley view than she was, so he was probably local or knew someone who was.

She swallowed the question as an irrational fear welled inside her. One that told her if she asked, she might find out exactly how true his statement was, and she wouldn't like the answer. Instead she said, "I had a lot of fun too."

He moved his hand to the back of her neck, and wove his fingers into her hair. Her pulse kicked into overdrive at the gentle contact. When he tilted his head in and kissed her softly, she swore her heart was about to beat its way out of her chest.

She parted her lips, and his tongue drove in. The kiss went from soft to hungry in instant. She rested her fingers on his chest, fingers digging into muscle, and groaned against his mouth.

When they finally split apart, her head swam, threatening to float away.

He traced a thumb over her cheek. "Thank you for the evening, Ella. I'm sorry it has to end."

"Why?" She shouldn't ask, part of her knew that. As soon as the question passed her lips, she wanted to take it back.

"Because." He put several inches between them, leaving a longing ache everywhere he'd touched. "I should let you get home."

Her chest deflated with hurt and disappointment. It wasn't an answer, and as much as she wanted one, she wasn't sure she'd believe whatever he told her. Still, she wasn't willing to let this connection slip away. She fumbled in her purse for a business card. He already knew where she worked, it wasn't like she was giving him any home information.

He held up his hands. "I can't."

Hurt welled inside, and she smothered it with irritation. "I'm not asking you for the rest of your life, or even the next month. Just offering company if you feel like it again." She held the card toward him. Why was she being so pushy? Still, something inside sparked with hope when he took the card and tucked it into his shirt pocket.

He closed the distance between them again, and traced a thumb over her bottom lip. "I can promise, I'll feel like it again. If you don't believe anything else I said tonight, believe that." He brushed his lips over hers.

She hated the finality in his statement, and the deep regret inside telling her she'd never see this man again.

****

Ella stared at the ceiling in her bedroom, thoughts a jumbled mess. Last time she'd looked at the clock, it read eight am.

She'd replayed the entire evening in her mind over and over since she and Josh parted ways. On her drive home. In between fitful bouts of sleep. She still couldn't make sense of any of the situation.

Even worse, the empty ache in her chest missed him terribly. How was that even possible with someone she'd only known a few hours?

Her work phone chimed and she rolled her eyes. She should be bitter that she was actually being called in on Christmas, but it wasn't like she had other plans. She grabbed the device and pulled up the new email.

Her heart leaped at the message in her inbox. A greeting card website return address. She pushed the hope back down. It wasn't as if it was from *him*. It would be a standard greeting from a colleague. Something they'd scheduled to send out to everyone in the office first thing in the morning. The logic didn't stop her from hoping to see Josh's name on the card when she opened the message.

The image on the front was pleasant, but generic. A couple of baubles nestled in green garland and surrounded by lights.

But the note underneath made her heart soar.

I wasn't going to email you. We're not supposed to ever see each other again. But in a week, if you're still interested in knowing why I sought you out, spend New Year's Eve with me. If you've forgotten me by then, I'll understand.

Either way, I'll always remember last night.

Josh

Underneath his name was an address, a restaurant name, and a time.

She sank back onto her bed, butterflies and sparks dancing through her veins. He wanted to see her again. She wasn't the only one who'd felt at least a little spark.

Hitting reply, she swiped out a quick message. Scanning it, she read, deleted, and retyped it several times before finally deciding on a simple,

New Year's Eve sounds wonderful. I'll see you then.

Ella

There, that didn't sound too needy, but still sounded genuine, right? Her smile grew. It had been eons since she felt like this about someone, and she'd only spent a few hours with him.

Her email chimed seconds later. Had he already replied? Disappointment and confusion pushed aside some of her elation. The message had bounced back as undeliverable.

He'd used a fake email address to send the card? Josh@cupidinc.luv. It certainly looked fake. That wasn't even a real domain. Was this a sick joke?

No. The fluttering hope in her chest refused to believe it. Second later she was seated at her desk, laptop open, and typing in the domain name, www.cupidinc.luv. The screen flickered, and a generic message popped up. It looked like a search engine box, but it said, *We'll help you find what you're looking for. Just answer our question to get started. What do you wish for more than anything else?*

Josh's words from the night before echoed in her head. *A cupid...until I find the life I was supposed to have...I make people happy.*

Confusion pounded in her skull. This was another part of the joke, right? Logic whispered back this was an awfully long way to go to prove an off-hand comment made in an empty restaurant. But there was no other alternative.

She typed into the box, *I want answers.*

Again, the screen flickered, and when it refreshed, she was looking at a Page Not Found error.

No, that wasn't right. She clicked back, but no matter what she tried in her web browser, she couldn't get the strange website to load again.

Her head throbbed with more questions than answers. Was the message actually from Josh? Would he even be there next week, or was this a bizarre prank?

And why did it feel like the answers were right in front of her, and she still couldn't see them? Last night, she'd just hoped for the chance to see Josh again. Now, even though New Year's Eve was only a week away, she didn't know if she could hold out that long for answers to this bizarre riddle.

Chapter Four

Josh sank into the battered sofa near the front window of the coffee shop. He flopped his head back, and stared at the ceiling for a moment, before focusing again on the woman across from him. "It's just for one night, and I'm not asking for anything extravagant. Just be vague, if anyone asks how I'm spending the evening."

Amanda took a long sip from her cup of coffee. "Don't make me say it. You know you don't want to hear it."

He did know. Irritation crept through him, not at her, but at the entire situation. She was talking about the rules. The same guidelines he'd always adhered to without complaint in the past. There were two very good reasons cupids weren't supposed to hook up with assignments. He waved a hand in irritation. "Yeah, yeah. Emotional connections formed in times of grief are unstable and frequently harmful, and blah, blah, blah."

It wasn't that he disagreed, but right now it was the last thing he wanted to hear. It had only been a week since he met Ella, and they hadn't done more than share dinner…and an incredible kiss. But he hadn't been able to get her out of his head since. It wasn't true love or anything as dramatic, but it might be at some point. Even if it never went further, he knew he'd regret it, if he didn't at least see how things played out with her.

Amanda set her cup down on the low table between them, leaned forward, and clasped her hands. "I notice you didn't mention reason number two."

Because he was trying to pretend it wasn't an issue. The reminder gnawed at him from the inside. It was a bizarre contradiction in the system. A lot of people had a specific fate—were even destined to be with someone—but it didn't mean things turned out that way. They were still allowed to make their own choices and decisions, and could end up completely side-stepping that future.

If he got attached to Ella, he ran the risk of interfering with her fate, assuming she had one.

He pushed back the doubt broiling in his skull. It didn't matter, because he wasn't looking to get attached. "I'm not ignoring any of the reasons."

"But you're going to do this anyway."

He raked his fingers through his hair, and focused a narrowed gaze on Amanda. Why did she have to be the voice of logic here? It was true, that was why he was talking to her, but she wasn't supposed to be so good at it. "It's not like we're hooking up," he said. "And she's not some grief stricken individual who's going to cling to the first guy she meets."

Amanda's brows rose.

He tapped his toes inside his shoes as he waited for a witty retort—or something. Anything. Finally, impatience won out. "I have the night off anyway. I'm just going to spend the free time with a friend. There's nothing wrong with that."

"All right." Amanda leaned back in her seat, expression blank and giving away nothing. "Then you're asking me to cover for you because…?"

Josh opened his mouth to reply, but couldn't find the words. Damn it. This should be an easy answer. Sometimes he appreciated how well Amanda knew him. She'd been his one friend since he'd arrived, and as two of the only cupids who had been in the job for so long, they frequently found confidences in each other.

But just this once, he needed her not peering inside his head. "Devin hooked up with an assignment."

She smiled, but the corners of her eyes still

tugged down. "Devin was one of the lucky few who got to go back to his old life. Are you thinking you want to go back to yours?"

He didn't. It had been a miserable existence filled with venom and hatred. "Please. Do this one thing for me, and I'll owe you anything"

She sighed, stood, and crossed the few short feet to sit next to him. "With Devin, I knew what his fate was. It sucked to push him in that direction and watch it eat at him before he had the answers himself, but I knew the payoff was worth it. With you, I don't have that information."

Of course she wouldn't. She'd been Devin's supervisor. Josh didn't report to her. "I'm not asking you to know."

Amanda rested a hand on his knee. "I don't know this Ella girl, but I'm sure she's nice enough." She'd have to be a good person to earn a cupid companion. "It's you I care about. Don't throw your own future away, because of a little misplaced lust. Don't play this wrong, because you're not thinking straight."

He clenched his jaw until it ached. He wasn't worried about his own fate. This was his decision. But could he live with himself, if this was the moment that stole her future from her, just because he wanted to see her one more time?

Chapter Five

Ella smoothed out her skirt for the millionth time since she'd put on the evening gown. She'd purchased the ankle-length sleeveless dress, when her best friend insisted every woman needed a black dress. But this was the first time she had an excuse to wear it.

Her insides fluttered, as she wove her way through waiting people and toward the front of the restaurant. No familiar faces stared back. Josh wasn't among them. She was early, though. Or maybe he'd already been seated.

She checked in with the maître de, who confirmed they had a reservation but Josh hadn't arrived yet.

"Thank you." She gave the man her friendliest smile, and moved back into the crowd. She needed a spot that would let her see the door, but keep her out of peoples' way.

After the bounced email and bizarre website incident, she'd dug some more into cupidinc.luv. A basic search yielded dozens of results, almost all of them pointing to conspiracy sites, or urban legend fact-checking pages.

People seemed pretty evenly split on the matter of whether or not cupids were a real thing. At the root of the rumors, whether people believed them or not, was always a story similar to the one Josh had told her.

As the minutes ticked away, she drummed her fingers against the small purse dangling from her wrist, gaze flitting to the entrance every few seconds. A glance at her phone told her it was almost twenty minutes past the hour. She dropped the phone back in her wristlet.

Doubt grew inside, pushing out the elation she'd let propel her here at the start of the night. Why had she thought this was a good idea?

Her phone vibrated against her leg, and she jumped, startled. A nervous giggle slipped out, and she glanced at the other waiting faces. Had anyone seen that? No, everyone was busy doing their own thing and involved in their own conversations. . Their dates hadn't bailed on them.

The bitter thought welled inside, as she checked the text message that had just come in.

"Shit," she muttered under her breath. The servers were down in the office. Her foul mood grew, as she shoved back through the crowd and toward her car. Shooting the restaurant one last glance, she headed toward work.

At least Josh hadn't shown and then left her with the bill. Even the couple of times that had happened to her in the past were enough to make her wary. If he was going to flake, it was better he not show at all, right?

Except the gnawing ache in her chest didn't like the reassurance. She'd only spent a few hours with him—the stranger she met in the parking lot, of all places. So why did it hurt so much that he stood her up?

The questions repeated in her head, circling and

taunting and mingling with her rationale that it didn't matter that he hadn't shown. It wasn't a big deal. She was better off working tonight anyway.

She let herself into the building. The dim after-hours lighting cast long shadows around her, as she made her way to the elevator, rode up, and crossed the lobby to the server room. If she couldn't bring things back online from here, she'd have to go to the data center, but odds were good she could fix everything from the office.

The process of rebooting the servers was simple. Which should have been nice, but it meant her mind was still free to wander over her failed evening, and try and make sense of her disappointment.

Not that she was reaching any new conclusions. It wasn't like she wanted to marry the guy, but if she had to be honest, another evening of his company, and maybe seeing where things went from there, would have been wonderful.

She slipped her heels off, and tucked them neatly under the desk. *Thank God. Those were killing me.* One thing to be grateful for tonight.

A loud ringing filled the building, a hundred phones vying for attention simultaneously, and for the second time that night she almost jumped out of her skin.

She took a couple of deep breaths to calm her hammering heart. It was just the front door. There was an intercom hooked up to the phone system, for after-hours deliveries, but no one should be delivering anything now.

Her racing pulse insisted she ignore the caller and pretend no one was around. Her curiosity had to know who it was, though. She pulled up the security feed on a different machine than the one she was working on.

A rainbow of emotions rushed through her, when she saw Josh standing at the front door. Hurt, longing, and on top of it all, irritation. Her annoyance smothered any other reaction. She snarled at the screen, and hit the speakerphone button. "Is this fun for you?"

Satisfaction sparked inside when he startled and then spun back toward the intercom near the door.

"Ella, I'm so glad you're here. I mean I'm not, but I was hoping I'd find you." His voice was the same smooth, confident baritone that sent fingers of tantalizing desire down her spine just a few days earlier.

She swallowed back the response and buried it in the sick pit of confusion growing in her gut. "Creepiness aside, I don't put up with bullshit like this...whatever you're doing. If your real date stood you up—if you're just screwing with my head—I'm not interested."

On screen he searched the lobby around him, until he looked directly at the camera. "You gave me your business card, your car is in the parking lot, and you said you were on call."

It was a good explanation, but it didn't sound at all like an apology or any sort of reason for not showing at dinner. Her frustration flowed. "If you really wanted to find me, I was sitting alone in a restaurant about forty-five minutes ago, feeling like the biggest idiot in the universe for thinking you were going to be there."

He ducked his head, and shoved his hands in his pockets. "I tried to stay away. I'm sorry, but I thought I was doing what was best for you. Except I couldn't leave things that way."

"Wow." Her laugh barked back at her in the empty room. "What was best for me? Turns out that line sounds even worse, when someone is feeding it to me directly. Way to twist the knife." She was letting more of her hurt show than she wanted, but she couldn't dial it back.

"Let me explain?" Pleading carried in his voice even over the crappy speaker phone, and tugged at the part of her that wanted this to be more than some kind of twisted... She didn't even know. No. She wasn't getting sucked into his stories, as much as they spoke to her sense of whimsy. "Is this like your bullshit cupid story? Because I'm not in as good a mood as I was that night."

His shoulders slumped. "You're right. I'll leave. Just remember what I said before. Regardless of anything else that happened or will happen, I wanted to see you tonight. I still want to see you."

Was he actually wounded?

Served him right.

She wanted to be furious. An emotional gash still sliced her heart, but he looked sincere.

"Wait." The word pushed past her lips before she could swallow it back. What was she doing?

Chapter Six

Ella walked toward the front door, even as her thoughts spiraled out of control. He wasn't begging, or making up excuses, or cajoling, or any of the things she expected to accompany someone trying too hard to make their lies believable. And if he meant what he said, he was exposing his heart. Opening up in a way she wasn't used to.

She still couldn't get past his bizarre story—everything he'd said about being a cupid, what she'd found online. Part of her wanted to believe in that magic as much as she wanted his words to be genuine.

He was pacing in front of the entrance, when the glass doors came into her view seconds later. She wasn't sure why she was doing this. Logic said she needed to avoid everything about the situation, and still she was compelled to talk to him face to face. To hear him out.

When she pushed one door open wide enough for him to step through, he looked up. Some of the stress vanished from his face.

"I'm still pissed off about being stood up." She crossed her arms to keep herself from fidgeting. Now that he was actually in front of her again, that tempting scent of leather and soap teasing her, images of their dinner on Christmas Eve rushed back more vividly than she thought possible.

He looked even better than her memory gave him credit for. He wore a suit jacket under his coat, and his white shirt was pressed, top button undone. His tie hung unknotted around his neck.

She'd been too furious to notice when she was watching him on the security camera, but he looked like he'd dressed for dinner too.

He kept his distance, toe tapping to a rhythm she couldn't hear. "You should be. It was an asinine thing to do. I had my reasons, but they weren't good. I'm sorry."

Each time he apologized, it kicked more of her irritation aside. A tiny voice asked, *What if you're reading his sincerity completely wrong? You stay single to keep from getting hurt.* Not completely true, but she knew the people around her saw it that way, and it was such a simple explanation, sometimes it was easier to believe it herself. "You said you wanted to explain."

His fidgeting stopped. "I do. But I don't think you're going to believe me."

So he was going to fall back on the ridiculous story. A spark of hope ignited inside. Part of her wanted him to make her believe. "I'll start for you. All that stuff you told me at dinner about being a cupid and dying twenty years ago—you're going to tell me it's true, right?" She tried to keep a skeptical tone in her voice, but the desire for something magical won out, and her optimism shone through instead.

"I am, and it is. According to my birth certificate, I'm almost fifty. But really, I was in my late twenties when I died, and I haven't aged since they brought me back. I won't until my contract with the company ends, for whatever reason."

"That sounds kind of final." She'd meant to keep the comment to herself, along with the concern it summoned inside.

"It's not as bad as all that. Like I said before, my job is to make people smile. It might be that they don't need me anymore, and I'll be free to live my own life. Or I'll figure out what I'm supposed to be doing with myself, and set off on my own. Or—" His brow furrowed. "There are a lot of reasons, but none of them is bad, depending on your perspective. I'm basically in this kind of holding pattern, until that happens. I don't age. I don't get sick. I can't die."

As much as she wanted to believe, this was all a bit much to swallow. "It's a good story. Why would that make it better to leave me alone in a restaurant, when *you* made the date?" She hadn't meant her question to sound so bitter, but she struggled to contain all the emotions swirling inside.

"Because if you have a different future ahead of you—and I'm not saying you do or don't; I don't get to know that kind of information—meeting up with me might have spoiled that."

"So you took it upon yourself to decide my fate?" She didn't know which bothered her more. That she had something like a fate, or that he thought it was his right to interfere.

"No. I mean, yes, kind of, but no." He raked his fingers through his hair. "No one's future is set in stone. There's just a more likely possible outcome for everyone. The thing is, knowing that, if someone starts second guessing all their decisions, it tends to screw with their head."

It was screwing with hers, and she still wasn't sure she believed it. "So you were going to stay away, and you changed your mind because of magic and fate and resurrection, and I still have a say in the matter."

He raised an eyebrow, and his mouth twisted into a smile. "Basically, yes. But on a not-so-basic level, the more I thought about it, the more I realized spinning my thoughts in knots, trying to figure out the right thing was the wrong way to go. You made the decision to have dinner with me, you chose to show up again tonight, and I asked both times because I wanted to see you. I figured that was really all that mattered. We were both here because that was what we picked."

Out of everything else swirling in her head, the confusion—the warring desire to put her faith in his explanation versus being logical—that was the one thing he said all of her agreed with. And it was a tangible reminder of why she enjoyed his company. "What if I don't believe your story?"

"Then I probably get to keep my job a little longer." He stepped closer, and rested his palm against her cheek. Heat flowed between them, drawing her longing to the surface. "As long as you don't doubt I'm here because I wanted to see you," he said.

Did that mean—? If any of this was real...he'd risked it to see her? She leaned into his touch, searing how real it was into her memory. "I don't doubt it."

"Good." He tilted his head in, and pressed his lips to hers. It was a feather-light sensation, whispering across her skin and singing through her veins. When she leaned into him, he slid his hand to the base of her skull, held her captive, and deepened the kiss.

Desire flared over her skin. She groaned against his mouth, his smell and taste filling her head. Her fingers tingled, as she looped them behind his head, clinging to the moment.

He drew a trail down her chin, along her jaw, and up to her ear, nipping with his teeth between kisses. His voice was low, vibrating through the sensitive skin when he spoke. "The other night, the last thing I wanted to do was leave you." He drew his tongue along the edge of her ear, breath hot and tantalizing. "If I'd been thinking, I would have spent the night wherever and however you wanted."

He glided his fingers down her spine, and she arched her back, pressing tighter against him. "I can't take back walking away or standing you up, but I'm willing to do whatever you'll let me, to make it up to you." His words caressed her cheek.

Fantasy teased her thoughts with vivid images of exactly what she'd like him to do. Arousal ached between her thighs, reminding her it had been ages since she was with anyone. Even longer since she'd been with someone who spoke so strongly to both her mind and body. Hell, it may have never happened.

She pushed his coat off his shoulders, and draped it on the reception desk. "What did you have in mind?"

He nuzzled her neck. "A lot of things that might get me slapped. But I'd be just as happy—in a different way, I'll admit—to spend the night talking."

"Maybe later." The rush of too many emotions colliding in her head blurred into intense need. She slid her frame against him, hip rubbing his hard length through his slacks.

His chuckle faded into a groan. "Am I taking you from work?" One hand glided lower down her back, to cup her ass.

She struggled to focus long enough to find a reply. "Crisis is over. I just have to watch for the next hour or so."

He pushed her back with his body, until she bumped gently into the front desk. "Are there cameras everywhere?"

With her mind tripping over all the places she

wanted to feel him and the fact there was too much clothing between then, answering his questions required more thought than she wanted to exert. She shook her head. "Front door only. They can't see in here."

He left one hand on her behind, and moved the other to her stomach. Palm flat, he inched up until he brushed the bottom of her breast. She gasped at the barely there contact. He dragged his thumb across her nipple through fabric, and wetness grew between her legs. When was the last time she'd been this turned on? She couldn't remember. Her hips swayed at the sensations, and a throbbing need below her waist begged for attention.

"You know"—he kissed down her neck—"if you don't stop me now" —his lips grazed her collarbone—"I'm going to push your dress out of the way, and figure out how many ways I can make you moan. And we're in front of these big glass doors. On display. For anyone to walk in on us."

She didn't care. Well, she might have, if it weren't the middle of the night, or if their offices were on the ground floor, but even then she wasn't sure. She pushed herself onto the desk, wrapped her legs around his, and pulled him so close she felt his heat. "You're drawing this out on purpose, aren't you?"

He dropped his hands to her thighs, grasped the bottom of her dress, and shoved it out of the way, as he forced closer between her legs. "Maybe. But I'm not patient enough to play much longer."

One hand returned to her breast, kneading this time. Pinching the hard nub of a nipple through her dress. The lace of her bra dug into the tender skin, drawing a loud moan from her. While he lavished attention on her chest, the fingers of his other hand danced along her inner thigh, up one side and down the other. She squirmed to get closer to his touch, but each time he neared her mound, he pulled away again.

When he finally made contact, she whimpered in relief. He moved one finger under the crotch of her panties, and caressed her slit. Her hips thrust forward, and he obliged, parting her folds. She cried out when he slid two fingers inside her.

He nibbled at the soft spot where her neck met her shoulder. "You're so wet."

"I think you had something to do with tha—" Her words evaporated when his thumb found her clit. He bumped the swollen button, rubbing tiny circles and then pulling away. He nudged her close to the edge of climax each time, before easing off.

He finally relented, grinding hard against her sex, and orgasm tore through her. The wave washed over her, lingering when he didn't let up. Cries tearing from her throat, she ground into his hand, vaguely aware of the sound of a zipper sliding down followed by foil tearing.

She pulled away from his touch when it became too much, and he moved his hand to her leg, thumb tracing her thigh.

He nibbled her earlobe. "You make the most delicious noises when you come. I want to hear you scream again."

There was no hesitation when he pushed inside her, burying his thick length to the hilt and stretching her out. She wrapped her legs around his waist and arms around his neck, thrusting against him in time to his frantic pace.

Every time he drove inside, he hit a spot that tingled through her entire body. His breathing turned into grunts, as he increased his rhythm. She tightened her grip on him, holding tight as orgasm built inside again. She cried out when she came again, clenching around his cock.

He bit into her shoulder as he pounded hard and fast, groans vibrating through her body. Somewhere through the euphoria, their voices mingled in a climactic chorus.

She grasped for breath and reason, as he slowed and then stopped but didn't pull out of her. She buried her face against his chest, struggling for her voice. "I, um... Wow."

He trailed his fingers through her hair, his heart hammering against her ear. His voice carried through her cheek. "Yeah, me too."

A sudden wave of uncertainty gripped her, and she failed to shove it aside. "Is this the only reason you're here?"

He placed a finger under her chin, and raised her head until her eyes met his. His voice was gentle but certain. "I meant what I said. Even if all you want from me is hours of conversation, I'm great with that." He brushed his lips over hers. "Not that I'm complaining about this. You're incredible."

Heat flooded her cheeks at the blatant flattery, and comfort settled in when he wrapped his arms around her. She wasn't sure what she'd done to deserve this moment, but she was going to enjoy it for all it was worth.

He kissed the top of her head. "Happy New Year, by the way."

She moved her head enough to read the clock. Sure enough, it was midnight, on the nose. "I can't think of a better way to ring in the new year."

Chapter Seven

Josh pulled up an office chair next to Ella's, until his knees brushed her leg. They'd broken apart long enough to clean up a little, and then she'd pulled him back to the server room. He was happy to follow, unwilling to call it a night just yet. If she was stuck here, even just for another half hour, he could keep her company.

She clicked through a couple of things on the screen, then spun her seat back so she faced him. "I'm still having a hard time believing your story."

He shrugged. "Because you're smart, and it's a ridiculous story. But," he added when she frowned, "it's true."

"I don't suppose asking you to prove it will do me any good."

He'd been thinking about that, and every time he believed he had a solution, it fell flat when he mentally followed it to a conclusion. "I can try, but you'll still have to take some of it on faith."

She intertwined her fingers with his, and rested both hands on her knee. "Do your best."

He nodded at her computer. "Search obituaries,

twenty years ago, in the Tribune."

She raised her eyebrows, gaze raking over his face for a moment, before she turned back to a computer. His gut turned in on itself when she pulled up the article. He'd read it all those years ago, after they'd brought him back, but after so long he'd forgotten how surreal it was. The picture next to the clipping was him, looking exactly as he looked now, but in a T-shirt. He scanned the first few sentences, and then had to turn away.

The words were burned into his memory anyway, even though the newspaper didn't tell the whole story. They said he'd been shot and killed by police fire, and that he wasn't survived by any family.

Ella turned to him, face pinched. "Is that really you?"

He swallowed past the lump in his throat. "Yes."

"What happened?" No judgment in her voice, only concern and curiosity.

He dug up the memory, surprised to find it still hurt to drag it to the forefront of his mind. Even after so many years. "My brother, Greg, had a problem. Serious addiction. It ran in the family—I don't know how I escaped it." That morning flashed through his mind as he spoke, playing out as if it happened just a few days ago instead of twenty years. "I begged him to go into rehab. To do something. And then the police knocked."

He dragged in a shaky breath, and pushed calm to the surface. "I didn't realize he'd held up a convenience store the night before and killed both the owner and his wife, trying to score enough cash for his next fix. When the police pounded on the door, Greg answered with a gun in hand."

Her forehead creased as he talked, and she squeezed his hand. He managed a grateful smile. "I don't remember anything after that, except waking up in the morgue. And spending the next several months denying any of it had happened."

"God, I'm so sorry." She scooted closer.

He pushed the fog of the past aside, and shook his head to come back to the now. "It's in the past, really. Though some days I still can't believe I got a second chance, away from all that. Apparently dying was the best thing to ever happen to me." He paused, as something occurred to him. "Until they assigned me to cheer you up."

Pink colored her cheeks. He adored that look on her. It was so natural. So much of what she did felt real, though. He could tell she was being herself, and even the things she hid didn't make her fake.

"What about you?" He didn't want to linger in the past anymore. That was a different life, and even if she wasn't a long-term part of his future—an idea he hated more and more each time it resurfaced—she was here now. "Tell me about the Ella outside of this office."

"I don't have anything nearly as interesting in my past." She gave him a reassuring smile. "Went to college, got an internship, moved across several states for a job in information technology, and here I am."

"What about boyfriends?" Morbid curiosity made him ask, but a hint of dark cloud still hung over him.

She ducked her head. "I haven't really had a lot. A couple of guys I thought I was serious about. But...I don't know. Dating just hasn't been a part of my life, and I haven't missed it, so I don't think about it a lot."

"What would it take to get you to consider it a little more frequently, at least in my case?"

The clouds lifted from her face. "What did you have in mind?"

160

"Anything that lets me see you again." Consequences be damned. "It doesn't have to be more than that right now, but I figure it's a good starting point."

"I'd love that."

He tugged her fingers. "How much longer do you have to be here tonight?"

The corners of her mouth pulled down. "Another hour or two. I have to monitor these updates, and make sure they don't bring the system down again. You can go if you like. I'm giddy that you're here, but I can't ask you to sit around and watch me work."

Something in his gut clenched at the idea of walking away now. It wasn't that he was worried about leaving her; he believed when she said she wanted to see him again. But there were consequences waiting for him back at the cupid offices, and he'd rather enjoy her company as much as possible, before he had to face those.

"You're not really working, right?" He held up his hands when she frowned. "I don't mean to sound rude. You said you're only monitoring things, though. So you only need to give it a little bit of attention?"

"It's true. This isn't really a hands-on process."

His cock stirred, as images of other hands-on activities raced through his mind. So tempting. He tried to be subtle about taking a few deep breaths to calm his heated pulse. "I'll keep you company until you're done here. I still owe you dinner, but this is a start."

As the minutes ticked into an hour, and then two, they chatted about anything and everything. Not just their pasts, but the now. Shared interests, that they both enjoyed high action movies with big explosions and just the right touch of love, and how they spent their free time.

Every time she laughed, or brushed her fingers

over his hand, or leaned into him, something in his chest ached. What was he going to do, if he had to walk away from her before they even made it past the getting-to-know-you stage?

Ella paused mid sentence, as a yawn tore from her throat. She covered her mouth, eyes wide. "I'm sorry. Don't take this the wrong way. I'd have fallen asleep ages ago, if you weren't here."

"I get it." He scooted his chair as close as he could, and pulled her head down to rest on his shoulder. Too bad there wasn't something more convenient in this room for lounging on. *I guess a sofa is counterproductive to a room full of computers.* He trailed his fingers through her hair. "I need to take you home."

She glanced at the screens one more time, never pulling away from him. "Ten more minutes. As soon as that bar there finishes, if nothing flashes or protests, I'm done."

Even as she finished explaining, her voice drooped. Moments later, her breathing evened out, and her weight slumped against his arm. *Angelic, even when she's sleeping.* Where had that come from? He shook the thought away. As soon as her work was finished, he'd wake her up, and make sure she got home safely.

The indicator she'd pointed out raced toward one hundred percent, and then announced it finished successfully. A hint of disappointment swelled in his chest. The night was over.

He moved to nudge her awake, and his hand passed through her.

The pressure of her body resting against his evaporated, and milliseconds later, she was gone. The server room vanished around him, and was replaced with his apartment. *Shit.*

As far as he knew, only *they* had the power to

do something like magically move people from one place to another in an instant, which meant he'd been caught potentially screwing with Ella's fate. His gut twisted in on itself. So much for avoiding reprimand.

Chapter Eight

Josh paced the length of his apartment, too many thoughts racing through his head to make sense of them. When he reached one wall, he spun and made his way back toward the other. According to Amanda, when Devin had done something like this, he'd lost his cupid status within hours. Sunlight streamed through Josh's window. Apparently he'd been doing this for hours, and still hadn't made any headway.

It wasn't that he was stuck. He was sure if he tried the door he could walk out. He jus wasn't sure what to do next. Bow to the people who had given him a chance—wait for them to make their move, or go after Ella.

He wanted to do the latter, more than anything, but unknown consequences stopped him. He'd never forgive himself if he caused something bad to happen to her.

Did he know anyone else who'd broken the rules in this way? No. Every other cupid he knew found their second chance through legitimate channels.

Jumbling his thoughts more than anything was a concern for Ella. She'd wake up alone, most likely back at her place, and not know how she got there or where he'd gone. And possibly missing out on her real future. One he hadn't fiddled with.

As his mind tumbled out of control, a single spot of reason broke through the clutter. *Stop.* He paused in the middle of the living room and breathed deeply. He'd already had this argument, and Ella agreed with his conclusion. Life wasn't worth living, if he spent the rest of it second guessing whether or not each next action was the one he was supposed to take.

What would he do, if he didn't have a list of cupid rules to follow? The question barely finished forming in his head, before he had an answer. *Make sure Ella's all right.*

The only contact information he had for her was her office, though. Knowing her home address hadn't been necessary to his assignment. Her work number would have to do. As he reached for his own phone to call her, it buzzed with a new message. His heart leaped, but he pushed the reaction back down. It wasn't going to be Ella. With any luck, she was still asleep instead of dealing with the kind of confusion she'd have to deal with upon waking up. On top of that, she didn't have any idea how to get hold of him.

The text was from Amanda. *What did you do?*

He gritted his teeth, and dragged his brain for the quickest, least incriminating answer. *Nothing. Talked.* Had some amazing sex, connected mentally in a way he hadn't thought possible—oh, and told her who he was, in such a way she probably believed him. But sure, *nothing* was a legitimate answer.

Amanda responded seconds later. *Your name is flying like a curse word in the office next to mine.*

What was he supposed to say? Saying he was going to push *their* rules aside was easy enough, but actually making decisions after that was still complicated. There were so many variables.

Another message came in from Amanda, before he could figure out his next step. *You slept with her?!?*

For the second time that morning, Josh's surroundings faded, and were replaced with something else. He was in his boss's office. Skinny, a few inches shorter than Josh's six foot two, and with a tendency to turn bright red, if he was experiencing any emotion, Bill was one of the nicest guys Josh had ever met.

Just now, he was almost fuchsia. "What the hell were you thinking?" Bill's voice echoed off the walls. "Telling her who you were? Not just telling her, but having her look it up online, as proof?"

Because when you were a cupid, Big Brother was always watching. Josh never had a problem with it in the past, but now it gnawed at his sleep-deprived senses. "I was thinking, 'Wow, let's find a way to get yelled at?'"

A bitter laugh accompanied Bill's sneer. "Seriously. Twenty freaking years, and now this? What happens if she tells people?"

Josh should feel remorse, or guilt, or something. He did feel bad for making Bill turn fluorescent pink, but that was the extend of it. Questions he'd asked twenty years ago, the ones shoved aside and eventually forgotten as he grew content, flooded his head. "So what if she does?"

"Excuse me?" Had Bill actually just sputtered?

"There are rumors all over the internet already. People who leave here undoubtedly tell their loved ones—it's not like you wipe their memories. So what if she knows?"

"The rules exist for a reason." A growl lined Bill's voice.

"I know." Moments ago, Josh hadn't known what his next steps were. Now there was no doubt.

"The rules exist to keep people from rushing back out into a life they're not ready for. To stop those of us lucky to have a second chance from blowing it frivolously. To force us to consider the consequences of our actions, when most people never do."

Some of the violent red faded from Bill's face, and his brows rose.

Josh took the silence as a sign he could continue. He never put so much thought into this before, but now that the words were spilling out, it made sense. "I appreciate that. Everything this place has done for me. But I don't need that kind of security anymore." If he said this, there was no turning back. The thought made him pause, as the words caught in his throat.

There was no turning back anyway, even if he didn't say it now. He'd know. "I quit."

"I—but..." Bill shook his head and blinked, as if trying to make sense of the situation. "You can't just quit."

"I can." Josh loved knowing this was an option, regardless of what anyone said. "This is all about teaching us to be responsible with our choices, without taking them from us. I'm making this choice. Take my cupid status away. Pull me out of this holding pattern that's a sorry excuse for immortality. Give me my real second chance at life."

Bill frowned. "I see. I don't approve of this."

"You don't have to." Josh took a step back toward the door. "Are we done here?"

"Once you step out the front doors, you won't be able to find the building again," Bill said. "Your stuff will be in that condo you haven't told anyone you bought a few years back, and we'll be gone to you."

"I know." Melancholy and nostalgia tinged Josh's smile. "Tell Amanda goodbye for me."

Seconds later, he stepped through the front doors of the high-rise housing cupid headquarters and their local apartments. He spun back around, ambivalence filling him when a concrete-faced insurance company building stared back.

He shook the sadness away, and pulled his phone from his slacks. His fingers brushed something cold, metal, and familiar. His car keys. A glance up and down the street confirmed that yes, his Impala was parked just a few meters away. At least he still had that. He typed out a quick message. He had a life to start living.

*

Ella stared at her phone, wristlet style purse, and car keys laid out on her kitchen table. She knew—*knew*, not just believed—she'd fallen asleep in the server room at work, head on Josh's shoulder.

So why the hell had she woken up in her own bed, in one very wrinkled little black dress, with all of her stuff waiting for her where she normally left it?

She'd been asking herself that question over and over for the last hour or two—pretty much since she woke up to the sunlight streaming through her window. It was easier than dealing with the bigger, more painful question of what happened to Josh.

Her phone rang, as if her staring at it for so long had made it nervous. She shook the ridiculous thought aside. With any luck, something else had broken at work. It would be a pleasant distraction.

"This is Ella."

"God, even your voice is gorgeous." Josh's familiar tone, combined with the blatant compliment, heated her skin and pushed her confusion to the back of her mind.

Most of it anyway. "And if we're going to keep running into each other, you're going to have to come up with a better lead-in than 'I can explain.'" She should be furious at him for vanishing—or whatever had happened, but she was just glad to hear his voice.

"I promise, this is the last time." His sincerity carried over the line. "Meet me for lunch?"

Reason tried to tell her she shouldn't— She pushed it aside. She was sick of being reasonable. This was what she wanted to be doing. "No."

"I—what?"

Giddiness flooded her. "I won't meet you somewhere. You owe me a real date. You can pick me up. At my apartment, not in an office-building parking lot."

"I'd like nothing better."

She gave him her address, told him to give her an hour to get ready, and disconnected. Flutters filled her heart and chest. This entire situation was absolutely ridiculous, but nothing had ever felt more right in her life. It was true she didn't know Josh well enough to start planning for a future, but for the first time in ages, she was interested in giving things a shot.

It didn't hurt that the entire thing came with just a hint of magic attached to it. She was going to enjoy the hell out of falling for this guy.

Epilogue

Ella blew at the loose strand of hair on her forehead, and then again when it refused to budge. Just inside the apartment door, she dropped the box she was carrying. Frustrated, she reached up, and rebound her ponytail. The June sun was making her T-shirt stick to her skin, but the final result would be worth it.

A pair of arms wrapped around her waist, and Josh kissed along the back of her neck. "You're sexy with your hair up."

She smiled at the now-familiar contact, and leaned back into him. "I'm hot, sweaty, and need a shower."

His fingertips traced over her stomach, the light contact both tickling and comforting her. "The last of the boxes can wait until the sun goes down, right? There are only a few left in your car."

For the first few weeks after he'd quit his job as a cupid, he'd grumbled about having to take a *normal* job, but she knew he loved his call center work and talking to people on the phone all day.

And they'd seen more and more of each other over the past six months, until they finally relented and realized neither one of them liked it when she had to go home at night. They were just finishing up moving her stuff into his apartment.

She intertwined her fingers with his. "I suppose it can wait. Why?"

The sound of the door latching shut echoed through the room, and he tugged her shirt over her head. "Let's solve the shower problem."

She laughed, as he tugged her toward the bathroom. He pressed her against the door frame, and kissed her hard before breaking away again.

He pressed his forehead to hers. "I love you so very much, Ella."

She sighed, and leaned her weight against him. "I love you too." She still wasn't sure if she believed in things like fate, but she knew without a doubt that she'd always be grateful for second chances at love and life.

The End

Caging the Wolf, A Snowdonia Wolves

Novella, by Sofia Grey

Jessie has fallen in love with the perfect guy, Levi, but there's one tiny problem. The blue-eyed hunk only exists in her dreams. That is, until he greets her in the local shopping mall. She'd swear they never met before, so how come he knows so much about her – and can tell her the naughty things they did in her dreams?

Chapter One

"You have got to be kidding me."

The nearby guy's voice rose, alarm rippling through his words, and then I heard a yelp. There must be a problem with one of the dogs, but I guessed in a pound this big, it was to be expected.

I shuffled the box in my arms and tried not to fidget. It was bulky rather than heavy, but I'd been waiting nearly ten minutes. If the girl didn't come back soon, I'd just leave it on the floor.

"*No.*" Alarm had risen to panic. What was happening? "No, please don't. Don't put me in there." Ice snaked down my spine at his shout, and I glanced around, wondering why nobody was doing anything.

"Help me. Somebody, please help me."

Instinct battled with common sense. This was a dog pound, not a torture chamber. It was probably just someone messing around.

As I thought that, a man in a white coat appeared in the doorway. "Sal?" He shouted. "He's down." His eyes sharpened when he noticed me. "Can I help you?"

Footsteps pounded down a hallway,

approaching us in the tiny front office. I shuffled the box some more. "I'm, uh, Jessie. I'm dropping off some bedding." His eyebrows dipped and I hastened to explain. "I'm moving out, and I don't need it any more. The girl I spoke to on the phone said you were always in need of blankets and quilts, you know, for the stray dogs."

I was babbling, like I always did when I was nervous. And for some reason I couldn't quite put my finger on, I felt very uneasy.

"Right." He nodded, but his attention leapt to the young woman who burst into the room. It felt distinctly crowded now. "We've got him, Sal." A grin broke over his face. "This is the one. Get on the phone. Call everyone."

I could have been invisible. "Should I just leave my stuff here? I've got some more in the car."

"Yeah, sure." They were already heading down another corridor, leaving me alone. I could hear the excited rumble of their voices and I puzzled over his words. *This is the one. Call everyone.*

None of my business. I dumped the box on the floor, next to a teetering stack of dog food cartons, and pushed out through the door. My car was around the corner, parked in my usual haphazard fashion, and I'd left it unlocked. I grabbed the second cardboard box from the back seat, and straightened up. I'd be back in a minute, so I left the door open. Nobody would steal this piece of junk.

To my right was a side door into the pound. It didn't say *keep out*, or *private*, or *staff only*, it was a lot closer than the main office, and this box was particularly heavy. Fuck it, I'd give it a try.

I tried the door handle and it opened. I peered through the gap. A long, grey-tiled corridor stretched away from me, animal pens on both sides, and most of them empty. It didn't look as though anything was running free, and so I slipped through the door, box in my arms. It stayed open behind me; I'd have to come back and close it.

The only dog I saw lay on its side in a cage way too small for its size, and I felt outraged on its behalf. It didn't even have room to stand. Was this really the best place for me to donate my stuff to? I'd left it too late to find anywhere else, and I wished I'd spent more time thinking this over. It'd been a last minute idea, something I excelled at.

I stood there, battling my indecision, and the dog lifted its head. Brilliant, sapphire-blue eyes stared at me.

"Please help."

That voice again, the guy I'd heard earlier. I looked over my shoulder, but the corridor was empty. The only other voices were in the distance, high and excited. My heart thudded against my ribs. Where was he?

"Um, hello?" My voice came out as a squeak, and I cleared my throat. Before I could try again, the dog shook its head and whined.

"You can hear me?" The voice sounded urgent.

Okay, this was weird. The other cages were empty, and there was nobody else in the corridor. "Where are you?" I clutched the box tighter. "What do you need?"

The dog yipped and I glanced down at it. At *him*. Don't know why, but I knew it was a *him*.

"I'm right here. Locked in this fucking cage."

Chapter Two

The first thought that leapt into my head was, his mouth didn't move. As if a dog could really be speaking to me.

"Cage?" I repeated, my eyes fixed on the beast behind the bars. It was enormous for a dog, with thick, dark fur, and a lighter splash of colour on its face. And those eyes. I'd never seen anything like them.

"You have to help me. I can't stay here."

I took a deep breath. If this was a stunt, if a hidden video camera watched me talking to a dog, I'd feel like a right idiot. A quick glance left and right showed there was a camera above the door. "This is a trick, yeah?" I jerked my chin at the camera. "I find myself on YouTube later?"

"No trick." The blue eyes beseeched me. "You're the only one who can hear me. All you have to do is unlock this cage, and let me out."

"Why are you locked up?" Why was I even replying?

"Because I made a mistake." He snapped the words out, and I realised I was hearing them inside my head. My spine prickled.

"Please." I couldn't miss the urgency in his voice. "In about ten minutes, all hell is going to break loose. There's going to be a media-fucking-frenzy here, excuse my language, and I really don't want to be in the middle of it."

I blew out a breath, and then dumped the box on the floor. Was I going to do this? "Are you talking to me? Is that why they've locked you up?"

"Yes. I'm talking to you. We've got about nine minutes left, so if you could just open this door, I'd really appreciate it."

"Where are you going to go?" I peered up at the video camera again. There's no way it could miss me. "I mean, where does your owner live? And how will you get there?"

"Eight minutes. Please. Just open the fucking cage." He sounded scared rather than angry, and I made a snap decision.

"My car is right outside, and the back door is hanging open. If you really understand what I'm saying, go and get into my car and I'll drive you away from here. Okay?"

"Yes. Please hurry."

The cage was fastened with bolts, top and bottom. They were shiny and new, and stiff to open, and I struggled with the first one. "I can't believe I'm doing this."

"I can't believe you heard me."

The top bolt squealed when I dragged it back, the noise ringing out in the quiet of the corridor, and I froze. The only thing I could hear was my pulse banging in my ears. I could do this.

"You're doing great. Don't stop now." The second one was easier. The moment it released, the dog shoved against the cage door and tumbled to the floor in a tangle of legs. "Thank fuck. I mean, thank you."

This was unreal. I shouldn't even be in this corridor, let alone releasing a dog, and my common sense screamed at me to run. The dog scrambled to its feet, and once standing, it was even larger than I'd expected. It took off, racing toward the door and I followed.

Chapter Three

The dog lurched onto the back seat, his legs giving way beneath him, and I slammed the door shut. I'd left the keys in the ignition, and seconds later I started the engine, and spun my aging car to face the exit.

"Go, *go*."

I didn't need him to urge me on. My foot slammed onto the accelerator and the car shot forward in a flurry of squealing tyres. The dog pound was at the end of a quiet road and it would take a minute to reach the highway. How soon would they realize he was gone? Would they come after me? My heart raced every bit as much as the engine.

I swung around a tight bend, way faster than I'd normally drive, and saw the dog moving in the rear view mirror. "You okay back there?"

"Yeah. Thanks. Really." His words slurred together and I glanced in the mirror again. Shit. Had he banged his head?

"You sure you're okay? We're nearly at the highway. Where do you want me to go?"

"They inj…" His head dipped, and then jerked

up again, as if he was trying to stay awake. "Doped. Fuckin' cat."

"Cat?"

His eyes were closed. "Ketamine."

"What?"

No reply. I reached the junction with the highway, and took the turn for home. I'd only gone a short distance when two brightly coloured cars shot past me, garishly logoed with the local TV station decals. I watched in my mirror as they swung onto the road to the pound. Holy fuck, the dog had been right. The *talking dog* that currently lay unconscious on the back seat of my car.

I tried to figure out a plan as I drove. I'd be home in half an hour, but I was leaving tonight. I had to be at the airport by seven this evening, and it was nearly noon already. Would that be enough time for him to wake up? What did he say? *Ketamine*? It sounded familiar, and I could Google it later.

Parking outside my shared house, I faced another problem. How would I move him inside? He looked heavy. Thankfully, when I opened the back door, he lifted his head and opened his eyes.

"Where are we?" He may have been awake, but his words were still slurred and the sapphire gaze was unfocused.

"My place. Do you think you can walk?"

"Uh huh." He slithered out of the car, to stand by my side, and I led him slowly to the door. I wasn't expecting my housemates back for hours. Just as well, really. If they heard me trying to have a conversation with a dog, they'd think me crazy.

The hallway was cool after the blazing sunshine outside, and I wondered how cold it would be back home in England. It'd be strange wrapping up in layers again, after weeks of living in shorts and T-shirts. My trip down under was almost over, down to a matter of hours. Would I come back to New Zealand one day? Maybe.

The dog padded beside me, looking more alert by the second. "Could I have some water, please?" His voice was clearer too.

"Of course." I pushed open the kitchen door and grabbed a bowl from the draining rack, before filling it with cold water from the tap.

He didn't speak again until he'd emptied the bowl, and the refill I gave him. Sitting on the floor, he pinned me with his gaze, sharp and alert again. "Thanks. I owe you. What's your name?"

I swallowed down my laugh at the absurdity of the conversation. "Jessie. My friends call me Jess."

"I won't forget your help, Jess. But you know you can't talk about this."

I snorted, my giggle escaping. "Like anyone would believe me. What kind of dog are you, anyway? Apart from the talking-variety."

He huffed a soft laugh. It made me tingle, every nerve ending suddenly aware of the delicious timbre of his voice. "I think it's time I went." He stood, stretched his front legs, and then shook his entire body. "Where are we?"

"Plimmerton. Do you, uh, want a ride somewhere?"

"I can run home from here, but thanks anyway."

Padding up the corridor beside me, he waited until I opened the door, and then paused on the doorstep, and turned to face me. He stepped closer and nuzzled at my hand. "Whoah." He jerked his head back, and stared at me, eating me up with his gaze.

The air felt charged, as though we were in the middle of a lightning storm and I felt the hairs stand up on the back of my neck. What just happened?

"My name is Levi. I'll see you again soon, Jess."

What? "Um, no. You won't."

The dog—Levi—cocked his head to one side. "Why not?"

"I'm leaving in a few hours. Going home. To England." His stare was unnerving, and I babbled to fill the silence. "I was only here on a work visa, and even though I might come back one day, it won't be for years. And I'm not sure this isn't all a hangover-induced dream. I'm probably going to wake on the sofa in a few minutes and forget all this happened. I mean, you're a talking dog. Either I'm dreaming, or I'm crazy. I think I prefer the sane-but-asleep option."

"I have to go. But for the record," he paused, his voice a low and seductive murmur. "I'm a wolf, not a dog. And I'll find you. I *will* see you again, Jess."

Chapter Four

Hours later, I twisted in my window seat and gazed at the final rays of light playing across the ocean beneath me. The afternoon had passed in a whirl of last minute packing and goodbyes, along with several glasses of wine. I'd not had the space to sit and think about the weird encounter with the dog. *The wolf.*

If it hadn't been for the bowl of water on the kitchen floor, and the clump of long, black hairs on my car seat, I'd be convinced it was a dream.

His last words echoed in my head, silky and all too enticing: *I* will *see you again.* I shivered, just thinking about his voice.

As the sun drifted low in the sky, my eyelids followed suit. Snuggling under the airline blanket, I settled down to sleep. With luck I wouldn't awake until we landed in Bangkok. My return flights had been cheap, but included several stops: Auckland, Sydney, Bangkok, Dubai, and finally, Manchester.

I dreamed of home, and Christmas shopping. I sat on a wooden bench in my local shopping mall, the giant Trafford Centre, and gazed at the opulent decorations strung from the glass ceiling. Busy shoppers hurried past me—the usual crowds—but even though I'd shopped here a thousand times, it now felt alien.

I felt, rather than saw, someone take the space next to me. A glance to my side revealed a young man. He sprawled against the bench seat, one arm insolently thrown across the back, as though we were a couple.

I gave him a proper look. Messy, dark hair fell to his chin, and thick stubble raked his cheeks, as though he'd stumbled here straight from his bed. A black T-shirt hugged his chest, and worn, dark jeans clung to strong thighs. The denim looked soft and much-washed, and I dragged my gaze up from his crotch, to meet twinkling—*startling*—blue eyes. Where had I seen eyes like that before?

A lazy grin broke out on his face, and my cheeks heated. He couldn't have missed the way I'd been staring at him. With his dark tan and perfect white teeth, he looked far too exotic to be sitting in a Manchester shopping mall.

"Hi, Jess."

The rational part of me questioned how he knew my name. The rest of me wanted to swoon at his voice. Deep, and husky, it reminded me of salted caramel chocolate—velvety, but with a dangerous edge. It also had a lilting accent that was familiar. He was a Kiwi.

"I'm sorry, do I know you?" My polite English upbringing stepped forward, even though I'd never seen him before. I couldn't forget someone so delicious.

His gaze dropped briefly, as though he considered how to reply. A smile tugged at his lips. "Not really. I'm Levi."

It was on the tip of my tongue to say, I don't think we've met, but something held the words back. He was familiar, oddly so. He continued to stare at me, amusement lighting his brilliant eyes, along with something else, an intensity that made my spine prickle.

"You're from New Zealand?" I blurted. "Are you here on holiday?"

"Kind of." He gestured to the shops around us. "I've never been here before."

"To the Trafford Centre? Or to Manchester?"

"Either. Would you show me around?"

Show a hot guy around my favourite shops? Shame it was only a dream. I smiled at him, and wondered where to begin. Something niggled. "How did you know my name?"

Levi pushed away from the bench to stand before me, tall and imposing, but delicious. He shrugged and held out a hand. "We met briefly, but you were, uh, distracted." Wiggling his fingers, he gave me an enticing smile. "Shall we?"

Still, I hesitated. I'd never conjured up such a gorgeous apparition in my dreams before, and I knew it was too good to be true. Would he morph into a psycho and toss me over the railings to the gallery below? "I don't usually hold hands with a guy I just met."

"I wouldn't want you to make a habit of it," he countered swiftly, "but it's solely for my benefit. I might get lost otherwise." His eyes widened with mischief. "Man, I could be stuck in here for weeks."

How could I resist?

Taking his hand, I let him pull me to my feet. His grip was firm and confident, his palm warm and slightly calloused, and the moment I stood beside him, he tangled our fingers together. It felt right. Good.

"Where to? What're you going to show me, Jess?"

"The Christmas tree. That's what catches everyone's attention the first time they come here."

He was tall, and I barely came up to his shoulder, but he matched his stride to mine, and we strolled along the upper level, dodging the other shoppers with ease. Like Moses parting the Red Sea, the crowd moved out of his way, and we walked easily.

A thrill bubbled in the pit of my stomach. This was so unlike me. Not only was he a complete stranger, but also completely out of my league. Six foot tall Adonis' didn't make a beeline for me. They paired up with Barbie dolls, in my experience, or cover-model look-alikes. My nose was a little too big, my freckles too ginger, and my hair a dull brown. I was spectacularly ordinary.

Levi squeezed my hand, and caught my attention. "How big is this place?"

His voice scrambled my thoughts, and it took me a moment to respond. "I read somewhere, there's three miles of covered walkways, with all the shops and cafés."

He gave a low whistle. "You could walk the length of Wellington in less than that."

"And you'd stay dry here." I glanced up at him. "And out of the wind."

This drew a laugh. "You've got me there." We strolled another couple of steps before he spoke again. "You like it here? With all these people?"

"It's one of my favourite places to shop. There's nothing like it in New Zealand."

"No, there isn't." He tugged me to a stop, and I peered up at him. "It doesn't have *this* though."

Chapter Five

I blinked, and everything changed. Instead of pretty tiles beneath my feet, there was now forest floor. Giant trees formed a dense canopy high over my head, lush vines twined around a nearby branch, and sunlight filtered through the treetops. It was noisy. A myriad of birds called and chattered, as they flitted above us.

Levi held my hand still, and I slowly turned to him. "Are we in the jungle?"

His eyes crinkled in the corners when he laughed. "No, it's the Rimutakas."

I recognised the name—the mountain range north of Wellington. I'd driven through the area, but it hadn't looked anything like this.

"We're well off the beaten track," he continued. "Few people have ever walked this path." He eased me closer, and then turned me to stand with my back against him, his hands caging my hips. "This is one of *my* favourite places."

I breathed in the scents of the forest, and gazed at the scenery. I'd never seen anything so wild, so prehistoric. I half expected a dinosaur to amble into the clearing. "It's beautiful," I said.

Levi rested his chin on my shoulder. "So are you."

It was just a line, I knew that. I also knew it was a dream. In the real world, hot guys like Levi didn't look twice at me. I determined to enjoy the moment, and when his hands shifted to rest on my stomach, I leaned back into the embrace.

His chest was firm, his abs flat and hard, and warmth poured from his body. He smelled good, of pine and green leaves, with a salty tang, as though he'd been standing in the sea. Delicious. Could he be any more perfect?

I yawned, my eyelids growing heavier by the second. "This is nice," I murmured. "I hope I dream of you again, Levi."

"You will, gorgeous. Look out for me."

****

I opened my eyes to find we were circling above Bangkok. The next hour was a flurry of leaving the plane, and traipsing through the airport to my connecting flight. Every step taking me closer to home.

I looked forward to seeing my family, and my dog, Charlie. He'd been my best friend since I was seven years old. In my head he was still a bouncy, lop eared puppy, intent on chewing my shoes and school bag at every opportunity. He was now a grizzled, grey-haired pensioner, in dog terms, but Mum assured me he was still fine. I'd missed him. It would be good to take him for a long walk in the woods near home.

In a flash, I remembered. *Walking through an ancient forest with Levi.* I couldn't help smiling. My subconscious had obviously been hard at work, mixing together a hot guy, and the weird talking dog, and throwing them together into a colourful dream. It had been so real. I'd felt the springiness of the forest floor, heard the raucous birds, and smelled the mossy, green-leaf fragrance all around me.

The dog *couldn't* have been talking to me. That was crazy. I must have been over-tired. Stressed. I'd had a moment of madness where I'd released a dog from the pound, and then taken it home. I'd been out in the sun too long.

****

The flights finally over, I stumbled down the exit corridor at Manchester Airport. The past thirty-six hours all merged together and it was only when I stepped into the Arrivals hall that I realised it was daytime. To me it felt like the middle of the night. My sleep patterns would be screwed for days.

I hugged Mum and let her welcoming chatter wash over me as we headed for the car park. "Sorry." I smiled while fighting another massive yawn. "It feels like I haven't slept in days. I'm convinced any minute I'm going to wake up and find myself back on the plane."

"You doze on the way home, love. We've plenty to catch up on, but it can wait until you've rested."

I'd emailed home every few days, Skyped weekly, and talked on the phone a few times. There wouldn't be any big news that I hadn't heard already. I knew about my cousin Sheryl's upcoming wedding, my friend's new baby girl, and that Jack Harper had stepped up his campaign to buy my dad's shop. What else could there still be to tell me?

I'd crushed on Jack for years, ever since school. I had a succession of pencil cases with our initials doodled on the outside. Jess and Jack—it sounded good. Mrs. Jess Harper had a nice ring to it. Only trouble was, he'd never seen me that way. To him, I was the shy, pig-tailed girl at the front of the class, while he hung in the back row with the cool kids. On the rare occasions he spoke to me, I either babbled like a lunatic on a full moon, or lost my tongue completely.

My big hope was that twelve months of living thousands of miles from home, would have made me interesting in his eyes.

When the steady movements of the car lulled me asleep, I thought briefly about Jack.

But it was Levi who greeted me in my dream.

Chapter Six

"Hey. There you are." Looking exactly the same as in my previous dream, Levi pushed himself away from the wall he leaned on, and stepped to my side. "We haven't finished the tour yet."

"Tour?"

White teeth flashed in a beguiling grin. "Three miles of shops." He spread his arms, and then hooked both thumbs in his pockets. "We haven't walked one mile yet, let alone three."

We were back in the Trafford Centre. The same wooden bench.

"This feels a little like déjà vu," I murmured. "Haven't we been here before?"

"Yep. You said we were going to see a tree, and then I distracted you."

I had to smile. "I think your tree was better than mine."

"Yeah?" He held out a hand. "Where else should we go then?"

He was difficult to resist. I didn't demur when he laced our fingers together. The excited thumping of my heart softened at his touch, and like last time, he smelled divine. "I like dreaming about you, Levi."

"Same." He cocked his head to one side, and sniffed the air. "Hang on. Can you smell popcorn?"

I shrugged. "The cinema is just down the mall. We could get some, if you like?"

"Really? I love popcorn. What are we waiting for?" He tugged my hand and with a giggle, I let him sweep me along. "Do you live near here?"

"Not too far. I live in a suburb called Stockport."

We queued up with the movie-goers, and inched closer to the busy popcorn dispenser. The questions continued, tossed so quickly I couldn't reply to them, before he asked the next.

How long had I spent in New Zealand? Why had I gone there? Would I go back? What did I usually do at Christmas? Did I have a boyfriend? Did I have a big family?

I couldn't help laughing, and he turned to me, a quizzical look on his face. "What?"

"I don't know what to answer first."

The part of me that recognised this was a dream, noted that we were no closer to the front of the line than we'd been a minute ago. The rest of me didn't care. I buzzed with the thrill of his attention, utterly enthralled by the novelty of having him by my side. People moved around us, endlessly shifting, like the incoming tide, and we stood still in the centre of it all. I stared at his face, wondering again about the brilliance of his eyes, the devilment in his smile. How would it feel to kiss him?

It wouldn't be real.

He doesn't exist outside my dream.

Unthinking, I licked dry lips and saw his gaze focus on them.

"The boyfriend question." Levi's voice

rumbled, deeper and even more dangerous. "Answer that one first." He leaned forward, and placed his hand on my arm.

"Here we are, love."

I opened my eyes to see Mum's smile. Where was Levi? I blinked and the world reasserted itself. We'd parked on the street outside our house. I'd been asleep in the car. It had been Mum touching my arm. I'd never been jetlagged before, never travelled far enough to cross several time zones in one journey, and now I understood why people hated it. I felt disoriented, as though I'd really been there at the Trafford Centre, and had been dragged back to wake here.

I yawned, and then got my ass moving. Grabbing my bags from the car, I followed Mum up the path to the neat brick terrace house where I'd grown up. A typical Victorian build, it may have been narrow, but it was deep, and spacious inside. Everything was familiar, from the untidy heap of shoes by the door, to the fridge full of homemade food. I'd enjoyed travelling, but it was good to be home.

Checking the time, it was only two in the afternoon. Dad wouldn't be home for ages, and Charlie with him. That was one advantage of having their own business: my parents could take the dog with them to work. They owned and ran a small hardware store, and it'd been in Dad's family for three generations. He liked to say that Morgan's Hardware still had the same values as when his grandfather first established the business, and he was probably right. Sometimes I feared it still carried the same stock.

Morgan's Hardware would be my legacy when they retired. I'd spent afternoons and weekends behind the counter since I first started school, and would do my homework in the back room while my parents served customers. The shop was as big a part of our family as

Charlie. That's why it was so amusing that Jack was determined to buy it. Dad would never sell.

At one time I didn't mind having my future mapped out, but these days I had my doubts.

Mum went back to work and I went for a long and blissful shower. That was the plan. I only meant to lie down on my bed for a few minutes, but I couldn't keep my eyes open. Next thing, I was back in the Trafford Centre.

Chapter Seven

Levi sat on the bench this time, sprawled as lazily as before, and his welcoming grin was a thing of beauty. "Sure is hard work having a conversation with you, Jess."

He didn't look put out, and I smiled back. I felt absurdly relaxed with him, as though I'd known him for ages, and it seemed natural to sit down on the bench at his side. He scooted closer, his arm brushing across my shoulders.

"So," he rolled the word. "Boyfriend? Yes or no?"

"Persistent, much?"

"Where you're concerned, babe, that's my middle name."

Babe? That was cute. I liked it. I decided to ask a few questions of my own. "How come I keep dreaming of you? And why do you keep asking about my, uh, status?"

He quirked his eyebrows. "I asked first."

Maybe he was my subconscious trying to tell me to have the guts to talk to Jack, to flirt with him. I took a rapid breath, and smoothed my damp palms on my jeans. "There's a guy I like."

"Uh huh." His fingers tapped a gentle pattern on the top of my arm. "And?"

"And I don't know how to talk to him."

"You're doing just fine as you are." His voice was silky, seductive and dangerous at the same time, and made the hairs on the back of my neck prickle.

"His name is Jack. And he's never even noticed me."

Levi went amazingly still. "Jack?"

"Okay, this is going to sound weird. I know you don't exist, and so I can say anything to you, without getting embarrassed. I can use you for practice." His eyes narrowed, but I pressed on. "I can pretend you're Jack, and you can tell me how I do."

There was a long pause, and then he rubbed his chin, as though thinking hard. "What's he like? Jack. Why do you like him so much?" There he went, asking me a cluster of questions all at once again.

"He's not as tall as you, and he's fair, to your dark. He's, uh, smart."

Levi made a circling gesture with his fingers. "Smart dresser, or smart in the head?"

"Both." Damn, this was difficult. "He's popular. Attractive."

After a moment, Levi's fingers resumed their touch on my arm, stroking a gentle pattern, back and forth. "Ever kissed him?"

My cheeks heated. "No."

"Dated him?"

My face burned, but I didn't look away from his gaze. "No."

He blinked, and his jaw softened, a tightness easing away. "Let's start with a kiss."

My heart stuttered and my mouth dropped open, before I realized and snapped it shut. "I don't think, I mean, I'm not sure…"

"Don't think," he murmured, and leaned into me, impossibly close. His eyes sparkled. They were so bright, I wondered if I could see my reflection in them. "Shh. You're thinking again." He lifted his hand and brushed his thumb across my lower lip. I felt the shockwave down to my toes. "That's better."

There was that delicious forest and sea fragrance again, as he dropped his head and pressed the tiniest of kisses on the corner of my mouth. I just had time to draw a breath before he covered my lips with his own. Awareness flooded me, every nerve and cell in my body leaping to attention. He slanted his mouth, and the pressure increased on my lips. This wasn't a kiss, it was a full body massage in disguise. I went limp, melting into his arms, wrapped tight around me. He kissed with precision, as dangerous and intoxicating as I'd imagined.

Then his tongue flicked against mine. I tasted green mint and something sweet, and I moaned, unable to hold the sound back. If I died now, I'd be happy.

All too soon, he withdrew. I was left gasping, my fingers clutching his T-shirt, and my brain in freefall. I didn't remember moving my hands, but I hung on to him now with a death-grip. Speechless, I noted the satisfied smirk on his face.

I lifted shaking fingers to my lips. They felt bruised, but in a good way. I needed to say something, but all my words were jumbled in my head. If I tried to speak it would probably come out as a series of grunts, and so I stayed quiet.

Levi rubbed his stubbled cheek against mine and set a new fire raging in my nerve endings. When had stubble ever been so sexy? How would it feel if he went down on me? My panties dampened at the thought.

"How far is it to Snowdonia?"

His question could have been in Swahili for all the sense it made. I ran a cautious tongue over my lips and then cleared my throat. "Snowdonia? Umm, a hundred miles. I think."

"Yeah." He leaned back on the wooden bench, creating a space between us, and my hands fell to my lap. I wanted to pull him back, but I wasn't sure I really had control of my body back yet. If I kissed him again, I wouldn't be able to stop.

Levi chuckled, and gave my hair a playful tug. "You weren't listening."

He'd been talking? I blew out a breath and tried to concentrate. "I'm sorry, what did you say?"

"Can we go to Snowdonia? I've a friend who comes from there and I'd like to see it."

Chapter Eight

A wave of sleepiness crashed over me, and I couldn't hide my yawn. "Can't you take us there? Like you took us to the Rimutakas?"

"Naw. I've never been to Snowdonia." Lifting one hand, he cradled my cheek, and I rubbed against his palm. "You want to sleep, don't you?"

I tried to deny it, but another yawn gave me away, and he smiled. "Come here, babe. Let me hold you."

Other boyfriends had cuddled either when they wanted sex, or as a brief treat afterwards. Neither of them had wanted to just hold me, and so I grabbed the chance with Levi. Of course, since he only existed in my imagination, he *would* be perfect. Amazing to kiss, and fantastic to snuggle.

I burrowed into his warm embrace, and couldn't help feeling sad. He was too good to be true. It'd be impossible to ever find a real guy like this.

****

The sound of the front door banging woke me,

and I sat up in bed, trying to figure out where I was. My old bedroom? Yes, I was home.

"Jessie?" My dad's voice rose up the stairs and I scrambled to my feet. I knew as soon as Charlie saw me, he'd bound up the stairs to greet me, only he didn't. Dad stood in the entrance hall, one hand on the banister, peering up, with Mum next to him. As I trotted down the stairs, I looked for my dog.

"Come here, Jessie-Bell." Dad swept me into a giant bear-hug. "We've missed you, little girl."

I hugged him back. "Lovely to see you, Dad, but where's Charlie?"

"He's here." Mum beamed at me.

I stared at my hound. Sitting on the mat by the front door, he cocked his ears and gave me his usual doggy grin, but didn't leap forward, didn't try to knock me over. His tail thumped, but in a subdued fashion, as though it was just too much effort. He was thinner than I remembered, his once-black muzzle now completely grey.

When I crouched, he licked my hands with all his usual enthusiasm, and slowly stood. Every movement looked stiff. I'd been gone a year, but my dog looked as though he'd aged ten.

"What's up with him?" I tried to keep the panic from my voice.

Mum came to fondle his soft ears. "He's getting old, love. Arthritis, bit of kidney trouble. He's seventeen now."

I thought back to all the phone calls, the skype sessions. "You never said he was ill. You didn't tell me."

"No sense in you rushing home." Dad ruffled my hair. "It was your time to spread your wings. You're back now, and he's still here."

I buried my face in Charlie's ruff. Dad was

202

right, but it nagged at me. What else had changed while I was away?

****

After dinner, I headed for the pub to catch up with my friends. Becca's parents owned the Bluebell, at the end of the street, and she'd spent as much time there as I'd spent in Dad's shop. As soon as I walked in, she ran to me and squealed in delight, abandoning the pint she'd been pulling. It felt good to sit down at our usual table with Becca, Clare and Neil.

I smiled at my friends. We'd been in a group on the first day of primary school, and had stuck together. Clare and Neil had been a couple since they were thirteen, and they were all like the siblings I'd never had.

"It's great to have you home again, Jess." Becca touched my arm. "Your face is so tanned. Are you like that all over?"

"It was the middle of summer in New Zealand. I wore shorts and T-shirts most of the time." I was glad of my thick fleece jacket now though, the change in seasons was as difficult to adjust to as the jet lag.

"Uh oh. Don't look right." Clare leaned into me and murmured in a low voice. "We have company."

"Well, the wanderer returns at last." I glanced up from my drink to see Jack Harper, with his usual wingman, Toby. Jack's blue eyes were dull compared to Levi's, but his smile was as confident. And what was I doing thinking about Levi? He wasn't real.

"Mind if we join you?" Jack tugged a chair to the table and sat, without waiting for an answer, claiming the space next to me.

Toby grabbed another chair, but hesitated when the only space left was next to Becca. She glared at him, but scraped her seat across the floor to make a little more room, before turning back to Neil. I was aware of the body language byplay from my best friend, but most of my attention was on Jack, the object of my lust for so long.

My hair was short now, I'd shed loads of weight while travelling, and I *knew* I looked my best. Would he finally see me?

Maybe yes. "Looking good, Jess. Welcome home." He took a swig of his bottled beer and grinned across the table at Toby, sitting stiff-backed next to Becca. "There's been some changes while you've been away." His voice was for me alone. "I can bring you up to speed later, if you like?"

This was unprecedented. I fought to keep the smile from my face, to play it cool. "Sure. What did you have in mind?"

"I've got tickets to the opening of a new club in town. Tomorrow night, you and me. What do you say?"

Chapter Nine

Jack didn't stay long in the pub, and I was still suffering from jetlag, and longing for my bed. A few hours later, when I finally sank into sleep, it was no surprise to find myself with Levi again. A lazy grin lit up his face when he saw me, and he patted the space next to him on the bench. I didn't have the energy to resist. It seemed entirely natural for his arm to drape around my shoulders, and for me to lean into him, my head nestling into the crook of his neck.

After a moment's hesitation, I rested one hand on his cobble-like abs. His chest was equally hard and muscled, and it should have been impossible to find comfort lying on him. Apart from his T-shirt, he wasn't soft anywhere. It felt right though, and when his fingers curled over my arm, pulling me closer, I let out a breath I hadn't realised I was holding.

I felt comfortable with Levi. Safe.

"What did you do tonight? Anything fun?" A hint of minty breath washed over me when he spoke.

"Dinner with my folks, then the pub with my friends." I smiled, remembering Becca's awkwardness. If I didn't know her better, I'd think she had a thing for

Toby. "Jack was there. He's asked me to a club tomorrow night."

Levi's arm tightened a fraction. "You going?"

"What do you think? And besides. I haven't been clubbing for ages."

"Uh huh. Did you go to Mighty Mike's while you were in Wellington?"

I frowned. The name was familiar. "Don't think so. What's it like?"

"As long as you don't go to sleep on me, I can take you there now. Wanna go?"

I forced my drooping eyelids open, and sat up a little. "Sure."

The world changed. From a brightly lit shopping mall to a dark cave in the blink of an eye. *The noise.* Fast, furious and energized, rock guitars and a wailing singer filled my eardrums. Rainbow-coloured strobe lights flashed and darted, and strange fragrances assaulted me. Sweet, like cannabis, but more potent, the smell made the blood zing in my veins.

"Wanna dance?" Levi's lips brushed my ear, and I nodded. We'd materialized on a handkerchief of a dance floor, already crowded with other rockers, but a space opened up, and we moved closer to the band. The lead singer tossed his mane of white-blond hair in time to his guitar riffs, and fascinated, I watched.

Levi took a position behind me, his arms around my waist, his chin on my shoulder. "Fuckin' love this song." His voice rumbled into my ear and we began to move to the rhythm.

I'd never danced quite like this before. Slow dancing with a guy was completely different. This was vigorous, sweaty and oh-my-god sexy. The bass beat echoed through my blood, the drum pounding a tattoo inside my head. I rubbed shamelessly against Levi's hard body and felt his even harder erection bumping my

206

ass.

I knew if I turned around, I could kiss him again. I'd been scorched by him last time; I'd be incinerated if we kissed again. It would be worth it.

The music slowed, the heady swirl gentling to an almost-ballad, and Levi held me close, hot breath on my neck and his teeth nibbling my earlobe. The rush of damp in my panties was unbidden. I'd never been so turned on. Was it something in the atmosphere? The cannabis-like smell? Or just the enticing combination of pumping rock music and the hottest guy I'd ever met?

Levi slid one hand beneath my shirt, his fingertips searing my stomach. If he hadn't been holding me, I'd have fallen to the floor. "I want you, Jess." His hand dipped beneath the waistband of my jeans, confident and utterly possessive. His words intoxicating. "If we weren't surrounded by a crowd of people, I'd show you just how much."

I wanted to play, to tease him back, and so I ground against his hard-on, enjoying his groan as it vibrated through me. "Is that right? What do you think I'd let you do?"

His voice was a growl in my ear. "I'd pop the button on your jeans." His thumb flicked at the metal fastening. "Slide down the zip, one tooth at a time." I bucked against his hand, my hips taking a mind of their own. In response, he slid his other hand to cup my suddenly aching breast. Both nipples firmed at the touch, both wanting attention.

I gasped, but then found my voice. "And then? How far would you go?"

"You wanna play with a wolf, baby? We play hard." *Wolf?* Was he in a gang? He continued, before I had time to process my thoughts. "Then, Jess, I'd slide my hand into your panties and finger you until you came apart in my arms."

A cascade of erotic images flooded my mind. I'd no doubt he could do that. I knew I'd let him. Here, on a busy dance floor, in downtown Wellington...Hang on. This was just a dream.

I'd been so wrapped up in his words, *his touch*, I'd forgotten he didn't exist outside my imagination. Disappointment lined my mouth with a bitter taste.

As though he recognised my confusion, Levi spun me to face him, and cupped my cheeks with both hands. The blue eyes seemed to glow in the dim lighting, and I stared, fascinated. "Before all that, I'd kiss you senseless."

The kiss was hard, dominant, and confident. I hung onto him for dear life, unable to think of anything but his lips and tongue, the hands gently holding my face. The utter possession of his moves.

When he lifted his head, I whimpered, bereft at the loss of contact. "When you go dancing with your boy tomorrow, remember how you danced with me, how I made you melt. You're mine, Jess."

Chapter Ten

Another club. More swirling, blindingly-bright strobes that swept across a packed dance floor. Techno beats this time, skinny girls wearing very little, and a different guy at my side.

I wondered if Mighty Mike's was anything like I'd dreamed. It was certainly nothing like Sx2, where I was now. This place was huge. Oceans of space for dancing, long polished steel counters, and a bar that ran the length of one wall, it gleamed and shone, and screamed *exclusive*. I'd already seen three TV celebrities and a clutch of pop stars.

"How did you get tickets to the opening night?" I had to shout for Jack to hear me, and he obligingly slithered closer on the padded bench seat.

"I know the owners. They gave me a couple of comps." His smile was white and predatory. It reminded me of a shark, zooming in on its prey. I had to wonder. If I'd said *no*, or hadn't seen him in the pub at all, who would he have taken instead? I shook the thought away. I was here now, I'd enjoy it.

Another couple came to sit on our bench, pushing us even closer together, and I felt uncomfortable. I hadn't seen Jack for a year, had barely spoken to him before that. I wasn't ready to sit in his lap. I stood up, and gestured toward the crowd on the floor. "Should we?"

"Damn right." He grabbed my hand and led me to the centre of the throng. There was no room to dance, and two people had already trodden on my toes on the way. Jack didn't seem bothered. He dropped his hands to my hips and began to sway to the beat, inviting me to move with him.

This was what I'd longed for so many times. A chance for Jack to notice me. So why didn't I feel more excited? He was handsome in a sharp-suited, clean fashion, his short hair precision cut, and trendy clothes immaculate. The cool boy from school had grown into a hungry real estate agent, his fingers in dozens of money-making pies—and my dad's shop was one of them.

Over dinner tonight, my parents had been pleased to hear I was going out with Jack. "Morgan's is going to be yours one day, Jess." Dad spoke slowly, his voice serious. "And with the economy the way it is, having Harper's money on your side wouldn't hurt."

"*Dad.*" I couldn't help laughing. "We're just going to a club. Nothing more."

Mum flashed a smile at me. "I met your Dad in a club. I was on holiday in Wales, camping in Snowdonia with my friends from school, and this handsome young buck wouldn't leave me alone. He even followed me back to Manchester and insisted I marry him."

I'd heard the story a dozen times before, but this time, something had jolted my attention. Someone else had mentioned Snowdonia. *Levi.*

Caught up in my thoughts, I didn't object when Jack turned me in his arms, to stand at my back. Maybe

I should have. "Relax, baby," he crooned in my ear. "You're so hot. I can't keep my hands off you."

When Jack bumped against my ass, his hands gliding down to rest on my thighs, it felt wrong.

This was how I'd danced with Levi.

In my imagination.

Levi didn't exist, but Jack did.

I wriggled free and turned to face him again, a gap between us. The music was far too loud to permit any conversation, and so I gestured toward the bar. He nodded, and followed me off the floor. Our miniscule space was swallowed up instantly by other partygoers.

The drinks were ridiculously expensive, and made more than a dent in my bank balance, but I didn't want to be beholden to Jack. It was also quiet enough here to be able to talk, to some degree at least. I chinked our bottles together and pasted on a smile.

"Why do you want to buy my dad's shop?"

Jack ran a hand through his hair, mussing the front of it. It made him look like a mischievous child. "I've a buyer interested." The shark smile returned. "I heard your dad is thinking of retiring soon, so it'd make sense to quit now, rather than losing this investment opportunity."

Retiring? That was news to me. "You might have heard wrong. Now I've got my business diploma, I'll be working for Dad. We've got plans to expand." I hadn't actually shared my plans yet, and they were still vague, but I wanted to quash any rumours of him retiring. That made him sound old.

Jack eased nearer, invading my space again. "Maybe we should compare notes."

"Maybe." I took a gulp of my beer. "Who's your buyer?"

He shook his head. "Sorry, baby. That's privileged information." His gaze dropped to my chest and then back up to my face.

Heat filled my cheeks and I was consumed with the urge to pour my drink on his head. I was fed up of being groped and eye-fucked by him, and the night had only just started.

All these years I'd lusted after Jack. What a waste. I wanted someone like Levi.

I want Levi.

When my phone vibrated in my pocket, I was glad of the distraction, but the text message from Mum, filled me with dread.

Charlie not well. On our way to Emergency vet. Pls call when you get this message.

I had to get out of the club. Abandoning my beer on the bar top, I grabbed Jack's arm and tugged him toward the cloakroom. It would be freezing outside, and I'd need my coat, so while I lined up to collect it, I phoned Mum. It dropped to voicemail. I rang Dad, and the same happened.

Fear lodged in my throat, and I shoved my phone at Jack, to show him the message.

"Who's Charlie?"

"My dog." I reached the front of the line and thrust my ticket at the clerk.

"So where are you going?" Jack held onto my phone, his brows tugging together into a puzzled frown.

"Where? I'm going to the vet." I bounced on my toes, mentally urging the clerk to find my coat, and find it quickly.

"It's just a dog, baby."

"He's *my* dog." I snatched my phone from his fingers and dialled Mum again. "And don't call me *baby*."

"Hey." He laughed, and took a step back, his hands held up in surrender. "Sorry, *Jessie*."

I pressed the phone to my ear, and heard Mum

answer. "Jessie?" Her voice was high and stressed. "We've just arrived at the emergency vet on Whitmore Street. Oh, love, he doesn't look good. Is there any chance you could get down here?"

"Whitmore Street." My coat appeared on the counter and I nodded a thank you to the girl, then I turned to find a quiet space. "I'll be there as soon as I can."

She'd already hung up. I stood there for a moment, fist pressed to my mouth, trying to compose myself. I sucked in a shaky breath, and then another. I had to get outside, find a cab, and get out of town and back to Stockport. The journey alone would be twenty minutes. Mum hadn't said *what* had happened, just those awful words: *he doesn't look good.*

I'd forgotten about Jack. He snaked an arm across my shoulders and squeezed me close. Maybe he'd help me get a cab. This part of the city was unfamiliar to me and I didn't even know where the nearest taxi rank was.

"Jessie. I get you're upset. Let's go and get a drink."

"I want a cab."

"What? You're leaving?"

I nodded. I was holding myself together by the finest of threads and didn't trust myself to speak.

"Jesus. This is the opening night of Sx2, and you're leaving it for a fucking dog?"

I wished I'd kept my beer. I could have poured it all over his designer shirt. Instead, I turned and pushed my way through the crowd to the exit. Jack Harper was a dick, and this had been a mistake of epic proportions.

I just hoped I could get to Charlie in time.

Chapter Eleven

I sat in the vet's reception area, one parent on each side, and waited for news. Dad had found Charlie lying motionless, and semi-conscious, in the back garden. They didn't know if he'd had a stroke, or a heart attack, or any number of equally dire alternatives.

It was serious. The vet diagnosed acute kidney failure, and had spent the last hour running tests and trying to stabilize him. I expected to be told at any minute, he hadn't made it.

Eventually, we were allowed to go and see him. He lay on his side in a cage, a drip connected to one paw. I fondled his soft ears and stroked his muzzle, smiling through my tears when he licked my hand. We had to leave him and go home, and the vet promised to call us in the morning. It was a horrible end to a rotten evening, and I wished I'd never gone to the damned club with Jack.

Seeing Charlie lying in a cage reminded me of the dog I'd freed from the pound.

Back home, I comforted myself by thinking about Levi. I longed to lose myself in his embrace, and he filled my thoughts as I went to sleep. If only he was real.

When I opened my eyes in my dream, and saw him sitting on our wooden bench, I stumbled forward and threw myself into his arms. The tears I'd been holding back escaped, and I sobbed against his chest, uncaring that I was making a fool of myself.

He wasn't real. *This* wasn't real, even if it was the most lifelike set of dreams I'd ever had. His woody fragrance, the muscles that bunched in his arms he wrapped them tight around me, and the softness of his much-washed T-shirt. It all added up to way more than a dream.

"Jess. *Babe.*" He stroked my hair, and ran one hand up and down my spine in a soothing motion. "What's the matter, my love?"

This was the intimacy I'd wanted from Jack. Fat chance. Another pang of despair for Charlie brought a fresh wave of tears. I was an ugly crier, always had been. Some girls could sob delicately and look fragile and pretty, but I went the full hog. Bright red nose, swollen eyes. Even perfect-Levi wouldn't find *that* attractive.

"Talk to me, babe." Worry lined his voice, and I sucked in a shaky breath.

"It's Charlie. My dog. He's very ill."

He held me even closer. "Poor you. Do you know what's wrong?"

"Acute kidney failure." My voice was wobbly.

"I'm sorry. I wish there was something I could do."

My tears were receding, but I kept my face pressed to his shirt. "I wish you could see him. I wish you were real."

"Do you know where he is?" His hands continued to soothe me. "You could take us both there. Just think it."

215

Did I want to go back to the vets? *Yes.* I squeezed my eyes shut, thought of the kennels at the back of the vet's consulting rooms, and opened my eyes to see Charlie staring at me.

"Hey." Levi dropped to a crouch and held one hand through the bars of the cage. His other held me, our fingers tangled together. "He's a handsome boy." Charlie sniffed him thoroughly, always suspicious of strangers, and then licked his palm. Accepted him.

Fear had taken root as a solid lump in my throat, and I could feel fresh tears welling. Levi squeezed my fingers. "He's strong, Jess. He won't give up without a fight." I hoped he was right.

Moments later, Levi slid his fingers through my hair, and tucked an errant strand behind my ear. "I'm sorry. I can't stay as long as I'd like. Go get some sleep now. I'll see you tomorrow."

"You'll be waiting on the wooden bench? Are you always there, Levi? I don't dream of anywhere else at the moment."

"Waitin' for you, Jess. Only you." He pressed the most exquisitely tender kiss onto my forehead and then disappeared.

I stroked Charlie's head some more. Was this the last time I'd see my dog alive?

Chapter Twelve

I surfaced slowly the next morning, my memories a mixture of fear and calm. Levi's soothing voice telling me Charlie was strong, mixed in with the desperate cab ride to the vet. I thought back to my disastrous date with Jack. If Mum hadn't sent me a text, how much longer would I have stayed in the club with him?

I shivered, and tugged the duvet higher. Everything had changed in my year away. Charlie. The idea of Dad retiring. Jack being a complete asshole. Even Becca acting oddly with Toby.

Was anything as I'd left it?

The news from the vet was hopeful. My dog looked a little stronger this morning, but it was still too soon to tell if he'd make it.

When I checked the calendar, it was two weeks until Christmas. Mum and Dad insisted I stay out of the shop until the new year, that I needed time to get used to being at home again. My friends were all busy at work, and after visiting Charlie, I had the day to myself.

It was typical December weather in Manchester, icy cold and overcast, and not pleasant to be outside. I found myself heading for the warmth and lights of the Trafford Centre.

The Christmas decorations were just as lush and colourful as I'd hoped, and after wandering up and down the galleries, I ended up at the bench close to the cinema. I had an odd, déjà vu moment, when I wondered if Levi would be there. How stupid.

Even though I knew he couldn't join me, I sat there and watched the world go by. Harried mothers with children clinging to their hands, office workers shopping during their lunch break, and bands of noisy teenagers all walked past me. Nobody I wanted to see, and yet I stayed. I felt closer to Levi when I sat there, and how crazy was that?

****

I watched my parents prepare dinner together, as they did most nights. It was one of their ways to unwind after a busy day, and was a routine as familiar to me as brushing my teeth in the morning. Was it my imagination or was Dad moving slower these days? His hair was more silvered at the temples, but his eyes were as bright blue as ever. Not as bright as Levi's, but I'd never seen anyone with peepers like his.

My parents had the perfect marriage. Even when they argued, you could see the love underscoring whatever it was they disagreed on. I'd never marry unless I found someone to love me as much as Dad loved Mum. A foolish part of me had hoped to find that with Jack, but I knew better now.

"Hey, Dad. I know you were Welsh, but did you come from Snowdonia?"

He turned and smiled at me, reaching for Mum's hand at the same time. "No, but my *Taid*—your great-grandfather—did. I'd been researching my family history that summer, when I met your mother. Why do you ask?"

A guy I've been dreaming about mentioned it. "No reason."

I caught up with Becca in the evening, and managed to grab half an hour with her, in a quiet corner of the pub.

"How was Sx2?"

I grimaced. "Not my thing. Not the club, or Jack." I looked up from my drink and met her sympathetic smile. "It wasn't a good night." I'd already told her about Charlie, but wanted to tell her about Jack face to face.

"I'm sorry, hun. I always thought he was an arrogant prick, but you never saw that."

I did now. "What's the deal with Toby? You like him?"

Her cheeks coloured and she fanned herself with a beermat. "Have you seen the boy play rugby? Jesus. He's fit."

"And?"

"And nothing. He hangs out with Jack. And no matter how much I might be lusting after Toby, that's enough to make me see sense. His first loyalty would always be to Jack-god's-gift-to-women-Harper."

I giggled, for the first time that day. "Are there any decent guys left in town?"

She shrugged and pulled a funny face. "Now you're asking." Fixing me with a smile, she raised her glass. "It's my day off tomorrow. Let's hit the Trafford Centre. We can go shopping, have a liquid lunch, and go the movies in the afternoon. What do you say?"

"You're on."

Chapter Thirteen

For the first night since I'd left New Zealand, I didn't dream of Levi. I tossed and turned in my bed, my thoughts consumed with brilliant blue eyes, and arms that could hold all my fears at bay.

Would I ever meet a man like that? Maybe I should go on holiday to Snowdonia and do some digging into my own family history.

The next morning, Mum gave me an update from the vet. Charlie was hanging on, and responding to medication, but the prognosis was still uncertain. Sadness draped around me like a blanket over my shoulders, but I tidied my hair, applied a little makeup, and went to meet Becca.

She hugged me. "I love your new haircut, by the way, Jess. It makes your cheekbones really stand out." My friend's mop of dark hair reminded me briefly of Levi, before I wrenched my focus back. Today was about spending time with real people, not mooning over someone who existed only inside my head.

Becca hustled me into her aging car, selected a noisy playlist from her iPod, and we set off for the short drive to the mall. The music was too loud to hold a proper conversation, but we had all day to catch up.

Over a platter of dim sum, we put the world to rights. Two glasses of wine probably helped, and I felt almost mellow as we wandered through the galleries, browsing the goods on display, and trying on a few clothes. Becca snapped up some leather boots in a Christmas sale, and I bought some more presents to add to the pile under the tree in Mum's lounge.

The movies would be a good place to chill out, and we headed for the booking office to check the timings. We had to walk past Levi's bench, as I now thought of it, and I gazed at it, as we approached. Instead of a hot blue-eyed guy, it was taken by an elderly woman with a mountain of shopping.

I paused, and checked my phone, in case there was any more news of Charlie, but there was none. While I stood there, lost in thought, Becca nudged me.

"There's a guy over there waving at you. Yum-*mee*. Look right."

What? I looked up, and saw Levi.

My heart thudded so hard that my ribs would be bruised. I must be asleep. But…memories of the day so far flickered through my head. No dream would be this long, this detailed.

"Now *he's* kinda hot." Becca's murmur shocked me into alertness. "Seems to know you."

Levi strode toward us, looking the same as in every other dream, yet subtly different. He wore a scuffed leather jacket over the T-shirt, had a pack slung carelessly over one shoulder, and a cautious look in his eyes.

This couldn't be happening. It just *couldn't*.

Had I gone insane? If I was hallucinating, then Becca was too. None of this made any sense.

He paused, a step away from us. "Jess." He was the only person who could say my name with so much feeling.

"Levi?" It came out as a squeak. "What, uh, why...I mean how? How did you get here?" I flicked my hand at the nearby shops. "*Here*." I repeated.

"Waitin' for you, Jess." He'd said that in my dream. I dug both fists into my temples. There had to be a rational explanation, I just couldn't see it.

"Um, if you're not going to introduce me, I'll do it myself." Becca thrust out a hand to Levi, who shook it firmly, his gaze never leaving me. "I'm Becca Maddingly, Jessie's best friend. And you would be...?"

"Levi Hapuku." He dropped Becca's hand and reached out to me. "We met in Wellington. You haven't forgotten me already, have you?" Mischief danced in his eyes, and I swallowed down the hysterical laugh that threatened to erupt.

"We did?"

He cocked his head slightly to one side, eyes searching my face. "We danced at Mighty Mike's. And went up the Rimutakas together." His hand closed around mine, and he tugged me gently into his embrace. After a long frozen moment, I snaked my arms around his neck and let him hold me. I was trembling from head to toe, but when I breathed in the oh-so-familiar forest scent of his skin, my racing heart began to calm down.

"I've surprised you." His voice rumbled over my head, and sent a fresh set of tingles through my blood.

"Yes." Everything about him felt familiar. Safe. Even if it made no sense. "I didn't expect to see you. Ever. I don't understand how you're here."

"I'll explain later."

Explain? How would he possibly be able to do that?

"Hey." Becca interrupted. "Instead of going to

the movies, why don't we grab a coffee? I can see you two might like some time together. We can all get acquainted."

"Sounds like a plan." I was glad when Levi replied. I wasn't capable of speech. God knew how I'd explain this to Becca, when I couldn't rationalise it myself.

I disentangled from Levi, and shoved my treacherous hands in my pockets. Left to their own devices they'd probably grab hold of him and never let go. Maybe I was psychic? Dad had always muttered about having a sixth sense he couldn't explain away, and I might have inherited that, although why it'd never manifested before was anyone's guess. Or maybe I was just crazy. First the talking wolf-dog, and now Levi.

"Where to, girls? I'm a stranger here." He hitched the pack higher on his shoulder, and smiled. *Jesus*. That smile was doing funny things to me. I shoved away the memories of dancing with him, of his molasses sweet voice in my ear, his hands on my skin.

Inside, I jumped up and down, and pointed at him, while squealing like a little girl. *You're real. Really real.* With Becca beside me, I had to behave normally, and try to pretend I'd met him in the usual way. All the questions I wanted to ask would have to come later.

Becca snagged us a table at the nearest café, chatting with Levi as we sat down. I followed in a daze and rapidly tried to pull myself together. I couldn't stop staring at him. I wanted to touch his chest, rub my knuckles across his delicious stubble, and to convince myself he was really there.

"So," she began in a bright voice. "You met in Wellington? That's cool. Are you here on holiday? Or did you fall madly in love with Jess and follow her half-way around the world?"

Levi's smile was for me alone. It promised sin and pleasure in equal portions, and I felt my cheeks heat. How did he do that? Just one look and I was squirming in my seat. "Something like that," he murmured. Dipping into the little bowl on the table, he pulled out four sachets of sugar and dumped them all in his black coffee. Becca and I both watched, bemused. "What? I need the energy." The lazy smile flashed again. "I've been awake for most of the past thirty hours, and I'm going to crash soon. Can you tell me where I can find a backpackers?"

I forestalled Becca's question. "They're called hostels here, and I've no idea. Where were you planning to go?"

He shrugged. "I've got friends in Snowdonia. I was heading there."

Becca leaned forward, her drink forgotten. "It's hours away, do you have a car? And if you're tired, you shouldn't try to drive so far." She glanced at me, and winked. "I could put up a folding bed for you above the pub if you like. It wouldn't be very comfortable, though."

Levi opened his mouth, but Becca continued. "Hang on. Don't you have a spare room at your mum's, Jess?"

They both looked at me, Becca the picture of innocence, and Levi with amusement. "Yes, we do. You're welcome to stay at my parents."

Fifteen minutes of small talk later, we all squeezed into Becca's car along with Levi's pack, and our shopping, and then we headed for home. We would have stayed longer, but Levi looked wiped out and ready to crash at any minute.

When Becca parked outside Mum's, she gave me a quick hug. "Come and see me tomorrow. I want to know *everything*." She'd be lucky. I didn't know anything myself. At least, not yet.

Of course, Mum and Dad were both already home, so there was still no chance to talk privately with Levi. I'd texted Mum to warn her, and they both came to meet Levi the moment we opened the door.

"Sorry about this," I muttered. I fully expected a cheerful welcome for him. My parents loved to meet my friends, and were usually perfectly genial hosts.

I closed the front door. "Mum, Dad, this is Levi." I was in the process of wriggling out of my coat when I realised my parents—and Levi—were all silent.

Dad sniffed the air, like a hunting dog scenting a rabbit. His eyes narrowed and he took a step forward. "Come with me, Levi. Let's go and talk in the kitchen."

Chapter Fourteen

Dad closed the kitchen door with a firm *clunk* behind him, and I was left staring at Mum. "What the hell? Levi only wants to stay the night, not move in or anything." Dad had never behaved like this before.

"I don't know, love." Taking my arm, she guided me to the living room. "He'll have good reason though. Let's give them a few minutes to talk before we go and rescue your boy."

I dropped my bags on the carpet and sank into an armchair next to the Christmas tree. As usual, it was completely overloaded with sparkly baubles and tinsel, and all the toys and trinkets I remembered from childhood. At least some things hadn't changed.

One spinning ornament caught my eye. A tiny wooden wolf, carved in intricate detail. We had a full set of these, had hung them up for years, and I'd never given them a second glance. Now though, I looked at it properly. That crazy talking-dog in the pound had been a wolf, I was sure.

"Mum, where did these wolves come from?"

She looked up from her phone. "They were a present from some of your dad's distant cousins. They were carved in Wales." I knew before she said it. "In Snowdonia."

"Levi has friends there. I don't think I've ever been."

"We took you when you were little. One of your father's family research trips."

"He doesn't bother with that any more, does he?"

Mum stood, and walked to the windows, to adjust the curtains. "No, love. He told me some secrets are best left hidden. I think he found something he didn't like."

"What, like a murderer or something?" My imagination ran riot.

Her reply was halted when footsteps sounded in the hallway, and Dad came into the living room, followed by Levi.

Dad smiled, but it looked forced. Behind him, Levi shuffled his feet and stared at the carpet. Anxiety clawed inside my chest at yet another outbreak of craziness. Did my father already know him? How could that be?

"It's getting late. Levi can stay tonight, and I'll drop him at the station in the morning." Dad's voice was gruff.

I took a deep breath, and pushed to my feet. "What's going on? You don't act like this with any of my other friends."

"Jessie," he began, but Levi interrupted, his gaze seeking me, and locking on to my eyes.

"She deserves to know, Mr. Morgan."

Dad shook his head. "I disagree."

There was something terribly wrong with this picture. Common sense told me to trust my father, but my gut screamed to go to Levi. I covered the few steps between us, and reached out to take his hand. His fingers instantly tangled with mine, and the butterflies in my stomach calmed at the touch. "Dad. I have to know, whatever it is. I know you're hiding something, but Levi is…" I groped for the right words. "He's important. To *me*."

"You met him an hour ago."

Time to face up to the crazy. I lifted my chin and met Dad's hostile stare. "I've been dreaming about him all week. Vividly. I know I'm about a psychic as a teapot, and I can't explain it, but it's like we've known each other for much longer." I swallowed hard. I loved my parents, and hurting them would be the last thing I ever wanted to do, but this had to be said. "I don't want to fight with you, but I won't let you cut Levi out of my life. Not when he's only just come into it."

Levi lifted his free hand and ran his knuckles down my cheek, mimicking the thought I'd had earlier. Soft and gentle, he soothed me even with the high tension levels in the room.

Dad blew out a noisy breath, but then Mum cleared her throat, and the room fell silent. "I dreamed about *you*, Alec. You came to my dreams every night after we met. You followed me back to Yorkshire and convinced me I wanted to move to Manchester." She stepped up, and slid her arm around Dad's waist. "You're not so different."

"I don't want our only child living half way around the bloody world."

"*Whoa.*" This was getting out of hand. "What are you talking about now?"

"Your father's worried that you'll follow me back to New Zealand." Levi's smile suggested he was joking, but his eyes darkened.

I laughed. "Talk about a whirlwind romance. Do I get a say in this?" My words hung in the air and I looked back at Dad. Lines dug into his forehead, and his jaw tightened. He didn't think it was funny.

"Levi looks as though he's dropping where he stands." Mum broke the silence again. "I'll make up a bed for him, and then we'll have dinner." She smiled at the man holding my hand. "I'd love you to join us. And then after we've eaten, we'll talk. *All* of us." Her last words were directed at Dad, who continued to hurl death-glares at Levi.

"Thank you, Mrs. Morgan. I appreciate your generosity." He squeezed my fingers, and didn't let go.

Chapter Fifteen

Dinner was subdued, and I spent most of the meal sneaking glances at Levi, sitting opposite me. I still felt like pinching myself. Part of me feared this might simply be another dream. He'd been polite and respectful, insisted on helping to clean up afterwards, and then had given me that pantie-quivering smile. Surely no man could be so perfect?

And now, Levi and Dad took the armchairs, while Mum and I shared the sofa, in the living room. I'd never seen my father so stressed. He wasn't able to sit for more than a few seconds. Instead, he paced, coming to a halt in front of the fire, and staring into the burning logs.

"I've never told anyone this story." He turned and gazed at Mum, but his eyes were unfocused. Snapping to attention, he looked at me. "You must promise to never repeat it."

Fear skittered down my spine, and I tucked my feet underneath me, feeling suddenly cold. "I promise."

Still he paused, as though trying to decide where to begin. "My father died when I was a small child. Mum never recovered, and only lasted a few years longer, so my *taid*—my grandfather—came back to the shop. He brought me up. He was a good man, but had one blind spot. He refused to talk about what had happened to my dad, so I went looking for my own answers."

His mouth twisted. "He'd been shot. Gunned down in a quiet country pub, with the group he was with. It was all kept quiet, but I found people willing to talk about it."

Nausea rose in my throat, and I pressed my hand to my mouth. Mum had said he found something he didn't like, and dear God, that was horrible. Common sense nudged at me a second later. What could that possibly have to do with Levi?

As though he'd read my thoughts, Dad gestured to me. "Go on. Don't you want to know *why* he was murdered? Hunted, and put down like a wild animal?" He cocked his head at Levi. "He knows."

Levi stood, and walked to the sofa, to crouch beside me. Catching my hands, he glanced over his shoulder at Dad. "You're scaring her." His face was serious. "Is that what you want?"

"I *want* her to be afraid of you. So scared that she never wants to see your kind again."

My gaze bounced from Levi, to Dad, and back to Levi. "What's he talking about? Will you tell me?"

"I'll tell you." Dad paced some more. "So there I was, digging back into my family history, tracking down a whole set of relatives I never knew existed. And when I asked my *taid* about them, he told me straight. Said he'd left Wales for good and didn't want to be a part of them anymore. They were freaks. Abnormal."

Levi's hands tightened around my own, and his breath hitched, but he stayed silent, his eyes tracking my dad.

"My *taid* just wanted to keep his family safe.

And he was right. If my dad had stayed here, things would have been so different."

"What has any of that got to do with Levi?" My voice shook.

"Because he's one of them." Dad made it sound absurdly simple. "I smelled him the minute he walked in."

"One of what?"

"Shifter," said Levi, his voice so low I only just heard it. He blew out a breath, released my hands and stood, approaching my dad. "I'm so sorry for what happened to your family. I understand why you fear my kind, but it's your heritage too. You have the bloodline in you, otherwise you wouldn't have scented me."

Something told me that when I asked the obvious question, I might not like the answer, but I had to know. "What does *shifter* mean?"

"Werewolf," snarled Dad.

"*No.*" Levi spoke over him. "Wolf shifter. We have some unusual abilities." He smiled at me, but it looked strained. "We can talk to our partners in our dreams." Turning back to face Dad, he continued. "We're stronger, and more healthy, and when we find our Mates—our life partners—we're faithful and devoted."

It was Mum's turn to stand. She went to embrace Dad. "Sounds like Levi is describing you, my love."

"Wait. What do you mean? *Werewolf?*" I had to be dreaming again. Werewolves didn't exist outside of horror books and movies.

Levi gave me a ghost of a smile. "It's very different. And if it's any consolation, I would've spared you finding out like this. I planned to tell you when we'd got to know each other better. When you trusted me."

My mind raced, but kept coming back to one freaky-ass word. Werewolf. I had werewolves in my family? I gazed at Dad, imagining he looked different. "Are you one?"

"No." He snapped the word out, but then hesitated. "My *taid* was a half-breed. He had premonitions. He knew the hunters were coming, and that's why he left. He thought he could avert the vision he'd seen, but he was wrong."

"It just happened later than he thought," whispered Mum.

"I hoped Jessie would find a nice young man one day. I never expected her to bring one of *them* home."

"It's probably because of Jessie's bloodline that she could hear me." Levi stuffed both hands in his pockets, and came to stare down at me. "I thought you were my Mate." He stumbled over the words, and then swallowed hard. "I must have been mistaken."

Chapter Sixteen

Levi's face was pale, his eyes unnaturally bright. There was no trace of his seductive smile, and his face was completely blank of emotion. He looked numb. Dragging both hands through his hair, he gazed down at me. "I'm sorry, Jess." A muscle flicked in his cheek, but otherwise he could have been a statue. "I'd better go."

"I can still give you that ride to the station if you want it." On the surface, Dad's offer was polite, but his hostility was only thinly covered.

Mum made a little surprised noise. "You can't be heading out now. There won't be any trains."

"I'm wolf," Levi murmured. "I'll be fine." His eyes continued to eat at me, and the intensity finally broke through my shock.

"You're leaving? Right now?" He gave a little nod. "But there's so much I don't understand. We haven't even talked yet." I didn't dare look at Dad, but I had the stupid notion that if Levi walked out now, I'd never see him again. "And this is Manchester." I improvised rapidly. "It's not safe for you to hang around the streets."

His eyebrows lifted a fraction. "Are you suggesting I can't look after myself?"

"No, I'm suggesting you're tired and jet-lagged." His eyes darkened. "And you don't have anywhere to go."

Levi ducked his head, and then reached out to touch my cheek. "Goodbye, Jess."

I couldn't watch him walk out. I grabbed his hand and clung to it like a lifeline in a rough sea. "Wait. Don't leave." He hesitated and I tried again. "Just stay tonight. *Please.*"

"Family means everything. It's not right for me to come between you and your parents."

He didn't sound as sure of himself, and so I appealed to Dad. "You said he could stay the night. That invitation still stands, doesn't it?"

Mum nudged Dad in the ribs. "Yes, it does. And right now, your father and I are going out. He promised we'd go late night shopping."

"I don't think I did." He sounded indignant.

"Maybe I dreamed it, but that's what we're doing." Mum gave me a quick hug. "We'll be a couple of hours. Plenty of time for you to talk."

****

I dug into the kitchen cupboard and found a bottle of Dad's single malt. Grabbing a couple of glasses, I headed back to the living room and found Levi examining the tiny wolves on the Christmas tree.

"Don't know about you, but I need a drink." I held out the malt, and after a moment, he nodded, and took a glass from me. I sloshed two generous measures, and then settled back on the sofa. I was acutely aware we'd only have the house to ourselves for a couple of hours, if that. They might come back early.

Levi prowled up and down, all lean muscle and grace. Just watching him move gave me chills of the very best kind. I quashed those thoughts and wondered where the hell to start. There was only one place.

"Why me?" He cocked his head on one side in a very canine way, and I tried to explain. "Somehow, you came into my dreams. You knew I'd dreamed about Mighty Mike's, and walking in the Rimutakas. And that bench in the Trafford Centre. But why me?" I took a sip of my drink, and rolled the liquor around my mouth. "I don't understand any of it," I finished, lamely.

"We met," he began, as though choosing his words with care, "in Wellington." He held up a hand when I opened my mouth to interrupt, and I subsided. I'd remember, surely. He was so distinctive, I couldn't possibly forget him. "I liked you. A lot." His eyes seemed to flash sparks in the flickering firelight. "I found you in your dream—and yes, I will explain that too—and I liked you even more."

Enough to buy a ticket to come here, to try and meet me in person?

Glancing down into his glass, Levi wouldn't meet my eyes. "I have contacts in Snowdonia, and I figured I'd try to see you before I headed there. It was just luck that we met in the mall."

There were so many holes in his story, it barely held together. Was he even telling me the truth? I took a drink and gazed at him. He stared back, inscrutable. I took another sip to give me courage. "The wolf thing. What the hell is that all about?"

"Your father might be mistaken."

That wasn't an answer. Dad's words buzzed in my head in an unrelenting chatter of background noise. *Half-breed. Freaks.* "He called you a werewolf, and you said shifter. You planned to tell me later." *When I trusted you.*

Maybe I needed to extend the hand of trust first.

Taking a deep breath, I spoke over the hammering of my heart. I'd never laid myself on the line before, not like this. "When I dreamed about you, I'd wake up and wish you were real. I've never met anyone I've been so...*connected* to. And now you're here, and, well, I'd like to take the time to get to know you. Properly."

Doubt flickered in his eyes, but he didn't move. I pressed on. "I know I never met you in Wellington, so please tell me the truth. I can't trust you if you're not honest with me."

Levi placed his glass on the mantelpiece, and then took a position with his back to the fire, arms folded. "We met at the dog pound."

The pound? I frowned as I thought back to that weird afternoon. "You weren't the guy I spoke to in the office." Something nudged at my memory, but I ignored it. "And I didn't see anyone else there."

"I asked you to help me."

Jigsaw pieces slotted together in my head. *Werewolf.* The wolf-dog I'd freed from the cage. He said his name was Levi.

I scrambled from my seat, unable to stay still. "Oh my God, that was you? In the cage?"

Chapter Seventeen

"Don't be afraid of me." I saw pain in Levi's eyes when he spoke. "I would never do anything to hurt you."

"That was you," I repeated. The wolf really had been talking to me. "They doped you with something."

"Ketamine."

"Oh my God."

He gave me a faint smile. "You already said that."

"It was really you."

"Yep, you said that too."

I blew out a breath, my head spinning. It felt as though the world was shifting beneath my feet. I wanted to run away and hide, but at the same time, I wanted to see him as a wolf again. It was the only thing that might convince me I hadn't gone insane.

"Show me," I whispered. "Please?"

"Are you sure?"

I nodded.

"I need to strip. Look the other way." His lips curled up, and I nodded again, but didn't move. He waved his fingers in a circle, and I tried to focus. *Turn around.* I moved to face the sofa and stared at the slightly faded cushions. How long would it take? Was he really going to change into a wolf? Anticipation skittered through my bloodstream, but for some bizarre reason, I was no longer scared. Nervous, yes. My palms were sticky, and my heart was racing, but I wasn't afraid of him.

Behind me, I heard a rustle of clothing. A soft *swish*, that could have been a T-shirt dropping to the floor. A rasp and scrape, repeated, and two *thuds*. His boots. The sound of a zipper, and then another rustling noise, the sound of denim being shoved down.

He'd be standing there naked. How pervy would it be if I turned to look? Very, I told myself firmly. I had to wait until he'd *changed*, however long that took. Something occurred to me. "Levi? I never thought to ask. It doesn't hurt does it? When you, uh…"

A sharp *yip* was my reply, and my heart almost stopped. Hauling in a ragged breath, I counted to three in my head and then turned around.

Levi had vanished.

A wolf sat in his place.

My mouth was as dry as the Sahara, and for a second I felt light-headed. How was this even possible? Everything I thought I knew was false. A memory of Becca flashed in my head, her sobs when she told me how she'd caught her boyfriend with another girl. "I saw them together," she'd cried. "No matter what I do, I can't un-see them."

I couldn't un-see this.

The wolf looked the same as the beast I'd released from the pound. Staring at him, I realised how freakin' big it was. Handsome too, with thick, dark fur, and the same brilliant blue eyes as Levi. Well, duh. This *was* Levi.

He took a step toward me, and then flopped to

the floor, to roll onto his back. Lying there, mouth open and tongue lolling, he looked harmless, and very friendly. What would his fur be like to touch?

"Can I stroke you?" He stretched out, the picture of innocence. His jaws were huge, and the teeth long and deadly, and if he wanted to, he could snap my wrists without even thinking about it. Even so, I still wasn't scared. I should have been running away, screeching, but I wasn't. Deep inside me, buried and locked down tight, was a spark of recognition. An awareness. Levi had talked about bloodlines, and Dad's heritage.

My father's words were: *My* taid *was a half-breed.*

If my great-grandfather had wolf-blood in him, that meant I had a trace of it too.

I dropped to sit on the carpet, and reached out to touch Levi's head. His ears were like velvet, the fur thick and soft, and I ran my fingers down his neck, to dig into the ruff. He made a rumbling noise of pleasure, and I gazed in awe. This was Levi. He was beautiful. How could Dad think him to be a freak?

He rolled to lie on his stomach, and then, without any warning, he just dissolved into a glorious rainbow of shimmering sparks. I sat spellbound, not daring to move, to even breathe. Next thing, Levi lay on his front, buck-naked, my hands on his bare shoulders.

In human form, he was even more devastating to my overloaded senses. Acres of tawny skin lay there, mine to touch. A tribal tattoo snaked down his spine, and another wrapped around his upper arm. He shifted position to rest his chin on his hands, and he looked up at me, the image of devilment.

"It doesn't," he said.

Huh? "Doesn't what?"

"It doesn't hurt. That's what you asked, a

minute ago."

I had, before my entire knowledge of science had been blown out of the water.

His skin was warm. I could touch him all day in either form, if he'd let me. Without thinking, I stroked the inked characters down the line of his back, tracing them with my fingertips. "I don't know what to say."

"You're still here. That's a good place to start."

Chapter Eighteen

"How do you do it? The changing thing?" I spoke quietly, unwilling to break this very intimate connection that had flared between us.

"I just think it, and it happens." Levi's voice dropped too, more husky by the second.

"It's incredible." I'd reached the curve of his waist, dangerously close to deliciously taut ass cheeks, and I began to caress upwards. I didn't want to stop touching him. "So there's more of you? Wolves?"

"We're all over the world. There've been shifters for so long, nobody knows when or where they first emerged."

"And yet you manage to keep hidden." I remembered something. "At the pound, the guy was calling in the TV reporters. Did they know?"

Levi scowled briefly. "No, that was something else. They thought they'd trapped a wolf, and I didn't get the opportunity to shift back to human form. There's been a lot of press coverage recently about people sighting wolves in the hills. It's crazy. If someone learns about us, we'll be destroyed."

I absorbed his words. "I saw something on the

news when I was there. I just didn't pay it any attention at the time. I wasn't sure if wolves ran wild in New Zealand."

"It's a growing problem for us, and it's never been before." He stretched under my hands, relaxing at my touch. "Someone is trying to expose us. And that cannot happen."

I reached his broad shoulders and the ends of his dark, rumpled hair. Stroking him was soothing my jangled nerves too. It was as though we'd woven a little bubble of calm around us, and I was loathe to break the spell. "You showed me. Don't you worry that I might expose you?"

The blue eyes were limpid pools. "Will you?"

"Of course not."

"You're amazing, Jessie Morgan. Not only do you have shifter blood, but you're the most beautiful girl I've ever seen. From the first moment I saw you, I wanted you."

My cheeks heated, and I looked away, my hands stilling on his back. He'd used that line on me in one of our dreams, and I was under no illusions. That reminded me. "Tell me about the dreaming thing. How does that work?"

"Ah, that." His shoulder muscles rippled, causing the ink to flex and reform. "I'll lie here all night, you know, letting you pet me."

I smiled. "Are you asking me to stroke you some more?"

"Was it so obvious?" His answering smile was a thing of beauty. I pressed my knuckles into his skin, and he gave a low moan. "That feels good, baby."

"Nice try, wolf boy. You were going to tell me about the dreaming thing."

He stayed quiet and so I sat back, and dropped my hands into my lap. He sighed, and pulled a funny face, and then in a sinuous move, he sat up and tugged his T-shirt across to cover his groin.

I gazed at his firm, muscled chest and perfect hard abs. He looked as though he'd stepped off the cover of a sports magazine, toned and lean. "The dreams," I prompted.

"Yeah. I guess some people are more receptive. It doesn't happen to everyone."

It wasn't really an answer. "Mum said she shared dreams with Dad." I thought some more. "Is this something you do with all the girls?"

"You mean lie naked on the floor while they give me a massage? No such luck."

"I think you know what I mean." I felt shy, and awkward, and completely out of my depth.

"There isn't much to tell." His fingers played with the edge of his shirt, and I fought to keep my gaze above his waist. "We connected so easily, and I couldn't stay away. I wanted to get to know the real you. See if you were as lovely as I dreamed."

The firelight flickered over his body, creating a golden halo around his hair, and casting interesting shadows over his face. I could stare at him for hours and not get bored. "Are you really heading up to Snowdonia? If I borrow Mum's car, I could drive you there tomorrow."

"Talking of your mum, they'll be back soon. I can't imagine your father would be too pleased to see me like this." He made no move to dress, but his hand fisted around the soft cotton of his shirt. "I want you, Jess. And I don't know how long I can keep my hands off you."

My heart skittered. The urge to kiss him was overwhelming, to see if he tasted as good in real life as he had in my dreams. My nerve endings all prickled in anticipation, and I licked suddenly dry lips. Was it me, or was it hot in here?

"Then don't," I whispered.

Levi's eyes darkened, almost burning me with the intensity of his gaze. "Come here," he growled.

I knelt facing him, in the V of his legs, caged by his strong thighs, and waited to see what he'd do. My heart thumped double-speed, and I had to wipe my damp palms on my jeans. I'd never had a man look at me so intently, as though I was the reason he drew breath, and it made me giddy. Lust arced through me in a fierce, searing wave. My panties were damp, my breasts heavy and aching for his touch, and he hadn't even moved yet.

With all the slowness of a man who had all night to play, he cupped my cheeks with both hands, and held me at the perfect angle to receive his kiss. Firm, blistering hot, and mind-meltingly good, his lips worked their magic on me, and I kissed him back just as hard.

This was better than I'd dreamed. This was real.

Chapter Nineteen

Levi kept up the pressure on my mouth, demanding and insistent. When he finally lifted his lips, it was to press them against my throat. "Take off your top. I want to see what it's hiding." His words vibrated against me, the stubbled jaw setting me alight.

My pulse sped into overdrive. With trembling fingers, I yanked my lightweight sweater over my head, and clutched it to my chest. I only had my bra underneath. A plain, white, cotton bra. If I'd had any idea of how today would play out, I'd have dressed with a little more care.

"Let me." His smile was enticing, but his eyes were hungry. He closed one hand over mine, and pushed my top to the side, to place it on the carpet. "Oh, baby. So pretty." He fingered the fine lacy strip across the curve of my breasts, the only adornment, and then, with care, folded down the cups to expose my nipples.

They plumped even further under his fleeting touch, and he smiled with pure male satisfaction. "You are so beautiful." He pretended to weigh them in his hands. "All pink, and pretty, and waiting for me."

Hot breath preceded his mouth closing around first one nipple, and then the other. Back and forth, he licked and sucked, driving me closer to insanity. Without conscious thought, I'd raised my hands to his shoulders, and I used him as an anchor, my fingers curling into the solid muscles. I needed something to hold on to.

I was drowning in pleasure. Surrounded by his green-woody scent, I knew if I ever smelled this fragrance again, it would remind me of this magical evening.

"Jess," he whispered against my skin, his teeth grazing the curve of my breast. I whimpered, actual speech impossible, and let my head loll. In a flash, he slid one hand under my neck in a move so possessive I should have complained. Laying a trail of kisses up my arm, he slid the bra straps down, and pressed his lips in their wake.

"You could drive a man insane, Jess. I don't know where to kiss next." He paused, as though thinking. "Here?" The shell of my ear. "Or here?" The base of my throat. "Hmm, maybe here?" The soft swell of my stomach. "I need you lying down."

I didn't care where he went next, as long as he didn't stop. I moved, with his hands guiding me, and our positions were reversed. He knelt over me. Skin to skin.

Deft fingers popped the button on my jeans, and then slid beneath the waistband, to dip under the elastic of my panties. Oh dear God, was he going to go down on me, here in my parent's living room, when they could be back any time? I wouldn't need much to push me over the edge, and if his touch went any further south he'd find how wet I was.

The zipper was next, and he opened it one tooth at a time, making me wait. His lips brushed the top of my panties, and then he paused. "Jess, I need to ask you something."

"What?" It came out as a squeak.

"Are you seeing Jack again?"

It took a moment before my scrambled neurons made the connection. I'd been to the club with Jack. "No." I sucked in a tortured breath. "He's a dick."

"Good." Levi lifted his head and scorched me with his gaze. "I won't share you."

His arrogance amused me. "Bit cocky, aren't you?"

The replying grin was smug and proud. "Baby, you ain't seen nothing yet." Before I could assemble a witty comeback, he yanked at my jeans and dragged them down my thighs. "Matching panties," he murmured. "Very pretty." He nuzzled them, and a second later, pulled them down too. I was helpless now, laid out before him, my jeans stuck at the knees. I loved every minute.

He cupped me in another bold, confident move, and my hips surged up, a rush of desire making me squirm. "Levi, please…"

"Please, what?" He stroked a circle around my clit, paused, and again. Teasing. Did I really need to spell it out for him? "Please, what, Jess?"

"Touch me." My lungs were struggling to re-inflate, and my pulse pounded in my ears, but I wouldn't move for the world.

"I am touching you, baby." He blew a hot breath over my pussy lips, and I shuddered. *Bastard*. I loved it. "You mean touch you here?" He dragged a finger along my slit, and I moaned. "Or here?" He slipped inside me, just a fraction.

So much sensation, but not enough, and he knew it. I'd never had a lover play with me before. I burned with frustration, my fingers clawing at the carpet, as I tried to form coherent words. Right now I could only moan.

"Hmm." Levi nuzzled my pussy, his tongue lapping at me. "You taste so good. Like the sweetest ice cream." Another lick that made me dizzy. "I want to make you come so hard, your legs turn to jelly."

His hands stroked the inside of my thighs, holding me open. I was helpless, and focused on one thing. My approaching orgasm. Never mind turning my legs into jelly, when this one hit, I'd melt into a sticky puddle all over the floor.

"Your clit is like a little pearl, all shiny and pink." Another hot breath made me tremble. "Ask me nicely, Jess."

He rasped a stubbled cheek over one hipbone, and I gulped. Speech. He wanted me to say something. "Please," I whispered, unable to say anything else. My vocabulary had reduced to one word. *"Please."*

There was a rapid lick on my clit, and then he closed his mouth around it and sucked. Hard. I cried out, pleasure sweeping through me in a relentless torrent. Lightning flashed behind my eyes, and every muscle in my body seemed to spasm at once. *Christ.* That wasn't an orgasm. I just died and gone to heaven.

Chapter Twenty

"So," murmured Levi, his lips vibrating against my inner thigh. "Jelly?" He nipped the soft flesh there and set off another shockwave of pleasure. "Or do I need another go? You did say I was cocky." His fingertips danced around my hyper-sensitive clit, not quite touching. "I like to deliver."

With an immense burst of determination, I grabbed at his head and tugged gently, pulling him back up my body. I needed to kiss him. Right now. He tasted musky, of me, I realized. Breaking off to draw breath, I ran my fingers through his hair. "Jelly. God, yes."

I loved the very wolfish grin he gave me. Pure, alpha male. "Come away with me. We can go to Snowdonia together." At that moment, I'd follow him anywhere. I nodded. His smile softened, and tenderness flickered in his eyes. "I have a confession."

This looked serious. I stole a kiss, and waited for him to continue. "I was going to walk away, try to forget I'd met you, rather than cause a rift with your parents. But now, I can't do that." He lifted a hand and dug it into my hair, closing his fist around the locks. "I want you too badly."

The mention of my parents reminded me they'd be home soon. Finding us semi-naked in front of the fire would not be good. I tried to think clearly. "I need to be home again for Christmas. That gives us nearly two weeks."

Levi held me close. I felt the steady thump of his heart, and breathed in the now-familiar scent of his skin. "We can do a lot in two weeks." His voice rumbled over my head.

"How long are you here for?"

"I've got a holiday visa, however long that is." He pressed a kiss onto my hair. "I just wanted to get here, the quickest way I could."

Huh? Something didn't add up. I backtracked the conversation in my head. "Why were you in such a rush?"

There was the tiniest hesitation before he spoke. "I couldn't wait to see you again."

"I thought you said you were here to see friends."

He sighed. I felt him tense, and then gather me tighter in his arms. "I came here to see you, Jess."

With so much delicious naked flesh in close proximity, it was difficult to think clearly. I must be missing something. "We met at the pound, and then in my, uh, dreams." I swallowed. That was a tough concept to get hold of. "And then you dropped everything to fly here, just to see me? Are you like a crazy millionaire or something? Nobody can afford to do that." I'd fallen back into babble mode. "Don't you need to get back for work?" I paused, and thought. "I don't even know what you do."

"I work in I.T., for my uncle, and he was fine about the time off." Levi's clever fingers were now rubbing soothing circles up my back. Distracting me. "And I had some savings. Enough to pay for a ticket."

More kisses rained over my hair. "No millionaires. I'm afraid. Not even close."

"Crazy though."

"Maybe a little. Crazy about you, yes,"

"If I hadn't been in the Trafford Centre today, we'd never have met. You took a huge gamble on me being there." Oops, that was another reminder of my parents. "We need to dress. My mum and dad will be back soon."

****

By the time my parents returned, we were fully dressed and sitting a circumspect distance apart on the sofa. Levi was showing me pictures on his phone of his home in a quiet suburb of Wellington. He told me about his job, creating and testing security systems for government agencies, and I realized he was even sharper and more intelligent than I'd assumed. He also helped at his cousin's recycling yard and volunteered for an environmental charity.

I felt dull in comparison, but he appeared to be entranced with me. He wanted to know about my friends, my life here in Manchester, my travels abroad, and my thoughts of New Zealand. I told him about my plans to work in Dad's shop, how I wanted a chance to use my business qualification, how I'd always planned to stay here.

Although Dad scowled, there were no further suggestions of Levi having to leave tonight. I was glad, especially when he began yawning. He looked exhausted, and no wonder. I'd been wiped out flying here, and I'd slept parts of the journey.

He sat on the edge of the spare bed and gazed up at me, and we shared a tender, chaste kiss. I was conscious of Mum bustling around, sorting out extra blankets in case he felt the cold. Like me he'd left the heat of summer behind, in exchange for a freezing English winter.

There'd been an uncomfortable silence when I explained my plan to travel with Levi the next day. Dad was clearly unhappy at my decision, and it tore at me. I tried to rationalise it to him. I liked Levi and I wanted a chance to get to know him. He'd travelled thousands of miles on the off chance of seeing me again, and it was plain rude to turn him away. I didn't mention the best orgasm of my life. I also didn't say anything about the intensity of the connection we shared.

Dad had one last try at changing my mind. "He's not normal, Jess. And his way of life is dangerous. No matter what he says, what you think, your *taid* was murdered. There will always be people who fear things they don't understand, and who turn their fear into violence. Hunters came after your *taid's* family, and he was there at the time." Dad stopped, his face tight. "I don't want that for you, Jessie-Bell. We came here so you'd be safe, and it's killing me that you might be putting yourself at risk."

I hugged my father. Right now, that was all I could do.

I couldn't tell him that giving up Levi was already not an option.

Chapter Twenty-One

There was some good news in the morning. The vet rang to say that Charlie was improving, and after a couple days more of monitoring, he might be allowed home. After a quick trip to see my dog, we loaded our bags into Mum's car.

Levi settled himself behind the wheel and flashed me a grin so sexy, it should've been illegal. "I've scored the pimp-mobile and the hot chick. What's next?"

I couldn't help giggling. "It's a fifteen-year-old Beemer, not a Cadillac."

"You haven't seen what I drive. A BMW is a step up, believe me."

It'd been uncomfortable leaving my parents, but Levi was steadily lifting my spirits. "Why don't we try to make it to the Welsh border before we stop for coffee?" I peered out of the windows at the white flakes steadily falling. "This is the heaviest snowfall in years, according to the weather service. Have you driven in snow before?"

"Baby, I come from New Zealand. We have some of the best ski-fields in the world."

He would certainly have more experience of driving on narrow mountain passes than me, so I settled back into my seat and scrolled through my playlist selection to choose some music for the journey. "Have you arranged to meet up with your friends when we get there?" I asked.

"Yep. I put a call in to Tammy. I'm a good buddy of her brother, Sasha, and she's sorted out somewhere for us to stay. We're heading for a village that sounds like *Bathe-Gelut*, and I've got directions written down. It's all good."

I was on a road trip with the hottest guy ever. We'd be able to get naked and have hot monkey sex without my parents interrupting. What more could I want? A nagging sense of disquiet sat at the back of my mind. I wanted my dad to like Levi, but I figured it would take time. I could either fret over that, or I could enjoy this stolen time with him. Another doubt crept in. He lived twelve thousand miles away. If I wanted to try and have any kind of relationship with him, one of us would have to relocate.

"Hey." Levi took my hand and squeezed my fingers, before resting our linked hands on his thigh. "Looks like you're thinking too hard again."

"Sorry, you're right. I'm borrowing trouble, as my mum says." I took a quick breath and decided to leave all the mental baggage for another day. "So tell me, what's it like being able to change into a wolf whenever you want to?"

"Pretty goddamn awesome, but it's normal to me. I can't imagine how you must feel, without an animal inside you."

He explained that although shifting between forms didn't take place until puberty, they were all aware of their inner wolves from their earliest memories. As we crawled along the congested

255

Manchester motorways, he told me about the Pack he belonged to in Wellington. It was nothing like a gang, as I'd first imagined, and more of an extended family group. Levi was excited to meet the Welsh wolves, and to see where his friend had grown up.

I began to relax, and managed to ignore the anxious prickle at the back of my neck.

Hours later, after several stops for coffee and to admire the spectacular views of the Welsh mountains, we hit a problem. The snow, much heavier here, had blocked some of the roads and we needed to divert. Our phones had no signal, and since we had written directions, we'd not thought to bring a map. The light was failing rapidly, and it would be dark within the hour.

The prickling in my neck intensified and I rolled my shoulders and tried to stretch, while scanning the road ahead. "What's the name of the village?"

"Tammy said it was *Bathe-Gelut*." Levi squeezed my fingers. "Next sign of habitation we'll stop and ask directions. We can't be far away."

"There's another junction here." I pointed to the sign, and laughed. "That might be how it's pronounced, but it's not spelled like that." The sign proclaimed: *Beddgelert – 10 miles.*

"Not far at all." Levi flashed me a grin, but he looked tired. "That freakin' diversion added two hours-"

The strange feeling in my neck exploded into a screaming warning and I clenched my fist on Levi's thigh, fear tearing down my spine. "Stop!" I cried, interrupting him. Without questioning me, he brought the car to a safe halt.

"What just happened?" He grabbed my hands. "Jess. Talk to me."

"I don't know." My heart hammered and my

lungs were struggling to draw breath. "I just knew we had to stop."

He smoothed the hair from my face, and waited until I'd calmed down. "Okay, let's take this next corner really slow, see what's up ahead." I nodded.

In the couple minutes that we'd been stationery, the snow had already covered the car. I'd never seen it so thick, so blanket-like.

Levi set off again, at a crawl. This was ridiculous weather for driving, and I feared if we didn't get there soon, we'd have to sleep in the car. This final stretch had been horrendous. Narrow roads that hugged the side of the mountain, with steep drops on the other side, hairpin-tight bends, and zero visibility. Maybe that's why I felt so odd? Travel sickness. Even as I thought that, I discounted it.

We embarked on the next blind curve, the wipers flying across the windshield, but barely keeping it clear of snow. Looming out of the white blur, was a hulking shape completely blocking the road. My heart leapt into my mouth.

Levi slammed on the brakes again. "What the fuck is that? Looks like a van, sideways, and covered in snow." If we'd been going any faster, we'd have hit it. I shivered at the realisation. My prickly sixth sense might have saved us being in an accident.

"Must have spun." Levi turned in his seat and looked behind us. "We'll have to back up. There's no room to turn around." He glanced back at the blockage. "We'd better see if the driver is still inside. They might be hurt."

He was right, and it made sense, but I didn't like the idea. I didn't want to let him out of my sight, not even for a minute. What was the matter with me? I was jumping at shadows.

Levi reached into the back seat for his leather

jacket, and I snapped into action. "I'm coming." I grabbed my own coat, a thick down-filled parka.

"Stay here, where it's warm and dry. No sense in us both getting wet." He was already opening the door, a blinding swirl of snowflakes pouring in, and he climbed out before I had chance to reply.

Common sense told me to listen to him. My gut told me differently and I scrambled to follow him, tugging on my coat as I went.

The BMW headlights lit up the stricken vehicle, and Levi went to try the driver's door. A couple of steps behind him, I was momentarily confused when another set of lights swept over the van.

Another vehicle was coming around the bend. And it didn't know we were blocking the road.

Chapter Twenty-Two

Engine noises. Metal on metal. A scream.

The world was filled with unearthly sounds. I didn't have time to react, to even think.

"*Jess.*" Something shoved into my side, sending me sprawling, face down in the snow. Levi.

Every atom of breath whooshed out of my lungs and the shock-wave reverberated through my entire body. I tried to process what had just happened. Another car had hit the BMW. Levi had pushed me out of the way.

I tried to inhale, but couldn't find my breath. Where was Levi? Was he hurt? Lights flashed, and over the buzzing in my ears, I heard voices. Shouting. I pushed to my knees and dragged in some precious oxygen. My chest hurt with the effort, but I took another ragged breath, and then another.

"Levi." I tried to shout his name, but it came out as a wheezy croak. "*Levi.*"

Suddenly there were other people, hands helping me to my feet, voices asking if I was hurt.

"Where's Levi? My boyfriend. He pushed me out of the way."

"Over here," a man's voice boomed. I staggered toward him. I had to find Levi. Adrenaline must have been coursing through my veins, because I didn't feel any pain, just the desperate need to find Levi. I'd never forgive myself if he was hurt. Why didn't I stay in the car?

I stumbled through the snow, a stranger's arm supporting me. It was only a couple steps, but felt like miles. I ran a dozen scenarios in my head. Levi was bleeding to death. Levi was already dead. I had to tell his family. I had to live without him. Pain filled my chest.

There he was. He lay on his side, fresh snow already blanketing him, and I dropped to my knees. "*Levi*. Babe?" I groped for his hand. *Please be okay. Please be alive.*

Time stopped for the longest moment. I tangled our fingers together, and leaned forward to brush the snow from his face. "*Levi*."

His eyes opened. Blinked. "Jess." He tried to sit up, groaned, and sank back down again. "Baby, you okay?"

I squeezed his fingers. "I am now."

Someone draped a heavy coat over my shoulders, and a blanket around Levi. He kept insisting he was fine, but when he tried to stand, he was in visible pain and our rescuers helped him to their car, a big off-roader. I clung to his hand. It was only when I sat in the warm, dry vehicle that I gave in to the shock. My teeth chattered, and I shivered from head to toe. I suddenly realised that Levi was talking to the strangers, and I tried to pay attention.

There were three guys, all young and strong looking. Each had the same brilliant blue eyes as Levi, and the same graceful way of moving. I tried not to stare. Were they wolves too?

"I'm Levi, and this is Jess." He hesitated, and then squeezed my fingers. "She's my Mate."

Mate? It seemed to hold some significance to the Welsh men, as they instantly relaxed around me.

"We're ten miles outside the village. Fastest if I shift, and run like that," offered the youngest. He gave me a shy smile. "I'm Dai Evans."

One the others clapped him on the shoulder. "Good lad. Get them to send the tractor to drag the vehicles clear. Morris is putting out some warning lights to stop anyone else from coming through."

Levi tugged me closer on the back seat of the car. "I'm sorry, baby. Did I hurt you?"

His concern brought tears to my eyes. "I'm fine, thanks to you."

With the help of the third rescuer, Taff, we pieced the events together. The van had swerved to avoid a fox, spun on the ice and got stuck. The driver had set off to get help, and this crew had been on their way to recover the vehicle. Coming around the bend, they'd been unable to avoid our car, smashing the passenger side of the BMW into the rock face.

Where I'd been sitting was completely mangled.

In the shunt, the BMW had lurched forward, and Levi had pushed me clear, taking the hit himself. The young wolf, Dai, was going to despatch the local doctor to come and check on Levi, and then they'd figure out if he needed to go to hospital. In the meantime, they kindly recovered our luggage, and gave us hot drinks, then left us alone while they worked to clear the road.

We huddled together, and I tried very hard not to cry. Levi's pained, wheezing breath scared me. I needed to talk, to distract myself from the realisation that Levi had risked himself to save my life. "You called me your mate," I whispered. "I thought I was a bit more than that."

"Ah yes." He ran his knuckles down my cheek. "There's something I should explain. It's not mate, as in friend." He paused, and I saw uncertainty in his eyes. "Some wolves," he continued slowly, "are lucky enough to find their true partner. Their *Mate*. Like your dad, when he met your mum." His smile was hesitant. "We mate for life."

"Oh." I tried to focus on his words. Thought about how good my parents were together, how happy, and still in love with each other. "And you think I'm your Mate?"

"I *know* you are." He drew my hand to his mouth and pressed a hot kiss on my palm. "When you freed me from that cage. My wolf recognised you as its own."

"Oh," I repeated, my mind spinning and Levi nipped playfully at my fingertips.

"You already said that," he murmured.

I pulled my wits together, as best I could. "So what does this mean?"

"That all depends on you, Jess. Whether or not you want to accept me."

A short while later, things went chaotic again. The local doctor arrived and checked out Levi. There were definitely some broken ribs, and most likely fractures to his sternum and collarbone. He needed an X-ray, to make sure his lungs hadn't been punctured, but apart from that he seemed to be fine. Luckily for us, the medical centre in Beddgelert could do this, rather than having to transport him to hospital—a near impossibility in this weather.

Wherever he went, I'd be holding his hand.

I couldn't be sure how I felt about the Mate issue. It was too big and complicated to think about right now, and so I pushed it from my mind. At least for the moment.

Chapter Twenty-Three

Our first night in a shared bed was not how I imagined. Despite Levi's protests of *feeling fine*, he'd been given strong painkillers and lay doped up and grumpy, while I tried to avoid moving. He was bruised from the neck down to his stomach, and I was terrified of hurting him in my sleep, if I rolled over.

"I want to hold you," he grumbled, and so we spooned together. "I wanted to turn your legs to jelly again tonight, and then fuck you into oblivion."

I stroked his hand where it curved around my breast. "Maybe in a few days."

"These damned drugs." His sleep-filled voice rumbled in my ear. "I don't think I can even stay awake long enough to come into your dreams. I'm sorry, baby."

My eyes filled up. "You have nothing to apologise for." From his slow, steady breathing, I figured he was already asleep.

I was still wide awake, and with too many thoughts tearing around inside my head, to sleep any time soon. Everybody here had been so helpful and friendly, wolves and non-wolves alike. We'd met

Tammy, the sister of Levi's friend, Sasha, and she'd been brilliant. She'd booked us a room in this lovely inn, and had promised us a guided tour of the area as soon as Levi was up and about. She was also organising the insurance on Mum's battered car, and sorting out a hire vehicle for us.

Our immediate problems had all been taken care of.

My thoughts returned to the man beside me. His body curled around mine, protecting me even in his sleep. Could I really consider a long-term relationship with him after such a short time? And if I did, would I move back to New Zealand with him? What about the shop?

The depth of what I felt for Levi was impossible to explain. I knew with a profound certainty that leaving him was not an option, so now I had to figure out how we could make it work. What would happen to Dad's shop? How would my parents cope with me living thousands of miles away?

I had no answers.

****

After breakfast the next morning, Levi went for a check-up with the doctor, and I had a little time to myself. I found a quiet spot and set up a Facetime call with my parents.

I told them of the accident. How Levi had saved me. How he wanted to claim me as his Mate, and how I wanted to say yes.

Dad looked sideways at Mum, and then back at me. "The day I met your mum, I knew she was mine. I would move heaven and earth to be with her, and I still feel the same." He gazed into the distance for a moment. Mum nudged him with her elbow and he met my eyes again. "I know how Levi must feel about you. I understand."

"And," piped up Mum. "If you feel for Levi even a tenth of what I feel for your dad, you'll be very happy with him."

Dad spoke again. "If you want to make a life together, Jessie-Bell, I'd be wrong to stand in your way. We'll figure it out."

The call over, I went back to our room, and found Levi sitting on the edge of the bed.

"Hey," he greeted me, and patted the space beside him. "C'mon over here. I think I'm dying of hypothermia and I need your body warmth to keep me alive."

I moved to his side. "If I want to hold you, will it hurt?"

"I'd be more hurt if you didn't."

We sprawled together, Levi propped up with a mountain of pillows, and he found a comfortable position where we could snuggle.

"I've been thinking," I began, watching the expression on his face. "If I became your Mate, what would that mean for us?"

Hope flared in his eyes. He slid one hand into my hair and cupped the back of my head. "It'd be tough. There'd be lots of hot sex."

I bit back my giggle. "Really?"

"Oh yeah. I'd also spend all my days telling you how beautiful you are, and how much I love you."

"Really?"

He huffed out a laugh. "I'm thinking it's a good sign that I reduce you to near speechlessness."

I grabbed my courage and held it tight. "I love you. I know it's early days, but I love you, Levi. I want to make this work."

"I love you too, baby. You've just caught

yourself a wolf."

I stole a kiss. "I haven't put you in cage."

He stole one from me. "Actually you have. But your love is a cage I never want to leave."

Epilogue

Two Weeks Later

When we returned to Manchester, it was to several pieces of good news. Charlie was home, and looked set to make a good recovery, and my parents had come to terms with Levi being my Mate. I think Mum had something to do with that, but Levi's willingness to risk himself for me, won Dad over.

That would be have been enough celebration for me, but Dad had some other news to share. He was planning to sell the shop—not to Jack Harper—but to the supermarket chain that wanted to open a branch of their DIY stores in the same street. Dad had been tipped off by Becca, who'd found out from Toby. This was why Jack had been so keen to buy the shop, in the hope of reselling it and making a quick profit.

"You're free to make your own decisions about your future, Jessie-Bell. Chaining you to this life isn't fair. And now I can retire early," he told us. "Very early. So if you do end up living half way around the world, we can come and see you."

"I've always fancied visiting New Zealand." Mum's smile was bright. "Maybe even living there one day."

When I'd come back home, just a few weeks ago, I thought I had my life planned out. The only wolves I knew, were the little wooden ones on the Christmas tree.

Now I had a real wolf of my own, and many Christmases to look forward to with him.

The End

Wolf for Christmas, a Fangs and Fur

Novella, by Sotia Lazu

Salina has earned her one-year vacation on Earth, damn it! She's been an exemplary sentinel for her pack, and saved all the universes.

Too bad she hasn't been very effective at kicking Aherin to the curb. Sleeping with the annoyingly persistent vampire was her one little lapse in judgement, and now he just won't leave.

As if that wasn't enough, her holiday plans are spoiled, her world is turned upside down, and she's going to miss out on a yummy family dinner, all because she's kidnapped on Christmas Eve.

Chapter One

Salina was about to enter her house, key poised at the lock, when someone grabbed her from behind. Her arms were pinned to her body with what could only be described as inhuman strength, and something soft tickled the side of her neck.

She cursed how the Earth plane had made her drop her guard. There was no way someone could've sneaked up on her back home. She would've been on edge, and smelled or heard them a block away. Then again, fighting for her life or her pack was a common occurrence in The Forest. South Kensington was entirely too tame, compared to that. Even downtown London was entirely too tame compared to any place she'd been, really, and at times kind of boring.

This wasn't one of those times.

She didn't panic. It wasn't the first time a certain undead *someone* was being an idiot. "Aherin, I'm not in the mood, and my parents are in town," she said, considering a head-butt. "You'll end up with a stake in your ass."

In a split second, a heavy piece of cloth was drawn over her head, blocking her vision.

She opened her mouth to yell, but no sound left her lips. What the hell? Was the thing hexed? Aherin couldn't be doing this. He'd never managed to keep her silent—and there was the small detail about him being unable to perform magic.

In theory, he could buy or steal magical items, but magic didn't exist on this plane. That was the entire point of the schism.

What had Aherin gotten himself into this time?

She'd get free first, and figure things out later. She kicked at her assailant, but what felt like a dozen hands grabbed her legs. *Ouch.* What was with the pinching? At least there was no groping.

Probably not Aherin, then.

"Let me go." She'd meant to yell the words, but they rattled inside her head instead. Despite her struggling, she was soon trussed like a Christmas turkey, her arms behind her back, elbows and wrists secured with thin yet incredibly sturdy binds.

Was it a stupid piece of string? She funneled all of her shifter strength into snapping it. Nothing. She couldn't break free from *a piece of string*?

Magic.

This had to be a full-on magic attack.

Her legs were bound at her ankles and knees with the same material, and she was unable to move them, though she still tried. She wasn't afraid for her life. At least not yet. Her attacker had incapacitated her, and it seriously pissed her off.

Salina tried to scream again. If she managed to make a sound—any sound—her sister would hear. Her kidnappers would have no luck against the both of them. The only other person Salina trusted to have her back in a fight was Aherin, when he wasn't too busy being a filthy perv.

Which he was, most of the time.

And what did that make Salina? She'd known what Aherin was when she...

Was this really the time to go down memory lane? She'd rather focus on her attackers. Kidnappers. Whatever. If this was another prophecy, she swore she was done with the pack. She'd move far away, and hide from it all—stupid older sisters, who brought temptation home with them, and even stupider black-eyed Irish vampires, who mojoed her into sleeping with them once and wouldn't leave her alone since.

This vacation on Earth was supposed to be her reward for her part in saving the universes. Was it too much to ask for a peaceful, merry Christmas with her family, after all they'd been through?

"Hey, assface," she tried to call out. Again nothing. *Bloody spell.* She bit her lips, furious at herself for letting Aherin's mannerisms influence her thinking. She'd known not staking his undead ass would lead to trouble. Yeah, okay, Aherin was one of the Balancers' golden boys, and had helped save creation itself, but couldn't he have gone away afterward?

It didn't matter they were on his plane of existence, and not hers. She was supposed to have a year to rest, and where did the Balancers find her a place? Bloody London, near bloody Aherin.

The growl in her chest made it to her ears. At least she had that.

She pumped her hips and tried to arch her body away from the grasp of whoever held her. Nothing. It was like fighting the Jaws of Life. Could it be a shifter from an enemy pack? They all united to defeat the vampire mage Acerbus, but maybe old feuds were resurfacing, now that he'd been dealt with.

She sniffed the cloth covering her head. Nothing but the faint smell of candy. What self-respecting kidnaper went around attacking people with a bag that used to hold *candy*? Didn't they know they were supposed to use more sinister props? She thrashed her head wildly, hoping for the off chance she'd make impact with sensitive cartilage, but all she got was light headed.

Like when Aherin started with the dirty jokes.

And he didn't have to stick around. Always there, underfoot, not letting her forget her single lapse of judgment. It had been *one night*, but he just didn't seem to want to move on. He kept rubbing it in, telling her she had to come to grips with wanting him. When she so totally didn't. Totally.

She realized she'd somehow gone from being angry at the ones holding her, to mentally jotting down ways of making Aherin pay for being the bane of her existence. Not a good road to go down. Whispers reached her ears, and she tried to focus on the hushed voices, but her usually acute hearing was dulled— probably by the same spell that wouldn't let her speak.

She stiffened as her world tilted. She was lifted in a horizontal position, and carried a short distance. Unseen hands positioned her sitting upright in a rather comfortable plush seat. Whoever this was, they hadn't walked here. How on earth hadn't her family noticed them? Other than her mother—who, though human, had surprisingly good instincts—there were two shifters and a vampire in the two-story semi-detached.

The pit of Salina's stomach fell with the sensation of sudden liftoff. She was still making sense of that, when she heard…

Nah. Couldn't be.

She tried cocking her head toward the source of what sounded like tiny bells. Was she losing it? First her voice, now her mind? She couldn't be hearing bells and jolly ho-ho-ho's. If it wasn't all in her head, where exactly was it all coming from? It sounded as if the bells were *jingling* all around her, right before a blast of air whooshed past her head.

The temperature dropped.

Were they entering a tunnel?

Where was she?

Whatever vehicle she was traveling in came to a sudden halt, almost throwing her out of her seat. She barely registered a strong arm grabbing her around the shoulders, to keep her from falling, when she heard clopping. Okay, those were definitely hooves. She was hallucinating. Had to be.

The thought of losing touch with reality brought tears of frustration to her eyes. It had happened to Xandra, Salina's sister, when she went after the vampire mage threatening to unravel their realm. Xandra told Salina she'd rather die than be unable to trust her instincts again.

Her instincts.

She could shift. She hadn't done so sooner, unwilling to reveal her second nature in case her attackers were human. Since they used magic though, all bets were off.

She wasn't surprised to find she couldn't turn into the wolf that had been her second nature since her eighth birthday. Another facet of the spell keeping her from defending herself. Whoever was doing this was going to pay. They were going to pay, even if they managed to kill her. Her family and pack would make sure of that.

Or Aherin would.

After all the times he'd been around when she wanted him gone, he chose now to oblige her?

Where was he?

The first tear that made it through the thick barrier of her eyelashes was also the last. Where had that cry for Aherin, of all people, come from?

She was pulled out of her seat and carried the same way as before. Despite knowing her voice was muted, she asked where they were taking her. There was no reply, of course.

After only a couple seconds, she was laid on her side on a cold, hard surface.

Like an altar.

Ritual sacrifice.

She almost sighed with relief. A quick death would return her soul to the Silver Pool her people came from, and was much preferable to losing her mind. Way better than having to sit back, unable to do anything to defend herself, and endure whatever the people holding her had in mind.

That didn't mean she'd go down without a fight. As soon as the binds on her ankles and knees were loosened, she kicked out her right leg. She connected with something solid, and then a *thud* sounded from what had to be ten to twelve feet away, followed by an *oomph*. Huh. She now knew two things. Her strength was returning, and she was in an enclosed space, assuming what she'd kicked had made impact with the far wall.

She sneered at how her would-be-killers would regret pulling her out of what was to be a quiet celebration with her family. And Rex. She was still amazed Xandra had convinced their father to allow her vampire mate to join their reunion. Then again, their father had mated to a human and agreed to follow his wife's customs. That was why Salina grew up in a family that celebrated Christmas.

Vox wasn't thrilled about his elder daughter's union with a vampire, but he wasn't able to ignore the wishes of the Balancers, who wanted Xandra and Rex to be together *forever*. It was the only way for the curse to be kept at bay.

So dinner would be Salina's mom and dad, her sister and Rex, and Salina.

Alone.

Since when did she feel alone, surrounded by her family? She hadn't seen her folks in the months after she and Xandra left The Forest; she should be jumping at the opportunity to spend some time with them.

But Aherin wouldn't be there.

Well, that was a stupid thought. Aherin had no business spending Christmas with them.

She kicked out both legs and tried to jump to her feet. Her first attempt failed, but she felt more of her natural strength rush in. Good. She'd concentrate on that, and not mentally kick her own butt for thinking of the annoying, stupid, insulting, *dead sexy*—

Her inner voice was obviously as out of whack as the rest of her.

Instead of arguing with herself, she reached with her senses to figure out where the rest of her attackers were.

"We mean you no harm, Ms. Crest. On the contrary, we're here to give you a gift," said a deep voice in an eerily soothing manner.

Yeah, well, he'd have to forgive her for not smiling and thanking him. It was probably the bag he'd pulled over her head. She focused on the voice, and tried to gauge the man's exact position. No way did she trust someone, whose idea of a gift included blindfolding and binding her. Unless it was all part of some sexy role-play. That might be interesting.

Aherin would be into role-play.

But she didn't care. At all.

Heavy footsteps approached, and she poised to strike.

"Careful, Santa." The tiny voice shattered her

focus, and reaffirmed her fears of losing her sanity. "She's got a wicked right kick."

Huh?

Santa?

A muted giggle scratched her throat, and soon turned into a hysterical, soundless fit that had her fighting for breath.

"Boys, take the sack off. The young lady is about to laugh herself to death." The commanding, deep voice was just to her right this time.

Someone undid the ties on her arms, and then several hands that felt too small to belong to adults rolled her on her back, and helped her sit up. Her back was propped against a wall. *Not an altar*. Someone removed the cloth from over her head. She squeezed her eyes shut, still cough-chuckling, as she refused to face the visual confirmation of her plunge into madness.

"Santa, is she all right? She's splotchy."

"At least she's breathing. Though it sounds like snorting."

Both voices were irritatingly high-pitched.

More tiny voices speculated on her condition, and Salina ventured to crack an eyelid open. It was dark, but her night-vision kicked in, only for it to be blocked by a large stretch of red.

When she looked up, her mirth vanished altogether.

Kind eyes looked back at her with concern. Kind eyes set above a perfectly white, curly beard. She'd seen the round face in books. Read about it being all jolly.

It was the stuff of legend.

"Oh, you have *got* to be kidding me," she heard herself say. Oh, yay. She had her voice back. Now she could give the Santa-look-alike a piece of her mind.

As if sensing her less than friendly intentions, the man moved out of reach, his impressive girth barely allowing Salina's gaze to wander over their surroundings.

A single candle burned to her left, its faint glow unable to dilute the darkness. Still, her nocturnal predator's eyes took in the dirt covering the floor around her and cobwebs decorating the stone walls. Leather bound books were stacked in ordered heaps around the room. One look over her shoulder revealed that what she leaned against was a large sarcophagus. She'd been here before.

She was in Highgate Cemetery. Specifically, Aherin's mausoleum.

"Aherin?" The word left her lips on a breath.

The infuriating member of the undead refused to move into an underground apartment, like the one Rex stayed in before his slightly lethal sun allergy thing was resolved. Instead, Aherin preferred staying in the mausoleum he'd been buried in for more than a hundred years, before Rex brought him back to life. Unlife. Whatever.

The point was she'd just *known* he had to be behind it all.

"I'll kill him," she muttered.

Relief warred with disappointment in her head. She knew she was safe now. Aherin would never hurt her. But to have her kidnapped? And on Christmas Eve? She'd kick his ass for that.

Love was making him stupid.

Her temples throbbed at the traitorous thought. Aherin didn't love her. He just hadn't been with a woman for over a century, and their one night of crazy sexcapades left him with a slight infatuation. He couldn't love her. He was a vampire, and she was a shifter, and the only two crazy kids to brave that combo were Salina's sister and Aherin's best buddy.

But again, that wasn't the point. He'd messed up her family Christmas dinner, and she'd find a way to punish him. An image of Aherin tied up, as she had been moments earlier, filled her head. Only, he was stark naked, his sculpted body bathed in the pale light of the moon. Her memory of the parts of his anatomy she'd seen months ago was detailed. Shamefully so.

She bet Aherin spent time thinking of how she looked that night too. Every time his gaze fell on her, she felt naked under his scrutiny. And the way he sometimes licked his lips. Slowly. As if savoring a favorite flavor…

She shook her head and turned her attention to faux-Santa, who towered over her, flabbergasted.

He hadn't stopped yapping, though she hadn't been listening. "…so now do you believe I am the real thing?" he asked.

"Run those arguments by me one more time, please." If her voice was back, and her kick could send people flying, maybe she could shift. She tried to call forth the wolf, but didn't feel the usual rush of blood in her veins. Nothing happened, so she did her best imitation of the innocent little girl act, while pondering the best way to run from the Santa-wannabe and his…*elves*?

Aherin had gone all out on this.

"What I am saying, Ms. Crest, it that I can recite every one of your letters to me from age five to eleven by heart. Your older sister's too. Why is it so hard for a shifter from the cradle of magic—one who works with vampires and has met the Balancers, no less—to believe in me?" He threw his arms in the air in resignation.

The mausoleum door banged on the wall, diminishing Santa's dramatic gesture. "I can smell you, little shifter. Did you finally change your mind and come back to continue where we left off?"

Chapter Two

"What the hell is going on here?" Aherin hadn't expected to find anyone other than Salina waiting for him when he kicked his door open. Hers had been the single scent to reach his nostrils, as he approached the tomb that had become his home.

But of course, Santa and his elves only smelled faintly of candy.

"Care to explain?" He arched an eyebrow at Saint Nicholas, and was about to go on a tirade about property law, when he took in Salina sitting on the ground. Forgetting his questions, he rushed to her. "Salina? What happened to you?"

He was kneeling down next to her, when she turned and punched him in the nose. She put her whole body behind her left hook, and landed him on his ass.

"Like you don't know." She hopped to her feet, and assumed the fighting stance that always made his desire for her soar. Legs spread at shoulder width, knees slightly bent, her weight perfectly balanced. She held up her fists, emerald eyes sparkling dangerously.

Finding his footing just as easily as she had, he raised his hands, palms facing her, to show he posed no threat. "I know them. Well, him." He pointed at Santa, who apparently saw that as his cue to cut in.

"Are you one"—he pushed his glasses a bit further up the bridge of his nose—"Aherin the Resurrected?"

So he had a nickname now? Cool. Still... "Oh, cut the fancy formalities, Nicholas. You know full well who I am. You wouldn't have met the Missus, if it weren't for me doing the introd..."

He trailed off at Salina's stunned look.

"I'm a romantic," Aherin said to her. "They were both jolly and both single. It was an obvious match."

Her eyes remained wide as saucers, but she waved at him impatiently. "Just tell me what's going on here. Who's he really? Did you hire an actor?"

Santa answered before Aherin could. "I honestly am *the* Santa Claus, Ms. Crest. Feel free to call me Santa." He glared at Aherin. "Both of you."

Salina looked at Aherin, and appeared to believe him when he nodded his confirmation. "And what do you want?" she asked Nicky—sorry, *Santa*. "Is it another curse thing? Did a reindeer go missing or something? 'Cause I'm supposed to be on vacation on this plane, and I'm not even the Balancers' favorite. Maybe you wanna check in with my sister? She's the one who usually takes on the hero stuff."

Even as she spoke, Aherin could see her assessing her surroundings. He'd seen her fight her way out of a couple extremely sticky situations, and knew she was about to wipe the floor with red velvet.

"Nothing like that, child." Santa's tone was casual now. "I'm here on my usual business, delivering Christmas presents. You"—he turned to Aherin—"were a very good boy-mpire this year."

"Boy-mpire?" Salina snorted. "That's not even a

word."

"I would not throw stones, dear. We have all heard your vocabulary, and I do not mean back when you were a cub." The playful glint in Santa's eyes belied his stern voice. "As I was saying, because of your being a *very* good boy-mpire, and helping avert the destruction of all universes, the Balancers have decided you deserve a present. I am here to deliver you that present: Salina Crest, if you will have her."

Aherin took half a step back and shook his head, dazed. He'd been in lust with the headstrong shifter since their introduction, and the more he got to know her, the more he fell for her. Shortly after she gave him her body and stole what was left of his mind, he'd informed her of his feelings in no uncertain terms. And she'd turned him down.

Repeatedly.

Salina was everything he wasn't and everything he wanted at the same time. Warm and soft, yet strong and unyielding when it came to her principles. Her laugh was as innocent and happy as a child's, but she could split a man in half without blinking, if he threatened those she considered hers.

Aherin had spent months wishing he could make the list of people she'd kill for. Maim for, even.

But he'd never expected her to be *given* to him, as if she were nothing more than an object. Surely Santa could see how crazy his offer sounded.

"Are you nuts? You cannot *make* me be his present." Salina had to be as stunned as Aherin felt, but she was rather vocal about it.

"I don't need the Balancers' help to land myself a woman, thank you very much," Aherin said. Though maybe he did, because he'd tried everything else, and Salina wouldn't give him the time of day. He knew her kind and his had always been at odds. It was why he'd initially suppressed his attraction for her.

Watching Rex and Xandra get over that same hurdle had been an eye-opener. And then seeing Salina bathe in the moonlight…

"Nope. Don't need anybody's help." His tone was more even this time, his mind soaking in the memory of her washing their enemies' blood off her creamy skin, smooth movements sending ripples across the black surface of the lake. Her hair shone almost white. She could have been a goddess. *Was* a goddess.

Later, when he'd had her by that lakeside, she gave herself to him with the same abandon with which she'd thrown herself into battle. Her eyes turned amber, her wolf close to the surface. He'd known her nature, had *seen* it on the battlefield, but that night he felt it too, and he was forever hooked.

Salina continued protesting, until Santa silenced her by raising his hand. Her lips kept moving, but no sound came out. Hex. Aherin could almost taste her frustration and saw she got more furious by the second.

"Mr. The Resurrected—erm, Aherin—the Balancers have decided to alter Ms. Crest's memories, so she loves you. She will, in fact, remember having loved you for a long time." Santa snapped his fingers in front of Salina's face. "You may voice your objections now."

"You can't be serious. Nobody messes with my mind. *Ever.* I'll kill you if I have to, Christmas be damned." She slashed a large 'X' in the air in front of her with her palms, and Aherin wondered if Santa knew how lethal those lovely hands could be.

Aherin knew her anger flared at the memory of her sister after Acerbus's spell, lost and confused and not knowing whom to trust.

Salina took a step to the side, away from Santa, and Aherin was enraged to see fear mixed with fury on her expression.

"How dare you?" He hissed the question instead of howling it, trying to keep his temper in check. "You come here, with the fucking blessings of the *Balancers*, to taint the only sunshine in my life? And...and you expect me to *want* that? This woman"—he cocked his head toward Salina—"fought for the world. For all the worlds. She and her sister almost lost their lives to maintain the balance your precious superiors value so much, and now you dare degrade her by wanting to rape her memory? Forcing her to be with someone she despises?"

Because she did despise his kind, if not him specifically. And in all honesty, he wasn't good enough for her, even if he denied it every time she said she could never be with him. That one moment in time they shared had been nothing but a fierce celebration of their survival—and maybe an outlet for her pent up frustrations. She was a force of nature, literally one with the universe through her ties to her wolf, and he was unnatural. He was dead.

Yet when she was near, he felt more alive than he'd ever been.

Like on that one night.

She saw him watching. He could tell the moment she knew. Her spine went rigid for a fraction of a second, and her palms hovered over her breasts, as if she considered hiding herself from his gaze.

She took a deep breath, and even from the shore he saw her dusky nipples harden, push out from the flawless curves of her small, firm breasts. They'd fit perfectly in his palms, those tits. Not that he'd get to find out. She was probably already pondering the best way to punish his insolence. Maybe she'd blind him, like the goddess Athena had done to Tiresias. Only, Tiresias had glimpsed the virgin goddess's naked body by accident, while Aherin hadn't even tried to avert his gaze from the exquisite body of the shifter bathing. Instead, he sat in the thick foliage surrounding the lake and took in the sight. If she was the last thing he ever saw, he'd make sure to commit her all to memory. Her slim waist. Her narrow hips. Her wide shoulders. Her body was full of angles, when he'd been brought up to consider curves attractive. Still, it was perfect.

She turned to fully face him, and he tensed in anticipation of her wrath. He was more than surprised to see a tiny smile play on her lips, as she glided a few steps closer. Close enough that, when she slid her hand between her long legs to cup her sex, Aherin saw her push a finger between her folds. He'd spent some time during their journey wondering what her pussy looked like, but he hadn't expected it to be completely bare.

"Are you coming in?" she asked. "It's divine."

He forced his gaze to the lake around her. It looked otherworldly, the dark waters, clear as a black diamond, reflecting the moonlight and odd patterns of stars hanging on this universe's skies. Then again, he was in a world other than the one he knew. He wanted to go in the water—a swim was all he'd had in mind before he'd seen her breaking the surface, tossing back her silver mane. Now all he could think of was getting inside her.

"I didn't know if you wanted to share." He stood and leaned against a tree. Was there a challenge in her eyes?

She shrugged. "It's a free world. Still. Thanks to us. I think we could reward ourselves with a little indulgence."

His sensitive hearing picked up the sounds of her sister and his best friend rutting like animals back in the cave. Maybe Salina could hear them too, though he wasn't sure how acute her shifter senses were in her human form. It wasn't the right time to find out. "Is this your idea of indulgence?" he asked instead. "A bath?"

She smiled, and took another step toward the shore. "Could be worse. At least I don't smell of blood anymore." She tilted her head to the side, arching the appetizing column of her neck. "Do I?"

"Can't tell from here." He lied. She smelled of the blood she'd shed, and her arousal, and Aherin didn't know which one drove him wilder with desire.

"Maybe you should come closer, then. Just to make sure."

Was she...flirting with him? He'd wanted her from the moment he laid eyes on her, but she'd cut off his advances, and they eventually settled into spending their time together exchanging barbs and jibes. He'd accepted that he'd never have her, and convinced himself he was all right with that.

The taunt in her eyes now looked too much like an invitation.

Aherin realized he'd untucked his T-shirt and unbuckled his belt. He forced his fingers to stop, before he also popped the buttons of his jeans. He needed to know what she was offering before he took the next step. "Careful what you wish for, little shifter. If I decide you smell delicious enough, I may eat you."

She grinned, and amber shone in the depth of her emerald eyes. "I'm the wolf, remember? I don't think you could eat me."

He'd proven her wrong minutes later. He ate her until she begged him for mercy, and then he took her. Tasting her, being with her, being *inside* her had been the pinnacle of his long existence. The way she came—and came undone—beneath him was the one truth by which he'd measure all others.

And the fatso in red wanted to fuck that up.

"I'll rip your heart out of your chest as many

times as it takes to keep you from changing anything about her." Aherin held Santa's gaze as he spoke, ensuring his words sank in. "Even if that means I never touch her again."

Santa pursed his lips and scowled, but it wasn't his reaction that surprised Aherin. It was Salina's arched eyebrows. What had she expected? That he'd jump at the opportunity to mess with her head?

"Honestly?" he asked her. "What sort of man did you take me for?"

She shook her head. "I'm sorry. I—"

"Never mind. I don't think I want to know." He huffed and crossed his arms over his chest.

She raised one hand slowly, as if to touch him, but never made contact. Her fingers just hovered there, above his arm. He wanted to pull her closer, but at this point, she might take it as an assault. She apparently believed him capable of anything.

He had been, the first time around. When Rex first turned him, the two of them lost themselves in debauchery and slaughter, and enjoyed it immensely. They hadn't lost their souls, or whatever people believed happened to humans when they turned into vampires. But they were invincible in an era when people died young, when pillaging was a more acceptable means of making a living than farming, and they'd enjoyed it all.

They'd cut down on mindless killing as the centuries went by and they'd had their fill of it, but he'd never fathomed consciously and actively trying to be good.

Then he and Rex killed the wrong man.

They'd been out hunting, when the hooded figure jumped in front of them from a nearby roof top. That stunt and his scent indicated he wasn't human, and they attacked him, believing another predator had invaded their territory. When they realized their mistake, it was too late. They still might've gotten off easy, if Aherin hadn't ripped the guy's head off.

His punishment had been to spend eternity dead, but not. Buried and incapable of movement, but thinking. *Thinking.* Planning how to destroy those responsible for locking him in a grave.

When Rex had brought him back to break a curse, a century or so into his sentence, Aherin wanted nothing more than to see the whole world crumble.

And then he'd laid eyes on her.

Salina had tossed her silver hair, her bright green eyes flashing with disdain. "He can't help us," she said. "And I'm not working with another vampire."

He'd do the fucking save-the-world thing all over again, if it meant fighting alongside her once more.

Santa looked at him, and Aherin poked him on the belly with his index finger. "Hear me, big guy? You're not scrambling her brains, so how's about you turn on your heel, and go where you're wanted?" He let his fangs show, in what he meant to be a ruthless grin.

Why hadn't Salina shifted and run—or better, shifted and gone for the throat?

The elves around them watched the interaction dispassionately.

"Aherin, you know you can't hurt me. Neither of you can. I'm eternal." Santa's words were smug, but his gaze flickered from Aherin to Salina and back again. "You should be thankful for what you're given. A shot at love, on your own terms. Who could ask for more?"

Anger diffused, Aherin shook his head. "I don't want her." From the corner of his eye, he saw Salina stagger, and her face fall. The dejection he thought he glimpsed had to be a figment of his imagination. Still, he added, "Not like this." It was a whisper, meant for her ears only, and he hoped it made a difference.

Santa frowned. "In that case, Ms. Crest, I'm afraid you'll have to follow your people's traditions when dealing with the undead, and exterminate him."

Santa was a twisted fuck.

"*What?*" Salina said.

Aherin growled. "Shit." He assumed a defensive position, still facing Santa. Salina might not share his feelings, but she wouldn't dust him just because Fat Nick said she should.

"The Balancers"—Santa intoned each word slowly and carefully, as if to chastise Aherin for his earlier insolence—"are concerned Aherin the Resurrected has only been behaving himself because of his love for you, Ms. Crest. Now that he has refused the opportunity they presented for him to have his feelings returned, he might go back to his former evil self, and be a threat to the world as we know it. The Balancers have done everything in their power to prevent an unraveling of the universes. They cannot show him lenience." He approached Salina, produced a stake out of thin air, and held it out to her. "Here. Do it quickly."

Aherin tried to step closer, maybe grab the weapon from Santa's outstretched hand, but an invisible force held him rooted in place. Unable to move, he watched Salina close her fingers around the piece of wood and twirl it in her grasp. Her elegant movements held a lethal beauty.

"Can't you just undo whatever mojo is keeping me from shifting? There's no reason to use this; my jaws should be enough," she said.

The words cut Aherin to the core. She'd told him time and again that he meant nothing to her, but he didn't expect her to so readily accept her role as his executioner.

"I am sorry." Santa shook his head. "He might survive an attack by your beast, while a stake through the heart is irreversible. The Balancers cannot risk it."

Aherin shivered at the evil glint in Salina's eyes, as she stalked toward him, stake held at shoulder height. This was it. At least he would go by her hand. He spread his arms and met her gaze.

"Aren't you going to fight me?" She tilted her head to one side, the movement reminiscent of her white wolf.

"No. If the Balancers want me gone, they won't stop till they get their wish. I'm not spending the rest of eternity on the run."

Her smile was sweet. Even flirty. "You weren't such a fatalist last time we were up against impossible odds. And look how that turned out."

That was true, but the situation had been different then. He pursed his lips, trying to think of the least sappy way possible to explain. "I was running with you then, not from you. If you're going to kill me, I'd rather you don't do it by talking me to death, love." Still, the strike didn't come. "Do it, Salina. I've been around for a thousand years, and been nothing more than a killer for most of it. You made me see there's another way. For that alone, I'm glad Rex brought me back. No better time to die, than when you've had your fill of life, and I've had just that. Aim well." He winked.

Not the best farewell speech, but it'd have to suffice. He found no reason to tell her that, though his heart had stopped beating ages earlier, he'd never felt it as empty as when she first told him he'd never get to touch her again. There was no time for him to even begin to explain his love for her, or how it would only cease when he was dust—let alone how empty such a promise might sound, since his dusting was imminent.

She wouldn't believe his feelings, anyway, and Aherin didn't want to go out with her rejection in his ears.

"Go on," he said.

Salina raised the stake, and gave him a ferocious grin.

He'd been touched by death before, but it had never looked so majestic.

Under a spell or not, Salina was managing to call her wolf. Her eyes had turned amber again, and her fangs jutted under her upper lip. She flared her nostrils, and he could see every muscle on her body poised to strike.

Here came oblivion.

Or not.

Just inches away from him, Salina spun on her heel and landed a round house kick in the middle of Santa's chest that sent his considerable weight flying. The moment he landed flat on his back, she was next to him, her boot's spiked heel poised over his heart.

"Don't even think about getting up. It may not kill you, but I bet it'll hurt like a bitch." She paused, as if considering her next words, and Santa grasped the opportunity to reason with her.

"Ms. Crest... Salina, think about it. If you do not destroy this creature, we will just have someone else—"

"You said the Balancers have done everything in their power to prevent an unraveling of the universes." She spoke dispassionately, tossing the stake from one hand to the other. Aherin loved the slight lisp her fangs caused. "From where I'm standing, all they did was choose the right champions. Aherin was one of them. If I kill him now, who's to say they won't come after me next?"

"There would be no reason for that; I assure

you. Once you dispose of him, the Balancers will leave you be. I understand you feel some sort of...camaraderie toward him, but it will not suffice to keep him in check. If you refuse to do the deed, I might be able to talk them into finding an alternate executioner—"

Quick as lightning, Salina bent down and dug the tip of the stake into Santa's shoulder. "Nobody messes with Aherin. He's mine." The plush fabric didn't even tear, but Santa winced.

Aherin raised both eyebrows. She couldn't have said those words.

She glanced his way and rolled her eyes. "He's mine to kill or let live. Unlive. *Whatever.* Tell your elves to stay back, or this will go down very badly for you. I'm feeling my wolf again, and you don't want me to let her out. Whether you're eternal or not, your little helpers are gonna have a really hard time putting your pieces back together." She stressed her words with a growl, and Aherin echoed her.

Salina went on. "I can't believe *you* are the children's favorite saint. I don't know why I ever bothered sending you letters."

Aherin could see she was fuming, and he was grateful not to be the cause of it. Of course, knowing her mood swings, he wouldn't be surprised if she were chewing him off next.

For now, Salina was locked on her target. "You come here and want to fuck up my memory, and when a vampire shows more compassion than your bloody Balancers, you want me to kill him?" Aherin chuckled at her use of his favorite curse, but she didn't seem to hear him. "So not happening," she said, with a growl.

Chapter Three

Santa frowned. A dry, burnt smell reminiscent of ozone battered Salina's nose, alerting her wolf to deception. She expected Santa or one of the elves cowering in the corner to turn the tables on her. She hunched her back, ready to launch if anyone so much as made a move. She'd meant her threat. She'd turn Santa into nibbles, if he hurt a hair on Aherin's head.

When she'd thought Aherin was behind this, she was ready to kick his undead ass. After the way he reacted when Santa offered her to him, though, she couldn't let anything happen to him.

She was so ready for someone to attack, she was almost shocked when Santa spoke. "You say he is yours. Will you be his champion, then?"

She sucked air through clenched teeth. "Who will I have to fight?"

"Him," Santa said quietly.

Salina applied more pressure on her stake. "What are you playing at? I just said I wouldn't kill him."

"No, no. You will have to fight his reputation. The Balancers want him destroyed because the scale of his life was tilted toward evil far longer than it has been tilted toward good."

Salina clucked her tongue. "Are you stalling? I'm not looking for a lesson in Aherin's history; I want to get us both out of here safe, and with the Balancers' promise they will leave us alone. You said I can be his champion. What does that entail?"

"You will have to give three compelling arguments in his favor. Three reasons why the Balancers are to trust that allowing his survival will not be harmful to mankind as a whole in the future. When left unchecked, this creature has—"

"He's not a creature. He's a man."

She expected Aherin to speak up, but he merely watched them, arms crossed over his chest. "Care to pitch in?" she asked. "We *are* negotiating for your life."

Aherin arched an eyebrow, pointed at his mouth, and shook his head.

"If you agree to do this, we do not want him interfering," Santa said.

Gee, thanks. Although, Aherin would be infinitely easier to be around if he didn't talk. His baritone and Irish lilt confused her libido as much as the muscled expanse of his back, stretching the tight shirts he favored.

Santa. She had to focus on Santa. "Don't think I didn't notice how 'the Balancers' became 'we,'" she said.

"They and I happen to be in accord on this. Aherin can be destructive beyond your wildest imagination. He spent more than four times your lifetime immobilized was because he killed one of the Balancers' own, endangering the core of creation. If he reverts to who he was back then…"

"He didn't do that killing alone. Rex was with him, and they gave Rex a mate." Sounding menacing while holding this awkward crouch was a feat, but she managed and was proud of it.

"Rex requested forgiveness and began his atonement the very second he realized what was at stake. This one threatened to—as he put it—finish the job."

Salina looked to Aherin for confirmation. His smug grin was enough of an answer. She saw right through his defiant act, but didn't doubt part of him believed he could take the Balancers on and win. Having seen him fight, she thought he might actually have a chance. She bit back a smile.

"Even so, it was more than a hundred years ago. Look at what he did recently. Does saving all universes ring a bell?"

"Are you undertaking the position of his champion, then?"

Santa needed an ass kicking. Another one. "I am. But we do this alone. You and I."

"And he. He is to remain where I can see him, until his fate is decided."

A choking sound made her spring up and turn toward Aherin, her foot still on Santa. One of his fangs had pierced his lips. The man couldn't keep his mouth shut.

She nodded, her foot still keeping Santa in place. "But your lackeys need to go. They're creeping me out."

Santa snapped his fingers, and the elves disappeared into the shadows of the mausoleum, as if they'd never been there.

It'd be cool if it weren't freaky.

"You may begin," Santa said.

Salina crossed her arms. "Okay. My first argument is the one I've already given you. Aherin fought to preserve creation. He didn't do that for me.

Rex was the one who asked him to."

"This further proves his moral compass is external. If it is not you, it is Rex. He does not choose to do good by himself. Not unless there is something in it for him."

"There was *nothing* in it for him when he helped us. He'd lost so much time, because of the Balancers, and all he wanted was revenge for the century he'd passed confined inside his own body. But when Rex explained—"

Santa looked up at her, eyes widened in surprise. "You really don't know, do you? It wasn't Rex's speech about becoming a hero that convinced him to help you. It was you. More precisely, his need to prove you wrong when you said he couldn't help you."

A muted growl from Aherin. He held his middle finger up at Santa. Salina cocked her head. He was cursing inside his mouth. She chuckled. "So he likes proving people wrong. Doesn't that mean he won't go bad seed again? That's what you expect of him, after all."

"Is this your second argument?" Santa asked.

For a man lying on the ground, with her heel digging into him, he certainly was commanding. And annoying.

"No," Salina said. "I still haven't wrapped up the first one. Aherin wasted a good chance to kill those who punished him so harshly. All he had to do was join Acerbus' ranks, and we might be in a completely different place now. Hell, all he had to do was sit back and wait it all out. He didn't. He chose the hard way."

"You are not listening to me. His choice was made by your appearance. By your long silver hair and bright green eyes. Am I quoting your thoughts correctly, Aherin?" Not waiting for a reply, he returned his attention to Salina. "I cannot quite recall the part

298

about your...athletic physique, but I know it was much ruder than the phrasing I just chose. Remember how the two of you celebrated your first major victory?"

Remember it? Forgetting had been the hard part.

"You know?" she whispered, unable to form proper sounds around the bitter taste in her mouth. How? Had the Balancers watched her and her vampire—?

Not her vampire. It had just been one night. One roll in the dirt.

A seriously enjoyable one, at that.

She felt invincible. They'd managed a great hit on Acerbus, reducing his forces by half, and had all made it out alive. She'd single-handedly decapitated the undead mage's second in command. Her wolf had thrilled at the kill.

Now the woman sought another thrill—a forbidden one. Shifters and vampires had been enemies since the beginning of time. Vampires were undead. Unnatural. The exact opposite of shifters, who shared an unbreakable bond with nature. When the schism had created the separate planes at humanity's dawn, vampires had chosen to leave other magic behind and stay with their food source. Magic was contained in the plane of The Forest, where her people and distant relations of her kind cherished it for what it was.

The force behind creation.

Salina had grown up listening to stories about the vile undead who defiled creation. She still remembered her revulsion when her sister chose to sleep with one. Although Rex had become an ally and a friend by then, Salina couldn't fathom her sister's willingness to open herself to him. It was sick and wrong, despite how sexy Rex was.

Sexiness wasn't enough of a reason to break one of the cardinal rules of balance. And if it were, and

299

Salina had been in her sister's shoes, she wouldn't have chosen Rex to break said rule with.

She picked up Aherin's scent again. She'd noticed how he watched her when he thought she wasn't looking. Not that he was any shier when she was staring right at him. The man was insolent, irreverent, and extremely funny—though she wouldn't tell him so to his face. Just as she'd never admit to finding him charming when he wasn't being an ass.

And smoking hot, if she was being honest. His black eyes and long lashes gave his pale face an almost haunting beauty. His mouth was hard, but his lips full, and when he gave her his lopsided grin, a single dimple formed in his left cheek. His jet black hair reached past his shoulders, always giving him a ruffled hue, as if he'd just gotten out of bed. And when he fought, it whipped the air around him, like a dark halo framing his head.

She dived underwater, enjoying the cool caress against her heated skin. The battle had awoken in her a hunger that had nothing to do with bloodlust. She'd hoped to assuage it with a swim, but the night air was fraught with want and promise and seduction.

And Aherin.

She resurfaced, pushing out her chest and throwing back her head, fully aware of the sight she presented. Her hair, unusual even for her family, had always been her pride. The wet ends swished and tickled her lower back, as she pretended to have just noticed his presence. A deep breath, a fake effort at modesty, and they were bantering. Innuendos went back and forth. Nothing out of the ordinary—naughty, but safe. She could stop it at that.

But she didn't want to.

The lake had done nothing to quell her thirst, and despite her better judgment, her blood boiled for

Aherin's cool touch.

When he finally stood naked before her, she studied him unabashedly. Nakedness wasn't something that fazed her kind, and Aherin's body was a work of art. He was tall, and full of muscle gained by his human years as a pirate. His long legs were sprinkled with dark hair, as was his chest. The hair trickled to a thin trail down his abdomen, and turned thicker around his cock, which stood long and thick, as if beckoning her.

Salina licked her lips, and waded closer. When the water was only a foot or so deep, she went down to all fours and crawled the rest of the distance to him.

She was surprised when he got on his knees and held her gaze, as he ghosted his thumbs over her pebbled nipples. Sex had always been primal with her pack mates. It was about lust and heat, and foreplay was a rare thing. As was eye contact. They didn't call it doggie style for nothing.

Aherin kept surprising her. The raw need in his dark gaze didn't match the gentleness of his touch. She didn't expect him to ask if it was all right, before his lips claimed hers—ask again while he rained kisses down her neck, to the sides of her breasts. Before taking each hardened peak in his mouth, and rolling his tongue over it.

Didn't expect him to tenderly lower her on her back, and crawl down her body, until his lips found her mons.

And—oh, God—she didn't expect what his talented tongue did next.

Most of all, though, she didn't expect her body to react to him the way it did.

That one night had haunted her dreams. It had revealed a level of passion she'd never experienced before. Until now, she conveniently attributed it to external factors. The moonlight, their victory, her crazy sister and his even crazier friend… They had all contributed to lowering her and Aherin's inhibitions. Aherin might have been attracted to her physically before then—he'd certainly botched several attempts at flirting with her—but that night had birthed his dumb infatuation.

Or so she'd thought till now.

She saw nothing but honesty in Santa's face, but was it true? Had Aherin always wanted her? Enough to fight on the side of the Balancers, despite hating them? Was that why he'd agreed to help them against Acerbus?

She looked up in time to see Aherin lunge toward them. She flinched, expecting impact, but his leap was cut short when his body flattened against nothing but air, mid-stride. An invisible wall? Of course Santa wouldn't be so reckless as to let him roam unrestrained. He'd stopped the fierce, angry vampire in his tracks—without so much as lifting a finger. Salina's gut clenched, as the reality of her situation sank in for the first time.

She and Aherin might not live through the night.

No. Someone would come looking for them. Her parents. Her sister. *Someone.* They all knew she was never late, unless she called first. Things were so much easier back home; there was always a crow-shifter nearby when one was needed to carry a message. Shit. Salina should've bought a cell phone by now. She'd been on this plane long enough to know they came in handy.

"Will you proceed to your second argument, or concede and take his life?" Santa's voice snapped her out of her musings.

"You said nothing about me being the one to kill him if we lose." She couldn't bring herself to kill him before. When she didn't believe him. If she did now, it would be like…

It'd be like betraying an ally. Yup, exactly like that. Because Aherin was nothing more to her than a team member. Even if he was telling the truth about being in love with her. That he had feelings didn't mean she owed it to him to return them.

"Being his champion also entails giving him what he deserves, and he deserves his ending to be by a hand he respects. Even one he holds dear." Santa's gaze softened, and Salina thought she saw pity in his eyes. So he already considered them a lost cause? That wouldn't do.

"Okay, then. Second try. If the Balancers believed he was so dangerous and unrepentant—is that even a word?—why didn't they kill him the first time? They had the power to, but they chose to hold him prisoner for what turned out to be a hundred years plus change. You don't sentence someone to being buried alive for that long, only to get him out of his hole for a couple months—during which he *saves the worlds. Worlds. Plural*—and then get rid of him. That's just mean."

"So," Santa said, "your second argument is that the Balancers are mean? High rhetoric is not your strong suit, I suppose."

Aherin snorted. His mute button wasn't pushed in all the way any longer. Tonight was so not her night.

"No." Salina hated feeling helpless. "My argument is that, for people supposedly there to uphold goodness and honesty and stuff, they're not being very good or very honest. And stuff."

"They are called the Balancers because their job is to preserve the balance, not protect individuals at the cost of the greater good," Santa Claus said. "Now, if you don't have anything else to add, let us move to the third and final argument. Why should Aherin's life be spared? Think hard, Salina. To keep him, you have to earn him."

His skin ran cool against hers, as his palms—rough from the sword—kneaded her flesh, ripping moans and groans from her lips. He hadn't even entered her, and she'd come twice, thanks to his talented fingers and mouth.

One fang grazed over the side of her neck, and her wolf roared her protest. She wasn't his to taste. Not like that. Her blood was too high a prize, even for earth-shattering sex.

"I won't drink until you beg me to," he said. "And I think you will *beg me, Salina."*

He never called her that. It was 'Shifter' or 'Growly' or 'Wolf Sentinel Junior.' Hearing her name roll off his tongue prepared her body for a new level of ecstasy. His voice was a purr, and it felt like a physical presence, a caress gliding down her body and to her aching core.

"Will you get it over with? It's almost daylight." She didn't fear he'd burn; her plane's sun didn't hurt him. She merely didn't want to miss out on this next part, because there was no putting it off. After the sun came up, reality would replace whatever this was, and the night they shared would forever belong to the past.

He could never be a part of her life.

Only, he had been, even before that. And the more she thought about it, the more integral a part she realized he was.

"Wait," she called out, more to the sky she couldn't see than to Santa. "Doesn't the number of bad guys he killed tip the balance toward him? Not even a little bit?"

"It would, if he had not been so cavalier with innocent lives in the past. You are not going about it the right way, Salina. You are his champion. You need to use what you know about him to plead his case, not what we all do."

She chewed on the inside of her cheek. What *she* knew about him?

She knew his black eyes could be incredibly warm. She knew he liked horses, and had hated the sea for the first few months he spent on the pirate ship. She knew he was smart and funny.

But those were all common knowledge.

"He's loyal," she blurted. "When you told me to kill him, he could have come at me. He didn't. And he never left the battlefield without making sure all of us were with him."

"Love can do that to a man." Santa's playful smile made her want to slap him. They were talking about Aherin's life, and he was joking around.

"You need something else," he said. "Something that makes him irreplaceable. Indispensable. Is there such a thing?"

Salina looked at Aherin in panic. He stood eerily motionless, watching her with what might have been calm acceptance. He'd never balked in the face of impossible odds. It hurt her to watch him give in now.

That was another thing she knew about him—he was persistent.

For the first few nights after they had sex, he came to her side of the cave again and again, each time with a different excuse for being there. First he was looking for his 'fancy' pen, which Salina had never seen and doubted existed. Then he insisted she join him on a hunt for their dinner. She had to come look at how big the moon was. See an exotic flower he found.

Have sex with him again.

Salina's response was invariably negative, but Aherin always followed up with the same question, whispered in her ear.

"Are you ready to beg me yet?"

Salina would scowl, yell, or toss him on his ass, and he'd leave with a smirk and a promise to try again the next evening.

Despite herself, she quirked her lips upward. He was a lousy liar too. His excuses never held water. Just the other day, he'd pretended to have found her hairpin in his mausoleum and returned it to her. Only the one she'd lost was a cheap metal, and the one he 'found' was white gold, according to Rex, who knew his precious metals.

Once they'd returned to London, he dropped all pretenses and just showed up in front of her when she least expected him, to ask if maybe she was up for some fun. He took her repeated rejections with a knowing smile and good humor. And then he tried again.

Despite his flat-out refusal to give up on her, she never felt pressure or discomfort at his advances. Just annoyed. And maybe a little flattered. As if she were the only woman in the world worthy of an ancient warrior's affections.

"He can be considerate," she muttered, knowing it wouldn't be good enough. Why not also tell *Santa*, of all people, that the murderous vampire he wanted to rid the world of was also an amazing lover?

Lover? Was that how she thought of him?

Nah. She just couldn't find a more appropriate word.

"Ms. Crest? The clock is ticking, and I still have presents to give out."

"Well, if they're as awesome as the one you had for Aherin, I'm pretty sure the kiddies can do without."

"Can I at least sit up? This floor is beyond uncomfortable."

And dirty, because Aherin wasn't exactly clean

and tidy.

Truth be told, Salina's leg was cramping with the awkward position, but anything to discomfort Santa even a little. "Bummer for you. You're staying put."

"Then wrap things up, please."

She was trying, damn it.

What did she know about Aherin the Balancers didn't?

His jet black hair was smooth to the touch. He'd said hers looked like blades when she spun around in the middle of battle. His looked like warm, live silk, pouring down to his shoulders.

Gods, he had wide shoulders. Despite forbidding him to bite her, she'd sunk her human teeth into the hollow of his neck, while grabbing onto those shoulders for dear life. While he pounded her into the damp earth.

She wrapped her legs around his slim hips, knees spread so he could reach deeper...where she burned for him. His cock was harder than any she'd ever had, unyielding as he thrust inside her with punishing force. Every few strokes, he stopped and looked into her eyes, and she had to buck her own hips to make him keep moving.

"I can take it," she whispered in his ear. "Give me everything you've got. I can take it all."

So could he. He could take her riding him as well as he'd taken the punches she'd thrown his way during their sparring sessions. And later, back on this plane, when he tried to kiss her outside her house.

"He's resilient, and he doesn't give up. He's kind, and not half the badass he thinks he is. He even saved a puppy from a speeding car last week. What psycho killer saves a puppy?"

Santa rolled his eyes. "If you will allow me the pun, Ms. Crest, you are chasing your tail. This is getting us nowhere. Unless you have a convincing closing argument, Aherin's fate is sealed."

No. He couldn't die. She couldn't kill him. "Maybe I should do what he said, and turn you into dinner. That should put your indestructibility to the test, huh?" She was going to go through with it. She was going to eat Santa, and let the Balancers come after her and Aherin.

Drawing in a deep breath to prepare for the shift, she called her wolf to the surface. It'd be awkward doing this in front of Aherin—what with the bone breakage and realignment involved—but he said he found her wolf form stunning. She was rather pleased he thought so.

She focused on the power, the raw hunger that came with the change, and tugged at her connection to her beast. Bringing her forth was usually a matter of seconds, even if the agonizing pain accompanying the process made it feel like it lasted for days.

Digging her heel harder into Santa's chest, she squeezed her eyes shut and mentally put her weight behind her grip on the wolf. Nothing. Salina's second nature was caged again. It slipped through her grasp, until she could barely feel her.

She howled in frustration at the moon she couldn't see.

When she looked at Santa, his eyes were narrowed. "You were going to back off our agreement," he said. "I thought you were a woman of your word."

The accusation choked her, despite being true. Or maybe because of it. "What about your word? Huh? When you first grabbed me, you said you had a present for me. Where is it? Is this it? Is my present having to kill the man—?"

The truth she'd denied for months hit her hard, like a bucket of ice cold water. There had been a point, after Aherin had agreed to help save all of existence, and possibly even before he ever touched her, when he'd become more than a vampire to her. Vampires were the sworn enemies of her people, but Aherin had proven trustworthy time and again. He was a friend. A companion. And somewhere along this evening, she'd come to believe his feelings for her were real.

Fuck, if that wasn't terrifying.

Aherin and Santa Claus were both watching her, the first with hope lighting his dark eyes, the second with mild interest. She'd left her sentence unfinished.

"I'm not killing him. I'll fight you, if I need to. I'll fight the Balancers. Go back and tell them..." She inhaled deeply, seeking the perfect wording for what she needed to express. "Tell them I care about him. I won't let anyone touch a hair on his head."

"So you are saying he is special to you?"

Salina frowned. "I'm not sure I'd go that far..."

"Pity. If he were special to a Champion like you—if there were an inkling his feelings were returned—the Balancers might feel more confident in his current reformation."

"Gods." Salina grinded her teeth. "You don't count his champion-ness... championity—you know what I mean. You don't count it as reason enough to let him live, but if I have feelings for him, he goes free?"

Santa shrugged as much as her weight on him allowed. "More or less."

The casualness of his answer threw her. She studied Aherin's face, and saw hope mingle with apprehension and defiance.

She'd forgotten to add being defiant to his list of unique attributes, though she doubted it would have helped his case.

"So do you?" Santa was squinting up at her.

"Huh?"

309

"Do you return Aherin the Resurrected's feelings? Are you in love with him?"

She was surprised by the bluntness of the question. Surprised, and a little scared. Now that it had been asked, she couldn't avoid answering it.

So did she? *Was* she?

She reflected on the roller coaster that had been her evening. From the moment she was sure Aherin had been her kidnapper, and she'd known she was safe; to her shock when he didn't jump at the opportunity to have her love him; to her initial dismay and following horror at the thought of the Balancers wanting him dead. By her hand.

Could she possibly be in love with him? A member of the evil undead, who'd until recently been punished for being more than willing to end creation? A fun and funny, creative man, who knew how to push her buttons?

She mulled over her reactions to him since their night by the lake. No, before that. Since she'd watched his blade slice through the mage's followers as if they were made of butter, the feral grin on his face matching her own.

He'd been magnificently lethal, and she'd had to squash the thought she might have found her match.

But there was so much distance between match and mate.

Wasn't there?

And she wasn't even in love with him. Couldn't be. It was as unnatural as he was.

Though nothing had felt as natural as having him inside her, his long, hard shaft stretching her just this side of pain. She'd wanted him to mark her that night. Her blood had called for him to pierce her flesh with his fangs. That was what had embarrassed her the most about it. She might have actually begged for his bite, if he hadn't been so cocksure.

Sexual compatibility didn't equal love, though. It was lust. Skin-deep and fleeting. Not like he was the best lover she'd ever had.

Which he was.

But she could easily find someone as good. She wasn't looking, but it was possible.

Or not.

Still, that wasn't the point. Aherin might have magic fingers, a talented mouth, and incredible stamina, but that wasn't what made her fall for him.

No no no no no. That was as good as an admission. She hadn't fallen.

Had she?

Eyes narrowed, Aherin watched her, as if reading her mind. That he might be able to, was the scariest thing she ever contemplated. She didn't know all there was to know about his kind.

Her fear had to show, because his nostrils flared, and his gaze turned more speculative.

"Salina, I am going to need an answer soon. Are you in love with Aherin?" She'd forgotten all about Santa until he spoke.

"I can't— I have to think…"

Think what? How she was always quick to snap at Aherin, even when he wasn't leering or throwing sexual innuendos her way? How her temperature and heart rate increased, when she caught his scent in the air? She'd convinced herself it was irritation at his persistence that caused it, but she might have been wrong.

She tried to remember her life before him. She was nothing other than a sentinel, her first thought in the morning and last at night being the preservation and safety of The Forest. Her carnal needs were met often and quite successfully by pack mates, some of whom went on to pursue a relationship with her, only to give up when she indicated she wanted nothing more than casual sex.

Salina's father had fought the pack leader to be allowed to keep his wife as mate. Whether by a stroke of luck as he claimed, or out of desperate love, Vox had managed to gain the upper hand and close his jaws over the other wolf's throat.

Instead of finishing the job and claiming pack leadership for himself, he let go, shifted back to human form, and kneeled before the larger beast. His strength and loyalty had won him the place of pack enforcer, but Salina wanted to be more than the enforcer's daughter. Unlike Xandra, who was born a wolf, Salina didn't shift until she was eight. Everyone in the pack believed she'd inherited her mother's singular nature, until her white wolf manifested. After that, Salina spent every waking moment striving to prove she was more wolf than anyone.

Salina had struggled to create a place for herself among the pack, and then to match her sister's reputation for worthiness as a sentinel. She'd breathed and lived for the pack, and had been more than happy not to know anything more until the end of her days and her return to the Silver Pool.

The infuriating vampire had turned her world upside down, and now Santa-fucking-Claus wanted to tip it over once more.

Salina clenched her jaw and squeezed her eyes shut. "How do I know if I am? In love?"

A desperate sound came from Aherin, and she saw him clawing at the invisible barrier holding him back.

"You know," Santa said sagely. "And if you are not, spare the man more misery, and take his second life. Your final refusal of him may tip him over to the dark side anyway."

At least they had cookies there.

Salina snorted. She'd been right to worry about her sanity after all. There was no way she was having this discussion or entertaining the thoughts she was.

But was being in love with Aherin so impossible?

Santa waved one hand, and Aherin flew across the floor and ended spread-eagle on the wall furthest from them. "I believe your answer is in your procrastination," Santa said. "It is obvious you do not see him as the potential mate he sees in you. The die has been cast."

A snap of his fingers, and the stake slipped from Salina's fingers with incredible force, rose, and turned so its point was level with Aherin's heart.

"I thought it might be easier for you both if you took care of this, but your indecision is not helping anyone." Santa pointed at the stake, and Salina saw it fly toward Aherin.

In her mind's eye, the sharpened piece of wood slid through the air in slow motion, but she knew reality was faster. And definitively more final. Aherin didn't spare a glance at the instrument of his impending death. He didn't flinch or close his eyes.

He gazed at her. With understanding.

He could always speak volumes with his eyes.

Salina realized she was frozen in place, this time by fear instead of a spell. "No." She tried to run to him, but Santa grasped her ankle, holding her in place.

"Why not, Salina?"

There was no time to explain. The stake would impale Aherin any moment now. "I can't—"

"Why not?" Santa's voice boomed beneath her.

"Because I love him," she cried out, finally breaking his hold.

"That, darling girl, is your real present." Santa smiled and, for a heartbeat, he was once again the jolly old man her childhood self had pictured. "You were too stubborn to admit the truth unless you absolutely had to, and you would never have the happiness you deserve until you did." He looked at Aherin. "I am sorry I scared you old friend. You should know I would never have hurt you. I owe you my marriage, after all."

And then he vanished. As did the stake. One moment it was inches from Aherin's chest, and the next it disappeared.

Aherin was safe.

Her boot no longer perched on Santa's chest, Salina lost her balance. She found her footing and looked around, bewildered. No sign of Santa Claus or his sleigh. Like with the elves, it was as if they'd never existed.

Aherin was there, though, and she just knew he wouldn't let her live down her admission.

Chapter Four

She was beet red and disheveled, and yet had never looked more beautiful. Aherin tried hard to think of something to say. Maybe something snarky, like how he loved being right.

Or maybe he'd cut the crap, and thank her for saving his life.

Better yet, just grab her and kiss her.

Salina snapped her head toward him. "*You*, wipe that stupid grin off your face."

Aherin felt said grin grow wider.

He cleared his throat to check if his voice box worked again. Satisfied with the sound that reached his ears, he puffed his chest and squared his shoulders. "So, you do love me."

"Shut up, Aherin. We need to get out of here. He may come back." Her voice wasn't all that steady.

"You know as well as I do he's not coming back. He's done. He gave you your gift and all. Gave me my gift too." He arched an eyebrow and crossed his arms. His hands itched with the need to touch her. To have her. To make her repeat what she'd been forced to admit to Santa. He could lower his arms, so the spell had worn off—probably broken as soon as Santa took off. He could approach Salina, but he wouldn't go to her this time. It was her turn. "You love me," he said again.

"I need to get out of here. People are expecting me." She mirrored his stance for a second, before slinking toward him, the sway of her hips too feline for a wolf, but perfect for the woman she was. Stopping a foot or so away, she looked him in the eye. "You're enjoying this way too much, you know."

Aherin shrugged. "Feels good finally getting something in return, after fighting for your attention all this time."

"Oh, I don't think you're getting anything. At least not tonight." She brushed past him, but Aherin grabbed her forearm and spun her so her back was to the wall. Still holding on to her, he shoved his knee between her thighs to pin her in place.

"Here is where you need to be. Whatever else you have to do can wait," he whispered in her ear. "We need to talk."

"Let me go." She made no effort to push him away. "We said too much tonight."

"Not to each other. After months of chasing you around, I hear you love me back, only you tell some other guy. Tell me."

She turned her face to the side and huffed. "I should've staked you when Santa gave me the option."

Aherin chuckled. "But then you wouldn't have me to play with. And you know I can be a good playmate."

"I'm not shopping for a playmate." And yet, she arched her back and tilted her hips to rub against his thigh.

"Too bad, 'cause you're stuck with me. I'm going to kiss you, until you're panting and lightheaded.

316

Then I'm going to take you. On the floor or where you stand, makes no difference to me."

"No." It was barely more than a whisper, but Aherin's resolution wavered.

"No?" He used his free hand to lower her palm to his crotch. Her eyes widened when she cupped him over the denim, but she didn't move, and he didn't make her. He wanted her and knew she wanted him, but she had to want to act on it.

"No." Salina shook her head. "I'm expected for Christmas dinner, and I'm already late. If you want, I can come by afterward, and we can talk."

He wouldn't allow that much time to pass. She was open now. Had said she loved him *now*. He had to make her own up to it, before she shut him out again.

"We'll talk now." He trailed his fingers from her arm to her shoulder, brushing her breast, before splaying his hand over her side. "The sooner I hear what I want, the sooner you'll be free to go."

"Later," she whispered, her breath tickling the shell of his ear. "Promise."

The prospect of there being a later for them almost made him give in, before Salina made a mistake. She pulled his earlobe between her teeth, and nibbled on it lightly.

A growl built in Aherin's chest. "You just killed any chance you had of walking out of here now."

"My mom is going to kill me if I don't show for dinner, and then my dad will make sure you can't...*delay* anyone again."

"I'll survive." He tilted his head and nuzzled her neck, inching his way down to her collarbone.

Salina let out a dramatic sigh. "It's your funeral." She grabbed a fistful of his hair, and guided his mouth lower.

"We really should talk first." He lowered her

neckline with his teeth until one bare breast peeked above it. Encircling one engorged nipple with his lips, he flicked it with his tongue. "Yeah. Talk." He withdrew and covered the naughty peak again, enjoying her frustrated huff.

"Okay, talk." Her eyes threw daggers.

"I didn't mean me. I've done enough of that. It's your turn. Tell me how you burn for my hot body, and how you want me to be your *boyfriend*." He sing-songed the last word.

Salina arched an eyebrow. She pursed her lips, then sucked in her cheeks. When she opened her mouth, she looked so serious, Aherin wished he could turn back time, so he could have gone on with the thorough shagging, instead of opening his stupid mouth and saying whatever it was that pissed her off.

But then he'd have to surrender his license for carrying balls, and he wasn't about to become her little bitch. He wanted her to tell him how she felt, and God damn him, if he hadn't earned it.

"You're right," she said, and his mind whirled.

"About…?" Damn it. He shouldn't have spoken. He should've played the strong silent type, and let her say her peace.

"Yes, despite it being a horrible, horrible thing, and despite your being undead, and your stupid smirking when I try to say something serious, I may sort of feel"—she sighed—"*feelings* for you."

He kept his expression stoic, despite wanting to pump his fist in the air and cheer. "And what do you propose we do about that?"

Salina rolled her eyes. "Nothing. Nothing right now, anyway, because judging from last time, you'll take forever, and we don't have forever. I'll meet my family for dinner, and maybe bring you a snack afterward, and we can take it from there."

"How do I know you won't come up with an excuse for us not to be together by then?"

"I didn't say we're together now."

He raised his head and looked down at her. "So, am I to be your dirty little secret?" If she said yes, he'd kick her out and then move where she'd never find him.

"I didn't say that either. It's just not going to be easy. We can't be walking around holding hands and staring into each other's eyes. Things are complicated."

"Are they?" He was seething inside. He'd never in his long existence given a flying fuck about what other people thought, and if Salina let something like that get between them, he wasn't sure she was worth his efforts after all.

She studied his face with an intensity he had only seen her use on the battlefield. When she smiled, it was either the most genuine smile she'd given him, or his eyes weren't as used to the dark as they were supposed to be, for a creature of the night. "Things shouldn't be so difficult. I mean, we already have Santa's seal of approval."

He bet that was something she'd never thought she'd say. "So?"

"I guess we can try. Rex and Xandra seem to have figured out how to balance things. Must be why the Balancers are fangirling over them."

He stifled a chuckle. "What exactly are you suggesting, little shifter?" He enjoyed how the word made her wince. "You'll have to put it into words. I need to know what you're agreeing to."

"I'm agreeing to trying to see if we can be together, you undead idiot." Her tone was soft.

"No holding back? No excuses?"

She brushed a strand of hair away from her face and tucked it behind her ear. "No holding back. No excuses." She closed the distance between them, reached for the waist of his jeans, and tugged until he was flush against her. The first touch of her lips to his lit a fire a mere inch from where her fingers still dug into his pants. A fire she stoked when her other hand sneaked underneath his shirt and trailed down his stomach, nails dragging against the sensitive skin.

He wasn't ready for their lips to part, when she broke the kiss and knelt down in front of him.

"Where are you going?" he asked.

"I have a debt to settle." Nimble fingers undid his belt and popped his fly, and the night air caressed his cock, when Salina pulled him out.

He let his head roll back, and groaned at the pressure of her palm around his shaft. "This isn't going to cut it"—he gazed down at her—"but you're on the right track."

Salina smiled and opened her mouth…

…and closed it around his cock.

She deep-throated him in one single wet gulp. Aherin grunted, as she closed her throat around his shaft, making him feel like he was about to burst.

She pulled all the way back. "How about this?"

Aherin hadn't the faintest clue what she meant.

"Will this cut it?" She tapped his cock with her tongue.

"Probably," was his not-so-bright retort, as she sucked his length back inside her hot mouth, licking the underside.

She sucked him hard for a while, rolling his balls in her palm, as she bobbed her head up and down. Aherin was close. Too close, and he bet she knew it.

He pulled her up by the hair. "I want to be inside you."

"Later. I have to go."

He didn't care. "Now. I can have you coming in a couple of minutes. As a matter of fact, I plan to."

"Right." She placed her hands on his shoulders and pushed him at arm's length. "You can show me later tonight."

For the second time that night, she tried to make an exit. Just like before, he stopped her. This time, though, he pulled her to the inside of the mausoleum. His grip solid at the small of her back, he fisted his hand in her hair and crushed his lips to hers with all the hunger he'd been suppressing for months. "I'll show you now," he whispered. He bit her lower lip, and when she gasped, invaded her mouth with his tongue.

She tasted like freedom and wildness. She tasted like the sun. She tasted like happiness he hadn't felt since his youth. It was different than before, because this time he knew she wanted *him*, and not someone to help her scratch an itch.

Her hands found their way inside his shirt, clutching at his back, pulling him closer. He wouldn't be close enough until he was inside her.

"Fuck it. Now." She untucked her blouse, and he let his fingers explore her body. The smooth back, marred by a single scar she earned in battle. The sleek line of her spine. The tilt of her perfect ass.

He wanted to take her. Consume her. Drink her all in.

He wanted her to beg.

The dilemma made his cock throb harder, and his head hurt.

Eh, he'd fuck her first, hear her beg him to drink her later.

"Where?" he asked.

Salina shrugged.

He wrapped an arm around her waist and threw her over his shoulder. "I vote sarcophagus."

"Eww." She giggled and punched his shoulder playfully. "You better not mean inside it."

"What am I? A savage?" He lowered her in front of the stone lid of the box that had contained him for longer than he wanted to remember. Time to exorcise those memories. "Pants off."

"Just like that?"

"You said you were in a hurry."

Salina hopped down and fiddled with the zipper of her slacks. She should've worn a skirt. Other than offering ease of access, it would do more justice to her long legs than dress pants ever could.

Though these showcased her ass brilliantly.

When she finally uncovered her magnificent buttocks, and began turning to face him, he walked up behind her and pressed his hips to hers, trapping her body between his and the stone slab. "No." One hand on the nape of her neck, he pushed her down.

She tensed against him and he heard her heart speed up, before she gave in and folded her long frame over the top of the sarcophagus.

"Good girl." Aherin dragged her blouse out of the way, so he could lick a trail up her spine. He wanted to tear the silk in ribbons for daring to keep him from her skin, but she wouldn't appreciate that, so he settled for pulling it past her shoulders and over her head.

She propped herself up on her elbows and waggled her ass against him. "You're already taking too long."

Oh, she'd regret mocking him. He pulled the waist of her pants lower, and ghosted his fingers along her inner thigh. Smooth and lovely. He'd bite her there too, later. Tomorrow, maybe.

She pushed back her hips, and he shoved two fingers inside her pussy without further preamble. The echo of her groan bounced off the walls of his tomb, and he closed his eyes for a long moment. He'd spent days fantasizing about making her moan, right here in

322

the only place on earth undisputedly his.

She was scorching hot around his fingers. And wet. Like liquid fire.

He wanted her to burn him, but first she had to burn for him. "I see you're ready." He congratulated himself for maintaining his composure.

"The last three months have been nothing but foreplay." The smile in her voice made his cock throb and pulse harder. She was right. There had been enough teasing.

Kicking her feet as far apart as they'd go with the slacks stretched between her knees, he withdrew his hand and shoved his cock inside her to the hilt. She clenched and made to withdraw from his invasion, but he held her in place, his fingers digging into her flesh. "You said you can take all of it."

She glanced at him over her shoulder. "Do your best, Dead-boy."

He threw his head back and roared with laughter, as he pulled out and drove back in with all his strength. Every thrust lifted her hips off the stone surface, but she pushed back, matching his fervor. His fingers raised welts on her ass, as he impaled her again and again.

The laughter surrounding him was too melodic to be his. She was laughing too, enjoying their fierce coupling as much as he was.

The scent of her blood reached his nostrils, and he stopped. "Are you okay? You're bleeding."

"Just a scrape." She pumped her hips. "Don't stop. More."

Oh, he'd give her more. He resumed his near-brutal rhythm, and draped his body over hers so he could lick the sweat off her neck. He pulled her head up and grazed the spot behind her ear with one fang. "Is this enough for you?"

"Never." She brought his hand to her mouth and sucked his thumb between her lips, slicking it well with her tongue.

It drove him crazy with desire. He could never have enough of her either. He slowed his movements almost to a halt. "I'll give you more." He traced the length of her body, all the way down to her puckered hole. "I'll give you more right here."

Salina clenched, but he pressed his thumb, slick with her saliva to the tight ring of muscle.

"You'll love it," he said.

She'd stopped matching his thrusts and now looked back at him, eyes narrowed. "You speak from experience?"

"That's a talk for another time." He withdrew his vampire fangs, and gave her shoulder a playful bite. "Relax and trust me."

"I'm going to regret this." Regardless, she ducked her head down, and pushed back, still tight, but allowing him to slide his finger inside to the first knuckle. "I don't know what I'm supposed to like about this."

He chuckled and resumed a steady rhythm of long thrusts in her pussy, trying to get her back to her previous level of enthusiasm. It didn't take long. When he circled her waist with his other arm and pressed on her clit, she bucked against him hard. He chose that moment to pull all the way out and align his cock with her tiny hole.

"You can forget about it." But she wrestled an arm free of her blouse and reached back to grab her ass cheek and open herself more to him.

Aherin rubbed his cock along her crack, spreading her juices. "I want to go in here, Salina. I want you to walk crooked and feel me inside you for days to come." He held his cock at her tight orifice and pushed forward a fraction of an inch, watching the muscle stretch white to fit the tip. "And I want my dick inside you, as your blood flows in my mouth." He pinched her clitoris with his index and middle finger. "Do you want that? Do you want me to make you mine?"

*

She heard the words but wasn't sure what he was asking. He'd shown her pleasure she'd never felt before, his finger and cock filling her up and driving her body wild. But make her his? What did that mean, more than letting him inside her body like she'd never let anybody else?

He pushed another fraction of an inch—or foot—of his impossibly hard cock inside her. It hurt, but the pain brought with it the promise of more pleasure, and she was done denying him and herself that.

"Yes."

"Yes what?"

The bastard wanted to make her beg. He'd promised she would, and she hated proving him right, but she needed...more. She needed more. "Please, Aherin. Whatever you want. Just...please."

"Please fuck you?" He bit her neck with blunt, human teeth, and a shiver run through her.

She knew the question for what it was this time. If she said yes, it'd be more than an admission of her feelings. More than granting him permission to her body. It'd be as close to mating as her kind practiced among its own. The mutual exchange of blood during sex sealed a lasting, unbreakable bond between partners. She doubted it meant much less to vampires. But if she didn't take Aherin's blood, it was one-sided.

That couldn't be binding.

Still, she understood its symbolic value for Aherin. By offering him her blood, she proved she wanted to be with him.

She pulled in a long breath and pushed back again, taking in more of his length. "Yes," she whispered, flipping her hair to the side and baring her throat to him. "Please take me. I'm yours."

He stopped, and for an instant, she was sure she'd said the wrong thing. Was she supposed to have played hard to get?

Then his fangs sliced inside the crook of her neck at the same time he buried his cock in her. She squeezed her eyes shut at the pain, but she'd asked for it all. She felt filled to the point of bursting, sure he'd split her in two if he began moving inside her. Salina expected her wolf to pounce at the intrusion, but the beast lay dormant, docile even. It wasn't the spell. Not any longer. The wolf welcomed the vampire just as the woman had. More, it submitted to him. Aherin would have a field day if she ever shared that realization with him.

His first pull on her blood made her head light with unprecedented euphoria. She understood bite-junkies now. There was no way one could willingly give up this sensation. He accompanied his second pull with a short thrust that caused surprisingly little pain and sent a tiny jolt of desire to her womb. When he sucked again, warmth spread in her belly, and wetness slicked the inside of her thighs. This time he withdrew more and pushed back in harder than before, and she arched her back to accommodate him.

Soon, he was fucking her ass with the same lack of restraint he'd shown when pounding her pussy, his fangs tore the edges of the bite ragged, and Salina was floating on a cloud of ever-increasing bliss. She'd never been high, but she guessed what she felt was the mother of all buzzes, short-circuiting her brain at the same time it expanded her senses.

The lid of the sarcophagus screeched, as it moved back and forth with their erratic coupling. Salina could hear Aherin's knuckles rocking against the stone, as he circled her clit. Could smell her own sweat and blood mingled with the combined scent of their sexes. Could hear the wind blowing the leaves outside.

If she could hear the world again, maybe it heard her moan and grunt, and mewl with the need to release the ball of fire revolving in her core.

She didn't care. Let them hear. That was as close as mere mortals could ever get to experiencing what she felt at this very moment, with a vampire invading her more intimately than any of her pack's laws allowed.

Fuck, was this…happiness? A tear of pure bliss rolled down her cheek. "More," she managed with a gasp.

Pinning her to him with enough force for both his hands to leave lasting bruises, Aherin took a step back. Her breasts rubbed against the cover of the sarcophagus, but it served to amp her need.

He slid his fangs out long enough to say, "Play with yourself," and Salina felt almost bereft until he bit her again, on the same spot.

She snaked her hand between her legs, and began rubbing her clit with punishing force, as Aherin pistoned inside her even harder.

One rough pinch on the tender button, and the waves of pleasure rocking her lifted her and sent her hurtling to her climax. Spots appeared behind her eyelids, when she squeezed her eyes shut, to keep her head from spinning. She had to maintain some semblance of control over her body.

Wolf for Christmas by Sotia Lazu

Aherin drew one last, long gulp of her blood, at the same time his cock pulsed inside her. The sensation of his cool spendings filling her made her give up trying to break out of her haze. Her lower body throbbed; her throat ached; her thighs, elbows, and most of her upper body were full of scrapes; but she and Aherin had redefined satisfaction, and as he pulled her up to him for an awkward kiss, she couldn't wait to repeat it.

He caressed the skin around his bite mark with his fingertips, and then took his time laving the wound with his tongue. "The bleeding's stopped," he said.

She'd expected it to. Soon it would look no worse than a hickey. Shifters didn't recover from wounds as fast as vampires did, but their bodies still healed supernaturally fast.

He gave her his T-shirt to wipe herself clean, but her thighs were still sticky when she pulled her slacks back, and she was glad her black top wouldn't show drops of blood from the myriad of her tiny, rapidly healing wounds.

"I have to go." She buried her nose where his neck met his shoulder, and inhaled deeply. Vampires were supposed to have little to no scent, but she could recognize his smell. She was sure her family would be able to recognize it too, all over her. "I need to find a way to sneak in and shower. Any clue what time it is?"

He shook his head, looking a little dejected for someone who'd just had mind-blowing sex and a meal all in one.

"We shouldn't have done this." She rubbed her forehead against his cheek.

He pushed her back harshly. "You can't take it back."

"What? Oh, no. I meant not tonight, and not without running water in the vicinity. As if being late isn't bad enough, my folks will know I was late because

I was getting my brains fucked out."

The tension seeped from his shoulders, and the familiar and gorgeous dimple appeared on his cheek. "You could skip dinner all together, and stay for another round."

She patted her ass. "I think it'll be a while before this is ready for you again. Or any other part of me," she said, holding up a warning finger, when he leered.

"Then I guess all I can do is kiss you goodbye and let you go face the music." He tugged her back to him from the waist of her slacks. "I'm starting to like these pants," he mused, tucking a midnight-black curl behind his ear.

"That's a pity. I was thinking of not wearing pants around you again, but if you insist…"

He stole a kiss from her swollen lips, and brushed his thumb across her cheek. "I can make a concession, if it means that much to you."

She sobered up. He meant that much to her. Much more than she'd ever dare imagine anyone but family would. He *was* family—even if she was half convinced part of her warm and fuzzy feelings toward him were because of his magic bite. She had a decision to make, and a lot depended on it.

"Well, I'll need to wear pants tonight at dinner, and you'll need to put on a proper button-down shirt, or Mom will pitch a fit."

His cocked his head, eyes shining with child-like glee. "Are you asking me to join you for dinner, little shifter?"

"Well, I'm not dealing with my parents on my own. They came all the way to this realm just so we could all have a nice dinner, and it's your fault I'm late." She watched, amused, as he used vampire speed to cross the mausoleum and wade through his clothes for an old-style ruffled-front white shirt. "Dashing," she said when he asked how he looked. In truth, he was smoldering hot.

"We should do something about that." Aherin pointed at her throat.

She ran her fingers through her hair a couple of times, and arranged a thick tress of it over her shoulder. "There." She smiled.

At the door, she took his hand. They were in this together now, and they could face anything.

Except maybe her parents. They might need the Balancers' help for that.

****

They entered her house, hands still linked.

"Aherin. You came." Xandra threw her arms around him, inadvertently disengaging his fingers from Salina's. "Rex is on his way. He'll be so happy to see you."

Salina glanced at the kitchen clock. 8:15 pm. Her kidnapping and…everything else had only lasted a quarter of an hour in real-world time. Would the weirdness of the night never cease? She tapped Aherin's shoulder and tilted her head toward the clock. His eyes widened in surprise, and he gave her a one-shouldered shrug. She smiled. One less problem to be dealt with.

Her relief was short lived, when Xandra flared her nostrils.

"You're shitting me," Xandra said. "You two?"

"And not for the first time." Aherin beamed a self-satisfied grin at both of them, and Salina smacked him in the stomach.

"Watch it, or it could still be the last. And my parents don't need to hear about it, either way," she said with a scowl she didn't feel.

"Mom and Dad are out back, braving the cold. Don't worry." Xandra looked at Salina's neck pointedly. "And I don't think it will be the last time." To Aherin, she said, "She doesn't know, does she? Do you know what kind of trouble you're in?"

"Huh? What'd I miss?" Worry crept in. Did her parents already know somehow? She could think of nothing worse.

"I thought she knew." Aherin turned his panicked gaze to her. "When I said I wanted you to be mine... You realized what that meant, right?"

Unease roiled in her stomach. There were no records of vampires biting shifters, and she'd never bothered to ask Xandra about the logistics of it all. She gulped, her throat suddenly clogged. "I thought it was a you being possessive thing. Sexy thing too."

Aherin's deep belly laughter made her scowl. "Then what?" she asked.

"Maybe I shouldn't be here." Xandra headed toward the living room.

Salina held up a hand. "Stay. I may need witnesses for when I kill him." She poked Aherin in the chest, cutting his mirth short. "What did it mean? Making me yours."

"It meant becoming my mate. Like your sister is with Rex. You agreed. You asked me to drink you. You said you'd be mine. That's almost the vampire mating oath verbatim." His voice didn't waver, but his face was even paler than usual, and he'd just fed on her, so it wasn't lack of blood.

"But I didn't bite you back. It wasn't binding."

"You didn't have to. I thought your sister told you..."

Xandra had tried to describe the vampire mating process to her, after she and Rex mated, but Salina had

331

a distinct memory of covering her ears and chanting, "Ew ew ew." She knew what being mated to him meant though, assuming the results on Xandra and Rex were the rule for such a union. As a vampire's mate, she'd live longer than even shifters did, and her vampire would become impervious to the sun. Good news all around. There was, of course, the small matter of forced monogamy, and the little bit about spending eternity together.

Should she panic?

She studied him overtly, from the tip of his black-haired head to the toes of his scuffed Italian-leather boots. He was hot, fun, smart, and kind—when not in a murdering mood. And he saved puppies.

And she was crazy about him and the things he did to make her body sing.

She shook her head. "I guess I could've done worse."

Aherin wrapped his arms around her and brought her flush against him, but she batted him away. "Not until we talk to my parents."

"Hello? Can I get in on this, please?" Xandra raised one hand. "When did the two of you become a thing? And where was I? Gods, I hope you don't cause another balance war. I'll stick up for your right to…fun, or love, or whatever, but I was hoping to sit this year out."

"Don't worry about it. Santa's got us covered. I better go get this over with, so Mom and Dad can yell, and then we can all eat. I'm starving." Salina made sure her hair still covered Aherin's bite mark, and gave him a reassuring smile. "Aherin will fill you in on our evening. Well, the PG-rated parts of it," she told Xandra, and made her way out of the kitchen.

She wished Rex was there already. Then she could point at him and say, "*He's* here. Why can't

Aherin be too?"

She halted at the screen door that led to the yard, unable to take a single step forward. When she felt a solid body press against her back, she took in a deep breath. "That was fast," she whispered as low as she could. "I expected my sister to have more questions. Especially about Santa."

Strong arms encircled her waist. "She said she can wait for the sordid details. I'm here with you, yeah?" Aherin matched her hushed tone.

She nodded, taking comfort in his strength and his familiar scent.

"Hey, you're back." Her mom dropped her cigarette butt and stepped on it. Salina pretended not to notice. After so many years, Rose still thought her daughters didn't realize she smoked. Salina didn't mind; being mated to a shifter, her mom couldn't be hurt by diseases that plagued humans.

"And you're dragging a stray behind you, I see." Her father's greeting had no bite. It was more of an observation.

"Yeah, well, I've sort of adopted him." She'd meant to keep her dad's simile going, but winced when she heard the words come out of her mouth. "Aherin and I... We're together now on. And you'll have to deal. Santa said he's my gift. And I'm his. So deal." She blurted the words in a single breath, watching in horror as her father's eyebrow reached for his hairline, and her mother's eyes widened in surprise.

"Is Santa really jolly?" Behind Salina, Xandra focused on the important stuff.

"So, I have to set the table for six?" their mother asked.

"Well, I hope he brought some beer, 'cause I'm not sharing mine," their father snapped, although playfully.

Salina blinked. Then she blinked again. Maybe this was a dream after all. Had they heard her right? "Aren't you going to make a fuss about this? I'm…canoodling with the enemy."

Her father grimaced, but his voice was calm when he spoke. "And don't think we're not going to discuss your lack of better judgment tomorrow. But tonight is Christmas Eve, and your mother and sister have spent time preparing dinner. One more vampire at the table isn't going to make much of a difference."

"Sorry I'm late." Rex held up a six pack of Guinness as he joined them. "Let's eat, drink, and be merry." He nodded at Aherin, as if he expected to see him there. "'Evening, mate."

There was Salina's opening. "It's not bad judgment, Dad. Santa himself said I should be with him. And it can work. Look at Xandra and Rex."

"As I said, we'll talk about it tomorrow. For now"—Vox turned to Aherin—"you're welcome to join us, as a valued ally." Her father led the way in, and they all followed him to the dining room.

"This was easier than I expected," Salina whispered to Aherin. "Though I'm dreading the little chat I'll have with them tomor—"

"Shhh. Listen." Aherin pointed upward.

When Salina did as he asked, she thought she heard clopping on the roof, and— "Are those bells jingling?"

"I think ol' Nicky bought us some extra time to get ready for your parents' inquisition." He kissed the crown of her head.

Oh, Santa was so getting cookies next year.

The End

Unleashed, A Fangs and Fur Novella, by

Sotia Lazu

Grayon is ousted from the only life he knows, for trying to do the right thing. The Earth plane is his punishment, and both his human and wolf nature hate the smell of London and long to return to The Forest, but for now he has to accept the hospitality of the local vampire Master and the annoying undead chick that comes with it.

Raven loves nothing more than control. Her life was all mapped out, as was her death. The only thing she hasn't planned for is this hot piece of shifter that grates on her nerves, with his cocky grin and sculpted body.

Vampires and shifters were enemies till recently, and some still consider this to be the case. It's up to Grayon and Raven to decide if they will hate each other or...

Chapter One

"—the fuck?" Grayon snapped his head to the right and winced when his vision blurred. "Bron, you here? What happened?"

His brother gave no response, and Grayon searched his muddled brain for a thread of logic. The darkness around him held no threat—not that he ever felt threatened—but it was unfamiliar. Where was he? He sniffed the air and let his wolf near the surface. The beast growled, always ready to take over, but Grayon suppressed it. He needed to use its senses, not give it free roam.

Pine and grass and something dirty. Murky. Was it smoke?

A fire in The Forest? Why weren't the werecrows spreading the word?

No fire. What invaded his senses was darker and oily.

He looked around again, this time careful to avoid sudden movement. He was in the woods, but not in The Forest. The canopy of trees hid the stars above, yet the call of the moon was different.

"Shit. Not another dog. Are you starting a

colony?" The husky female voice came from straight ahead, just a few feet away, but all Grayon could make out was a dark shape. To access his night vision, he had to give his wolf more leeway, and that wouldn't do until he'd assessed his situation.

He could still smell her, though, and he knew this scent. Kind of. Beneath a light fruity aroma, the tang of magic was free from all animal traces. This could only mean one thing.

He was on the Earth plane.

The realization opened the floodgates for memories to come pouring in. He and Bron talking. About Candia. Bron loved her, and she returned his feelings. But she'd been promised to Grayon.

Grayon's head throbbed. His heart hurt. His body ached with the effort to keep the wolf down.

Chivalry had gotten him ousted. To Earth.

Where fucking vampires roamed.

Right on cue, the one in front of him took a step closer. Grayon jumped to his feet. The only vampires he knew had fought on his side, after their kind and his became allies. That had been back in his plane, though. For all he knew, this bloodsucker was out for Grayon's blood.

"Chill out, pooch. I mean no harm." Her giggle grated his nerves.

"I'm not a dog, and I doubt you could hurt me, Deadgirl." He hunched his shoulders and lowered his body mass, preparing for a fight, if that was what she sought.

He relaxed when she stepped out of the shadows and within his field of vision. She barely came up to his clavicle and had to weigh less than a werefox in animal form.

His smirk was still forming on his lips, when she swept his legs from under him and landed him on his ass. His head thunked on a tree root. "*Ow.*"

The vampire came to stand next to him. "See? I can totally hurt you." She was even shorter than he'd thought and balanced her weight effortlessly on chunky six-inch heels. Tight black leather stretched over her generous curves, and the tips of her jet-black hair were bright blue.

"What? You got a concussion now?" She nudged him with the toe of her lace-up boot.

Grayon growled. He rolled to the side and was back on his feet in no time, glad his head and sight were now clear. "Next time I'll be ready, bloodsucker."

It seemed as good a line as any, to end the unpleasant exchange with. He made a show of turning his back to her and hoped she couldn't tell he had no clue where he headed. At least he had a plan. Once he put some distance between himself and the annoying female, he'd try to figure out exactly where the witch's spell had landed him. He was pretty sure it'd be a terrible place. After all, the witch followed Xenon's instructions, and Grayon was in the pack leader's shit list these days.

"Like you know where you're going." The vampire's voice came from ahead, and Grayon cursed under his breath. "I heard that," the vampire said.

"Good. Now hear this too. Go the fuck away, or I'll rip your head off."

"Rude."

By the time he realized she was rushing him, he was on his ass again.

"You weren't ready this time either." She crossed her arms and looked down at him.

He stood and dusted the seat of his pants. "What the fuck?"

"You say that a lot."

Okay. That was it. He called the wolf enough

for his night vision to kick in. Didn't hurt that it made his eyes look big and yellow. *Scary fucking eyes*, Rex called them. Maybe they'd scare this vamp too.

They didn't.

"So cool." She got in his face. "Can you—like—change any part of your anatomy at will?"

Grayon growled.

"Yeah, you said that already."

This was stupid. He grabbed her biceps and lifted her, so they were eye to eye. "What's the matter with you? Do you have a death wish?"

She kicked him in the balls.

He bit down on the howl of pain that forced its way up his throat, and managed to keep his hold on her. "Will you fucking stop this? I can tear you limb from limb. I can snap you like a twig." Just in case, he held her at arm's length.

She gave a shrug. Well, she tried to, but his grip turned it into a tilt of her head. "I'm cool with that."

So she did have a death wish. Pity. Now he took a good look, he saw she was beautiful under the layers of makeup. Her dark eyebrows and long lashes framed eyes as green as emeralds. The curve of her cheek was soft, and her lips were plump and kissable.

If she weren't a vampire and he wasn't in the most fucked up situation ever, he might go for it. As things were, he'd rather be an ass. "What happened? Tired of eternally roaming the earth?"

"I'm not *that* eternal. I'm only twenty five."

He snorted. "For how long?"

"Nine months."

"You mean—"

She arched an eyebrow. "I was turned on my twenty-fifth birthday."

"You're a fledgling?" He'd been dropped *twice* by a fledgling? What the fuck was wrong with him?

He'd held his own in a fight against two old-ass vampires more than once. This plane of existence was messing him up.

She twisted and brought her knees to his chest. "I can still kick you."

Grayon let go, but she didn't give him the satisfaction of falling. She tilted upright, but her feet still didn't touch the ground. She hovered in front of him, as if suspended by unseen threads.

"This is creepy," he said. "Now I'm going to go, and you're going to stop bugging me, before I show you what pain is."

She laughed, the sound too bitter to be coming from someone so young. "Oh, I know what pain is. I know what loss is too. And death. Have you ever died, doggie?"

"No." Why was he answering her? Why was he even talking to her?

She smiled, and her green-green eyes shone. "I hope you never do. It's really no fun. And you're not going anywhere until you register. Rex will kill me if a lone wolf starts wreaking havoc in his city."

He knew Rex. Hell, they'd formed a tentative friendship, once Grayon got over the fact Rex was one of the undead, and Rex stopped calling him *fleabag*. Grayon supposed there could be more than one vampire called Rex, but seriously, how many males would lack the good sense not to keep that name for eternity?

"This is Rex's city?" he asked. "Is Rex tall, dark haired, and as annoying as you?"

"Yup, but he's British-annoying." She grasped his arm. "Ready to go?"

He tried to shake her off but couldn't get free, even though her fingers barely circled half his wrist. "Go?"

"To Rex."

341

With no further explanation, they were leaving the woods and earth behind, and flying toward the night sky.

Chapter Two

The shifter was big. More than a foot taller than her five-five, with shoulders as wide as a Mini Cooper and hands that could span her waist. The shifter was also gorgeous, and Raven wanted to kick herself for her juvenile behavior.

It wasn't her fault. It was the stupid rules. When she moved to London, to act as a liaison between the American vampire council and the British clans, she was warned about the local master's girlfriend being a shifter. Now that The Forest and Earth had an open gate between them, more shifters could show up, and not all of them would be friendly like Xandra.

So when Rex told her to go watch the gate, she went, and she watched, and she was ready for a fight.

She wasn't ready for a three-hundred-pound mountain of muscle, or for those wide lips that curved so beautifully when the shifter sneered at her.

"Hey," she called to him, but the wind forced the words back to her.

He looked at her, no fear evident on his face. He was one cool dog, if flying over the Big Ben didn't faze him.

"What's your name?" she mouthed.

He shook his head and tapped his ear with his free hand. Couldn't hear her. She'd solve that. Still steering them through the air, she slowed down enough for momentum to bring him next to her, and wrapped her arm around him. It was like hugging stone, and she had to make conscious effort not to hump his leg.

She climbed up his body until her lips touched his ear, and then repeated her question.

The shifter went rigid against her, before whispering, "Grayon." The word brought to mind an enormous gray wolf, roaming the forest and howling at the moon. It fit him.

"I'm Raven." She felt his eyebrow rise against her skin. "I swear that's what my mother named me."

"Well, it fits you." He didn't say more, and neither did she.

She thought of things, though. All sorts of naughty things she hadn't done in a long while, and some new ones she might like to try with him.

Grayon. She whispered the name, liking the roll of the *R* on her tongue.

"What?" He sounded grouchy, but she didn't let it get to her.

Grouchy or not, he was warm and hard, and smelled like the woods and life itself. Raven had never in her life been spontaneous. She'd planned everything, including her death and turning. It was the only way she knew to live her life. The stupid blue highlights that would disappear during the day were the wildest she'd ever been, but now she had the urge to stray from her course.

It was lucky she saw Xandra and Rex's place when she did, or she might have done something stupid.

Something she'd have no doubt enjoyed.

Chapter Three

Grayon's feet hit the asphalt before Raven's did. He stumbled and pulled her down with him. He managed to roll so neither of them plunged to the ground face first. That he landed on top of her was a happy coincidence.

She took a short, unnecessary breath, and Grayon found his gaze glued to the pale round tops of her breasts, pressing against the square cut of her neckline. She was a tasty morsel all right, and if she were anything but a vampire, he might try something. The world was changing, but he wasn't ready to risk permanent shunning from his pack.

Raven huffed.

He wasn't very discreet with his ogling.

"Will you move? You're squishing me." She jumped up as soon as he was off her. "This is it." She pointed to a red-brick house.

After she'd called this Rex's city, Grayon expected to be taken to a castle or something. The two-story semi-detached was anything but palatial, but the garden was filled with flowers, and their aroma was the first thing Grayon liked since he landed on this plane—

other than the accidental bump-and-grind with the vampire.

He let her lead the way and ring the doorbell.

Barely a second passed, before Rex appeared at the door. He did a double-take and smirked. "Never thought I'd see the day you'd leave the wilderness for the clean London air, wolfboy."

Grayon tried to scowl, but he was smiling when he shook the proffered hand. "You're lucky you don't have to breathe, vampire. This place reeks."

"It isn't that bad, when you get used to it." Xandra pushed past Rex, and before Grayon knew it, he had an armful of petite blonde shifter. Not that long ago, he'd kill to have her clinging to him, but now she was Rex's mate, and there was no messing with that.

She let go and took a step back. "So glad you're here, big guy. Tell me about home. Actually, you know what? You're staying for dinner."

Grayon didn't miss her questioning glance at Rex, as she pulled him inside the house, nor the tiny nod he gave as a response. Someone had finally tamed her. Her face looked relaxed, and Grayon knew he could never have made her this happy. Shifters and Vampires had been enemies for ages, but Xandra and Rex made their love work.

And Grayon wasn't able to get a mate from his own pack, or to keep the one promised to him. "I don't want to impose"—not that he had another option—"but I may need to stay a little longer than that."

Another exchange of looks.

"Raven, take Grayon to the second guestroom," Rex said. "I'll help Xandra with dinner. We'll see you two in an hour."

How very domestic it'd all sound, if something in Rex's voice didn't indicate the hour wasn't so they could prepare food, or for Grayon to make himself comfortable. His house, his rules, though.

Grayon nodded. "Thank you." He followed Raven up the stairs, trying to look anywhere but at her leather-clad ass.

"This is me. No windows." She pointed at a closed door to her right. "And this is where you'll be staying." She stopped in front of the room next to hers and waited for him to step inside first. "Beddings and towels are in the cupboard across the hall. Bathroom next to it. Don't mix up the two doors in the middle of the night."

He turned to snap at her, but the smile on her lips was teasing, not mean. It suited her.

"I'd say change into something less woodsy," she said, "but unless you can make a toga out of the curtains, you're stuck with what you have on."

"I could go naked."

She flared her nostrils. "Rex won't appreciate it, but if you have to…"

He might not be allowed to fuck her, but he could like her spunk. Yes, that was all he'd like about her.

And the jiggle in her gait when she walked away, leaving him in the painful blankness of an unfamiliar room.

The white walls and metal bed felt sterile, as did the table right beneath the single window. Heavy drapes that matched the wall-to-wall carpeting blocked out the night sky. Grayon needed to see stars. Smell the night. Opening the window wouldn't suffice.

He thundered down the stairs and out the door, barely aware of voices trailing after him. He'd lost The Forest. His brother. The only home and family he'd ever known.

He turned his face to the moon and funneled the agony and uncertainty that clenched a fist around his insides into a long howl.

"Shut that blasted dog up," came from somewhere to the left.

A hand clasped his arm. He looked at the slim, pale fingers and shook his head. "I don't belong here."

"None of us do." Raven hauled him back inside and locked the door behind them.

Xandra handed him an armful of clothes. "These are Aherin's. They'll be a little tight, but you should be good for length."

Aherin. Rex's best friend. Great fighter, though as annoying as Rex. "Is he… gone?"

"Yes. To the Bahamas, with Salina. Dad is super psyched both his daughters ended up mated to fangers."

"He never said anything to me. Just that you both decided to stay on Earth. And that you're happy." He tucked the clothes under his arm and tugged at her ponytail. "I'm glad he wasn't lying."

Xandra cupped his cheek. "Grayon, I'm sorry. Not that we didn't work, but— You know."

He smiled. "I know. Thanks for the clothes."

Rex leaned against the doorframe to the kitchen, arms folded over his chest. Grayon nodded at him on the way to his room, and Rex returned the gesture. They both knew who Xandra belonged with, and tonight Grayon realized he didn't mind. Weird how things worked out some times.

He shed his dirty clothes and squeezed his legs in the pants Xandra gave him. They were no material he was aware of—tight and thick but stretchy. Maybe a little flashy. How did the vampire walk around with his junk showcased like this? The shirt that came with them was long and billowy. Too frilly for Grayon.

How much would Aherin miss the pleated collar?

Not much.

Grayon ripped it off, and was left with a deep *V*. He could breathe in this. He pulled his boots back on and felt like himself again.

"Nice." Raven's voice came from behind. She had a knack for sneaking up on him. It helped that he'd left the door open.

Shifters were cool with nudity. It came natural to a species that changed form at will and wasn't really into looking for their discarded clothes in the woods. They dressed for the sake of hygiene and to protect their bodies. He'd have to remember he wasn't on his plane, and people here didn't approach sex as casually as his kind did.

"Which part?" He turned to see her purse her lips.

"All of it. The outfit is a little pirate-y for you, but it works."

He let himself relax but should have known better.

"I chose it myself," she said, barely containing a giggle.

Of course she did. To make fun of him. He'd have to ask Xandra what pirate-y meant.

Raven licked her lips. "Have to admit the result isn't what I was going for, though."

His gaze followed the tip of her tongue along her pink lower lip. He had the urge to taste it. Taste her. "They're waiting for us," he said.

Chapter Four

He wasn't supposed to look good in that. Yeah, it was Aherin's, but he'd bought it for Halloween. Lycra pants should make Grayon less sexy, not unbearably so. They hugged his long, muscular legs and made her want to rake her nails down his thighs. And when the shirt rode up, she saw his rock-hard ass and... God, the man was huge everywhere.

Raven wondered if she could fit him inside her. Vampires were resilient, so maybe if she was well prepar—

What the hell was she thinking? She didn't think like that, especially about a huge-ass werewolf. And what sort of name was Grayon?

The annoying sort.

She looked across the table at him. Dinner was steak and fries, Xandra's go-to meal, and Grayon's fork and knife lay discarded by his plate. He held the slab of beef in both hands and accompanied every second bite with a groan of appreciation. *Ugh*. His pecks, visible through the torn neckline, bunched as he tore into his steak. It was hard not to stare at how his shoulders stretched the shirt. When she tried, she found her gaze glued to his wide palms and long fingers. He brought one hand to his mouth and wrapped his luscious lips around his thumb. Flicked out his tongue, to catch a drop of steak sauce.

Raven had wished for very few things in her life—that her tumor was operable, that her father was around, that her mother wasn't an addict—but now she wished she could feel that tongue and fingers between her legs.

"You're not hungry?" His steel-gray eyes bore into her. "Sorry. Forgot you don't need to eat."

"But I want to." She shoved a handful of fries in her mouth. What was wrong with her? She didn't get flabbergasted over any pretty guy that crossed her street. She was a big bad vampire, and nothing scared her. Not even the intensity of his gaze.

She chewed and washed it down with a gulp of ale. Fun that she drunk, now she'd died. "I feel more of the taste than you do. Than *humans* do. I guess your taste-buds are better than theirs."

Grayon nodded.

"Food holds no nourishment for us," Rex said, "but we can still appreciate a nice piece of meat." He gave Xandra a look that had her blushing to the roots of her hair.

Raven found it endearing how the two were so into each other. She never had that kind of relationship with a guy. She'd dated, but not seriously; it'd mess with her studies. She had a plan—she'd study her ass off and become a doctor. Maybe help people like her mother, who couldn't shake their addictions.

If she had more time, she might have helped herself too, but she didn't have time, and she'd never become a doctor, and she'd missed out on her life for nothing.

Grayon covered her hand with his, warmth

seeping into her. "You okay?"

How bad was it when a *stranger* noticed? "I'm fine. Sorry. Short trip down memory lane."

Xandra squeezed her shoulder. Raven tensed for a split second, before forcing a smile on her lips. Shifters were so tactile. Like cuddly animals. That was the only way she saw them, not as friends, companions, and—

"So, big guy, what brings your overly exercised ass to Earth?" Rex asked.

Raven wasn't the only one who noticed his ass, then.

"I'm going to need a real drink for that. Not this foamy water." Grayon shook his empty beer can.

Rex chuckled and left the table, to return with a bottle of Glenfiddich and a couple tumblers. She'd heard of it but never tasted it. Less than a year ago, she swore she'd never touch alcohol. Now she found she liked its taste on her tongue and its burn down her throat. Plus, drinking as much as she pleased and walking it off in minutes was like an *up yours* to all the pain alcohol caused her, growing up.

Rex filled a glass for Grayon and one for himself.

"Don't us girls get any?" Raven asked.

"Xandra hates the stuff, and it's twice your age. You can't have any till your palate is more refined. Be a waste of time now."

She pointed at Grayon. "So *his* palate is refined?"

Rex snorted. "Hardly. But by the look in his eyes, he needs it."

"I might need it too."

Rex studied her face. "Maybe. But not tonight. You get some when you're ready to talk."

And there they went again. Rex had accepted

her into his house and taken her under his wing, no questions asked, but from time to time there was this nudge. Just a reminder he'd one day flat-out ask about her, and she wouldn't be able to refuse.

At first she hadn't shared her past with him and Xandra, *because it was him and Xandra.* She'd known about vampires for months before her turning, but her maker hadn't said much about shifters, other than they weren't to be trusted. When she was done with her training, parts of which included techniques for fighting hostile shifters, she was told there was now a truce, and she had to work on it.

Her maker shipped her halfway across the world, to live under the same roof as someone supposed to be her enemy. Who could relax in that environment?

As time went by, she got to like the diminutive blonde who could kick a master vampire's ass, but by then Raven had created a mystery around her. The truth would be a letdown. She was so stupid.

"I was ousted from The Forest," Grayon said.

Raven forgot her self-flagellation and focused her attention on him.

"Bron, my brother, told me he and Candia were in love. They wanted to mate, but—"

"But Candia was promised to you," Xandra said. "When your family and hers allied."

Raven ignored the stab of jealousy. Seemed alcohol had some effect on her, after all. "Can I have subtitles with that?" she asked in her most disinterested voice.

Chapter Five

The little vampire had teeth, but now he'd seen her pain, this bored façade wasn't convincing.

Grayon sniffed the drink in his hand. It smelled like an evening by the fire. He liked that. "My father and Xenon fought for leadership of the pack. Xenon won, but instead of killing my father, he offered him an alliance. It was a political move—my family comes from old blood and owns vast hunting grounds. To seal it, he promised his newborn daughter as a mate to me. I was two at the time, and unless Xenon produced a male heir, this put me next in line for pack leader." He took a tentative sip of his drink. Just what he needed. Strong enough to make his tongue tingle. He downed a longer gulp.

"Candia and I grew up together. We always knew we were to be mated, but... it wasn't there. I didn't know, but my brother fell for her, and she for him." And Grayon never noticed. "Xenon follows tradition. His word is his contract. There was no telling how he'd react if his daughter told him she meant to break his promise. I had nothing to lose"—he stole a glance at Xandra—"so I went to Xenon and said I wanted out." He polished off his drink and held his glass out for a refill.

"And here you are," Raven said.

"Here I am."

"Was there an official ousting?" Xandra squared her shoulders, her sentinel training showing. "He'd need the Balancers' ruling or a fair trial by the pack elders. Was my father present?"

Grayon shook his head. "Just Xenon and his witch."

"That's against protocol. I'll go see my father. I'll—"

"No, Xandra. It's better this way." Bron could be happy with Candia, and Grayon would be out of their way.

"But it's not right." This came from Raven. "They can't just throw you out, without following the right procedure. You didn't even know where you'd land. Didn't have time to pack. There might have been a less friendly vampire, waiting for you at the portal."

"There are *less* friendly vampires than you?" Grayon smirked despite the direness of his situation.

She glowered, but the corners of her lips tugged upward. "Whatever. I don't care. But it's still wrong."

It was. Wrong and unfair. But Grayon had been nothing but a pain to his family, breaking the Balancers' rules and trying Xenon's patience whenever possible. He hated that his fate had been decided. When he fell for Xandra, he was determined to mate with her and bear the consequences, but she didn't feel that way about him. Sex was sex, and love was love, and what they had was sex. Her words had ripped out his heart. The first time he smelled the vampire on her, he was mad with jealousy, but seeing her here, Rex's hand on her knee, he only felt a dull ache in his gut. Not because he'd lost her, but because he couldn't have what she did.

He looked at Raven, who glanced between him and Xandra and arched an eyebrow. Let her draw her own conclusions. Grayon, Xandra, and Rex knew where they stood.

"Well, I have to go back to patrol," Raven said after a heartbeat. His heartbeat. She didn't have one, because she was a vampire, and he'd better remember that when he thought of how expressive her eyes were.

"Grayon, feel like shadowing her? She'll fill you in on how things are here, and since you're staying, you'll need a job," Rex said.

"He'll slow me down." Raven's protest was weak.

Grayon threw back his second glass and stood. "I'll try to keep up." He stretched and scratched his stomach.

Her gaze followed his hand. So the little vamp wasn't entirely unaffected by him. This could provide a fun distraction. Sexual tension made banter more interesting, even if it could go no further.

And, boy, was there tension.

****

"I follow a different path every night, but the goal is the same. Make sure the surrounding area is clear of vampires outside Rex's rule, and end the night at the portal. Find signs of a newcomer? Track them down and bring them to Rex. He's the ultimate authority on the paranormal scene here." Raven strode ahead, never glancing back at him.

Grayon snorted. "Rex, Master of London."

"Of the entire United Kingdom, to be precise."

This time he laughed. "We're talking about the guy who couldn't be convinced to be in charge of twenty sentinels?"

"Huh?" She turned on her heel but didn't stop moving. She walked backward, watching him.

"Never mind. Reminiscing."

Her focus slashed to the right, and she disappeared inside an alley. She was too fast for him to follow in human form, even when he called his wolf to the surface, but he turned the corner after her anyway. He didn't have to go far. She was by a trash can at the end of the block, and she wasn't alone.

She hovered a few inches above ground, a man dangling by her hand. Grayon stopped a couple feet away and watched as she shook the human. Raven's fangs were out, and judging by the stain in the guy's pants and the smell of urine, he knew they weren't fake.

"You touch *any* woman again, and my face will be the last thing you see," Raven hissed. "I'll tear out your throat. I won't even drink your filthy blood; just have you watch while it spills on the ground, until your worthless life is spent."

Grayon took a step closer, and one of the garbage bags by the wall moved. Not a bag. A woman.

He rushed to her and helped her up. Her face was paper white, except for the blood on her lips and the angry bruise on her cheekbone, and she trembled like a leaf.

She winced away from him when their gazes met, and Grayon realized he'd allowed his wolf too close to the surface.

He forced the beast down and took a step back, open palms in the air. "I'm not going to hurt you." He kept his voice calm, though he wanted to rip to shreds the man who'd hurt her. "I only wanted to make sure you're okay."

"Will she kill him?" she asked in a heavy accent. She sounded the tiniest bit hopeful, and Grayon couldn't hold back a grin.

"Not tonight, but she'll make sure he never comes near you again. Right, Raven?"

"Right."

"I'll never go near her again. Please don't kill me."

Raven held on to the worthless sack of bones for a couple of heartbeats and then dropped him to sag on the dirty street. He got his footing and ran away without a backward glance. Raven turned to the woman with a sweet smile. "Is there someone we can call for you?" she asked.

"No. My family is in Poland. He brought me here. Promised me a job. But he—" Her sob broke Grayon's heart.

Raven gathered the woman into her arms, her gentleness surprising after she'd made a grown man piss his pants. "Look at me, hon," she said.

The woman sniffled and pulled away to meet her gaze.

"There is an abused women's center a few blocks from here. Tell them Raven sent you. They'll take care of you. Do you have papers?"

The woman shook her head. "Thomas has my passport." She tilted her head toward the direction the man fled in.

Grayon stepped next to Raven. "Tell us where to find him."

Chapter Six

Why did he have to be kind hearted on top of hot? So unfair.

He insisted they walk the woman—Raven didn't do names; they were so many, she couldn't afford to get attached—to the shelter, and then joined Raven in raiding Thomas's place. The sleaze-ball wasn't there, but Raven and Grayon found his two partners and a dozen women's passports.

She wanted to tear the men limb from limb, but Grayon held her back. He had a better suggestion, he said.

She didn't know if it was better, but it was fun watching them go to the police and turn themselves in for human trafficking.

"You all right?" Grayon asked, dusting his knees.

She hadn't expected him to clear the fence of Richmond Park with a single leap. Another impressive thing about him. "Sure. Now, don't go chasing down the deer, or the royal army will be all up our asses."

He grabbed her elbow and spun her toward him. "I'm serious. This night can't have been easy for you."

"How do you know about things here, anyway? How are you not all googly-eyed at the cars and the shelters and the all-night stores?" She looked at the trees behind him. Easier to focus on the foliage than on his eyes. She felt naked under that gaze.

"Raven—"

She shook him off and started toward the portal. "No, seriously. I mean, you don't use cutlery, but you're clearly civilized"—

"Gee, thanks."

—"and you take everything in stride. It's like you've been here before."

He caught up with her and matched her stride. "I have. Before the truce. Jumped on an opportunity to get away from everything for a while. It was an undercover mission. The Balancers sent me to keep tabs on Rex, before he was called to save the universes."

"Cool."

"Yeah, he made me on my first day but let me trail him for a few moons, while he visited the least respectable establishments he could find. My reports were not appreciated by Xenon."

She could see that.

"Do you do this often? Go after men for hurting women?" he asked.

"When I can. May as well put this new strength and shit in use, right?"

"Right. So it's not personal at all."

She was that transparent, huh? "It's cheaper than therapy."

Grayon snorted. "More fun, too."

"Yeah." She sniffed the night air, careful not to let the mix of scents overwhelm her senses. Once was once too many, as she'd realized the first time she inhaled deeply after her turning. Without a self-imposed filter, the stimuli could short circuit her brain long enough for an attacker to take advantage.

She looked at Grayon. She doubted an attacker would take his chances with him around. She'd bested him because he'd underestimated her, but she doubted he'd make that mistake again.

"Want to talk about it?"

His question startled her. "About what?"

"Where you just went. Why you trawl the night for wrongdoers. Why you shut down when I mention it."

She shrugged.

"Tell me anything," he said.

"I was dying when Vassili found me." She hadn't meant to answer him, but once the first words were out, she couldn't stop. "Brain tumor. He was in the hospital for a snack—blood bank, not a human—and heard me groan as he passed by my room. I didn't know vampires existed, but there was something about him... I asked him to kill me. He wouldn't. He started visiting. Feeding me his blood. It didn't do much for the cancer, but it strengthened the rest of me.

"His visits were the highlight of my day. My mom never came to see me. We didn't see each other much since I left home, and I didn't reach out when I was diagnosed. Vassili came to read to me every night, and every night I asked him to finish me off. I was done fighting. I was so tired. When he refused to kill me, I decided I wanted to be like him. He wouldn't hear of it."

"Was he in love with you?"

"Nothing like that. I reminded him of his little sister. Same hair and eyes. Same stubborn streak, he said."

"I wonder why he'd call you stubborn."

They were almost at the portal, and she turned to scowl at him. His expression was so serious and open, she had to look away. "I found a discarded razor and hid it under my mattress. When Vassili came to wish me a happy birthday, he found me with my wrists sliced."

"And he turned you." No judgement in his voice.

"And he turned me. And he trained me. And then he sent me here."

Grayon nodded.

"He couldn't face me as a vampire, I think. He liked caring for me temporarily, but not on a full-time basis." She kicked a patch of grass. "Story of my life. And unlife."

She didn't realize she'd stopped walking, until Grayon circled her and stood before her. She raised her gaze to his, and found him studying her with an intensity that warmed her chest and turned her legs weak.

"What?" She had to say something. Cut the moment short, before she let him see more of her.

"For a vampire, you're all right."

She batted his arm, lingering a second too long on the hard muscle. "You sure know how to make a girl feel special."

His gaze turned smoldering, and Raven gulped.

"We'll revisit that at a later date," he said. "It's been a long night, and there's no trace of an intruder. I say we go back."

Good idea. "I need a hot shower and a long sleep."

"Lead the way."

*

He wasn't used to following, but the view made up for it. Whether Raven always swished her ass this way or was still getting used to her sky-high heels, her every step made her round buttocks jiggle and Grayon's cock threaten the integrity of his pants.

Her ass took his mind off everything else he *didn't* hate about her. She was strong and didn't hesitate to do the right thing. Vampires were supposed to be self-serving—it came with immortality—but she hadn't hesitated to jump the guy in the alley and risk exposure, when she saw the young woman in danger.

And how she dealt with the two men in the apartment… Grayon did his part, punching and kicking, but he let her run the show. And she was glorious. He'd never expect a woman of her petite stature to command fear the way she did.

But her strength wasn't only a result of her turning and training. It came from inside.

Grayon hadn't missed the way her spine tensed when she spoke of her past. Her voice was impassive, but there was more to the story. More to her.

He couldn't waste time figuring her out. He had to be a model representative of his pack long enough for word to get back to Xenon. Then Grayon would ask Xandra to arrange him a hearing. He'd fight his way back to The Forest and resume his life, this time with nobody ruling his destiny. There was no room for a fiery little vamp in this plan. Not even one with an ass like that and eyes filled with secrets and pain.

Chapter Seven

The shower was supposed to calm him.

He was still dealing with whiplash from finding himself in the Earth plane, let alone sharing lodgings with two vampires, but it wasn't his nerves he wanted to soothe. Those were taken care of by the night-long trek through the city and the ass-whopping he and Raven had dealt.

It was other urges that needed taming, and he thought the quick rub under the water jet would tide him over till morning.

But it didn't.

He blamed his superhuman hearing for that. He could make out the creaking of Raven's bed every time she moved, and she moved a lot. Short, quick pumps. Sheets rustling. And was that...? The tiniest moan reached his ears, muffled but distinct.

Fuck.

Raven was either hard at work polishing her shoes in bed, or she was pleasuring herself, and there was only a thin wall between them. He flared his nostrils. He could smell her too. The undertones of magic were mixed with the heady musk of raw desire.

His wolf jumped up, rearing to burst through him and tear his way to her. His skin felt too tight to contain him, and he was glad he'd gone to bed naked, or his body heat would burn through the clothes. He tossed the sheets aside and crossed the room, to plant both palms on the wall.

The wolf twisted inside. Howled to be set free. His nails grew, scraping indentations in the plaster, and it took all he had to drive the beast back down. He never had trouble controlling his second nature before, but Raven teased the animal as much as she did the man.

He let his head drop forward, but the cold surface did nothing for the fire inside, as Raven's moans grew in urgency and volume.

Xandra and Rex would hear her.

A growl spilled from Grayon's chest.

Why did he care who fucking heard her?

"Grayon?" The word was whispered, but he heard it.

The wolf howled again. Clawed its way out.

Grayon forced himself to the window and moved aside the heavy drapes. Rays of morning sun spilled inside the room. He couldn't go out now; if he lost control of the wolf in broad daylight, *in fucking London*, there'd be chaos.

He let the curtain fall back in place and took a deep breath. The beast wanted to be unleashed, and he'd have to do it indoors. Not like he turned into a mindless monster. He was a housetrained wolf. One who was done waiting.

Grayon fell on all fours, letting the change wash over him. It wasn't painful if he rode it out instead of trying to hold it back. He shook his head, feeling his ears prick. His mouth and nose elongated, and his limbs were realigned. For a second or two, his body turned fluid, allowing the beast to fill him and take over.

He shook his head.

Buzzing. Came with the change.

The female vampire smelled good. Delicious.

Worse—familiar.

She called to him.

He padded to the door. Whined. Turned back. He couldn't go to her. Shouldn't. He paced a circle around the room. And another. And again. Head and tail low. Hear her better. Feel the ground. No threat there.

He flicked out his tongue. Taste the air. Taste her scent.

Vampire but more.

Not food.

Something else.

And calling to him.

*

"Grayon?" Raven said again.

She had no clue what she'd do if he answered, but she had to know if he heard her. What would he do if he did?

Unsatisfied and embarrassed, she slid her hand out of her boy shorts and listened. His breathing had changed. The rhythmic inhale and exhale was what got her hot and bothered to begin with. She hadn't been this close to a breathing man in a while. The memory of his incredible body didn't hurt. And those eyes were dangerous. She could lose herself in them.

She wanted to touch herself again, this time to completion, but curiosity took over. For a second he'd sounded right next to her, but not anymore. He was panting now, and...

It took a second to pinpoint exactly what was

off, but the mental picture of a big, shaggy dog flashed before her eyes, and it all clicked in place.

He'd shifted. Crap. Rex would kill him if he ruined the carpeting. Why would he shift? The human nature was supposed to be prevalent. There was always a reason behind the change, even if that was to frolic under the moon. But this was the middle of the day, and Grayon didn't seem the frolicking type.

Was he about to run off again?

Without much thought, Raven got out of bed and pulled on a tank top, before leaving her room.

She called his name once more and gave a soft knock on his door, but the only sound that reached her was that of his beating heart. Faster than before.

She had to go in. Make sure everything was okay.

"It's me. I won't hurt you, if you don't attack me." She wouldn't hurt him anyway. Just subdue him, if need be.

Raven turned the handle and nudged the door open, careful not to seem threatening. She'd been told shifters didn't completely lose their human nature in their animal form. Their instincts took over, but the beast wouldn't do something the man didn't agree with. And deep down, Grayon didn't want to kill her.

She tried to remember that, as she looked into the bright-yellow eyes of a two-hundred-pound gray wolf.

Grayon was at least twice the size of any wolf she'd ever seen at the zoo. Bigger than werewolves on TV. His fur was more silver than gray, but it was his canines that drew her attention. Those things were longer than her fingers.

"*Fuck.* Nice doggie." She took a step back, trying to figure out the best strategy. Should she close the door and let him wreck the room, if he so pleased, till she got Rex and Xandra? Should she try to talk him into changing back?

Should she pet that gorgeous pelt?

The wolf tilted his head, studying her.

"Grayon, Rex will pitch a fit if you go feral on me. What happened? Change back, and we'll talk about it."

The wolf lowered his butt, as if to sit, and Raven only got a split second to realize he was going to leap, before he landed on her and sent her sprawling across the hall. His weight pinned her to the floor.

Raven was about to deal him a blow, when she realized he wasn't attacking. He wagged his tail like a dog and burrowed his muzzle in her neck, to sniff her. It tickled and was so far beyond weird, there was no name invented for it yet.

She dug her fingers in his back, meaning to dislodge him, but his fur felt like silk beneath her fingertips, and she let herself luxuriate in the feel.

"You need to let me up now," she said.

He gave her a wet doggy kiss across the face.

"Yuck. Grayon, off. Roll over. Go away. What's the matter with you?"

She had no warning other than a spiking of heat where his body touched her bare skin, and then she wasn't pressed down by a humongous wolf, but by a very big, very naked man.

Grayon's human face looked down at her, but his eyes were still ringed with yellow as he lowered his head and closed his lips over hers. He wedged one hand behind her neck, to pull her closer, and Raven let him, because her brain had stopped working. Everything she was, everything she had, focused on the demanding tongue tracing her mouth, on the soft lips that pulled sighs out of hers, and on his unique scent of trees and clean air and fresh-cut grass. He smelled like *life*.

He rolled to the side, taking her with him, and dragged his free palm up her leg and then higher, under her top, to cup her breast. She was amazed at the gentleness his large hands were capable of. He rolled the nipple between his fingers. Pinched it.

She moaned in his mouth and dug her nails in his shoulder when he let go of her breast to caress her belly.

He was hard and long against her leg. If she let this go on, they'd soon be rutting like animals. On the floor. Out in the corridor, where anyone could walk in on them.

Rex and Xandra.

Rex could walk in the sun since mating with Xandra, but they still preferred to sleep during the day, since the night was best for prowling the city. Their bedroom was in the cellar, but that wasn't far enough for them not to hear the sounds of longing and need that tore from her throat.

Grayon inched his hand inside the elastic band of her shorts, spreading her thighs apart with his knee. His touch burned her skin and warmed her core. His heartbeat reverberated through her ribcage. Her body hummed with unspent energy. If he so much as tapped her clit, she'd come apart. He pumped his hips, and his cock nudged her inner thigh. God, he was so big. He'd rip her in two, but she'd enjoy every second of it.

If she let him in.

"No." She pushed him with her vampire strength.

Grayon flew off her body and landed hunched over by her feet. He straightened, caught her gaze, and smiled.

She got a good look at his body in all its glory, and committed it to memory—the muscles rippling under the tan skin; the dark hair on his chest, thinning to a sprinkle down his stomach, and the short thatch around his cock; his long, thick shaft standing at attention and glistening with precum.

He rolled his shoulders and then held out a hand for her. "Let me help you up."

As if he wasn't stark naked and hard.

She took his palm, hopped up, and dusted the seat of her shorts.

As if she didn't want to hump his bones.

He smiled again and turned toward his room, allowing her a good view of his wide back and that ass she was dying to bite. "Sleep tight, little vampire."

"Yeah. You too."

As if that was an option.

Chapter Eight

This time Grayon kept the wolf at bay while Raven got herself off. He needed his hands too much, to let the beast take over. The memory of her lithe body writhing beneath him taunted him. He pulled on his cock in time to her moans, and came shortly after they stopped.

No matter what she said or how she ran off, for a while there, she'd responded to him with a heat no vampire was supposed to exhibit. It was a pleasant surprise and a welcome break from his new reality. Not that he'd pursue it further. Their attraction played no part in the grand scheme of things. Fucking hot or not, that kiss was nothing but a brief distraction.

What amazed him was that his wolf had scented her arousal and stepped back for the man to take over. That wasn't usual. His wolf's first instinct around fangers was to attack, and it had taken getting to know Rex and Aherin and fighting alongside them for weeks, before the beast was at ease around them.

But he didn't mind Raven. He was playful when he jumped her, and she knew, or she'd have kicked him away. Weird, but not enough to keep him from drifting off. Unlike vampires, shifters weren't purely nocturnal, and he was worn out.

And hard again.

He was still hard when he got up at dusk, and was extremely grateful when Xandra knocked on his door to bring in his clothes, clean and dry. Clothes at The Forest were made of organic fibers that smelled and felt infinitely better than those on the Earth plane. More importantly, his pants were of a thick enough material to hide his raging hard on, unlike those flimsy things he wore last night.

He heard Raven head downstairs and felt a pang of disappointment that she didn't stop by his room. Eh, he'd put their interlude behind him. She probably chose to forget it.

In the bathroom, he checked himself out in the mirror. His beard had grown. It grew faster here than at The Forest. Inconvenient. He found disposable razors in the cabinet and took care of that, before joining the others in the kitchen.

He found Raven, Rex, and Xandra at the kitchen table. The scent of blood and something bitter wafted off the mugs the vampires held. He scrunched his nose at the coffee maker. How did people consume this murky concoction? He filled a glass of water and grabbed a slice of pizza from the counter. Now *this* smelled nice. Nice and meaty.

Rex glanced at him, and one corner of his mouth twitched. "Enjoy your rest?"

Grayon looked at Raven, who avoided his gaze. "Can't complain," he said.

Raven ducked her head and took a sip of blood. Her hair and mug hid her face, but not before Grayon saw her grin.

"Some noise kept me up," he said. "It sounded like someone trying to rub off a stain."

"Or something," Xandra added, straight faced.

"Could be a threat. We need to be vigilant. I say we expand patrol round the clock for a few days. Grayon and Raven, you take the night shift, since Raven can't do days. Xandra and I will go out in the mornings." Rex looked very satisfied with himself, and Grayon arched an eyebrow.

Was Rex pushing for him and Raven to be alone at the house?

"But no supernaturals are out in the morning." Raven seemed perplexed.

Xandra shrugged. "I guess we'll find another way to fill our time."

****

"I guess it's really important to Xandra and Rex that we're on good terms, huh?"

Grayon looked at Raven like he hadn't heard what she said.

"Xandra and Rex?" she said. "Inventing a threat, to get us to spend time together?"

"So it's not just me who noticed."

"Nope. Not just you." She'd have to be blind not to see the looks between the mated couple, but she kept her snarky demeanor contained. Grayon would be her patrolling partner for however long he was here, and they had to keep things civil. Besides, snark led to temperatures rising, and she already had a hard time keeping her clothes on around him.

"Let's go this way." He took a sharp left.

Camden was that way, and a trip in the clubs wasn't a bad idea. Prime feeding spots for vamps. Rex had approved hunting, as long as there were no casualties, but her kind could use the reminder that someone was watching.

She hurried to match his stride without snapping her ankle—not that she'd have lasting damage, but *ow*. "What's the rush? We have all night."

"We don't have to stay outside the entire time. There's two of us now. We can work faster and maybe have some fun." The brief glance he threw her over his shoulder made her step falter. There was pure hunger in his eyes.

Have some fun? Was he saying—?

He headed for a building with a flashing red sign promising all sorts of debauchery. "Besides, I didn't get much sleep yesterday."

Yeah, neither did she, but she wasn't sure they'd rest if they went home early. And was that such a bad thing? Sure, their kinds had been enemies once, but not any longer, even if people like her maker insisted that was the case. The frickin' Master of the city was mated to a shifter. Why would it matter if Raven slept with one? She was no longer the timid med student who cared about saving the world, and yet she did more for that world now. She deserved *some* concessions.

"Coming?" Grayon stood at the opening of the club door, he and the bouncer looking at her with matching perplexed expressions.

She'd bypassed them and kept walking, lost inside her head. "Sure. Sorry. Thought I heard something over here."

Grayon didn't seem convinced by her lie. He studied her with narrowed eyes, as the bouncer stepped aside to let her in. The loud noise that passed for music threatened to blast her eardrums, but she managed to tune it down, if not out.

"You okay, little vampire?" Grayon whispered in her ear.

She had enough of this little-vampire shit. "Don't let my size fool you, pooch. I can cause more pain than you can imagine," she replied in the same hushed voice.

"*There* she is." He chuckled. "I was afraid I broke you yesterday."

So they acknowledged *yesterday*? It wasn't some hormone-induced aftereffect of his shifting? "You'll have to try a lot harder than that, to break me."

Wrong thing to say. She saw it in the pursing of his lips, before he even said, "I'll keep that in mind."

"Is that a threat or a promise?" Shit. She had to learn to keep her mouth shut.

With a speed that could match her own, he grabbed her by the shoulders and spun her around. Before she could shake him off, he had her face pressed against the nearest wall, Grayon's body draped over hers. He took hold of her wrists and raised them over her head. She was more than a foot shorter than him, even in her sky-high boots, and his erection dug into her back.

She wanted to climb higher on that mother-fucking wall and feel him against her ass. She put up a semblance of a fight, but Grayon didn't let go.

He pumped his hips, so she felt his entire length. "You tell me if you feel threatened, *little vampire,*" he growled in her ear.

"Not even a little bit"—she craned her neck and rubbed her cheek against his stubble—"but points for trying."

He let go of her with an uproarious laugh. "Yeah, you're fun."

Raven followed him through the crowd, smiling. This was the first time anyone said something like that to her. Usually she was stuffy, boring... predictable. A control freak.

Felt good to be stepping outside her comfort zone, though she'd still rather be roaming the streets than in a nightclub.

Grayon put some distance between them, but with his height, he stood out above the swarm of undulating bodies. Raven spotted him making a beeline for a group of women about her age. Dressed in the bare essentials, they swirled their drinks and swayed to the music.

And they watched him like he was lunch.

Raven stopped trailing him. Nobody would notice in that chaos, so she hovered a few inches above the ground and zeroed her gaze in on him. He reached the women, and Raven's blood boiled. His body language screamed *seduction*, and his eyes held the same dark promises they did when she lay pinned beneath him.

The dirty dog was shirking his responsibilities, to get some tail.

And how stupid was she, for pretending his lack of vigilance was what bugged her?

Grayon wrapped one arm around the woman closer to him and buried his face in her neck.

Raven couldn't look. She didn't want to see him make out with the gorgeous stranger. With anyone. Stupid, *stupid* for allowing herself to want him, and even stupider for feeling this territorial over someone who could never be hers. As she turned away, something glimmered in her peripheral vision. She whirled back toward them, and saw the woman's eyes flash an eerie green. Her friends giggled and nudged each other, but the smile on the woman's face was no longer flirty. It was pained.

Grayon lifted his head and looked straight at Raven. He gave a weird little nod that might mean *follow me*, and led the woman toward the exit, his arm still circling her waist.

Chapter Nine

Grayon pushed Sibyla out the door and inhaled deeply. Even the stale London air smelled fresh, compared to the stench of sweaty bodies inside.

Yet another reason to count himself lucky—tonight's patrol was done.

Sibyla had joined the vampire mage whose quest for power had threatened to destroy all realms. She turned against her people and wounded Xenon near-fatally. As a sentinel, Grayon had spent months looking for her all over The Forest. He'd had to sample her poison, to be able to spot her faint scent. When he picked it up tonight, he couldn't believe his luck.

The door whooshed open again, and he turned to see Raven slip out. Her lips were pursed in annoyance. "Our job isn't to find you bed warmers, *doggie*. We're supposed to be looking for paranormal activity."

He let out a chuckle that sounded loud as a gunshot in the quiet of the night. "Guess you don't recognize her kind." He jabbed Sibyla on the ribs with his fingers. "Whistle for the lady?"

"Fuck you." Pity there were no *S*'s in that, or

she'd have made his point for him.

"Sibyla is a weresnake."

Raven gave him a blank stare.

"She shifts into a snake," he said.

Raven huffed. "I get what a weresnake is. I just can't believe she's a *were* anything. She smells normal."

"That's the thing about them. They assimilate in the environment and have little-to-no smell of magic." Sibyla tried to pry his arm off her waist, and he squeezed tighter. "But they can't shift while someone's holding them."

"Thank fuck for that. I hate snakes." Raven chewed on her bottom lip, while she studied Sibyla. "Are you registered?" she asked.

Grayon laughed. "If she was, she'd have been shipped back to The Forest. People are looking for here there."

Sibyla twisted in his grasp and hissed. "You're out of your jurisdiction, Sentinel."

"Yeah—well—I'm not, and I'm taking you to the Master." Raven reached for Sibyla's shoulder before Grayon could stop her.

Sibyla darted her head down, and Raven jumped back, clasping her own wrist. "The bitch bit me."

Shit. "Raven, sit down."

"Like hell I will." She swayed on her feet and let go of her arm, to touch her forehead. "What—"

Grayon barely had time to grab her, before her eyes rolled back and she flopped against him.

Great. He had both arms full, and Sibyla wouldn't stop thrashing and kicking.

"I'll bite her again," she said. "Then I'll bite you."

He head-butted the side of her skull as hard as he could, and she went limp. He wouldn't mind two gorgeous women pressed against him under most circumstances, but this was the exception.

He gently rolled Raven to the ground. "Her bite releases a paralytic toxin. It'll wear off soon, and in the meantime, I've got you. I'll take you home. I just have to secure this one first." Raven couldn't move, but he knew she heard him. He ripped his shirt into long strips, and used one of them to tie Sibyla's arms behind her back and two more to cover her mouth, so she couldn't bite him. Then he threw her over his shoulder and did the same with Raven.

Now his head was squeezed between two exquisite asses. He was one lucky bastard.

He let the wolf out enough for his supernatural speed to kick in, and ran back to the house, mindful to avoid prying gazes.

He kicked open the front door and hollered for Xandra.

She rushed up the stairs from the underground bedroom she shared with Rex. "Bring the house down, why don't you?" One glance at Grayon's cargo, and the snark was gone. "What happened? Is Raven okay?"

"She will be, or Sibyla's dead."

"Sibyla?" Xandra helped him unload the unconscious weresnake. "You found her? That's huge. It could get you back—"

"Contact Xenon. Tell him I found his traitor and demand a hearing." Grayon was already heading upstairs. He rearranged Raven in his arms.

"And Raven?" Xandra called behind him.

"I'll take care of her."

*

She didn't need to be taken care of. She wasn't a child. She was a scary vampire, and she'd prove it as soon as she could move again.

When she collapsed behind the club, terror gripped her insides. She remembered the days the tumor consumed her brain, leaving her helpless.

She remembered being helpless long before that.

Grayon could have left her behind, but he didn't. He carried her in those big, hard arms of his, even though she was a pain in his ass. She hoped she didn't drool on his back while he rushed them home.

He held her pressed to his chest, and she let his scent wash over her. Seep into her pores. He smelled so good. Grayon and leather and clean sweat. She wanted to make him sweat, and not with the effort of bringing her home before sunrise.

God, she couldn't move her *eyeballs*, but she was thinking of sex with a shifter? And one about to leave for good, if the hearing he requested went well.

"Raising your body temperature will help," he whispered in her hair. "I'll run you a warm bath. No funny business."

She tried to shake her head. Form the word *no* with her lips. Nothing. It was like being buried alive inside her own body.

Grayon laid her on his bed, and she reeled. He'd strip her. She was helpless and at the mercy of a very large, very strong man she'd only known a couple days. A man she was exceedingly attracted to, but that didn't lessen her horror at how exposed she was and how easy it'd be for him to—

No. The way he'd treated the woman yesterday, he'd never take advantage of Raven. If he did, she'd kill him as soon as she regained control of her body.

Grayon made quick work of her boots, then undid her leather pants and pulled them down her legs, never touching her skin. He left her underwear on and moved to undo her bustier. The laces in the front gave him trouble, and he let go with a frustrated sigh.

"I'll never hear the end of it, but I need to do this," he said. Then he grabbed the two sides of the thing and pulled until the laces snapped and air caressed her breasts.

"Shit," he whispered, and she heard him walk out of the room.

Raven hadn't cried since the first time her mother chose a random man over her. She didn't even cry when she was diagnosed with terminal cancer; she just shook her head at the irony of a life that allowed her to get out of the shit she'd grown up in, only to land her the final blow.

She cried now, though. Silently and without tears, she cried for the fear and loneliness she'd tried so hard to ignore for years. *Please don't go. Don't leave me here. Please, Grayon.*

As if summoned by her thoughts, he appeared over her and wrapped her body in a warm, fuzzy towel. He took her to the bathroom and only uncovered her to submerge her in hot, bubbly water that smelled of roses. Except for the being-paralyzed part, this could be a romantic date.

He sat by the tub, holding her head out of the water with a palm at the base of her neck. She was grateful. Vampires couldn't drown, but having water fill her nostrils wouldn't be pleasant, even if her lungs didn't work to suck it in.

She didn't know how long they stayed there, but the water was room temperature when he lifted her out. He draped the towel over her again and patted her skin gently. "I'm sorry. I have to do this." He sounded really sorry, and warmth that had nothing to do with the bath spread in her belly.

Grayon took her to her bed this time, and called

Xandra to change Raven into a dry pair of boy shorts. Once Xandra was gone, he closed the door, and Raven heard the rustling of clothes. "I don't have underwear, but I'll keep the sheets around me," he said.

Raven didn't get what he meant, until he slipped in bed next to her and turned her so her back was flush against his chest. He pulled a blanket over them and folded one arm around her waist. "Shifters can maintain a higher body temperature than humans. I'll warm you up. Try to sleep. You should be back to normal in a few hours."

Raven tried to figure out how long that would be. No way would she manage to drift off when she couldn't even shut her eyes.

His warm skin and the weight of his arm made her feel safer than she ever remembered being. If she could, she'd laugh at the irony. She'd never felt safe around men who were stronger than her—had seen up close how strength could be abused. Grayon wouldn't hurt her, though. Not physically.

He could still break her in a million pieces inside if she let him close enough, but for now, she'd allow herself the respite of a living hard body against hers and the odd sense of freedom that suffused her in the steely prison of his arms.

*

Grayon couldn't tell if she was awake. Her stillness worried him. The effects of the poison were temporary, and the sun was still high in the sky, but his heart sank more with every second that ticked by. Shouldn't she be up by now, yelling at him for being naked in her bed?

Which led to another question. Why wasn't he hard?

His body reacted to her from the beginning, yet now, with only a bunched-up sheet between him and her perfect ass, his cock was on strike. Was something wr—

Raven arched her back and let out a little moan.

Nope. Nothing wrong with him. He was hard as a rock now. He withdrew his arm and inched toward the wall, allowing some space between them. "You okay? Can you move your arms and legs?"

She stretched on her back and raised her arms over her head. "Yes. Thank God." A breast peeked from under the covers, but she didn't move to hide it, and he kept his gaze to her face.

Her pupils were dilated. He'd been too panicked to notice earlier, but it had to be an effect of the poison.

"I didn't think I could sleep," she said.

"I couldn't tell if you did." He gave her an easy smile, while his heart thundered in his ears. She was fine and looking at him with those big, green eyes, and her breast would fit perfectly inside his palm—it had before. He wanted to pinch the pink tip, but this was not the right time.

His beast howled inside.

Entirely not the right time.

He should be getting up and away. She should be kicking him out of her bed.

Instead, she rolled to the side, to face him. "Thank you."

He shrugged one shoulder.

"No, really. For bringing me back. For warming me up. For everything."

"I couldn't leave you there. Rex would have my ass, remember?"

She let her hand hover over his forearm for a heartbeat, before ghosting her fingertips over his skin. "It wasn't just that you helped. You were—" She snorted. "I've learned to see the worst in people. You could have... done things. I wouldn't have been able to stop you."

Grayon recoiled. He didn't know what hurt more—that she considered him capable of such treatment, or that she'd been conditioned to expect it. "I should go, since you're okay." He sat up, but she pressed him back down on the mattress.

"Please don't leave me. I was so scared when I couldn't move. I couldn't fight." She turned her gaze to the ceiling. "My mom was nice. I think she loved me. But she was weak and would do anything for a hit. Her taste in men was bad. *Bad.* I had to always be on the lookout. Never got a full night's sleep. Was always ready to bolt. One time I wasn't fast enough."

Grayon growled, and it wasn't the wolf part of him.

She shook her head. "He didn't do much. Too drunk for... *that.* But he was big, and I was fourteen, and he touched me and made me touch him."

An iron fist clenched around his chest, making his heart ache and his lungs cry for air. He wanted to yell. Curse. Find the man and make him pay. Fucking *end* him. His gut instinct told him this wasn't what Raven needed, though. She needed him to hear her out, so he kept silent, man and wolf vowing to keep her safe at whatever cost.

"He passed out cold at some point, and I ran to my mom. She didn't believe me. She called me a slut. Said I seduced him. That I wanted to make them all love me more."

What mother could say those words to her little girl? What mother thought that of the child she raised, when that child went to her for help? Grayon was enraged on Raven's behalf. He wanted to erase everything that ever stole the smile from her face.

"That was the day I realized I was on my own," Raven said. "He wasn't the last man to come to my bedroom uninvited, but I'd learned my lesson and kept a knife under my pillow. As soon as I hit sixteen, I got emancipated. I worked at a diner to put myself through school. It took longer than it should to graduate, but I didn't give up. All I did was eat, sleep, work, and study. No partying. No fun. A couple of boys that didn't last long. I'd have time for everything else later. When I got in premed, I thought life was finally paying up its debts to me." She gave a dry chuckle. "I guess cancer didn't get that memo."

Chapter Ten

She studied his eyes, challenging him to look at her with pity. If he did, he was out of there. She didn't want him to be sorry for her. She didn't know why she said as much as she did. She was only supposed to explain why the paralysis had freaked her out, but then she'd bared herself to him, and his lack of a reaction unnerved her.

"You can talk now," she said. "Or not. Whatever."

Grayon gathered her close and tucked her head under his chin. "Little vampire, none of this was your fault."

What a shitty thing to say. Of course none of it was her fault.

She knew that.

But maybe sometimes, alone in bed, she wondered if she did something to make her mother's boyfriends come on to her. If she'd somehow sinned and her tumor was a punishment. If she was broken.

She buried her face in Grayon's chest and allowed herself a luxury she hadn't in forever. She let the tears roll unchecked down her cheeks, until they emptied the pain from her soul, if only for the day. She felt light and new. Newer than after her change.

She fell asleep with wet eyes and a smile on her face, while Grayon caressed her hair and her back.

Raven woke up with what felt like a black hole in her stomach. The house was quiet—no sounds from Rex or Xandra—so it was still day. A dull throb nagged between her legs. It wasn't the first time her bloodthirst mingled with another base need, but this time was different. She could sate one hunger.

Sometime in her sleep, she'd climbed on top of Grayon. The sheets had slipped away, and his cock pulsed against her pussy. She wished she were naked too. She looked up and saw him watching her. His expression was unreadable, but his heart thudded under her chest.

He emanated a quiet strength. No, a *vibrancy.* He was vibrant, and when she was with him, she hummed with his energy. She needed to feel him inside. Screw logic and ancient feuds, and screw being cautious her entire life. For once, she'd go after something, not because it would be beneficial in the long-run, but because it fucking made her feel good. She licked dry lips and propped herself on her elbows. The sprinkle of hair on his chest grazed her nipples and made them stand erect. Or maybe it was the vein on his neck that had that effect.

"Raven..." His deep bass resonated in her core.

"Mm-hmm?" She gyrated her hips once and was thrilled when he thrust against her.

"You haven't thought this through."

"I've done enough thinking for two lifetimes." She sat up and slid along his length, once again marveling at his size. "Now I want to feel."

He drew his gaze from her eyes to her lips, down to her exposed breasts, before he looked away with a groan. When he spoke again, it was through clenched teeth. "You don't know what you're asking. Shifters and vampires… I don't know how my wolf would react. He might take over and attack you."

"Liar. Your wolf acted like a pup around me. He'd never hurt me." She didn't know where this confidence came from. She hadn't been turned down before, because she'd never approached a man. She'd been too busy building a future.

Grayon's pupils were dilated, and his breath came in short bursts. He flared his nostrils. "I'm trying to do the right thing, Raven, but I'm holding on by a thread. Move your ass one more time, and that thread will snap."

She swiveled her hips. "You mean like this?"

His growl bounced around the small room. He grabbed her ass with both hands and spread the cheeks. "Last chance to stop this," he whispered. "Then I take you."

She grinned around elongated fangs and dragged her nails down his chest. "*Snap.*"

*

He skated his palms up her back, tangled his fingers in her hair, and pulled her to him for a kiss. He could lose himself in her mouth. He'd thought it'd be weird, kissing a vampire—expected her skin to feel waxy. But it wasn't. She was living porcelain, though nowhere near as fragile.

She gave as good as she got, nipping his lips and sucking on his tongue, as if her unlife depended on it. She let out a tiny mewl when he traced her spine with one hand. He bunched her underwear in his fist. One sharp yank, and the elastic snapped. A second, and he shredded them and tossed them aside.

He cupped one firm breast and flicked his thumb over the nipple. When she moaned into his mouth, he twisted the hard bud. Rubbed it between his fingers. She felt different to any female he'd bedded. She had less muscle tone, but that wasn't it. The undercurrent of power beneath her skin was nothing like that of a shifter. He wanted to experience more of it.

Raven broke the kiss and licked a path down his throat. She moved lower, until his cock nudged her entrance. He'd felt how wet she was and smelled her arousal, but her bare pussy teasing his cock tested his self-control. His need for her overcame all but the last traces of his reason.

She sliced a thin line over his nipple with one fang. It barely stung, but he wasn't thrilled with the idea of a vampire spilling his blood. Until she closed her mouth over the cut and swirled her tongue over it. He'd heard vamp bite released some sort of endorphin, but this was incredible.

"Fuck." He wanted her now. Wanted to flip them over and pound her into the mattress. But he wanted to see what she had in mind more.

"That's the plan." She raised her hips over him, but he stilled her with a hand on her hip.

Foreplay wasn't a big thing in The Forest. A good run or fight or laugh—anything that got the blood pumping—was enough of a lead-in to the main course. Sex was easy fun. But Raven used to be human, and for all he knew, she hadn't been with anyone since her turning. "We should take it slow. I can prepare you." If he only got this one time with her, he wanted it to be memorable.

She shook her head, her face pinched in concentration.

"Sure you can take me?" It'd kill him to stop

now, but he would, if she wasn't into this.

"Yeah, yeah. We both know you're huge. Now stop talking and let me do this." She closed her eyes and lowered her hips an inch.

Grayon hissed and clenched his hands into fists, to keep from thrusting up and burying his length inside her.

It was an eternity before she moved again, taking in another fraction of his shaft. He held his breath and watched her face for signs of discomfort, but all he saw was a half-smile, as she kept moving. Slowly.

*

Grayon's size was daunting to look at, but Raven was glad she hadn't let that stop her. Every inch of him that sank inside her stretched her further, but the pain was worth the pleasure of being so completely full. She'd die again, this time a happy woman.

She finally took in all of him and opened her eyes to see raw desire in his gaze. The sheets were torn next to his thighs, his fingers digging into the mattress. Yellow ringed his pupils, but he was all man between her legs, the beast at bay. However much this affected her, Grayon was right there with her. She sat still, unwilling to move and break the spell.

His heartbeat echoed off the walls around them. She could hear his rugged breath. The creaking of his knuckles, as he squeezed his fists harder. The blood rushing in his veins.

And she wanted all of it.

"Touch me." Her words came out in a rough whisper, but he heard.

He palmed her breasts again. Hefted their weight. Brushed her nipples with the pads of his thumbs. Every move of his fingers sent a jolt of lust to her core, and she rocked against him. She kept her moves slow at first, tentative, but when he ran his hands up her thighs and urged her on, she lifted her hips almost all the way up, before gliding down again. And again. Getting bolder with each thrust. Soon she was riding him in earnest, chasing her release.

He sneaked his thumb between her folds and found her clit. She couldn't remember the last time someone else's fingers were there, but no touch had ever been this electrifying. A twist, a pinch, a harsh rub, and the torrent rising inside her burst into an explosion of pure pleasure that had her shaking. She folded her legs around his hips, to anchor herself, and realized they were no longer on the bed but hovering above it.

Grayon arched his back, hips jerking, hands clutching at her flesh. She rolled them over and lowered them to the mattress, still riding out her orgasm.

Correction—*orgasms*.

A second came in the wake of the first, as Grayon thrust inside her with brutal force. No human could take fucking this incredible specimen of a man, but Raven wasn't human, and she was extremely happy about it. In the morning, she wouldn't even have bruises to tell of what happened between her and Grayon.

The thought sombered her and brought forth the bloodlust sex had kept at bay. Tasting his blood before had teased her taste buds. It was thicker and warmer than human, and it was infused with the magic of his realm. Magic banished from the Earth plane.

Grayon kept lunging inside her, and another tremor ran through her limbs. She had to have more of him. Now. She clawed her way closer and sank her teeth into his chest, above his heart. His blood filled her mouth like he filled her, and she sucked greedily.

Grayon didn't try to stop her. He grabbed a fistful of her hair and held her in place, as he pistoned his hips harder than before, until he came inside her with a roar.

She retracted her fangs. His scent surrounded her. His blood was sweet and spicy on her tongue. His cum dripped down her thigh.

And still Raven wanted more.

Whatever this was would be over the moment he walked out her door, and she'd make the most of it for the few hours they had.

He collapsed on top of her and rolled to the side. "You bit me." He glowered, but a smile tugged one corner of his lips.

"Yeah. Sorry. I was starving, and I lost control."

"I'm still bleeding."

She licked the bite marks closed, though his shifter constitution was already healing them.

"Next time, ask first," he said.

That was it? No yelling at her for taking liberties?

And—wait... *Next time*? There would be a next time? They had to talk about this.

He kissed the tip of her nose and lay on his back, one arm folded behind his head. "Wake me up in fifteen."

"Huh? Why?"

"That's how long I need till I can go again."

She snorted a laugh and turned to drape a leg over him. A powernap would be perfect right about now. They could talk later.

Chapter Eleven

It felt like forever since he'd woken up with a woman in his arms, fitting perfectly against the contours of his body. Especially one this amazing. She'd exhausted him, and he'd loved every minute of it.

He caressed her thigh. His heat and blood had warmed her, and he hated getting out of bed, but he had to. His wolf insisted it was night out, and he had to talk to Rex about patrol. He wouldn't mind taking it on himself this once. Raven could use some rest.

Grayon slipped out of bed, careful not to wake her. He wasn't yet at the door, when he picked up a voice he knew too well. *Bron.* Had Xenon sent him? Did Bron tell the pack leader the truth? *Shit.*

He hurried to pull on his clothes and rushed downstairs, making as little noise as possible.

"You fucker." Bron wrapped him in a bear hug. "You did it. Don't know how you found the snake, big brother, but Xenon sent me to say all is forgiven. You can come home."

Grayon's heart lifted for the briefest of moments, before his stomach dropped. Yes, he missed The Forest and his pack, but he didn't want to go just yet. Not when there was a woman upstairs who spoke to man and beast like no other had.

"What are you waiting for? Say goodbye, bring Sibyla, and let's go. This place reeks." Bron scrunched his nose and tapped his foot.

Xandra sniffed the air. "It's not that bad once you get used to it. Maybe Grayon could stick around a bit longer. I'm sure Raven could use the company."

"Raven?" Bron asked.

Xandra nodded. "She's—"

"She's this annoying vampire I've been patrolling with," Grayon said. "She guards the portal, but she's too green to do this by herself. I could stay a few months. Show her how to do her job right." He was already ousted; if it looked like he left the pack leader's daughter to hook up with a vampire, he'd be shunned.

And he was lying to himself. This wasn't the reason he downplayed his entanglement with Raven. He didn't want Bron and Xandra to know what he and Raven shared in her bed. It was too new for him to define it, and he wouldn't talk to anyone about it till he and his vampire figured out where they stood.

His vampire.

Bron pulled him closer and inhaled deeply. "Green or not, she's all over you. I see you haven't been wasting your time. This why you don't want to leave? To spend more time with your new girlfriend?"

"She's not my girlfriend. It was a one-time thing. Didn't mean anything. Of course I wanna leave. Nothing keeping me here." He tried not to wince as the words left his mouth. They tasted bitter with betrayal. Being inside Raven felt like returning home, and he wanted to keep that to himself and cherish it before he could share it with the world. After all, he didn't know how Raven felt. She might have been seeking the thrill of a wild night with a shifter. "I just thought I'd help

Xandra and Rex, because they took me in after Xenon"—he spat out the name—"tossed me on my ass."

"Xenon regretted his rash decision. He knows you're the best sentinel he has right now, and the alliance is in place, since our families will still merge when Candia and I mate," Bron said.

Xandra shook her head. "You should go, Grayon." Her eyes were sad.

Was it because he was leaving? She had to miss The Forest too, and he was part of it. A reminder of home.

But she wasn't looking at him.

He followed her gaze and spun to see Raven a few steps behind him. Her hair was mussed with sleep, but her eyes were hard and alert, her expression carved in stone. "You don't need to prolong your stay for my sake. I've been doing fine, flushing out the crap in this city. I was off my game last night, but it won't happen again." She turned and climbed the stairs, her posture stiff.

He couldn't even watch her ass sway. Guilt made him drop his gaze. She'd heard him and thought he'd rejected her. And he still stood here, like an idiot.

"Tell Xenon I need more time," he told his brother.

"To chase after a fanger?" Despite the derogatory term, Bron's tone held no judgement.

"You may want to leave out that part," Xandra said. "I'll help you bring back Sibyla, and I'll tell him I need Grayon one more day. He'll take it from there."

Grayon took the stairs up two at a time, and reached Raven's door just as she slammed it in his face. He knocked, trying not to drive his fist through the wood. "Raven, let me in."

"Can't. Busy, reading the Asshole Sentinel's

handbook," she called back. "Wanna grow up to be as awesome as you."

"Come on. Open the door. I didn't mean those things."

"I don't care." She sounded so dispassionate, he wondered if she was telling the truth.

"Please let me explain." He almost fell forward when she threw open the door.

The way her green eyes blazed, she was as affected by their love making as he was. And she was furious. He wanted to talk, to tell her he hadn't been ready for what he found in her. That she'd surprised the fuck out of him by being so fun and smart and sexy and amazing. She made him reconsider all he'd been taught about her kind. He'd found warmth in the most improbable of places, and he—

"Well?" She crossed her arms.

"I'm in love with you."

She took a step back, eyes wide. "What the fuck, Grayon?"

"I am. I know it's too soon, and I know it's weird, and I know you may not believe me after what I said downstairs, but you're the reason I don't want to go back. And not because you're a hellion in bed."

A half-smile appeared and disappeared on her lips. "Not what you told Big-Guy junior. I'm apparently a useless nuisance, and you have to help me improve."

"I didn't want to tell my brother and Xandra before you knew. And now you do, you decide if I stay or go." If she told him to leave, he'd never return to Earth, but he'd always carry Raven in his heart. Once upon a time, he believed he was in love with Xandra, but the thought of not seeing her again never sliced him as deep as the fear of losing Raven.

She narrowed her eyes and pursed her lips, and his heart shattered.

*

This wasn't happening. Grayon—huge, gorgeous, fucking sex-god Grayon—was in love with her?

Did her freaking heart just beat?

He was looking at her like a puppy—*ha*—who'd munched on her favorite boots, and she wanted to pull him inside and go for orgasm three million and ninety-six.

But could she fall for him?

She studied his gray eyes. She glimpsed his soul in those eyes, and it was as beautiful as his incredible body. Hard to keep a glare in place, when she saw he meant what he said.

When she heard him talk to the other two shifters, her worse fears came true. Grayon treated their night together as if it meant nothing. He flat out said *she* meant nothing. And the insecure girl whose own mother never made her a priority believed she'd been alone in thinking there was something between them.

She wasn't experienced, but she knew her body, and Grayon played it like a fiddle. That wasn't what had her gaga over him, though. It wasn't the expanse of his back or the muscles bulging in his arms and shoulders. His cock was pretty magical, but not enough to steal her heart.

Those eyes though—the way they bore into her, as he took her to new levels of ecstasy… She could fall in love with those eyes.

She *was* in love with them. With him.

But the way he acted, he deserved to wait a little longer before she admitted it aloud.

"You want me to go," he said but didn't move.

"No."

He arched an eyebrow. "No?"

"Nope."

"Because…?"

"You're kinda okay in the sack?" She giggled when he reached for her, but he silenced her with his lips over hers.

Chapter Twelve

"You can forget about it." Xenon's voice boomed in the clearing. "I'm not losing another sentinel."

Grayon wasn't cowered. He could take the Alpha in a one-to-one fight, and they both knew it, which meant it wouldn't come to that. "You had your pet-witch kick me to the Earth plane." He itched to resolve this. Xenon had him requesting audience for days, and Grayon missed Raven like crazy.

Xenon frowned. Shadows fell on his face and hid his charcoal eyes, but Grayon felt the weight of his gaze. "What are you talking about? You said Candia wasn't your true mate, and I had Moira send you to your destiny."

He was passing off Grayon's ousting as a favor? Grayon's wolf growled, but Grayon hushed him. "You didn't know where I'd land," he told Xenon. "You didn't care. I owe you no allegiance, but I ask for your permission out of respect. Let me join Xandra and Salina for a year." He'd come up with a more permanent solution by then.

Xenon huffed. "I confess I was enraged.

Nobody turns down my daughter. But I knew that day would come. Moira had a vision a while ago. She told me you'd break your word out of love, and that I was to send you after your fate when you did." His grin looked genuine and smoothed the lines off his face. "I'm not as stupid as your brother and Candia believe me to be. I saw the looks they exchanged, even as pups. I couldn't break our families' agreement, but your doing so saved my daughter from a life she didn't want. She's happy, and I'm happy. I had to make it look like I punished you, though. Need to be the firm hand this pack needs."

Xenon might not be the strongest of wolves, but the bastard sure was the best for the position of ruler.

"I still want to go."

The Alpha shook his head. "The schism between the realms happened for a reason. All magic but that of the undead is supposed to stay in The Forest. Too many of us move to Earth, and balance is lost. That's too dangerous for me to allow. The Balancers themselves allowed Xandra and Salina to leave The Forest; I can't take a risk with you."

Grayon growled in frustration. He was moments from ignoring Xenon's wishes and fleeing these lands for good. Putting effort into keeping his voice reasonable, he said, "My destiny, which you so gallantly led me to, is not in The Forest."

"Then bring her with you."

That was a possibility Grayon hadn't considered, but— "The pack will never go for that."

"*My pack* will do what I tell them to. This conversation is over. Go back to Earth and bring your female to The Forest. If you're not here two sunsets from now, you'll be considered a defector, and this time your punishment will be real."

Grayon nodded. He'd convince Raven to join him in The Forest, or he'd disobey his Alpha's direct orders and weather his wrath.

****

Raven paced the area of the portal. She felt Grayon as if he were right beside her, but it'd been this way for thirteen nights, and he still hadn't returned. When she picked up his scent, she thought her mind was playing tricks.

The air simmered and crackled between two old oaks. *The portal.* A tear through the fabric of creation, yet all that was visible was a ripple like a thick current of air.

And Grayon stepped through that ripple.

He was no more than ten feet away, but the distance seemed vast.

She flew to him and tackled him to the ground, like the first time they met. "*You're back.*"

He was saying something, but she couldn't hear with her lips pressed to his. She searched his body with her hands, tearing his clothes in her frenzy to touch him. Feel his skin. She'd been cold since he left, and vampires weren't supposed to feel cold.

Grayon didn't seem to mind her attack. Devouring her mouth, he slid his hands up her thighs and under the hem of her skirt. He wedged his hand between their bodies, shoved aside her boy shorts, and pushed two fingers inside her.

God. She was never wearing pants again.

She moaned in his mouth, and he slipped his tongue between her lips, as he thrust his fingers in her pussy. He kissed and stroked her slowly, going deep enough to bring her to the edge but not fast or hard enough to let her rumble over it.

"I missed you, little vampire. Missed feeling you squeezing me. Missed your taste on my fingers. On my lips. Missed you writhing against me." He spoke against her lips, bringing his free hand up to toy with one nipple.

"I missed you too, Grayon. So much." She pumped her hips, riding his hand. Her fangs elongated. She wanted to bite him. Have his rich blood in her mouth. Down her throat. His cock throbbed against her thigh. His fingers weren't enough. She wanted him to fuck her. Now.

She ripped open his fly and freed him, but he wouldn't let her remove his hand from her pussy. He rubbed his fingers against the bundle of nerves inside her and pressed his thumb to her clit. And again. More. Until her orgasm came crashing down on her, making her body shudder with its force. Every nerve ending felt raw. She was spent and exposed.

The sounds of the forest rushed in. Water trickling. Leaves swishing. An owl. Something scurrying away. *Foxes*? For once, she wasn't overwhelmed by the stimuli. Grayon's heartbeat, thundering like a drum, anchored her. She scratched his chest, raising welts. Needing to feel that sound. To be lost in it. The smell of wet earth and night and blood filled her nostrils. Her head spun, and so did she.

Grayon rolled them so she lay beneath him, and drove inside her to the hilt. Her body wasn't used to his size. Her walls, still fluttering with her orgasm, clenched around him before yielding to the intrusion. He took her on the matted grass, until her limbs were heavy and her head light. As he drove her body to new heights of pleasure, one thought rang in her mind. *Yours.*

By the time he let his own release take over, and shuddered above her, she didn't even have the strength to bite him. He lowered his head for one last, deep kiss, and then tumbled to the side and pulled her to him.

"Me too," she managed to whisper through dry lips.

"Huh?" Even his confused expression was gorgeous. The man had the bone structure of Adonis.

"I'm in love with you too," she said. "Didn't have the chance to say so before, but—"

His laugh sounded like a howl, and when he looked at her, his eyes were ringed with yellow. "Come with me," he said.

Strength was just returning to her legs. "I'll need some time before I can do that again."

"I mean The Forest. I'm not allowed to stay here, but you can come with me."

She blinked at him lazily. This required too much thought, and thought killed her buzz. "How much time do I have to decide?"

"Till tomorrow night."

Crap. That was soon. "And if I don't?"

His face darkened. "I'll stay. I'm not losing you, whatever it takes."

He'd be a fugitive. For her. "Can I come back and visit?" She had no family. No friends, other than Xandra and Rex. Her maker had shipped her off. Leaving this place wasn't what scared her. Leaving her life behind for a man did. Could she move to a new place, where she'd be an outsider—an enemy—and trust Grayon's love to last? She'd seen love go south before.

Grayon watched her, glee fading from his expression. "What's wrong?"

"What if you change your mind?" she asked.

"About us?"

"No, about leather pants being in fashion. *Yes, about us.*"

He sat up and looked down at her. "Raven, my people mate for life. When we meet the one whose soul speaks to ours, we're done for. It doesn't change, and it doesn't end. I want you with me for as long as I live, and may the Balancers help anyone who stands in the way of us being together."

Her vision was blurred. It took a second to realize she'd teared up.

"You're mine, Raven, and I'm yours."

"I'm yours, and you're mine." She didn't know what made her say the words, but they were heavy with a presence of their own. For the first time in her life or unlife, she wasn't untethered. She was linked to someone she trusted not to hurt her.

And for the first time ever, she felt free.

****

They didn't take as long as Xenon allowed Grayon. They said hurried *goodbyes* to Rex and Xandra, packed Raven's things, and rushed back to the portal. Grayon was equal parts eager and worried about this new beginning. He squeezed her hand and pulled her through to his realm.

Bright sunlight greeted them, and Raven let out a terrified squeal. He shielded her body with his, searching their surroundings for the threat. It had to be really fucking scary for his woman to react like this. Then it sunk in.

"The sun here won't burn vampires," he said.

She glowered and slapped his arm. "You could have said so sooner."

Xandra had told him something else he should share with Raven, but he'd wait until after they were mated.

"No sun will hurt you again, nightwalker." The woman's voice made the hairs on Grayon's arms stand up. He turned to see Moira, the pack leader's human witch, perched up on a log, watching them.

"What do you want, witch?" He spat out the question. He never liked her, but Xenon heeded her advice on everything.

Raven took a step toward Moira. "And repeat what you just said."

"I said you're safe from the sun now. Vampires and shifters mating may have drawbacks, but it also has perks for both." Moira's blue eyes sparkled with mischief. There was no malice in her gaze, but that didn't reassure Grayon.

"We're not mated yet," he said.

The witch laughed. It sounded crystalline and carefree. The sound was fitting to her appearance. She was over fifty—that Grayon knew; she might as well be over a thousand—but seemed to be frozen in her early twenties. "I see you're in for a lovely surprise. Anyway, I'm here to make sure you're settled in nicely."

"We're staying at my family's home," Grayon said. He didn't want to face Raven, afraid of the questions he'd glimpse in her eyes. They'd said the mating words, but hadn't done the ritual. Though they'd had sex…

Perhaps the ritual was just for show? This'd be an uncomfortable discussion.

"Right. I'm not needed any longer." Moira hopped down from her perch.

"Xenon sent you to tell me we're mated, didn't he?" Raven asked, surprising Grayon.

The witch smiled. "Why would he do that?"

Grayon's mind raced. The Alpha never did something without good reason. Then it dawned on him. "Because I can't challenge him for pack leadership if I'm mated to a vampire."

Moira arched both eyebrows. "Huh. Imagine that. Well, have a great life kiddies." She waved at them before flickering out of sight.

"So we're mated for life?" Raven asked.

He couldn't read her tone. Was she horrified at the possibility of being tied to him forever? Would she run away if he said *yes*? "We could go back to Earth and wait for sunrise, to check," he said.

She gave a roll of her eyes. "Nah. I guess I'd rather risk *forever* with you than burn to a crisp."

"Well, if those are your only choices…"

"Shut up and take me home." She tangled his fingers through his and pulled him closer for a quick kiss.

He already was home, because he was with her, but he didn't want to sound sappy.

"Gladly," he said, and led her to their *ever after*.

The End

Courting Mortality, Brothers of Fate # 1,

by Allyson Lindt

When it comes to the destinies, fates, and curses that come with being a demi-god, Eli got screwed over. He's spent eternity thwarting the same family curse that granted his brother, Loki, ever-lasting fame. As long as Eli doesn't fall in love, no one gets hurt. His plan to stay single and detached has worked for several millennia.

And then he meets Marley. She's making him abandon all his resolutions, except the one that never lets him forget the curse. Falling for her means her death, and he won't let that happen.

Chapter One

As you are, for all of time
To taste neither love nor death
When you find the one worth more than life
She'll draw her last mortal breath

Eli dropped his phone back into its cradle, and rubbed his face in exhaustion. He could call the shipping company all day long, and still get nowhere. It wouldn't matter how many people he reamed for the critical-but-delayed, package. He'd still wouldn't get it today.

His brother's voice drifted in from the outer office, and he growled. Loki was the last thing Eli needed. Especially Loki's jokes, with sexual harassment written all over them. Sometimes Eli wondered how that man actually owned his own company.

"And she says '...isn't *choking hazard* the warning label they put on tiny objects?'" Loki's laughter floated through the office.

The laugh that joined in—pleasant but sarcastic—made Eli pinch the bridge of his nose. It was the best way he'd found to suppress any other reaction. For instance, the way his imagination careened out of control and his cock sprung to life when he heard Marley's voice.

"I bet that ruined your plans for the night." She must be back at her desk.

"Not really. I have other talents." The confidence in Loki's voice never wavered.

Eli stood and made his way into the main office. He needed to talk to her anyway. Kicking Loki out of the office was just an added benefit.

The bad jokes and innuendo continued as Eli crossed the short distance to Marley's desk. With the four-foot high cubicles, it was easy to see what most of the people in the room were up to. Or at least, if they had their attention on their computers. Most of his people had their heads down, headsets on, to take support calls. Marley didn't work the help desk, though. She fixed the issues that couldn't be resolved with a simple phone call.

For instance, it looked like her current task was to keep Loki busy. Or maybe it was the other way around. Marley leaned back with her hands on the arms of the chair. The posture accentuated the way her T-shirt hugged her breasts. She shook her head, attention still focused on the man standing next to her.

Loki looked up. The corner of his mouth pulled into a smirk when he saw Eli. His gaze shifted back to Marley in an instant, and he leaned on the cubicle wall, closing the distance between her and himself.

Her full lips twisted in disbelief. Her voice didn't carry as far, but the subtle sarcasm was enough to reach Eli's ears. "Lucky her. I guess that's why they say, 'Those who can, do. Those who can't, make up euphemisms about why size doesn't matter.'"

Eli should tell her to get back to work. Over the

centuries, he'd watched his brother destroy countless lives, both literally and figuratively. Loki had never hesitated to kill, maim, or render someone psychologically crippled, if it suited his purposes.

Eli definitely saw the appeal in Marley. With full breasts, round hips, and a narrow waist, she haunted plenty of his fantasies. The way her plump lips pursed when she was annoyed and curved when she smiled short-circuited his thoughts. Her sense of humor and intelligence, though—the sharp wit and ability to think through anything—were what drew her to him the most. And made her far too independent, compared to the women his brother usually preferred.

Eli had gotten used to a lot of things in his long life. That people actually knew who Loki was, where very few even realized he had brothers. That Eli had needed to shorten his name—Byleist—to something easier for modern tongues to wrap their brains around.

But Loki's repeated attempts to hit on Marley still set Eli on edge. Eli didn't seen himself getting over that any time soon.

Loki didn't flinch at her slight. "You're good. I almost bought that. Have dinner with me."

Marley's, "Seriously. Again?" echoed Eli's thoughts perfectly.

Loki moved around the cubicle wall, and his leg brushed hers when he sat on the edge of her desk. "The odds are, the more times I ask, the better my chances you'll say yes."

Eli had stepped in on Marley's behalf the first dozen or so times this had happened, but she'd asked him to stop, and said she could handle it herself. Even now, he had to force himself not to say *something*.

He'd tried to tell himself it wasn't jealousy. He knew it was, though. Even if he couldn't have Marley, everything about her called to him, and most of the time, it took all of his restraint not to step in on her behalf when some unworthy dickhole hit on her.

"Game theory doesn't work that way." She sat up, and moved her chair back a few inches. "The odds are the same, every time you roll the dice. Besides, no-chance-in-hell multiplied by not-in-this-lifetime-or-the-next will always equal zero."

Eli couldn't completely hide his smirk, and had no desire to hold back his pointed reminder. "Don't you ever work?"

Loki winked at him, before turning back to Marley. "I'll be back another day."

There were lots of things Eli was grateful for, and at the top of the list was that his brother owned his own antique store, instead of working for the family business.

Some days Eli questioned why a family of gods—his family—did something as banal as running an insurance underwriting firm. Logically, he got it. Over the centuries, as their followers had dwindled and life had become more structured, Eli and his family had to do something to stay busy. The demand for miracles, and the destruction of entire sects of opposing tribes, had really sloped off. Since Eli's father, and really most of his family, were gifted with the ability to control the elements, they knew more about acts of God than almost anyone, so they'd just gravitated toward insurance.

Marley spun in her chair the moment Loki was gone. She tucked a strand of black hair behind her ear. "I don't suppose you're in such a splendid mood because my cable came in?"

Her teasing pulled him back into the conversation, and reminded him of why he was actually at her desk. "About that."

Her brows knit together, and she studied him for

a minute. "Good thing I don't have a hot date tonight."

He agreed, though his reasons didn't have anything to do with work. He beat back the emotional response to her retort. Even if she wasn't vehemently opposed to getting involved with people from work, hell, even if he wasn't her boss, his fate wouldn't let him do more than relegate her to daydreams. "The hubs came in. The cable and connectors weren't with them. Tomorrow morning."

Her shoulders slumped. "We've got less than a week before the move."

He knew. Everyone knew. The countdown reminders went out every morning via email. Their branch of the company was moving into a new building over the Christmas break, which meant all the network wiring had to be in place before a single workstation was set up. As IT director, it was his job to make sure it got done, and he knew Marley could handle the work fine on her own. Or, she would've been able to, if she'd had the time they'd been promised months ago. No one could wire the entire place by themselves in just a few days. Sure, he could summon lightning, fly, and even heal people and sometimes bring them back from the brink of death. However, even as a god, he didn't have the kind of power it would take to pull off a miracle like wiring and testing an entire building in a single day. He couldn't make the cables appear out of thin air. He didn't have the power to materialize them into the places they needed to be.

"I'll help." He knew she wouldn't let him do the work. It would be a blow to her pride. He wasn't sticking her on the job alone, though. Not this late in the game. "We'll probably have to pull an all-weekend shift, but I promise I'll comp you for it."

She shook her head, but a smile had crept in, erasing some of the frown-creases in her forehead. "I guess I'll have to make sure I'm not out too late tonight."

"I hope not." He couldn't keep some of his relief from leaking into his voice. He should want her to find a nice guy and settle down. At least her life wasn't at risk, with someone else. Not the way it was with him. That fact still didn't console him. Fortunately, they had work to do, and it was a nice distraction. "Planning meeting, my office?"

She didn't protest, and moments later she was perched on one of the chairs while he thought aloud, and made notes on the white board. "Supposedly, the missing bits will be in by eight tomorrow." Since they'd been scheduled to arrive today, and nobody had been able to explain to his satisfaction why the shipment was delayed, he'd demand blood if he didn't have the waylaid packages first thing in the morning. "So I figured we could start at ten."

"We want to get it done this weekend, right? Why wouldn't we start at eight? Or seven, with prep. We're already looking at living there all weekend. Might as well pick up those spare hours at the end of Sunday," Marley said.

He hated the idea of making her give up her weekend for work, but didn't mind spending some uninterrupted time enjoying her company. "Seven it is. I'll bring the coffee."

"You do know how to treat a girl." She leaned on the desk, arms crossed, enhancing the seductive curve of her breasts.

She had no idea. He'd jump at the chance to show her exactly how he wanted to treat her.

*

Marley watched Eli sketch a rough outline of

the new building floor plan. When he'd come out of his office, he'd looked like a spring ready to snap from the tension. He was slowly relaxing. His arms were loosening up, and his movement becoming more fluid, which was nice. With short, platinum hair, striking blue eyes, and a slender form that looked as if it could wind its way through anything, she always enjoyed watching him work. He was even more attractive, when he was in his zone. The way he sank into the explanation, and passion drove his every movement.

When she'd started the job, she'd felt guilty about staring. After all, mixing business with pleasure had cost her last job—hell, almost her entire career, and it hadn't even been *her* pleasure. When she'd interviewed with Eli a couple of years ago, she'd been broke, frustrated, and at her breaking point. Her former boss made sure she didn't get any good references, so she'd started telling potential employers they couldn't contact her last manager. That had just made things worse.

When Eli had asked why someone with her qualifications was looking for work after so long, she'd told him the truth, unfiltered. Flat out. She'd been fired for refusing her manager's advances, and if that was going to be a problem, they could cut the review short and not waste the next hour of their lives. He'd hired her on the spot.

Since then, she'd recognized the fact that there was no harm in appreciating how good he looked. About six inches taller than her meant he was the perfect height. His button down shirts didn't hide his defined arms, and heaven knew she fantasized about him binding her arms back with his tie. Besides, they hung out on weekends a lot—as friends of course—and he was even sexier in a T-shirt and a pair of jeans.

On top of all that, he was smart. She didn't have

an issue with the occasional intensely graphic dream, as long as that was all it was. She'd do the same if he were a random stranger on the street.

"And no, I promise this isn't the Death Star." His casual joke dragged her back to the work-half of the conversation. With some guys, she'd think it was self-effacing. With him, she knew to step back, and look for the hidden humor instead.

"Are you sure?" The retort slid from her tongue with little thought. "Because I'm thinking, if we fired at that exhaust port there"—she nodded toward a random spot on the rough map—"we could blow up the whole ship. No more wiring to do. Problem solved."

His deep rumble of a laugh sank into her skin, tempting her. "If we're going that route," he said, "we'll just have the rebels take out the entire thing for us, and spend our weekend marathoning some real movies instead."

"I'm in. Unless you have a hot date." Sometimes she wondered why he didn't date more. Why a guy like him was still single. For the most part, though, she took it for granted that he could frequently make room outside of work for the way their bouts of geekiness played so well off each other.

He shrugged and made random marks on the white board, instead of looking at her. "Last woman someone tried to set me up with had the ability to wipe out an entire city block with the wave of her hand, and no idea who Admiral Ackbar is."

She laughed at the exaggeration of what he called a cursed love life, appreciative he'd built on the Death Star joke. "You poor thing. Don't worry. Somewhere out there is a woman who gets your references. You'll find her."

He met her gaze for the briefest moment, before looking away. "I hope not."

Super weird. She shook off the questions his comment raised, and hopped to her feet. The joking was fun, but she had to get things back on track. As much because of time constraints, as because she needed a distraction from the part of her wishing they had plans together tonight, that might take them into tomorrow.

She grabbed the dry-erase marker from him. As her fingers brushed his, she tried not to linger on the warmth that raced between them. It didn't matter how many times she joked about his only having the one marker, he'd never gotten more, which made her wonder if he appreciated the excuse to share as much as she did. His heat brushed her bare arm, as she sketched in a series of outlet spots. She nudged her rambling thoughts back, and stepped away again.

"If we drop near these spots, it should keep the signals strong, and minimize the boosters we'll need."

He cocked his head, studying it for a moment. "And this is why I'm glad I hired you. Let's do it."

They spent the next several hours tossing ideas back and forth, peppered with jokes and obvious as well as vague references. Marley's cheeks ached from laughing.

Eli's phone vibrated on his desk, as it had so many times while they talked, and he glanced at it. His mood flipped from happy to sour in an instant. "Fucking asshole." His quiet curse filled the room.

"What's wrong?" Her question was sincere. She didn't want to see him upset.

"Nothing." He sank into his chair, and raked his fingers through his hair. "Just fucking asshole is all. I should let you get home. Let you enjoy your night, before you surrender your freedom."

She took note of the time. *How did it get to be so late?* The light banter with Eli, the way they joked and slid from one topic to the next, was just so easy.

She should at least try to remember why it was a bad idea to have a crush on her boss. She summoned a pleasant expression, and stood. "I *should* probably get home. See you tomorrow?"

"Bright and early." Anticipation mingled with his teasing.

Or maybe she just wished that was what she heard. Not that she needed to be hoping their attraction went both ways. The last thing she wanted was to lose another job over a little flirting. Except unlike last time, she'd be the one to blame.

Chapter Two

Eli wasn't surprised to see Marley's car already in the parking lot of the new building. He was five minutes early, and she'd still beaten him. He balanced the coffee cups on top of each other, while he flipped through his key-ring for the right key. Normally he'd nod in the right direction, and command the keys to float over and take care of the rest. But he didn't know who was watching. At least the electronic locks would be in by mid-week. Unless his brother decided to play another *prank*.

The reminder of the text from Loki yesterday sent a rush of irritation through him. The cock-up had actually visited a warehouse halfway across the country, just to distract the person shipping Eli's cable long enough to cause another day's delay.

Eli paused inside the front entrance, and inhaled deeply. The entire place had the lingering scent of sawdust and paint, and it was nice, just this once, to smell it overlaid with the familiar zing he associated with Marley.

"Hello?" His greeting echoed through the empty halls.

"Conference room." There was way too much cheer in her voice, given the hour. Unless she'd found that hot hookup the night before after all.

He swallowed the surge of envy, and followed her voice. When he rounded the corner at the end of the hall, he paused in the doorway. She was sitting on the row of cabinets against the back wall, legs swinging, arms on the counter top, every inch of her gorgeous body extended and accentuated. Even with a hoodie hiding some of her curves, it was a struggle for him to force his gaze to her face. The cold from outside still dotted her cheeks with pink, and her lips curved into a smile when she saw him.

"Morning, sleepyhead." Her cheer was contagious. A part of his mind asked what it would take for him to bring a bigger smile to her face. Pulling off her sweatshirt. Sliding his hands up her stomach. Stroking and caressing every inch of her, until she wore a giant grin the rest of the day, and then some.

Which he wasn't going to do. He banished the thoughts, crossed the room, and handed her drink over.

A soft sigh escaped her parted lips, when their fingers met. "Your hands are warm."

His hands were always warm. A side effect of being the son of Fárbauti. His father was named after the lightning that struck dry brush and caused forest fires, and while Eli hadn't inherited all of his family's gifts, he still had that heat flowing through him. Not that he was going to tell her that. "Or yours are cold."

He covered her hands, sandwiching them between his palms and her coffee cup. A new type of heat seared through him at the contact. It was accompanied by the desire to pin her to the counter, and let his fingers roam over every inch of her until they were both hot and spent.

He tried to be subtle about pulling away,

needing to get some space between them, before his imagination drove out of control. "I'll put the hubs in the server room." Strain tinged his voice. With any luck, she hadn't noticed.

"All right." Creases lined her forehead, and he saw the corners of her mouth tug down, before she hid her lips behind her coffee cup.

It didn't take as long as he'd hoped to relocate the boxes, but he still couldn't rein in his rambling thoughts. He couldn't shake the questions about whether or not she'd actually gone out the night before. Normally he didn't care whom his employees dated, or how they spent their free time. Marley was different. She occupied his thoughts when she shouldn't.

There were more important things in the universe than the fleeting nature of lust. Except in his case. Where any feeling that became more—love for instance—had the potential to kill that one woman...

A sickening creak filled the room, and he winced at the now crushed rack component in his hands. He had to have squeezed too hard while he was lost in his thoughts. Fortunately, they had extras.

"Tell me that arrived broken." Concern tinged Marley's joke. "There's no way you just crushed a solid steel shelf component, right?"

Shit. He hadn't meant for her to see that. Could he just laugh it off? He set the metal cage aside, and turned to face her. "I didn't like the way it was looking at me."

Her uncertain laugh filled the room, and summoned more of his regret and frustration. "Seriously, are you all right? I mean, I don't know, you seem...off this morning." She leaned against the door frame, gaze raking his face, and concern clouding her expression.

"Everything's fine." It took more willpower

than it should've to force his tone to stay even. "We need to get to work."

She didn't step aside. "Soon. First tell me what's up today? Don't give me this 'nothing' bullshit. Is this more serious than you're telling me? Shit, they're not going fire us, if we don't get this done. Are they?"

No. He knew for certain no one was letting him go. Not that he wanted to explain the ins and outs of that to her. He could just picture the conversation now. *No, we're not getting fired, because my father is an ancient god, who didn't know what to do with his life besides start a property and casualty underwriting company, and no one else in the family knows how to make the computers sing the way I do.*

Then she'd want to know why he was making shit up instead of giving her straight answers. No, he wasn't having that conversation. "No one's getting fired."

She uncrossed her arms, and some of the tension drained from her face. "So what is it?"

Nothing he was comfortable telling her. And yet, the words slipped out before he could think them through. "Not that it's any of my business—"

"Let me stop you right there." She held up a hand, palm toward him. "If you start a sentence that way, you know it means you shouldn't even be thinking whatever you're about to say, right?"

He probably knew it better than she could imagine. "Exactly." He brushed past her, a surge of want flowing through him when his shoulder met hers.

She grabbed his sleeve. "But it also means I'm not letting you walk away without finishing your statement."

Damn it. Maybe if he got this off his chest, he could admit to himself he was being jealous and irrational, and then they could get back to work. "There's no inappropriate thought. I promise. You seem like you had fun last night."

"I guess you could call it that." She relaxed further, teasing sliding into her response. "And what's all this 'it's none of my business,' crap? First, since when do we pull punches with each other?"

His thoughts ground and clicked on her words, as he searched for hidden meaning but didn't dare find any. "I don't—"

"I'm not finished. Second, I went out to try and unwind, some painfully-persistent guy hit on me with some of the cheesiest lines ever, and I'd rather put it behind me."

Relief flowed through him, tempered by his need to keep his reactions under control. "I'm sorry it wasn't a great experience."

She tightened her grip on his arm. "I'm not."

He shouldn't ask, but lust-driven possessiveness pushed the question out anyway. "What happened?"

"Nothing specific. Nothing horrible. I just would've rather…" A flush spread over her cheeks and she ducked her head. "Nothing. You're right. We should get on this whole work thing."

*

Marley had almost verbally slipped in the server room. She was still trying to wrap her brain around the fact she'd seen Eli crush a quarter-inch thick piece of metal like it was paper. There had to have been a week point in the rack, but the sight still had her distracted.

On top of that, after her abysmal encounter at the bar the night before, the coffee, and the spark she swore was tangible flowing between her and Eli that morning, she'd almost confessed she would have rather have spent the evening with him than cruising any bar. But she wasn't crossing that line. Toeing it, maybe. She wouldn't deny that. Smudging it? On occasion. Jumping completely over it? Not today. No, wait. Not ever. Right. She had to remember that.

Fortunately, once they started working, things went back to normal. She crimped connectors on the cables he measured out. With no eye contact, it was easier to pretend she wasn't attracted to him, and just talk.

"At least tell me Mister Last-night didn't do what the previous guy did." His teasing laugh fell short, and he snapped his mouth shut when her head shot up.

Please don't let him be talking about... "Which last guy?"

He glanced in her direction before turning back to his cable. "The one who wanted pictures."

She never should've given him so much detail after that date. She'd done it because she liked the idea of him making a similar request, and had been trying to judge his reaction, but that didn't mean it was a good idea. "It wasn't like that."

He put down what he was doing, and gave her his full attention. "Is something wrong?"

"No." She turned back to the cable, crimping as furiously as possible while still being accurate. She wouldn't look at him from her spot on the counter, pretending it wasn't a big deal.

Eli extracted himself from the spindle and snakes of wires, and crossed the room. He took the crimpers from her hand, and set all of her work aside too. "Except you just crimped an RJ45 onto that cable instead of an RJ12. What's up?"

Oops. She never made mistakes like putting a network connector on a phone cable. Her pulse raced through her veins at his light touch, making it hard to think. She needed to look away, but his gaze held her captive. If she'd been drawing a blank before, it was nothing compared to now.

He'd put the thought in her head. The reminder one of her dates had asked for pictures when he'd dropped her off. Told her if she wasn't going home with him, she at least owed him a topless shot to keep him warm that night. And part of her had never shaken the fantasy of doing that for Eli.

The temptation of turning him on, without ever touching him. "You're telling me you can't guess?"

The corner of his mouth pulled into a lazy smile. "I'm telling you I don't want to guess."

She couldn't ignore the mental images of what it would feel like if he leaned in and kissed her. "I just... It's not as though I had a problem with the request from Mister Send-me-pictures. Just with the requester."

There, that hadn't been so bad. They could gloss over it, laugh about it, and go back to work. Except she'd rather they took a break and got down to other things instead.

"Really?" His thumb stroked the inside of her wrist. Did he know he was doing that? She sure as hell did. The feather-light sensation spilled through her, desire growing between her legs. He stepped closer. "Who would it take, then? Just out of curiosity."

They needed to get this project done. To step away from this line before it was too late. Who was she kidding? It had been too late months ago. At least for her. "Well, I'd have to like the guy first. Actually being attracted to him helps." Would Eli have any idea she was talking about him? What the hell was wrong with her? And why couldn't she stop?

His voice dropped an octave. "And I would assume you can't dive straight into things. You'd want seduction. Teasing. The right words to set the mood..."

Even as she told herself to back away now, images raced through her thoughts, of stripping in front of the camera, one piece of clothing at a time, knowing Eli was her audience. A hands-off, private show where she'd caress herself, pinch her nipples, slide her fingers between her legs, and get off on the idea that she could turn him on that way.

The vivid image wouldn't leave. Her sex whimpered for attention, and her breasts ached to press into his palms.

Chapter Three

Eli had two choices. Back away—and there was no way he could hide how hard he was if he did—or go with the flow until Marley told him to stop. As long as he remembered this was only a physical response, nothing more than lust, and let her call the shots, it would be fine.

His cock strained against his jeans when she licked her lips. Well, not completely fine. He needed to do something about his body's response, even if he was ignoring his reservations. Screwing her was a bad idea for more reasons than he could list. But things would be mostly fine.

He stepped closer, holding her gaze. "In other words, in order for you to text a guy sexy pictures, you'd want a genuine lead in. For example, 'if I were there right now, I'd slide up behind you, and trace the back of your neck with my lips.'"

A tiny mewl, so soft he wasn't sure he heard it, tore from her throat. "That's a good start." Her voice was low and husky.

He raked his gaze over her, pausing on her chest before looking her in the eye again. "Say this unnamed guy followed up with more. For instance, 'next I'd slide my hands up your stomach...'"

Her breathing sped up, but she didn't pull her hands out of his grip. "From the right guy, especially if I was imagining him there, that would do something for me."

His dick throbbed at the thought of being on the receiving end of those pictures. Or better, pushing between her legs and making the hypothetical conversation a reality. Which sounded like the most incredible idea ever, but he was pretty sure it was because all the blood had rushed from his head. He needed to decide now. Could he risk this with her? Could he keep her on staff, keep her friendship, keep her alive...if he let things get physical?

Her frown contradicted the fact her chest was still heaving. She pulled her hands from his, and disappointment welled inside him. She scooted sideways on the counter, and hopped to her feet, not making any more contact between them.

He forced his voice to remain steady. "So really, all you're asking for is a gentleman who isn't afraid to pin you down in the bedroom, but still has more consideration for those around him than for himself."

"Exactly." The word was flat, and she wouldn't look at him. The flush on her lips and the pink in her cheeks proved she was as turned on as he was. All he had to do was tug her back into the conversation. Push things a little further.

The decision over whether to nudge things further or back away now warred in his skull, until he shook his head. "Too bad for Mister Last-night he wasn't that guy."

"Yeah. Too bad."

He turned away, and took a deep breath to clear his head. It didn't help. He yanked the last of his restraint up past arousal and desire, and forced his voice to stay steady. "If you have enough of those crimped, we should drop them before we make more, or we'll get a big tangled mess."

"Sure. Good idea."

He couldn't ignore how the disappointment and confusion in her tone matched his thoughts. He'd heard it enough times, relating to failed projects, that it tore away another chunk of his resolve. This was the right way to go, though. They didn't need to do something she'd regret. He'd be worried about the other consequences, those related to his curse, but he knew better than to call lust anything other than what it was.

He still couldn't look at her. It would take at least a couple of minutes to subdue his cock's raging want. He nodded toward the cubes they had agreed to start wiring in. "I'll drag everything over."

He knew the busy work he was doing, fiddling with nothing in particular, wasn't fooling her. What had he been thinking? Just a couple minutes of harmless flirting, and he'd almost blown a fantastic working relationship. Behind him, he heard the shuffle of her doing what he'd asked, but silence filled the remaining space between them. This was going to be awkward, unless he brought it under control now.

"Marley, listen." He turned to face her. "I didn't—"

"Don't." The single word was clipped. "Whatever that was, whatever it is you're thinking, whatever you're about to say, don't make it worse. It's done. It's over. It was what it was. And now this is a different time and place."

"I didn't—"

"Please?" She finally met his gaze.

The desperation in her request devoured him. He didn't want to leave things unresolved, but since he wasn't sure what to say anyway, and he didn't want to refuse her request... "Done."

"Thank you." Her sad smile left a gaping wound in his chest. Seconds later, her emotion vanished behind a mask of business. "I'm going to run line for the first block of cubes. Feed me the right cables?"

The builders had wired the walls, but it was up to Marley and him to do the external work. Along each section of wall in the office, there was a single panel with multiple outlets. A latch allowed them to open it up and add more if they needed, as well as get to any wires to troubleshoot.

She sat on the ground, legs crossed, and held out her hand. He passed her a cable, cut the right length to run under and reach the first cubicle in that block.

He knew the conversation was over. She wasn't going to mention it again, and probably preferred to forget it had happened. But he couldn't stop it from replaying in his mind, the fantasy ending in a different way each time, but always with clothes coming off. She fed the cable through the bottom section of cubicle, and pushed it until it hit its next exit point—a built-in spot in the metal trim, for electrical and network wires.

Even now, quiet, composed, engrossed in her work, she was gorgeous. Each movement enhanced the way her waist slid into grabbable hips, and her tendency toward biting her lip when she was focused threatened to make him hard again.

Her fingers brushed the electrical outline on the cube trim, and a sickening crack filled the room. She fell back, head slamming against the floor, and the lights blinked out.

"Marley?" Panic crept into his voice, as she lay there. Unmoving.

Shit. He dropped to his knees, ignoring the jolt that reverberated through him, and pressed his fingers to her throat. No pulse. "Marley." He scooted closer, fear gripping his insides.

Her chest wasn't moving. He leaned his head down, ear next to her face. She wasn't breathing. Her heart wasn't beating. Damn it. Had he done this? Was it the curse?

No. He took a deep breath, and forced the irrational thoughts aside. It had been seconds at best. And it wasn't his fault. It wasn't as if he'd fallen for her. Faulty wiring had caused this—and for some odd reason the breakers hadn't flipped until it was too late—and he needed to save her now.

He cradled the back of her neck in both hands, and rested his thumbs in the hollow of her throat, directly below her jaw where her pulse should be. He turned his attention inward. There was the spark he needed. Not too much. Nothing to jolt her. Just enough to massage her system back. It wasn't all science. He had just enough power in him to draw her soul back from the edge of death, on top of kick-starting her heart.

His heart rested in his throat. Even though he knew bringing her back should be easy, fear stole his confidence. A chill swept his entire body. Ancestors, don't let her be gone. His chest clenched, as the idea that he might not be able to revive her took shape in his mind.

He had to, though. He closed his eyes, and let tiny pulses of electricity flow from him to her. Seconds ticked away, and…nothing. Frustration crept in. He could heal any injury she'd sustained, and keep her from suffering brain damage.

Unless she didn't want to come back. No. Marley was too full of life for something so fatalistic.

She still wasn't responding. Anger surged. She couldn't be dead. Please. Ancestors help me. He'd never forgive himself or the fates, if she didn't wake up.

*

Marley gasped for breath, and her eyes flew open. She struggled to drag in more oxygen. Why the hell didn't she feel like she couldn't breathe? She drew in deep swallows of air. Something pounded inside her skull, hammering and splintering already fractured thoughts.

"Marley!" Eli's frantic voice sliced through her confusion. Gentle palms rested against her cheeks, drawing her further out of her own head. "Breathe. Slowly. Just relax."

She couldn't. Nothing made sense. What had she been doing? Why was there a giant, gaping black hole in her memory? Snippets rushed back to her, snapping into place.

Eli pressed close. How desperately she wanted to toss decency to the wind, and just let him have his way with her. Oh, God. Had they...? Had they what? Why couldn't she remember?

"Look at me. You need to calm down." Eli moved her head, forcing her gaze onto his face. "Breathe in, just once."

She focused on his voice. His gorgeous blue eyes. Because it was easier than falling into the pit in her head. She did as he said.

The corner of his mouth tugged up. The cobwebs cleared some more, but not enough. It felt like a million ants were dancing under her skin.

"Now let it out slowly."

She obeyed again, repeating the action several times, until she could form words. "What happened?"

He chuckled, and offered her a hand. Why had she been lying down? As she sat, she did a quick check. She was fully clothed. Her head hurt like hell. And it was dark in the room. "And why are the lights off?"

He shifted from his kneeling position to sit on his ass, across from her. "Something wasn't grounded. You were electrocuted. It..." He closed his eyes and swallowed. "It knocked you out. Blew a fuse. I'm just glad it wasn't worse."

She rubbed her arms through her sweater. Something about his words made ice run through her veins. She should go to the emergency room, but that would mean admitting something severe had just happened. The idea made her as uneasy as the missing last few minutes in her memory. A tiny nag tickled the back of her thoughts. Electrocuted, blank memory. Was it even more serious than Eli was saying? But he wouldn't hide something like that from her. Right?

She tried to stand, and her equilibrium made the room tilt and spin in protest. She sank back to her knees, and pressed a palm to her forehead.

"We need to take you to the hospital." He rested a palm against her cheek. "You're done working for the day."

His concern warmed her as much as his touch did. But her headache was already evaporating. It was almost as if his fingers were sapping away the pain. Not that such a thing was possible. It would be as ridiculous as wondering if he'd just done something like bring her back to life.

Sure, there was enough electricity running through those wires to stop a heart—that was safety one-oh-one when working with live wires. But it wasn't like Eli, or anyone, had the power to bring people back from the dead. She'd just gotten a little dizzy. "I'll be fine. We have too much to get done."

"Marley, no. Rest here for a couple more minutes, and then when you feel well enough, we're going to the hospital."

"No." She resisted the urge to lean into his touch. The longer his hand lingered, the more her pain evaporated. She almost felt back to normal. "I'm not leaving this half-finished mess."

"I'll take care of it." His thumb trailed along her cheekbone, stroking softly.

His concern warmed her further. Pride surged inside. She wasn't going to let a little tiny shock keep her down. Besides, she felt a lot better. He was overreacting; she just needed to sit for a minute. "I'm fine." She kept her voice firm. "And I'm not going anywhere."

He opened his mouth, and she held up her index finger. "No," she said. "I know you're the boss, but this is my project, and I intend to see it through."

"I don't—"

She narrowed her eyes.

He shook his head, still caressing her cheek. "All right. But the moment you wobble again, the workday is over."

She stood slowly, hoping she wouldn't falter, and even more concerned he'd decide she couldn't handle work after all. The room wasn't spinning anymore. Good. "But I will let you leave the circuits off until we're finished. We can get LED lanterns or something in here, right?"

Chapter Four

Marley scooted on the carpet, until her back connected with the wall. Every inch of her ached from bending, crawling, and feeding cable through small tubes for the last however-many hours. It was dark outside, and a couple of LED lanterns around them provided the only light in the building. The rush she'd felt after her post-electrocution dizziness passed had evaporated hours ago. But at least Eli finally stopped hovering and treating her as if she were made of porcelain.

While she'd really enjoyed the attention, she knew she shouldn't have.

He sat across from her, the lamplight casting his features in shadows, making the scruff of his unshaven face look even more rugged. Damn it, why did he have to be handsome and considerate? Why couldn't he just be an asshole boss like most of them?

The reminder that he was her supervisor snapped her back to reality. "We're more than half done. That bodes well for our schedule."

He glanced at his phone before dropping it back into his pocket. "And it's not even ten. Wow. I owe you dinner. And then we'll get back to it?"

She nodded. They'd made headway, but not nearly enough that they'd be done before tomorrow, if they called it a night. "Anything but pizza."

"You love pizza."

Just the word turned her stomach. "Yeah, but last night...cold pizza, warm beer, and a live band that was louder than they were talented—I'd just rather walk away from that memory for now."

"All that on top of the asshole. No wonder your night was a bust." He stood and offered her a hand up. "Note to self and all that."

At least if she was blushing, the dim light would hide it. She tried to be subtle about pulling away, before they could do an encore of the awkward moment from that morning. She might not be able to say no this time. "I want to get the west section prepped while I'm still thinking about it, and then we can break."

His gaze raked over her, lingering on her face for a moment. "All right. Tell you what. I'll order dinner and finish up in the executive office, and we should be done about the time the delivery guy arrives."

"Who are you going to get to deliver out here so late?"

He winked. "I know people. Trust me."

They hashed out a few more details, and he walked away to finish his tasks. The silence sank in around her for the first time that day, and gave her thoughts a chance to ramble. Combined with exhaustion, her brain did something she never let it do. It wandered into thoughts of what it would be like to spend time with Eli outside of work. Not as friends, but more along the lines of how different the night before would have been if he'd been her date.

She let her mind trip lazily over the delicious thought, while she worked. It was easier to lose herself, when she didn't have to worry about her attraction to him being written all over her face. With no one to see her gaze drifting off to nowhere, it didn't matter.

She would've invited him in at the end of the night. There was no question there. Offered him a drink. Maybe slid up next to him on the couch. Before today, she'd wondered if he'd be the one to make a move, but after the incident on the counter, there was no doubt he'd take charge if the situation was different.

"You okay?" His concerned voice broke into her rambling thoughts. She scrambled to her feet, and whirled to face him, pulse kicking up another notch. "I've been calling you."

She stashed the images in a mental side-drawer, and gave him what she hoped was a neutral smile. "I'm fine. Just engrossed."

"I see that." Was that awe? "You did all this in twenty minutes?"

She looked around the room, surprised herself. She'd been so lost in thought, she hadn't realized she'd finished prepping the quadrant, and then some. "I guess."

He stepped aside, and gestured toward the other end of the building. "Food's here."

She fell into step beside him. The familiar scents of lemongrass pork and curry wafted over her, and her stomach growled in response. He'd ordered from one of her favorite places. "I didn't know they delivered."

He shrugged. "The owner owed me a favor."

They reached the office that would be the CEO's after the move, and she paused in the doorway, any response evaporating. He'd lined the walls with a handful of flashlights—she had no idea where he'd gotten the extras—all pointing straight up like electric candles. A blanket sat in the middle of the room, with a

437

neat arrangement of takeout and two place-settings. A wine bottle even sat in the middle, adding an elegant feel despite the paper cups.

Had he brought all that with him? Bribed the take out boy to pick it up? She didn't care. She wouldn't be able to drink more than a cup, since they still had work to do, but the gesture still warmed her.

"I figured we might as well pick the nicest room in the building for dinner since there's no furniture anywhere, including the kitchen. Sitting on the floor in here should be a lot more comfortable than the cold tile in there." He waved a hand, and it seemed to grow brighter in the room, as if all the lights cranked up a notch. "Take a seat." He rested a hand at the small of her back, and nudged her forward.

She burned the memory of his touch into her thoughts, along with the entire setup. It was an incredible feeling, and a lot better than focusing on whether he'd really just made the flashlights intensify. She desperately needed to find a guy who got her on this level, and wasn't her boss.

*

Eli leaned against the wall, watching Marley talk. They'd cleaned up dinner at least an hour ago, and he knew they needed to get back to work, but he couldn't bring himself to interrupt. They both sat on the blanket, less than a foot between them, and she was as animated as he'd ever seen her. Arms moving and eyes bright, even in the dim light.

"No. I'm serious." Her smile was gorgeous and genuine. "My grandfather would tell these bedtime stories, every time he visited. Bible stories. But only the ones with dismemberment or beheading. Who needs Grimm, when you've got gentiles and worshippers alike getting their heads chopped off?"

He'd always been a fan of the brothers Grimm. Their version of the stories was more accurate than anyone else's up to that point in history, and no one had told the tales quite the same since. Still, she had a point. "I can't argue with that. It definitely sounds like a way to scare someone straight."

She laughed—that was an amazing sound. "It didn't work on me, but I'm odd."

"In the best way possible." He couldn't tear his gaze from her face.

She met his eyes, and pink flooded her cheeks. She ducked her head. Her voice dropped in volume, but her enthusiasm didn't vanish. "What kind of stories did you grow up on?"

The single question brought his entire universe crashing back into focus. There'd been hundreds of tales over the centuries. He'd watched people write down the original history, and then witnessed as it warped and mutated over time, as each story was retold, and the occasional new one was created.

But one stood out over all the others. A reminder of why it didn't matter how much he adored Marley. Even if she weren't off limits for professional reasons, there could never be anything more than a physical relationship between them. "There was one…"

She looked up again, eyes soft and curious. She scooted closer on the blanket. "Tell me?"

He shouldn't. He should put everything away now. They had a deadline to meet. They had… Every excuse evaporated from his thoughts, when she leaned forward, arms resting on her crossed legs and attention focused intently on him.

Maybe repeating the curse would help him get his thoughts back in order. "All right," he said. "But there's no beheading, or other body parts being cut off."

At least he hoped not. The sudden thought terrified him, and he squashed it. He'd never forgive himself.

"I'm sure I'll live."

He hoped so. He dredged up the thousands of years' old memories. "My grandmother used to tell me this when I was very young. We'd sit around the fire every year at holidays, and beg her to relate the story."

"You and Loki?"

"And our other brother Helblindi."

"I didn't know you had a third brother."

Most people didn't. Hell, most people didn't know Loki had any brothers at all. They thought Eli's brother was the son of Odin. Stepbrother to Thor. As if. Sometimes Eli hated that no one knew his history, but at least he hadn't been written into comic books and films with an entirely different bloodline.

"Blake manages affairs overseas. Maybe someday you'll meet him. Anyway." Eli breathed deeply, and let his memories drift back. "She'd always start off by reminding us we were the stuff of legends. That brothers born in threes—it never happened in our family. The oldest was always meant to take the reins of the household, and the youngest to explore the world. But when there was a middle brother, balance was disrupted."

Her brow furrowed. "That's a little harsh."

He'd never thought of it that way. "I guess. I'm the youngest, so I didn't mind." At least, he'd never minded until just a couple of years ago, when a frustrated brunette sat across from him in a job interview and told him outright that she'd be one of the best employees he ever had, but there was some shit she wouldn't tolerate.

"It's just a fairy tale anyway, right?" She almost sounded like she was trying to convince herself.

It was so much more than that, but he didn't

correct her. "There was a poem she'd recite. I can't remember all the words, but she'd chant it in front of the fire, the words mingling with flame. Sometimes I swore, if I stared at the flames long enough, I could see them becoming real. The words." He shook his head to clear away the vivid memory. He hated to lie to her. He remembered each verse as if it were in front of him. But speaking the words always felt like giving them power. At least speaking all of them. There was one verse she had to hear.

She stared at him, mouth barely open, eyes wide. "What was the general idea then?"

He swallowed. "No one would be suited to take over family affairs, unless he proved himself. Instead of assuming his birthright, the first brother would hop from wife to lover to wife, traveling the world, drifting for ages, until he finally found the woman who could calm his heart."

"Helblindi." She repeated the name flawlessly, even though she'd only just heard it.

He nodded. "The second brother would know fame. Celebrity like none of us had ever imagined. And it would change him into something none of us recognized."

She looked like she wanted to speak, but she snapped her mouth shut again. Silence hung between them, until she finally asked, "And what about the youngest?"

The words flowed to his lips without thought. After centuries of pondering them, he knew them better than his own name. "As you are, for all of time, to taste neither love nor death. When you find the one worth more than life, she'll draw her last mortal breath."

"Wow." Her single word was shaky. "Harsh. But it's just a fairy tale, right? Meant to scare you as a kid, by being vague and threatening?"

He forced something genuine into his smile. "Sure. Absolutely."

She caught her bottom lip between her teeth. "Still, it's not a very nice thing to tell a kid."

Or to burden an immortal soul with. "It is what it is."

He wished to everything ever it wasn't. Now more than ever, he wished it wasn't real. But the scare that morning… The rest of the curse was true. And he wasn't willing to take that chance with her. He didn't dare fall for Marley and risk her life.

Chapter Five

Cold flushed Marley's cheeks, and jarred her back toward consciousness. She and Eli had worked for a few more hours the night before, including testing every last connection in the executive offices twice. When exhaustion had become impossible to ignore, they agreed to nap for a couple of hours. But she was certain they'd fallen asleep several feet apart.

The familiar scents of new paint and recently unwrapped everything filled her head, but she wasn't ready to open her eyes yet. Every moment of the night before was seared into her thoughts. And even though it was cold in the building—no heat plus an overnight snowstorm meant it was probably almost freezing—her back and arms, and everywhere Eli touched was warm.

She wasn't sure when she'd curled up against him, or who had pulled the blanket from dinner over them, but she wasn't complaining. She let sleepiness have control, and stretched back against him with a sigh. His arm snaked tighter over her hips, fingers brushing the bare skin above her jeans, where her hoodie had tugged up during the night.

Floating in that wonderful haze between

wakefulness and sleep, every touch lit her thoughts on fire as much as it warmed her skin. He moaned and pulled her closer. This was incredible. His palm glided up to her stomach, and his warm breath caressed the back of her neck. Was he awake, or was this all just a reaction for him?

His forehead rested against the back of her skull. "You're freezing." His soft words barely reached her ears. "I know a cure for that."

The innuendo sent need and a wash of images surging through her—letting him warm her up. His skin pressed against hers. Those skilled hands searching out her buttons.

Her every nerve ending pleaded for more. She pressed tighter against him, and the hard length digging into her butt. "I'm listening." She wouldn't open her eyes. Wouldn't destroy this moment by letting reality seep in completely.

Desire surged between her legs, and her head swam with images of their clothes coming off, his mouth roaming her body, and his thick cock—currently pressed against the small of her back and tempting her—as it dove inside her.

His hand brushed the bottom of her breast, and she arched her back with a moan. When he glided higher and caressed her nipples through the fabric of her bra, the dampness in her panties grew. Her hips rocked, her ass grinding against his erection.

Something whispered at the back of her mind. A reminder that she shouldn't do this. Fuck it. She wanted him, and she knew the attraction went both ways. She was tired of hiding behind the past. Eli wouldn't threaten her job, and she needed to stop using her fear as an excuse. Even if there was nothing between them beyond the physical, she was going to enjoy every minute of it.

She reached a hand behind her, seeking him out by touch alone. His groan echoed through every inch of her, and sent pleasant chills over her skin when she grasped his cock and stroked through his jeans.

"Stop." His arm fell away, and seconds later cool air flooded in around her, chilling everything he no longer touched.

"What?" Confusion flooded her, and she rolled into a sitting position so she could look him in the eye. "Did I misunderstand?" Keeping her tone clinical and cool was the only way she could keep the hurt from leaking into her voice.

"No." He turned away. "I shouldn't have done that, though. I'm sorry."

What did that mean? "So we were both good with it, and nothing's wrong, but it's not right?" Uncertainty and doubt twisted her gut in on itself. It took every ounce of her control to keep her tone steady. Even then, she wasn't sure she managed.

"You should get home." He folded the blanket. "I can finish up here."

The ache of rejection grew in her chest. None of this made sense. "No." She stood in front of him, forcing him to look at her. "We don't operate this way. Talk to me."

His gaze bored into hers. "We do this time. The conversation is over. I've got this. Go home."

His cold command destroyed the wall of composure she was building around herself. She narrowed her eyes, and tried to obliterate any feelings using anger. "You're the boss."

*

Eli wanted nothing more than to call out, apologize, and spend the rest of the day with Marley.

The only thing that kept him from stopping her, from pinning her to the wall and stripping her down, and doing everything to her they both wanted, was his fear of what it would cost her.

Seeing her hurt, betrayed expression was better than seeing her dead.

He tried to lose himself in his work. The hours ticked away, as he finished his wiring and cleaned up the traces of their presence in the building. But he never managed to banish the images of Marley from his thoughts.

The entire drive home, fantasy taunted him. Of christening one of those executive offices. Stripping her clothes off a piece at a time. Kissing along her bare breasts. Hearing her gasp, as he tasted her nipples. Tasting every inch of her skin. Sliding his cock inside her. Watching her ride him. Drinking every gorgeous curve, and making her moan until she was spent from pleasure.

He pulled up in front of his house, unable to shake the images. It was true there was nothing he wanted more… Except for her to live.

What he needed was a cold shower, and something to distract him.

He stepped through the front door, and a growl slipped out before he could stop it.

"Late night?" Loki lounged on the living room couch, ankle crossed over the other knee, and arms stretched across the back.

Eli tossed his keys on the stand by the entrance way. He was rarely in the mood for his brother anyway, but knowing he'd been responsible for the delayed cable… For Marley losing her weekend. For— "Get out."

Loki didn't move. "How's your top worker? A little extra tingly after yesterday?"

A denial rushed to Eli's lips, and he cut it off. He rolled the words over in his head, looking for the angle. It was easy enough to assume Loki thought they'd slept together, but denying it meant admitting he'd at least had the thought. Not that he could deny it at this point, but he was going to try. "I don't know what you're talking about."

"Charged. Lit up. Electric?"

Rage roared through Eli. He should've known the accident yesterday morning was more than just shitty wiring. He crossed the room in a few short steps, grabbed Loki by the front of his shirt, and hauled him to his feet. "You asshole. Stay the fuck away from her."

Loki laughed, and held up his hands. "I don't know what you're talking about."

But he did. Eli knew it. An entire family of people who held the gift of elements—specifically electricity. It wouldn't have taken anything for Loki to shock Marley. It would've been a passing thought. Eli had no idea about the why, but the verbal taunting was too much to ignore. Except it didn't make sense. "Why Marley? I thought you liked her."

"She's fine, I guess. It's you I don't like. This will make you miserable. She's just a casualty."

Right. The drawback of having a brother who was not only immortal, but had zero regard for human life. Every couple of decades, Eli managed to forget about that. Fury poured through him. "Don't go near her, or her environment, again."

Loki wrenched out of his grip, straightened his clothes, and stared back, eyes cold. "Or what?"

"Or I'll find a way to make your eternity a living hell." Energy crackled over Eli's skin. Sparking and flickering. His clothes might not survive. He didn't care. He wasn't going to rein the fury in.

Loki patted him on the shoulder, and stepped

around him. "Like yours is? At least I know you've got practice."

Eli snarled. Keep this verbal or make it physical?

"I'll make you a deal." Loki cut him off, before Eli could swing.

Eli turned to face him, rage gnawing at his senses, roaring to be let out.

"I'll stay away from her. I'll even resist the urge to off her just to see how you react, if you keep your distance from her as well." Loki smirked.

No. Not in a million— Eli cut off his own rampaging defiance. "Deal." The single word sounded foul as it struck his ears. He'd intended to anyway. Besides, as reason clawed its way back into his skull, he remembered the best way to win an argument with his brother and piss him off at the same time was to concede.

"Wait, what?"

"I'll stay away from her, if you will. It's a deal."

Loki's mouth worked up and down, but no sound came out. He held up his index finger, and then dropped it. Finally he shook his head and turned away. "Good. Enjoy the rest of your weekend."

As Loki walked out the front door, Eli collapsed onto the couch. None of it made any sense. Why had Loki tried to hurt Marley? All that, just for a bargain he knew Loki wouldn't uphold?

He had no intention of keeping his promise to Loki, either. Even if he needed to keep some distance between himself and Marley, he needed to also make sure she was safe.

He needed to find a way to keep her from the harm of his curse, and everything else associated with his family. Maybe it was time for him to move on. Leave the family business behind. Make up his mind about whether Marley was safer with him keeping an eye on her or just leaving her to her own life.

Chapter Six

Marley had never been a fan of company Christmas parties. The first time she'd gone to one, she'd been nineteen and working the help desk for her college. All those years ago, it had sounded like a good idea. That had been the day she realized a lot of her coworkers were different people when they were off the clock. And drunk. And had nothing in common with her outside of knowing the people at the core of the gossip about who'd tapped whom in the copy room. No office party she'd attended since had been any different.

The reminders of why she hated these events raced through her mind, as she leaned against the bar in the Brazilian grill. She watched her colleagues filter in, and gather in packs of two or three. She twirled her straw in her Diet Coke. She'd been tempted to ask for a shot of rum in it, but these weren't the people she enjoyed drinking with.

Except the one person she couldn't locate. The only reason she hadn't ditched the party and just gone home. She hadn't seen Eli for the last three days; he'd only corresponded with her via email, and hadn't come out of his office while she was in, because he was *busy*.

She knew it was bullshit, and she intended to call him on it. If this was the only place she could track him down—short of going to his home, which was next if it came to it—then she was waiting here until he showed up. Confronting him over email didn't feel appropriate. It was too easy for him to brush her off. To avoid looking her in the eye.

She figured this was her best chance. Lots of people, no room for a scene, and nobody really paying attention to them anyway. And it was his father's company. He wasn't going to flake out on a holiday party for his own family's business.

An hour became two. She told about five million people—or ten, she lost count—that yes, it was cold, and yes, she thought it might snow and give them a white Christmas, and of course she was excited their work week ended today, because movers were relocating everything to the new office starting tomorrow.

Thinking about the new building dredged up memories she wasn't sure she wanted, but couldn't help sliding into. As people gathered for dinner, she still hadn't seen Eli. Had she missed him? If he was working to avoid her, it would be easy to do in this crowd.

She grabbed a table with some of the people on her team, unable to keep her gaze from roaming over every face in the room, over and over again. Dinner came and went.

The room grew quiet, heads and chairs all swiveling in the same direction, when Finlay Ugagnkin, the company CEO and Eli's father, stepped to the front of the room. Most people just called him Mr. U. Marley had wondered since the first time she met the older man, if Eli would age that gracefully. Finlay—he insisted people call him by his first name—had the same platinum hair and strikingly pale eyes as Eli, and as far as Marley could tell, not a single wrinkle on his face. He might as well have been in his mid-thirties. Lucky guy.

Finley rambled through his standard spiel. She liked that he thanked everyone for their hard work, and let the entire company know what their year-end profit sharing would look like. It wasn't a bad speech. She just had other things on her mind.

"And before I let you all get back to your conversations"—Finlay's voice took on a serious tone.

Marley snapped back to attention at the shift in mood. If the room had been quiet before, it was deathly silent now. At least she hadn't been the only one who'd heard the change in his voice.

—"I have an announcement to make. I have to admit, I've known this day was coming for a long time, but I still hoped it never would."

Her brows rose, and her gaze locked on Finlay. That sounded serious. He'd just told them they'd had a record year with revenue, so it couldn't be about the company. But knowing what it *wasn't* about didn't alleviate the tension suddenly crawling under her skin.

"Eli." Finlay gestured toward the back of the room. "You're not making me do this alone."

Marley turned with everyone else, as the familiar figure pushed away from a wall and wove his way through tables. Her stomach flipped in on itself. Maybe she shouldn't have eaten that...well, any of it. He looked amazing. Button-down shirt with no tie, untucked from his jeans, and all of it hugging that incredible form she hadn't been able to get out of her head since waking next to him.

She swallowed her desire, and kept her gaze fixed on the center of attention.

Finlay gave Eli a quick handshake and shoulder

clap, before turning back to the room and speaking. "I couldn't be more proud of my son. And not just because he's done things with this company's technology no normal person could accomplish. He's excelled in so many ways most fathers only hope for."

Eli's smile was casual, but never shifted. If the compliments embarrassed him, it didn't show. Marley tried to convince herself it was coincidence his wandering gaze never landed on her.

Finlay continued. "So I admit, I begged and pleaded and bribed him when he handed in his resignation, earlier this week. Today was his last day with us."

Marley's stomach dropped into her shoes. A loud hum echoed in her ears, drowning out the sudden rush of whispers. Last day? No warning? Her mind whirled with confusion. It couldn't be because of her. Could it?

She'd thought they were friends. Talked about everything. And she hadn't had any clue this was coming. Had she read their entire relationship wrong? A tiny voice in the back of her head asked if this opened the door for things to happen between them. Her doubt shoved the hope aside. He hadn't warned her at all.

The room erupted in confusion. People congratulating Eli. Others giving him their goodbyes. Dragging him further from her with every moment that ticked by. Her brain worked on overdrive. She was stunned and hurt at what had just happened, but she still just wanted a few moments alone with him. When she saw him break away, she managed to excuse herself and do the same.

"Eli." She caught up to him as he stepped outside. The snow had just started. Even though the sun had set already, the streetlights reflected the clouds in the sky. Flakes drifted through the air, melting before they touched him. That was an illusion, right? She was just imagining he didn't have a single spec of snow on him?

"I have to go." He wouldn't look at her.

"Bullshit." She grabbed his arm. "You can give me two minutes. You owe me that at least."

He finally met her gaze, and her chest felt like it might shatter. There was so much sadness and regret in his eyes. "You're right. I'm sorry I couldn't tell you."

"Not even a hint?" That wasn't what she wanted to say. She needed to ask what this meant for him and her. If she was never going to see him again, she might as well find out if there had even been a chance of *them.*

He shook his head. "I'm sorry. There wasn't time."

The apology wasn't what she wanted to hear. "About this past weekend."

He pulled out of her grip, and stepped back. "It was nothing. A slip is all. I need to go."

She stood in the falling snow, watching him walk away, struggling for any words to bring him back. But the finality in his voice... She didn't know what to do with that. She didn't know how long she stood there, before someone joined her outside. And then a couple more people. Apparently, the party was over. She shook more hands, walked to the parking lot with a group of people, and dropped into her car, mind still a blank.

The lot emptied as she stared at the snow building up on her windshield. A whisper of resolution wormed its way into her thoughts. No. This wasn't the way it was going to happen. She'd hidden from a lot of things in her life, but she couldn't ignore this connection with Eli. If he wasn't interested, he'd have to tell her. This quiet brush off wasn't going to cut it.

She took a deep breath, and pulled onto the road. Several inches of snow were already packed into the asphalt, so going was slow. She didn't care. She was heading to his house, and she was going to say what she needed to.

Chapter Seven

Eli paced the length of his living room. The hurt on Marley's face was etched into his thoughts, taunting him with every step. He hadn't turned the lights on yet. The falling snow and clouds reflected the glow through the large windows framing his living room enough to keep him from tripping on something.

He should've broken ties with her sooner. Months ago. He knew the consequences, and he'd still let himself get lost so deeply in how much he wanted her, he was second-guessing his decision to never see her again. It wasn't as though he had to confess his undying love to her. Or dying love. Whatever. Maybe just a night together would have been enough to sate his curiosity. Probably.

Not that she was a one-night-stand kind of woman, but he also knew the idea wasn't completely foreign to her.

He shook his head to banish the thoughts. No. It was done. It was over. He'd made the right choice. He could build his own start-up. He had the connections, the ideas, the funding. And he'd always wanted to…

Something disrupted the peace outside, and he

paused. The crunch of tires on snow. He wouldn't look. Whoever it was, it wasn't for him. Seconds later, a knock filled the empty room. After countless weekends of having her over for weekend movie marathons, he only knew one person who knocked instead of using the bell. He didn't know if he should groan, or praise his ancestors.

He yanked the door open. Marley stood on his front porch. Snowflakes dotted her hair and eyelashes. She looked at him, jaw clenched and eyes hard. "You have to hear me out."

He could've argued, but the desire wasn't there. Stepping aside, he gestured her in.

She hovered in the entryway, chewing on her bottom lip, her eyes searching his face.

"I'm listening." It was the best he could manage. Even in her winter clothes, she was gorgeous. Cheeks flushed, a rainbow of emotions on her face, accentuated by that stubborn streak she only showed when she really wanted something.

She took a step closer, and then another, until she stood toe to toe with him. His breath caught, and he clenched his hands, forcing them to stay by his side.

Her fingers interlocked at the back of his neck, frigid against his hot skin. She rose on her toes and pressed her lips to his.

He wouldn't kiss her back. He wouldn't give into this, or admit she tasted incredibly, and made his pulse race and his cock beg for relief. He wouldn't—

Fuck it all. He tangled his fingers in her hair, and yanked her head back for a better angle. She whimpered, and ground closer. He dove into the kiss, tongue finding hers, exploring her mouth.

He nudged her back against the wall, and then pressed into her. Her body yielded and molded to his. His body begged to be closer to her. Pleaded with him to rip away irritations like clothes, so he could feel her skin against his.

He wasn't sure where he found the will, but he managed to grasp the sanity he needed to step away.

She looked up at him, eyes wide, and drew a finger along his cheek, "I knew I wasn't the only one who felt it."

Was he going to have to hold an intelligent conversation? The blood had rushed from his head and into his lower extremities, and he wasn't sure that was an option. "You're not the only one."

She licked her bottom lip, holding his attention captive. "And now you've eliminated the one thing that was holding me back. I want to know why you resigned, but by hell I want you more."

Not the only thing keeping them apart. The thought nudged the back of his mind. The cruel, horrible reminder. "Marley, it's not that—" His words vanished in a groan when she slid against him, hip grinding against his arousal.

Some of the playfulness slid from her face. "Tell me you want me to leave. Say it, instead of dancing around it. Tell me you're not interested, and I've read us completely wrong. Do that, and I'll go."

"I can't." No, that was the wrong answer. He needed to do exactly what she'd just told him to. Except, instead he said, "Tell me what *you* want."

"You."

"Me too. You have no idea how much." That wasn't right. What was he doing? And why couldn't he take it back?

She traced a line down his chest, until her finger stopped at his waistband. "So what's stopping you from taking advantage of me?"

Death. Misery. A thousands of years old curse. "Not nearly as much as should be. I'm seconds away from stripping you naked, one piece of clothing at a time. I want to run my hands over every inch of your bare skin, caressing and pinching, and drinking in every moan. And I desperately want to explore every switch you have, until you scream so loudly, the neighbors know how much you're enjoying yourself."

She tugged at the button on his jeans, but didn't undo it. The bravado had vanished from her voice, replaced with breathlessness. "I like the sound of that."

He couldn't stop this. His desire was too strong. But he could at least set some boundaries. "You have to promise me something first."

"I'd probably promise you my soul right now, if that's what it took."

That was exactly what he was hoping to avoid. "Nothing that severe." He nipped at her bottom lip, and his senses flared to life again. "Promise me, whatever happens here tonight is just physical." He trailed his lips along her jaw and up to her ear, whispering, "Everything else, work, emotion, who we are outside of this moment, gets checked at the door."

She hesitated, and he swore his pulse ground to a halt.

"I promise." Her quiet voice barely reached his ears.

*

The promise was harder to force out than Marley thought it would be. She shoved her doubt aside. It wasn't like she expected—or wanted—more. Sure, the attraction was there, and three years of flirting and getting to know each other both mentally and emotionally had amped up the tension between them, but they'd never been more than friends. Her staring, lusting, all of it, had never been more than physical.

When Eli kissed her again, every inch of her whimpered with need. His mouth glided along her jaw. Each light sensation traveled along her skin, making her nipples ache, and dampness grow between her legs.

He shoved her coat to the floor. Disappointment flooded her when he stepped back, but the heat in his gaze deepened her desire. "Ancestors, you're gorgeous." His voice had dropped an octave. "I want to see more of you."

Was she blushing? How could she not be? Or was that just the pulse of want flowing through her? "Turn on the lights." She tried to keep her tone playful.

He shook his head, and then intertwined his fingers with hers. "I have a better idea." He tugged her toward the living room, and the large wall of windows, where the moonlight, reflected off the snow, spilled across the carpet. His breath was hot against her skin, when he stepped in and traced a line along her ear with his lips. "Strip for me. A single piece at a time."

Her pulse ratcheted up at the idea. "What if someone sees me?" Not that there were any houses nearby, and the road was blocked by trees. Besides, did she really care? The throb below her waist, the slickness the idea caused... She liked the thrill and the risk of doing something so indecent.

He let go of her and put a couple feet between them. "You don't have to."

She really might do anything, if he kept his hungry gaze trained on her like that. She kicked aside her shoes and socks first. He raised an eyebrow when she slid her hands down her sides, and then to the middle of her sweater, and undid the buttons one at a time. The knit caressed her hyper sensitive skin, when she slid the top down her arms. She'd never realized something like this could make her so wet. So strung out with need.

460

"Jeans next." There was no room for argument in his demand.

She bit her bottom lip, and pushed her pants to the floor. She tossed the discarded clothing aside, hyper aware of how exposed she was in just a bra and panties.

"So sexy." His words were almost a growl. "Now your bra."

Seconds later, the lacy lingerie joined the growing pile of clothes. The cool air in the room was a sharp contrast to the flush over every inch of her body, and her already hard nipples stiffened more at the light caress. She wanted his hands on her. Flowing over her bare skin. But this attention was incredible too. "What now?" she managed.

The corner of his mouth tugged up. "Play with your breasts for me. Show me how you like to be touched."

She glided her hands up her stomach, ignoring the plea from her aching clit that she pay attention to it instead. She cupped her breasts, and pinched the twin nubs. Rolled, caressed, and tugged.

His moan sent tingles rushing over her. "Are you wet?"

She nodded, not sure she could find her voice.

"Check for me," he said. "Slide your fingers between your folds. Slowly."

She kept one hand on her breast, while the other moved down. A whimper tore from her, when she brushed her swollen clit. Her fingers were coated the minute they dipped under her panties. She closed her eyes and focused on her surroundings. His voice, her own touch, the attention.

"Keep going." His voice was closer this time, his breath hot against her neck, but no other part of him touched her.

Her already racing heart spun into turbo mode,

when his fingers brushed her hips, and seconds later elastic scraped down her legs. She continued to stroke her aching button. Resisting the urge to go faster. When his lips brushed her thigh, she cried out. His tongue flicked over her wet fingers and sex, and her legs almost gave out from the sensation.

He pulled her hand aside, and wrapped his lips around her clit. Orgasm climbed through her, and she rocked against his face. Her head felt like it was full of helium, and she didn't have the voice or enough presence of mind to make any sound beyond groans of pleasure. He shoved two fingers inside her, hard and rough. She cried out in response, as the climax crashed over her body.

Her pussy clenched around his fingers, and she shuddered with pleasure, as he continued to lick and suck her, pumping in and out. She tried to pull away when his touch became too much. He grabbed her hip with his free hand, drawing the orgasm out, until she didn't know if she could stay upright on her own.

He finally drew away, and stood. "Look at me."

She realized she'd had her eyes clenched shut the entire time, and forced them open. He stared back, his gaze intense and holding her captive. She heard the distinct sound of a belt buckle, and realized he was undoing his pants.

"I want you riding my cock. I want to fuck you until you scream. And I want to hear you come again."

She managed to find her voice. "That's a big list."

"I'm sure we'll manage."

The confidence in his voice glided over her bare skin. "Do you have a condom?"

He shook his head. "We don't need one. I promise."

She'd heard that before. "Because you're some

kind of magical god, and can't get me pregnant or give me anything?"

He smirked. "Exactly."

She didn't know if it was the heat of the moment, or something deeper, that told her he was being far more serious than she was. She was on the pill, so pregnancy wasn't a concern. He didn't date enough for her to worry about STD's, so she would be safe. "You're lucky I trust you."

His hands rested on her hips. He spun her away from him, and then pulled her back to his front. The rough cotton of his shirt bit into her skin, and his cock dug into her ass, hard and demanding. "You have no idea how lucky I am."

He rested his hands on her stomach, and worked them upward. A new wave of lust increased her ebbing arousal, when he cupped her breasts. His rough fingers found her nubs, and sparks of pleasure and pain rolled through her with each squeeze. She rocked against him in time with his ministrations.

She didn't have time to be disappointed when the attention stopped. He tangled one hand in her hair, and yanked her head back. He kissed and bit along the soft flesh where her shoulder met her neck. With his other palm, he found her spine, then moved it over her ass, and between her legs. "You're still so wet." As he spoke, he nudged her forward. Her breasts flattened against the glass. When had they moved so close? The cold glass was another layer of exquisite agony against her tender nipples.

His fingers slid inside her easily. He pumped slowly, cock digging into her ass cheek, teasing.

"I thought you wanted to fuck me." She liked the way the crude language tasted.

"Hmm... I like the way you say that." His lips vibrated against her shoulder. "I want to hear it again.

Beg me."

"Fuck me, please?" She wiggled against him, and felt his shaft pulse in return. "Fuck me hard and fast, Eli. I want you inside me. Please?"

Hands on her hips, he guided her back a few steps, and then pushed her forward. Her palms flattened against the window.

The head of his cock nudged her, and then he thrust forward without further warning. Her moan mingled with his, as he stretched her out. The slow teasing was gone. His pounding was fast and frantic. Her breath came in short gasps, as he hit her at just the right angle. "Come again for me Marley. I want to hear you scream."

She was so close. Her head swam, and every inch of her hovered on the brink. He dug his fingers into her hips, slamming her hard. When he found her still tender clit and massaged it, a scream of pleasure tore from her throat. Somewhere in the midst of it, she heard his grunts grow frantic and fast, and then melt into a long groan as he peaked as well.

The pace slowed, and she knew she couldn't stand this time. He slid out of her, and seconds later, wrapped his arms around her, keeping her from collapsing. He sank to the floor, helping her down, and pulled her into his lap.

She curled up, and rested her head against his shoulder

He brushed a loose strand of hair off her forehead, and kissed her lightly. His thumb traced tiny circles over her spine. "I'm so glad you came over tonight." The hunger was gone from his voice, but the commanding power remained.

She smiled, and rested more of her weight against him. "Me too."

Chapter Eight

The storm had cleared up at some point during the night, leaving the sky black except for the shock of white moon, and the snow untouched in Eli's back yard. Like the front of his house, two entire walls of the bedroom were floor-to-ceiling windows. All he could see beyond the glass was a blanket of white over the trees that spanned most of his back yard.

Moonlight splashed across the form next to him. She was still wrapped in sheets, but she'd kicked off the blankets sometime during the night.

He'd have to say goodbye soon. He studied the way the cotton draped her naked form, hugging every seductive curve. He wouldn't let himself admit he was going to miss her. That thought led to others, with more dangerous consequences.

His hand hovered less than an inch from her face, as he followed the line of her cheek without ever touching her. Her dark hair spilled out over the white pillow cases.

"Some people think that's creepy." Her mouth curled into a smile, but she didn't open her eyes.

"Waking up at this unholy hour?" He couldn't

help his smile at the teasing note in her voice. But he wouldn't lean in and kiss her. He'd gotten that out of his system.

"Watching someone sleep." She finally looked at him, grin in place.

They'd spent half the night exploring each other. She made the most incredible noises when she was turned on. They were even better when she came. But it should have been enough to get her out of his system. The only reason he hadn't already sent her home was the roads were dangerous. Or at least, that's what he tried to tell himself. "I was going to wake you up."

"Mhm..." She sat up, and the sheets fell away, exposing her bare breasts and perfect skin.

He struggled to keep his attention on her face. "But I know you don't have work, so I thought I'd let you sleep."

She ducked her head. "I haven't slept that well in a long time."

He wanted to ask her to join him in the shower. To make one last memory. But he'd already pushed the limits of their relationship too far. He needed to stick to the same promises he'd coerced from her. "Can I make you breakfast?"

She shook her head, and scooted to the edge of the bed. "I'm good. Thanks. I should let you have your privacy back." If she noticed her clothes were folded on the chair next to her instead of still strewn across the living room, she didn't say anything. He hadn't been able to sleep, and the few times he'd managed to extract himself from her, he'd paced with no purpose, before crawling back into bed and wrapping himself around her again.

She dressed in silence, not looking at him. Every inch of his instinct begged him to say something.

To make the situation better. But he knew this was how it had to be. He had to let her go. He hated to be that asshole. But at least she'd still be alive at the end of the day.

She stood, and impulse snaked through him. He shot his hand out and grabbed her wrist. "Wait." When she didn't struggle to break away, he tugged her back to the mattress.

He knelt in front of her and rested his hands on her cheeks, forcing her to look at him. He let the sincerity fall into his voice. "I'm so glad you came over last night. That we have this memory. I will never, ever, forget it. Or you." He kissed her hard, searing the moment into his thoughts, where he knew it would stay. "I'm sorry that's all there is. That I can't give you more."

She pulled away, and gave him a weak smile. "Yeah. I get it." She didn't look back, as she made her way to the front door. The latch clicked. Seconds later, her tires crunched on the frozen snow.

He flopped back against the pillows. Only a selfish fucking prick would have taken that from Marley last night knowing it could never be more. Ancestors, he was an asshole. Then again, so was whoever had cursed him, so at least it ran in the family. He lay there, until the light started to creep over the trees and the clouds drifted back in. With any luck, Marley was home by now. He hoped the plows had cleared away enough snow, she'd make it safely before the next storm started.

And he needed her to hate him as much as he hated himself. Then at least she wouldn't be back. She'd be safe.

Lightning cracked across the sky, drawing his attention to the windows. He frowned at the electrical activity. That wasn't normal this time of year.

Especially as a lead-in to a blizzard.

His phone buzzed, and he reached for it on the nightstand, out of habit. He rolled his eyes when he saw the text message was from Loki.

And then he read it.

You broke your promise.

Eli's chest almost caved in on itself in fear. Another slash of lightning split the sky, followed by ear shattering thunder. *Marley.*

He didn't have time for a car. He pulled on whatever clothes were within reach, and flew out the front door. His feet left the ground as he picked up speed, and he soared at low altitude toward her apartment. At least she liked to take the back roads. He wouldn't have to worry about anyone seeing him. Not that he cared right now. Maybe the message was just meant to tease him. To see how he'd react. But knowing his brother, Eli couldn't take that chance.

The snowdrops melted and evaporated before they reached him. He cut a horizontal path through the storm, three thoughts looping in his head.

Please let it be nothing. Let me be overreacting. Let her be all right.

*

Stupid, myopic, narrow-minded, moronic, melodramatic… Marley's list of insults faded into a mental roar. She wasn't sure if she was talking about herself or Eli. Elusive, vague, possibly stuck in a fairytale from his childhood. That was Eli.

It had all clicked for her in the last twelve hours. The odd comments he'd make about hoping he never found the woman of his dreams, his insistence there was nothing between them, and the haunted look he'd had when he told her the story on Saturday night. He thought that stupid curse was real. The last thing she needed was that kind of baggage in her life. Especially if it belonged to someone else.

Snow fluttered onto her windshield, and she turned on the wipers. Large, fluffy, white flakes seemed to appear out of nowhere, blanketing the road within minutes.

A pushover. A coward. Indecisive, and too quiet for her own good—that was her. She hadn't even tried to argue. Just sat back, and let him make the rules. Not that she wanted to be with a guy who wasn't interested, but everything he did, all of his actions said he was. She'd just accepted his brush off without questioning it, though.

And she was nobody's booty call. Fury and hurt rushed through her. She wasn't going to let this eat at her. She was going back.

Except, the roads had gone from clear to covered in several inches of snow, almost faster than she could blink. She slowed, eyes focused on the road. Maybe she'd go back after the storm let up.

Lightning reflected off the clouds hiding the sky, adding an eerie glow to the dawn, for the briefest second. Something cracked nearby, louder than a gunshot, and Marley's heart hammered in her chest. She didn't like this weather. She gripped the wheel until her fingers ached, squinting through the falling white. Maybe she'd be better off without her headlights. There was no one else on the road, and with the sudden storm making it so dark, all they were doing was reflecting back at her.

Another crack lit the sky enough to blind her further. Her eyes grew wide, and she slammed on the brakes when she saw the tree just a few feet in front of her. The car slid toward the fallen trunk, not listening to her attempts to avoid the obstacle. She spun the steering wheel with the skid, the way she'd been taught, and the car listened. It drifted away from the tree at the last second. It tumbled over the drop-off, and her world tilted as the vehicle rolled.

Marley's world went black.

****

"Marley." The voice clawed at the edges of nothing fogging her brain.

She knew that voice, so why couldn't she remember?

"Marley!" He was persistent.

Eli. Right. He sounded worried. Snippets of memory floated back to her. He should be. He'd been an asshole.

"Open your eyes. Talk to me. Something."

It sounded like a reasonable request. Her skull screamed in protest, as she forced her eyelids open. More of her world crawled into focus. She was cold. All of her. Except the warm bits on her neck and cheeks where his hands rested.

"Thank you." Relief shone through his concern. A smile cracked his solemn expression.

She shifted to sit up. It didn't hurt the way it should. Wait, why should it hurt? She looked around her. She was sitting in the snow, several feet from her car, which lay on its roof. Was she thrown clear? Red splattered the ground. So much red. She raised her hand to her head, and brought it away sticky and covered with... Was that blood? It couldn't be her blood. She felt fine. "What are you doing here?" she asked Eli. "What am I doing here?"

He opened his mouth. A giant white ball of light slammed into his gut, tearing him away from her, and tossing him back several feet until he collided with a tree.

"Fuck, you're persistent." Loki floated to the ground next to her, feet never touching the snow.

Wait, floated? Ball of lightning? She had to be hallucinating. She remembered the tree in the road. Was she unconscious?

Loki's gaze raked over her, chilling her more than the snow she sat in. "I was worried about you. I wasn't ready for this to be over quite yet."

What? Out the corner of her eye, she saw Eli pick himself up. His posture shifted, every muscle tense, eyes tight.

Loki held up a hand. "Time out."

She had to be dreaming. That was the only explanation for this bizarre scene. She was really lying unconscious in her car. She hoped someone would find her soon.

Eli didn't relax, but disbelief marred his expression. "Are you serious? I don't care what the fates say; I told you what I'd do to you, if you touched her."

At least in her dreams, Eli was still sweet. Overzealous maybe, but sweet.

"Ditto." Loki smirked. "And we should get to that. But someone wants an explanation. I'll give you a minute to tell our lovely guest what's going on, and then we can resume seeing if one of us can die."

Wow, she was screwed up in the head. She looked between the two of them. Eli tense, fury etched in his icy expression. Loki calm, still floating—possibly chuckling? Terror slid into her veins. If this wasn't a dream, she was fucked. If this was real, she didn't want an answer from Loki. Something about his demeanor terrified her.

Then again, if she wasn't dreaming, Eli had been holding back some pretty significant things too.

Chapter Nine

Marley looked back and forth between the two brothers again. Even if this was some sick, twisted dream, she wasn't going to cave to the creeping fear inside. She locked her gaze on Eli. "Tell me what's going on." Her voice cracked, and she hid a wince. "All of it."

Eli's fingers twitched by his side, and he bounced on his toes. He took a step closer, and she narrowed her eyes to keep him at arm's length. Part of her wanted the comfort he could provide. But she wasn't going to sink into it. Even if they'd had that kind of relationship—the kind where he wrapped her up and kept her safe, instead of just listening to her vent on a bad day—she wouldn't let that happen right now. She needed answers.

His entire frame shook when he exhaled, but he never relaxed. "The story I told you the other night? The curse about the three brothers? It's actually about me. About all three of us. The first time I heard it was thousands of years ago, when I was just a kid."

Loki laughed. "You actually told her the story already? And neither of you has…" His chuckle echoed over snow and trees. He looked at Marley, something icy hiding in his eyes. "You know a curse isn't meant to be straightforward, right? You're familiar with Grimm. Aesop. Disney? You never take that crap at face value, especially if you've only heard part of it."

She struggled to wrap her thoughts around the information. Thousands of years ago? Aesop—like the fables? The answers should be right there, but all she could think was these men were trying to tell her they were actually immortal. Or at least really, really old. The last twenty-four hours had to be getting to her. Unless this was all a joke.

The new idea gnawed at her thoughts. They'd said his name was Loki. As in the trickster god. What if this was all some sort of elaborate hoax? Because that's more logical? She ignored her own, nagging question.

"We're gods." Eli interrupted her spiraling thoughts. "All of us. Loki wasn't inconveniently named by parents with a sense of humor. He's *the* Loki."

"No." She shook her head. A tiny voice in the back of her mind insisted she listen. That she take him seriously. But it was insane. There was no way this was real. Was it all just a joke? The resignation at the Christmas party. The night before, with Eli. Was it all some sort of cruel prank she didn't understand? Were there wires holding Loki up? She glanced at him out of the corner of her eye, not wanting to study him too hard and prove her theories wrong.

Terror snaked in to join her doubt. No. People didn't float. Gods didn't walk the earth working tech jobs, and she was afraid of a shadow. It was nothing. So why was the fear under her skin more convinced by their stories than her rationalizations?

"Marley?" Eli took another step forward. At least the concern in his voice was familiar.

And maybe part of the same sick joke that

landed her here. She boxed her cowering nerves in the back of her mind, and stood. She wouldn't look at Loki. Whatever he had to do with this, it was all incidental. Eli had been at the heart of it the entire time. Playing...some kind of sick game with her. "I'm calling the auto club," she said. There. That at least sounded like a rational thing to do. She should have done it to start with.

Her feet sank into the snow, as she trudged in Eli's direction. She tried to ignore that hers were the only footprints in the clearing. That her car was the only vehicle. She didn't look at Eli, as she brushed past him and headed for the slope leading to the main road.

"You even brought her back to life. Twice." Loki's taunt hit her back. "And she still doesn't believe you. How incredible is that?"

He was just spewing words. It didn't mean anything. She repeated the mantra over and over again, as she made her way toward the highway. The fact his words made her gut clench, and her head ache, and her logic wonder if he was telling the truth, didn't mean anything.

And she definitely wasn't the tiniest bit disappointed Eli wasn't coming after her. No. That didn't hurt most of all. She didn't care what he did with his life. He'd made it clear she wasn't a part of it.

*

Eli watched Marley climb back toward the street. Every inch of him pleaded to go after her. To wrap her up. To comfort her until she was calm, and then talk her through the truth of who he was, slowly and rationally. To run her a bath. Rinse away the tension and the grime. Make lo—

He cut the thought off, before it could manifest

completely. That was a dangerous path to go down. In fact—he turned his attention to Loki—he had other priorities. Like keeping her alive. His desires weren't as important as her survival

He sneered, and balled his hands into fists again. Even if it wasn't the curse, the accidents all hinged on Loki. And that meant, because of his own interaction with her, Eli had put her in danger. He wasn't going to let her suffer again, but he could turn his frustration on Loki. "Seriously, what's your issue with her?"

Loki rolled his eyes. "I already told you. I hate seeing you happy."

Eli roared and lunged. He had to make sure she was safe. That this wouldn't happen again.

Loki shook his head. "Not today. Probably not for several centuries." He vanished before Eli reached him.

Chapter Ten

Marley pulled on her favorite bathrobe, and tried to sink into the fluffy terry cloth. She toweled her hair dry, scowled at the fog on the mirror, and left her bathroom behind. The shower hadn't helped chase away her confusion. Was ten am too early to drink?

She made her way to her living room. When she'd climbed back to the road, leaving Eli and Loki in the clearing, she realized she didn't have her phone on her. She normally kept it mounted on her dashboard when she drove, because she liked listening to music in the car but hated morning radio programs.

There was no way she was walking back into that clearing. Her logic circuits couldn't handle that sight again. Especially as other pieces of her memory started to click into place. Odd things she'd seen Eli do in the past. Accepting she'd watched him crush steel plates, and make flashlights glow, and get knocked into a tree by a ball of lightning and not die, meant admitting to concepts she wasn't ready to deal with.

So instead of calling the auto club, she'd walked until someone picked her up. She'd been covered in blood, so that had taken a while.

It was nice to finally be home. She just wished she understood what had happened. She still couldn't wrap her brain around what took place in the clearing. And she couldn't get rid of the pit in her gut, either. Couldn't ignore how incredible the night before had been. And how it was apparently a lie. Or a joke. Or something. She didn't even know anymore.

Part of her brain asked why someone would set up such an elaborate prank just for her. Or for anyone, really. Unless she was on hidden camera. She resisted the urge to look around her.

That same part of her insisted she couldn't rationalize this away. The pieces didn't click into any explanation other than the one Eli had given her. But gods? No. It wasn't true. She was remembering things wrong. She'd rolled her car. Even if she had walked away unscathed, she had to have hit her head, for there to be so much blood. Never mind that she hadn't found a wound. Her memory couldn't be trusted.

A knock on the door jerked her from the rationalizations. Eli? No. She shoved the hope aside. She didn't want to see him. Not ever again. Even though just thinking something so final pricked her eyelids. It was probably a...

She didn't even know. Her gut flipped in on itself and she pulled her robe tighter around her, when she opened the door and saw who was on the other side.

"I had to make sure you were all right." Loki's cold tone didn't match the sympathetic statement.

Ice snaked down her spine, erasing the warm comfort of the shower she'd just left behind. "I'm fine. Thank you. But I think you need to leave." She swung the door shut as she talked.

He didn't say anything else, and the door latched shut between them. She snapped the deadbolt into place, and an irrational fear pulsed inside. Why didn't she have more locks?

"I'm not a vampire." Loki's voice startled her, and she whirled. He stood in the middle of her living room. "You don't have to invite me in. Knocking was only a courtesy."

Her pulse screamed into overdrive, carrying a whisper of terror with it. She swallowed it all. How had he done that? A magician's trick or something. There was no way Eli's story was true. Was there? "How did you know where I live?"

He held up her phone. "You left this in the clearing. Who actually keeps their own address in their contact list?"

"What do you want?" It was the most she could manage without her voice shaking.

Phone still in his hand, he sank onto her sofa, and leaned back. "You're a really rude hostess. Aren't you going to offer me a drink?"

She forced steel into her voice. Whoever this asshole thought he was, she wouldn't be intimidated. "You're not a guest. Answer my question or leave. Both, preferably."

"Smart, mouthy, obnoxious... No wonder Eli loves you."

Love. The word slid past her entire jumble of thoughts, and tugged at her heart. She pushed the reaction aside. "Eli doesn't love me. Eli is terrified of commitment."

Loki shrugged. "Believe what you want. You're right about the second one..." He trailed off. "Anyway. All that matters is you believe it, and so does he. It means I succeeded."

He was being cryptic, right? There was no way she was just being dim. His words didn't make any sense. Was he insane? Normal, rational people didn't break into their brother's employee's apartments.

Right? Especially not to make vague small talk? She needed to get him out of here. He'd tossed her phone on the coffee table less than a foot away. If she called the cops, would they get here before he could do something?

Call Eli.

She banished the thought immediately. Trusting Eli hadn't done her a lot of good to date. Not if he was keeping things from her like being a god who had a psychotic brother.

Loki stood, and was directly in front of her in a few short strides.

Panic joined her mounting fear, and she stepped back. Or she tried. Her feet wouldn't move. Her panic grew. She tried to put her arms up, to twist, to turn, but it was like something invisible had bound her.

He traced a finger down the side of her face, over her jaw, and along her collarbone. His touch made her skin crawl. An odd tone lined his voice. "I only ever wanted one date. Just to give you a test-drive. But no, you had to fall hard and fast for my brother from day one."

She hadn't fallen for anyone. Well, maybe she had, but not that quickly. She struggled harder, but nothing moved. His tone terrified her. What was going on?

"Don't misunderstand." He dipped his head toward hers, and trailed his nose along her neck, breath hot as he spoke. "This isn't some misplaced crush. I just wanted to know if you were any good in bed." He tugged the edge of her bathrobe. It wasn't enough to pull it open, but it left more of her chest exposed. "Not that it matters now. The game is almost over. Or at least, your part in it is."

"What game?" She could still talk. Every inch of her itched to recoil from his touch. What was he going to do with her? Helplessness made her pull harder at her invisible bonds, but it didn't do any good. Shit, he really was a god. Or something equally terrifying, and he had her bound and helpless.

"Life. Yours, anyway." He smiled, and she swore he was part wolf at that moment. Looking to play with his food before he killed it. "Everyone's life is a game." He traced a finger over her lips. "Here's the thing about the *curse*. Eli is a bit narcissistic." He chuckled. "I guess it runs in the family. But he hides it better than the rest of us. He's only ever focused on that one verse. The one bit he thought related to him."

Reality sank deeper the harder she tried and failed to break free of whatever held her prisoner. Every moment spent with Loki stole more of her hope, and she was pretty sure snapped another thread of her sanity. But at least while he was monologuing, he wasn't doing anything else. "What are you talking about?"

"He always ignored the part about ruling our father's kingdom. Dad can't stay in charge forever. Eli always glosses over the bit that says the first son to discover his happiness will rule the kingdom, with his partner by his side. He ignores it, because he's already decided he's destined to lose his true love, if he ever finds her."

Loki tangled his fingers in her hair and kissed her hard. He pressed close, every inch of his hard frame rubbing against her. His tongue forced its way into her mouth, as he held her captive. Her skin threatened to crawl away from both his touch and the power in it.

He broke away and stepped back. "Meh. Not sure what the big deal is about you." His gaze raked over her. "But Eli's not as bright as he thinks he is, so to each his own. The thing is, he thinks confessing his love to you is going to kill you. That whole, 'She'll draw her last mortal breath' thing. It doesn't mean death. It means your immortality. I'm not guessing this. Not the way he did. I know. It's happened before.

"But this works in my favor—his belief of your impending doom. As long as you don't believe he loves you, and he won't admit it to himself, you'll just die when I kill you. BAM!"

The shouted word made her jump. Tears of fear pricked her eyelids. He was insane. A mad god held her captive in her own living room. Her heart threatened to hammer out of her chest. "If he doesn't believe it, you don't have to kill me."

Loki smirked and winked at her. "Nice try. Thing is, even if he won't admit it, it's true. He almost burst a blood vessel just watching me flirt with you, and sweetheart, you're not close to worth my time. Watching you die…that's going to devastate him. It'll be centuries before he even looks at another woman the way he looks at you. And that's plenty of time to make sure he's not the heir."

She licked her lips. It was the only thing she could do, besides talk. "But he doesn't love me. I promise." It hurt to say, but she was certain. "And I'm never going to see him again."

"You're right again about that second point." He rested a palm on her bare chest, directly over her hammering heart. "But this time, he won't be able to bring you back. I know how to stop that from happening."

*

Eli sank back against his door, frustration pumping through him. He needed to keep his thoughts busy. He needed to not think about Marley. And he needed to find Loki. He could fly, but he didn't have his brother's ability to teleport. So he'd spent the last several hours calling everyone he knew—every place Loki might be—trying to track the fucker down.

Nothing.

He had to find him. Had to make sure Marley was safe. His phone buzzed in his hand, and he looked at it in an instant. The text from a blocked number made his heart sink and every inch of him ache in frustration and fury.

You should have stayed away.

No. Bile rose in his throat. It wasn't real. The message was a joke.

His toes twitched in his shoes. Except he couldn't take that chance. He burst through the front door, flying toward Marley's apartment for the second time that day. He reached her apartment within ten minutes, the longest of his existence. His heart sank when she didn't answer his knocks. He tried the doorknob. It was unlocked.

He rushed into the apartment, and froze just a few steps in. Marley sat in an easy chair, bathrobe spilling open, empty prescription and vodka bottles on the table in front of her. No.

He closed the distance between them without another thought, and pressed his fingers to her throat for a pulse.

Her skin was cold. She wasn't breathing. She didn't have a heartbeat. He closed his eyes, and repeated the gesture that was all too familiar after the last week. Hands at the back of her neck to hold her head steady. Thumbs against her throat, near the veins.

He reached inside her, looking for the spark he needed to pull her back. She can't be gone. This isn't real.

He couldn't find what he needed. That tiny warmth that would indicate she was still connected to her life, however tentatively.

He dove deeper. It had to be there. He had to pull her out. He rested his forehead against hers, despair sinking into him. "Please wake up, Marley." The words spilled out without him processing them. "Please. I love you so much. You can't do this. I'm not worth it." He pressed his lips to hers. But there was nothing there. She was gone.

"Wow. You're a real romantic, aren't you? Too little too late, eh bro?" Loki's taunt shoved Eli's grief aside, and replaced it with rage.

Of course his brother was here. Eli knew surrender wasn't Marley. That she'd never have done something like this to herself.

Something inside Eli snapped. Eons of fury, frustration, and putting up with Loki's shit tore through him. He lunged at Loki, unfiltered rage driving him. He wrapped a hand around Loki's throat, pouring all of his power into the grip, and slammed him in into the nearest wall. He wanted to threaten his brother, but was too furious to find his voice.

For the first time in their existence, he swore he saw fear in Loki's eyes. Good. Loki needed to pay. Marley's was the last life he would destroy.

"Eli." Marley's familiar voice speared through his haze, and he swore his heart stopped. Some of his fury evaporated in confusion. His grip loosened, but he didn't let go of Loki.

Loki's fear vanished, and was replaced with irritation. "Ancestors damn it." His body flickered into the ethereal, and then re-solidified under Eli's touch.

"You're not leaving. Not yet." Marley's voice was cold.

Eli didn't know what was happening, but he knew Loki wasn't going to live through it. He tightened his grip again.

"Stop." Marley's hand rested on his arm, her skin soft against his, calling to his heart. A familiar, but foreign electricity seeped into him. Why did she feel powerful? Marley didn't have that kind of touch. "Eli. You and I need to talk." To Loki, she said, "And I really should let him kill you. Not that I could stop him."

Loki shrugged. "It doesn't really work that way."

"I didn't think immortality was an actual thing until today," Marley said. "I was wrong. Maybe you are, too."

Was this confusion what Marley had felt like in the clearing? Except the pieces were clicking in Eli's head. The things Loki had said about the curse being more than it seemed, the specificity of the words last *mortal* breath, it was all starting to make sense. He'd revel in Marley not only being alive, but possibly being immortal in a moment. First he had to get rid of the immediate threat. "Explain after I destroy him."

Her attention never left Loki. "If you come near me again. Or my family. Or anyone I've ever said hello to on the street. You'll regret it." Her voice was low and threatening when she spoke. Emanating a kind of confidence Eli had never heard from her. He was used to self-assurance, but not like this.

Loki didn't even flinch. "You're not that kind of powerful, hon. You're just a baby in the grand scheme of things."

Eli squeezed his neck again. Loki's taunt ended in a strangled, choking gag.

Marley frowned. "Try me and find out. Or I can let you two fight it out now."

Eli smirked at the implication she wouldn't ask him to stop.

"You'd kill your own brother?" Loki asked him.

He still wasn't sure he believed it, but Eli had the upper hand—the woman he wanted was by his side. Smiling at Loki, Eli dropped his grip on his brother's neck. He balled his hand into a fist, pulled back, and let the punch fly.

Loki's head bounced off the wall with a satisfying *thunk*. He raised his fingers to his split lip, and brought them away covered in blood. Shock and disbelief marred his expression. "How did you...?"

Eli didn't know. He shouldn't have been able to draw blood so easily. When they were younger, Helblindi had been able to keep Loki from vanishing, and that had was the only way Eli had ever been able to hurt Loki. Helblindi wasn't stronger; it was just a different gift.

Did this instance have to do with Marley? Eli would ask for answers later. Right now, he knew she was safe. He growled, and Loki vanished.

Eli spun to face Marley, not sure what to say. He couldn't lose her again. Especially now that he'd figured things out. She was here. Safe. And in his arms. He tunneled his hands in her hair.

She pressed a single finger to his lips, before he could kiss her. "You're an ass. You never stopped to think falling in love might not mean death and eternal misery?"

Loki had known. Apparently for a long time. That's why he'd worked so hard to drive Eli and Marley together, to make sure Eli fell but didn't admit it before trying to take Marley out of the picture. It was an idea intricate and twisted enough it had to belong to Loki.

But that also meant Marley really was Eli's for eternity. "I'm a little slow sometimes."

"As long as it's only sometimes." She brushed her lips over his. "And I love you too."

Relief coursed through him, rapidly joined by lust when she shifted her weight against him. "You heard that?"

"Only kind of. I think whatever this magic, voodoo...whatever it is, was still sinking in. I wasn't completely back from the dead yet."

He didn't need to hear anymore. He crushed his mouth to hers, memorizing every taste and sensation. His cock hardened, straining to get closer to her. This was incredible. He still wasn't sure what to do with the knowledge Marley might be like him now—immortal, destined to be by his side.

Chapter Eleven

The new sensations coursing through Marley were incredible. She'd actually been able to stop Loki from leaving the room. Had the power to take that kind of control. Electricity filled her veins, whispering promises of what she was capable of. Showing her new layers of color she'd never seen in the world.

And none of it compared to Eli's hungry, demanding kiss. She dove into the attention, and returned his intensity. Her skin hummed to be closer to him. A giggle slipped out when he shifted to abruptly sweep her off her feet. He pressed his lips to hers again, as he cradled her. His eyes were soft, but that same domination she remembered from the night before hid behind his compassion.

"This time, you're not leaving in the morning." In a few short strides, he'd crossed her apartment to the bedroom, and sat her gently at the edge of the mattress.

She snaked a hand up the front of his jeans. "I wouldn't give you a choice."

His entire body jerked, when she caressed his bulge. She teased through fabric, arousal growing with his every response.

"Ancestors, Marley, you're killing me."

She took the hint, and slid down his zipper. When she wrapped her fingers around his shaft, he sighed and swayed closer. Her gaze met his, as she glided her tongue over the head of his cock, light and teasing. He shuddered when she took his length in her mouth. She wanted to fuck him again. To feel him inside her. But she wanted to taste him first. Eternity meant they had time.

She moaned, letting the vibrations run along his cock. He rocked against her. When she caressed his sack, he inhaled sharply. She sucked and licked, slowly letting him increase the rhythm.

He pulled out abruptly, and dropped to his knees, so he was eye level with her. "Your mouth is amazing." He kissed her hard, tongue diving in and owning her. He pushed her bathrobe off her shoulders without interrupting the kiss. One palm cupped her breast, kneading and sending daggers of want through her.

Going down on him had already made her wet, and the new attention amplified it.

He broke away, breathless, and rested his forehead against hers. "But I need to be inside you again. I want to watch you as you come. See that incredible expression of pleasure, when you reach the brink and I push you over the edge."

"You have too many clothes in the way for that."

He gave her a wicked grin, and shed everything. He nudged her back on the bed, knee between her legs and brushing her swollen sex. "Problem solved."

She wasn't sure how he managed it, but seconds later, he was on his back with her straddling him. His hands rested on her hips, and his cock poised at her opening.

She grabbed his shaft and stroked, letting his head bump her clit. His grunts matched her heavy breathing, letting her know he enjoyed this as much as she did.

He covered her hand with his. "I was serious." He glided his dick over her slit and thrust inside her hard and fast.

She sank into the pleasure, rocking against him. He set the frantic pace. His groans grew shallower, and she could tell he was close. She cried out in surprise when his thumb found her clit. He pressed tiny, hard circles around the engorged nub. Orgasm washed over her suddenly, stealing her breath. She clenched around his cock, milking him.

He pounded inside her, not letting up on her button until he came, filling her and thrusting, until he was spent.

She rested against his chest, memorizing every sensation. His heartbeat. The warmth of his skin against hers. His cock softening but not sliding out yet. His hands on the small of her back, holding her close and wrapping her in a familiar and incredible safety.

"You're amazing." His soft words melted into the peaceful aura around them.

She smiled against his chest. "I'm pretty fond of you, too."

They both lay there for a while, not talking. Marley wrapped herself in the soothing rhythm of his chest rising and falling. She could get used to this. Who was she kidding? She already was. It felt like she'd been missing this for ages.

"Are you asleep?" Eli's question rumbled through her ear.

She rolled off him, and rested her head on his shoulder. "No. Just enjoying the moment. I'm not really...like you now. Am I?"

"Hard to say. I've found you electrifying since I met you."

She laughed and draped a hand over his chest. "That's corny, and I'm serious."

"I thought it was clever." He rested a hand on her cheek, thumb stroking her skin.

A current raced between them, like a pulsing wave of static electricity. It only lasted a few seconds, but she knew she hadn't imagined it. "What was that?"

"You're definitely not mortal anymore." He tilted his head up enough to kiss her on the forehead.

She should be more surprised. In the last few hours, she'd discovered gods were real, one wanted to kill her, and one had been keeping his distance to keep her alive. Oh, and then there was the one who signed her paycheck.

It all still sounded ludicrous. But knowing she was one of them now somehow felt right. She snuggled closer to Eli. Or at least, knowing it was because he was her eternity felt right.

She'd adjust to the rest as time went on. Apparently she had a lot of that in her future.

The End

Seducing Destiny, Brothers of Fate # 2,

By Allyson Lindt

The vengeance of the gods has ripped love from Blake three times. He's not making the mistake of falling for a mortal again. He's shelved his personal life and dedicated the rest of eternity to ensuring those individuals with a destiny are able to fulfill it. When he meets the curvy, gorgeous Luci, memories of his past surge back to haunt him, and when a goddess from another pantheon tries to kill her, he's forced to admit fate may not be done with him yet.

Denying that his attraction to Luci and her voluptuous figure is anything but physical, Blake's racing against time and doing everything in his power to figure out why the gods want her dead and to keep history from repeating itself.

Chapter One

The world is yours, as you search for her soul
No lover shall bind you to the land
The one you discover, who quiets your might,
Will bring your journey to an end

Blake stepped into the local coffee shop the hotel concierge had recommended, and breathed in the heady scent of espresso roast. Thank the ancestors he wasn't one of those gods who didn't get to experience the effects of caffeine and alcohol.

The landscape inside was familiar, even though he'd never been in the place. A glass case, only half full of pastries; eclectic furniture; a gaggle of people in suits, waiting for their drinks and more concerned about their phones then their surroundings—

Hello, there. His gaze lingered on the woman at the front of the line. Her slacks and matching jacket hugged generous curves, the clothes not too snug but not so loose her figure was obliterated. Styles and fashions changed as the decades and centuries passed. Some for the better, while he wasn't so fond of others. However, a sensual woman with a Renaissance body always made his blood roar.

The way she worried her bottom lip, chewing on the plump swell, erased his dread about the looming interviews and sent desire rolling over his skin. No glow surrounded her, so she was mortal. Not that it mattered; he only wanted a distraction for the next night or two, while he was in town. She'd be a pleasant contrast to the dragging nation-wide tour that had been his last two weeks.

He stepped up next to her. The faint scent of plum and mint greeted him, carrying mental images of her joining him in the bathroom. Him lifting her onto the sink. Cupping that full ass. Finding out what her mouth felt like. He stowed the fantasy and flashed her a winning smile. "May I buy you a drink?"

In heels, she was only a few inches shorter than his six-two. She looked up, eyes wide, and his breath caught at the hazel pools staring back at him. Déjà vu scurried through his veins, overlapping the present with a memory he couldn't quite grasp. Flickers of sensation danced over his body. Lips pressed together. Bare skin gliding against his. Heat, and heavy breathing, and passion. He mentally shook aside the sensation.

She looked over her shoulder, and then back at him. "You're talking to me?"

Amusement joined his swelling lust. "I am."

She looked around again. "You're sure?"

The next register opened up, and she stepped forward and placed her order. He handed his credit card to the cashier. "This is together. Give me a large house roast."

"No, it's not together." The woman handed over her money. The cashier looked between the two for a moment, and then totaled out the first purchase before ringing up Blake's. The attractive businesswoman gave him an unapologetic shrug and set her laptop bag on a nearby table. "I appreciate the offer, but I'm fine. You know this is a coffee shop, not a bar, right?"

He leaned against the chair next to her. She was an entertaining combination of unsure and confident, which did more to wake him up than the coffee would. Some gods had the ability to influence those around them—to change someone's mind with sheer will. His gifts tended more toward weather control and keeping his counterparts from performing tricks, but he didn't mind. The journey was as much fun as the destination for him. "I don't see why mornings should be left out, just because it's not happy hour yet. But if a bar is what it takes, can I buy you a drink tonight?"

She pursed her lips, but the corners of her mouth twitched, a smile threatening to destroy her stern expression. "I'm not much of a drinker."

"You're making this difficult for me." He wasn't annoyed. In fact, he'd rather stay here the rest of the morning, instead of making his meetings. "What do I have to do, to get your number?"

Her brows rose. "You could ask? Or come up with a corny line. I suppose there are a lot of options."

"Would any of them work?"

She took her drink from an employee and set it on the table next to her bag. He grabbed his as well. Pink dotted her cheeks, and her pupils were dilated. "Probably not. But I'm enjoying your efforts," she said.

Too bad. It would have been fun to find out what she sounded like when she was turned on. He didn't have time to keep up the game, though. His first interview was in fifteen minutes, and he still had to walk back to the hotel. He extended his hand. "I'm Blake, by the way."

"Luci."

Two hundred years ago, or even one-hundred, he would have kissed her fingertips and bowed. He settled for focusing on her warm grip when her palm rested against his. Another shock of recognition spilled through him. An image from centuries ago, of a woman in a kimono, black hair flowing around her shoulders. He stowed both the memory, and the pang of longing it dragged with it.

He gave Luci a brief nod. "Thank you for keeping me company this morning, Luci. Enjoy the rest of your day."

She furrowed her brow and studied him for a moment, before stepping back. "Same. Nice to meet you, Blake."

For a moment, when her hand drifted to her bag before snapping back, he thought she was going to hand him her number after all. He was pushy by nature, but he knew when he'd been shot down, and he as a rule he never had to beg. He resisted the desire to glance at her one last time as he strode out the front door. It would have been fun to actually get her information, but it still would have just been a fling, and he could grab one of those somewhere else. A tiny whisper told him it wouldn't be the same, and he shoved the nagging aside.

He stepped onto the street, and pinpricks of electric sparks singed his thoughts, yanking his attention from Luci. Another god was nearby. Caution surged through him. It was an eerily familiar aura. Even before his brain registered a name, his muscles tensed, and his gut churned.

Another zing flooded his head. He scanned the area, and his gaze landed on a woman across the street. Morrigan. Her eyes were so pale, it was evident even with the morning sun casting her in silhouette. She looked up at Blake, smirked, and then faded from sight. The crowds milled in to fill the empty spot, no one even flinching that a woman had just vanished before their eyes. Morrigan being here definitely meant something.

But was it fuck-me bad, or was it maybe-he'd-finally-get-his-hands-on-her-long-enough-to-obliterate-her good?

****

Luci shut her laptop and blew her bangs out of her eyes. So much for getting a little work done before her interview. Normally, she would have worked from home that morning, and then made the hour drive for her appointment. With construction going on, she hadn't trusted travel time. She decided to work in the coffee shop down the street for a few hours, before walking to her meeting spot.

That had been the plan, anyway. The reality was, for the last two hours, her mind repeatedly drifted back to Blake, and not just the eerily comforting sensation of déjà vu that washed over her when they shook hands. She'd almost said his name before he did, but it would have come out Blaine, not Blake, and she had no idea why. Tall, blond... holy hell, she wanted to find out of his chest was as solid under that shirt as it looked. She'd been about two high-speed heartbeats away from giving him her number.

Reality had crashed back in before she made that mistake, though. Gorgeous guys weren't interested in chubby girls unless they wanted something they couldn't get anywhere else. Blake almost screamed, 'I'm hiding secrets.' He was too much like her ex. She wasn't making that mistake again, and not just because she couldn't foot the legal bill. Emotional attachment was a luxury she could live without.

She stepped into the hotel lobby, where her appointment was taking place, and approached the front desk. "I'm looking for Mr. Ugagnkin." Her tongue stumbled over the combination of letters. At least she knew she was pronouncing it right. She'd made his assistant repeat it, to make sure she got it right. She'd tried several times to hint she'd like his first name, but it hadn't been forthcoming.

"He asked that people wait for him over there." Reception nodded at a cluster of chairs across the room. "He'll be with you soon."

"Thank you." Luci had to perch on the edge of the seat to keep from sinking into it and wrinkling her suit. This entire job setup sent a weird vibe through her. Each individual piece was okay on its own. The company was in another city but was hiring contractors nationally, to telecommute, with zero in-office hours. Her interviewer was talking to people in a hotel lobby, because his in-town office reservation had fallen through at the last minute. The pay-scale was at the top end of the industry standard, and she'd been told she would never talk to anyone or need their contact information, during this project, except her direct supervisor or his assistant. All her requirements, changes, and quality-assurance results would flow through Mr. Ugagnkin.

Putting all the components together made her think someone was hiding something. Finding a new contract had been slow going, though, and the pay was good, so she'd stashed her reservations at least until she could talk to this Ugagnkin guy.

The minutes ticked away. She glanced at her phone. Her appointment was almost half an hour ago. This was ridiculous.

"Luci?" A tenor she'd heard before cut through her rambling thoughts and squeezed her pulse back to its high-speed trot from earlier. She looked up to see Blake a few feet away. He looked even better than he had this morning. That wasn't fair. "Lucinda Tansey?"

And he knew her full name. That should have

her concerned. Unless... Crap. She'd been hit on earlier by her possibly new employer, and she still fantasized about being pinned under that sturdy frame. She pasted on a smile. "Hello?"

"I'm Blake Ugagnkin. I'm sorry to keep you waiting. The last interview ran over."

Of course it was him. She struggled to push aside the vivid images in her head—him stripping off her clothes a piece at a time, her dropping to her knees and dragging down his zipper—and failed spectacularly. She stood, used smoothing out her suit as an excuse to wipe off her palms, and shook his hand.

The moment she touched him, a flash of images raced through her head. Memories of a dream she'd had most of her life, except this time the other person had a face. Blake's. She wore a kimono, and he stood behind her, untying the pieces one by one and draping them to the side. Sliding the silk down her shoulders.

She pushed the thoughts aside and steadied herself in the now. "No worries. I guess that means you have my number after all." Why had she said that? She hid her cringe. "I mean, I've got time."

His hand lingered in hers, as he studied her face and then shook his head. "I should make it clear what happened this morning doesn't impact this at all. I hope it won't color your decision, if we decide to make you an offer."

If they were going to be working in the same office, he'd definitely have her leaning toward a yes answer. She forced the thought aside—not an easy feat, given the weight of his gaze raking over her. "Of course. The past is in the past," she said.

Except for maybe the occasional after-hours fantasy.

Chapter Two

Blake kept his attention focused on Luci's face. He wouldn't let his gaze fall lower, to the silver locket nestled at the top of her cleavage. "Picasso was as much about commercial mass production as Andy Warhol or any modern clip art collection."

"That's a bit dismissive. Cubism was about taking three-dimensional objects and representing all their facets simultaneously in two-dimensional space." There was no irritation in her voice.

He had no idea how they'd gotten on the subject of art, but he was thoroughly enjoying the conversation. "You talk about it as if you knew the guy. Unless you were there, you can't say for certain."

She rolled her eyes, and laughed. "Because you were good pals with him? Besides, art is as much about interpretation as anything. You might see Warhol as simplistic, but those bright, vibrant representations of pop culture got people to pay attention to the medium."

"I'll agree with that. When it comes right down to it, for you or me, it's about what the eye appreciates." This time he didn't stop himself from looking her over. "A stunning Raphael or Renoir."

She blushed but didn't look away. "Masters of the human form and color and techniques. Definitely beautiful work."

When he'd seen her sitting in the lobby, it would have been so much easier to tell her 'thanks, but no thanks.' Except, in addition to being distractingly attractive, she was also the most qualified middle-tier developer he'd talked to in four cities. That didn't mean he had to cut the conversation short just yet, though.

He needed to stow his lust and hope she accepted his offer. Without the various pieces of this project, he and the other gods supporting this venture couldn't compile a system to record all the gods who had passed, vanished, or turned against the fates. Nor could they identify the vast list of mortals who might be in line to take some of their places and ascend.

Eternity was at stake. "Do you have any questions for me?"

Luci never broke eye contact for more than a few seconds. The uncertainty that had hovered around her in the coffee shop vanished when she launched into her presentation. "I'd like to know a little more about your company. What do you do?"

The truth wouldn't do. "We engineer resource-maximizing convergence, to continually enhance accurate scenarios." His nerves twinged at the meaningless, memorized bullshit. How had he never realized before how terrible that sounded? It didn't matter. Everyone would hear the same information. It was safer that way.

Her lips drew into a thin line. "How long have you been in business?" she asked.

"I started the company when I was in my twenties." That was almost true. He'd started *a* company, and one venture had melted into the next over the centuries, as times and necessity changed. The words still tasted wrong passing his lips.

"I see. So... the company's about five or ten years old?" Skepticism coated her words.

He gave her his warmest smile. "Not as new as you might think, and I guarantee we're stable."

"Of course." Her tone was flat. "I think that's all my questions."

He wasn't ready to stop chatting with her yet, and his desire only had a little to do with not ending the meeting on a sour note. "Listen, I'm really enjoying this, and I think we still have more to talk about. Interview-wise, of course. I was going to grab some lunch before my next appointment. I'd love it if you could join me."

Her frown deepened, and she fiddled with the strap on her laptop bag. "No, thank you. I won't take up any more of your time."

How had that gone downhill so fast? He stood as she did, keeping his voice pleasant and friendly. "This is the part of the conversation where I tell you I'll be in touch, but I'll be honest. I haven't talked to anyone who comes close to your qualifications. The contract is yours, if you're interested."

She shook his hand. Despite the warmth missing from her expression, her touch still lit his senses on fire, and sent vivid images of her and of his past racing through his thoughts. "Thank you," she said. "If you can email me a copy of the offer, I'd like some time to think about it."

That wasn't what she was supposed to say. Not as though he had a choice. "Of course." He pulled a business card from his wallet and handed it to her. He resisted the urge to tease her about having his number now as well. The flirting didn't seem to be working out. "My direct line. Reach out with any questions, and I hope to hear from you soon." As he said the words, he realized just how much he meant them. Because he needed her on board. Not for any other reason.

****

Luci was glad to be back home, so she could dive back into her job search. She didn't like to be out of work for too long—it ate into her savings. She stripped off her jacket the moment she was inside, and peeled off the rest of her suit as she strode toward the bedroom. Why was she even considering Blake's offer? The money was good, but every time he told her something new about the job or the company, her bullshit meter ticked up another notch.

When he'd invited her to lunch, she almost thought he was interested despite his disclaimers. Even if she did let herself believe the desire in his gaze was real, she wasn't in the mood to pick at a salad in a crowded restaurant, just so no one would ask if she was sure she needed a side of fries with that burger.

She hung her suit in the closet and snagged a pair of her favorite jeans. The ones with the tears right under her ass, because of the way she'd worn the denim out. She grabbed a tank top from her drawer and tugged it on as she made her way back to the kitchen table— the most comfortable spot for working in the one-bedroom.

Time to do some digging and find out if Blake's answers were bullshit, or if she was just being paranoid because of her experience with Craig. She plucked a bottle of iced tea from the fridge and settled in to do her research.

She didn't want to find out Blake was a fraud. Despite everything, she enjoyed the conversation with him. The way they'd flowed from technical questions to pop culture, to music, to art had been the most fun she'd had talking to someone in a long time.

An hour later, her head spun from the circles she'd run in, chasing invisible trails. She'd found several references to Blake's company, all for different functions and businesses, but each time she followed a new link, it dead-ended.

She needed to just tell him no and find a different contract. One that probably wouldn't pay as much and almost definitely wouldn't include the mental stimulation or eye-candy, but it wasn't like she had either of those things before this morning.

Her thoughts ground to a halt when the next website loaded. A phone number and an address. Disappointment nudged her senses. Blake had said he only had one office, and it was in Nashville, Tennessee. This was in Tampa Bay, Florida. Maybe it was just a coincidence, and the two weren't related at all. Best way to find out would be to call and ask if the place had anything to do with Blake. She hesitated with her hand over her phone.

She was being stupid. She needed the answer. Putting off the call wouldn't change what she already knew—taking this job was a bad idea. She sucked in a deep breath and dialed the number.

"F and M Communications." A pleasant voice greeted her.

Maybe she should have thought more about what she was going to say before she placed the call. "May I speak with Blake Ugagnkin?"

Silence greeted Luci. She checked her phone. The call hadn't been dropped.

"Blake—?" The pleasant voice snapped off. "I'm sorry, he's not in this week. Can I transfer you to someone else or give him a message?"

"No. Thank you." Luci disconnected. It wasn't proof of anything. So he worked in an office he'd implied didn't exist. No big deal. Except, combined with everything else...

She couldn't do this. The pros didn't make up for the risk she'd take signing on. That was a practical business decision. The best one she could make. Even if nothing was there, her uneasiness was enough to make the job a must-avoid. She could find another one.

Chapter Three

"Thank you for your time. I'll be in touch." Blake shook the hand of the contractor he'd interviewed. As soon as the man was gone, Blake sank back into the hotel-lobby sofa. He raked his fingers through his hair and exhaled. This guy had looked good on paper, but he'd shown up in a battered T-shirt, cut-off shorts, and reeking of... Blake wasn't even sure. Weed, beer, and sweat. But the job didn't require people to be presentable, just accurate. The meeting had consisted of an hour and a half of stories about past clients, and how stupid they'd been. The best thing about the interview was it had been Blake's last for the day.

His phone vibrated in his pocket, and he grabbed it. The device was set to remain silent, except for priority messages. He dialed into his voice mail and listened to the short message from his brother and business partner, Eli—Byleist, as he'd been known when they were younger. Eli was one of the first impacted by the old myths and curses, and was proof results could vary from the assumed interpretation.

The message was short. "One of your

appointments is digging. She talked to Freyr's office. Call me."

Uneasiness danced through Blake's joints like a million tiny jolts. When Eli's fate had played out the way it did, Freyr had become the company's most vocal opposition. In the past few months, his people had become increasingly aggressive and violent in response, hunting down mortals and weaker gods on the list, and eliminating them. It shouldn't matter that one of Blake's applicants had called, though. Given his encounter with Morrigan this morning, Blake's location wasn't a secret, and that would make it simple to figure out who he was interviewing if Freyr cared.

So why couldn't Blake sit still? He dialed Eli's number, and drummed his fingers against his leg while he listened to the rings.

"You got my message." His brother skipped the formalities. After centuries of working together, they didn't usually bother with things like hello.

"Fill me in."

"This woman is on one of our outlying lists, and now they know who and where she is." Papers shuffled in the background. "Lucinda Tansey?"

Fuck. Dread spiked through Blake, and he clenched his empty hand until his knuckles ached. That meant she played a part in the prophecies. A mortal with a destiny, and very susceptible to things like death until her fate came to pass. "I thought we vetted all the applicants against known names."

"We found this reference buried in a filing cabinet from decades ago. We wouldn't have known to look, if your person in Freyr's office hadn't given us a heads-up when Lucinda's name set off their warning bells."

This was why they needed to make everything digital. Exactly the reason he was hiring contractors.

Because there was too much to keep track of on paper. "What tier is she?" That would determine if her ties to the myths were significant, minor, or just a remote possibility.

"We're still digging up information about what her fate may be, but she's designated as significant. Could be a clerical error or..." Eli trailed off. They both knew that wasn't the kind of risk they could take. "I can send someone for her this afternoon."

The correct answer was yes. They needed to dispatch a local operative, to start surveillance and intercede as needed. If Luci accepted the contract keeping an eye on her would be easier. Then again, if Freyr decided she was an immediate threat, an operative might not be able to step in quickly enough.

"Helblindi"—Eli's sharp tone carried over the line—"make a call."

"I'll handle it myself." Blake shouldn't have said that. What was he going to do? Follow her around like a stalker? An operative could take care of that. Or Blake could knock on her front door and tell her, *'It's possible you're being hunted by a powerful god because you may or may not be a threat to his future'*?

There was no scenario he could picture in which that went over well. It didn't matter. He'd figure out it. His cock stirred at the thought of seeing her again. Her sarcastic laugh. Her witty comebacks. Her gorgeous curves. Long forgotten emotions he'd locked away—he thought forever.

Since he wasn't one of those gods who could teleport or fly, he had a bit of a drive ahead of him. With any luck, it would be enough time to think up a plan and convince his mind to stop taunting him with graphic fantasies of stripping Luci down, one piece of clothing at a time.

508

****

Her pizza was here. The knock on the front door pulled Luci from her job search. She hadn't told Blake yet that she wasn't accepting his offer, but she would. First thing tomorrow morning. Well, not first thing. Maybe later in the day, to make sure he wasn't busy and...

She shelved the rambling thoughts that had assaulted her since she made the decision not to take the contract, grabbed the money from the table beside her, and crossed the living room. She opened the door. When she registered the sight in front of her, she frowned.

The woman on the other side looked up, pale eyes wide. "I'm sorry. I was looking for Joey?" She trailed her finger along the edge of her collar.

Who? "You have the wrong apartment." Discomfort rolled over Luci. Something about this woman made her grind her teeth. "I don't know him." She pushed the door shut. It was abrupt of her, but her skin crawled, and the urge to bolt surged through her.

"That's all right. You'll do."

The knob was yanked from Luci's hand, jarring her wrist, and the door crashed into her arm before colliding with slammed into the wall. A sharp gust shredded through the room. Her hair whipped in her face and stung her eyes. The slam echoed off through the room, and just as suddenly as the wind kicked up, it vanished. She shoved strands of brown out of her field of vision.

Her visitor stood immediately in front of her, smile in place. Pale blue eyes searched Luci's face. "It really is you. It's been a long time."

The run-anywhere-but-here instinct pounded inside Luci until her head ached. What the hell was going on? "Morrigan?" She didn't know this woman's, but the name had popped into her head, associated with those pale eyes, and felt as real as Luci's swelling terror.

"You remember me." Morrigan sounded smug. "You're really"—she looked Luci over again—"kind of bland, aren't you? Not that it matters." She held up her right hand, thumb and middle finger pressed together, as if she were going to snap.

"Enough." A roar filled Luci's ears and skull, and Morrigan stopped moving. It wasn't just her snap that froze mid-air, but her entire frame, down to a grotesquely stalled smirk.

Luci blinked, to clear her eyes and thoughts, but it didn't help. A jumble of questions assaulted her mind, mingling with a fear she didn't understand. When she focused again, she wasn't sure she was seeing right.

Blake had Morrigan pinned to the far wall, his hand at her throat. Her feet dangled so her toes only brushed the carpet. "Leave." His voice was low and threatening, rolling on a breeze that didn't have a source.

Terror spilled through Luci. Whatever this was, she wasn't going to put up with it. Her apartment was a wreck, and she had no idea who these people were. This was too much. "What the *fuck* is going on?" she screamed.

Blake glanced back at Luci and then at the blue-eyed lunatic. Morrigan dropped, landing lightly, and dipped her head toward Blake's. "Catch you later, lover boy. Good luck with this." And then she vanished.

Luci shook her head. There was no way a woman had just disappeared from her living room. She looked at Blake. Why hadn't he answered her? Why was he even here? "Blake?"

He frowned, not meeting her gaze. "We need to

get you out of here."

"What?" With the strange woman gone, Luci's terror ebbed, leaving room for confusion and frustration. "No. Answer my questions. Who was that? Why are you in my apartment? And why the fuck would I go anywhere with some guy I've only known for a few hours, and don't even trust?"

The creases in his brow deepened, and was that hurt in his eyes? Good. Served him right. He shook his head, and a blank mask slid onto his face. "You come with me, or stay here and the next one who comes for you will kill you. Decide now."

She sank to the couch and rubbed her hands over her face. He was lying. This was some sort of... She didn't even know, but it wasn't real. So why did every inch of her tell her to do what he said?

Chapter Four

An hour's drive to find this place, and Blake still hadn't figured out what he was supposed to say. Morrigan provided an ice breaker, but seeing her had summoned centuries of demons, rage, and grief. Blake would have ripped her to pieces right then and there if it was within his power to do so.

Despite his ultimatum, no part of him was willing to leave Luci to her fate. He racked his brain for a next step. "You're being hunted by powerful gods, because you may or may not be a threat to their future." It sounded just as crappy and crazy when he said it aloud.

Her raised brows and twisted mouth indicated she felt the same. "You're insane. I don't know what kind of game this is, but I'm calling the cops unless you leave right now. Hell, I'm calling them anyway. Was that even a real job interview this afternoon?"

Her distrust left an ache inside, but he ignored it. "You can't call anyone. Just listen. Morrigan—or someone like her—will be back." With any luck, it wouldn't be her. He didn't need to see the past repeat itself.

She stood, crossed the room to the kitchen, and grabbed her phone. "I'm calling the police."

"Hear me out." Despite the adrenaline racing through him and the desire to get her to safety *now*, he forced his voice to stay calm. "Please." He had no idea why it was so important to him she listen. With anyone else, he'd have already tossed them over his shoulder and spirted them away to safety regardless of what they thought of him. Mortals were fragile, and he wasn't a god known for his patience. But it was important she trust him, even though he couldn't explain why he was being irrational about that. "If I can't convince you, I'll go." He couldn't though. There was no way he was leaving her.

She clenched her jaw and crossed her arms. Seconds ticked away, and the uncomfortable silence grew. "You have two minutes."

Great. That didn't make it any easier to come up with an explanation. Fuck it. He held out his hand, and with a flicker of concentration, summoned a ball of electricity and let it float about an inch above his palm.

A gasp strangled from her throat, and her phone clattered to the table. She snapped her jaw shut and closed the distance between them. "Bullshit. That's a trick." She pushed up his sleeves.

When her skin met his, a shock of familiarity seared through him, and images flooded his thoughts. Random snippets he couldn't make sense of. Memories of a woman he'd known almost two centuries ago. A nightgown. A high collar. Her soft gasps, as he stripped away her clothes, mingled with Luci's sigh in the now and dragged him from the vision.

He found his voice. "It's not a trick. It's real." He pulled off his suit coat, draped it over the back of a chair, and rolled up his sleeves. "See? It's just me."

"Can you vanish like that woman did?"

"No. Teleporting isn't in my arsenal."

She made a sound that was half huff, half sniff. "You need better tricks."

Wounded pride swelled in his chest. "I have better tricks." He closed his eyes, bowed his head, and inhaled deeply through his nose. He summoned an image of the afternoon sky, heavy with clouds blocking most of the sun. Electricity and water broiled through the air. Through his eyelids, he saw the light fade. He looked at Luci again, as a clap of thunder rattled the windows and echoed off the walls.

She squeaked and jumped. Her hand flew to her heart, and she met his gaze. "Did you do that?"

That was a better response. He smirked. "We need to go now. I'll explain everything I can, once we're safe, but that requires you to follow me."

*

Luci looked out the window—rain hammering against it from a sky that had been bright blue seconds ago—then back at Blake. She still had no idea what to believe, but she didn't know of a single magic trick that could make it rain in an instant. The flash of images she'd seen when she touched him... they'd felt like her memories. They couldn't be. Was he doing something to her head? Hypnosis, maybe. That made more sense than a random god having it in for her and Blake coming to the rescue.

Even knowing all that, she couldn't convince herself to send him away. It had to be better than waiting for some vanishing woman who could summon wind from thin air to come back and kill her. "All right. I'll go." Luci expected more anxiety at speaking the words. Instead some of the fight escaped her, and relief sank in.

He pulled a blank card from his wallet, intertwined his fingers with hers, and tugged her toward the closet. What the hell?

"I can't teleport," he said as he passed the credit-card sized object over the knob, "but this always gives me a doorway home." He opened the door, and her eyes grew wide. Instead of coats and jackets, an entryway stretched out in front of her.

He pulled her hand. They stepped into the new room, and the door swung shut behind them. This was too weird. She didn't know if she should freak out or just enjoy the madhouse. She whirled and yanked the knob. The other side was an unfamiliar street, instead of her living room. "How did you....? What...?" She didn't know what to say. Nothing in her scope of experience prepared her for this.

"It's magic." He flashed her a broad smile.

She might have to start believing that or lose her mind.

"You're back." A female voice interrupted Luci's thoughts. A woman tossed her arms around Blake's neck, and he returned the hug. "You're early," the woman said.

Jealousy speared Luci, leaving a sharp pain in her lungs. That was ridiculous. She didn't care who Blake had waiting for him at home, even if the woman was tall, thin, and almost glowing.

"We need to rethink our plans." Blake stepped out of the woman's grasp.

Another man joined them. He looked a lot like Blake but not as broad in the shoulders, and instead of a suit he wore more casual jeans and a T-shirt. He glanced at Luci before turning back to Blake. "You got there in time. I have more information about her relevance."

Luci was a guest, and it was true she had almost

zero idea what was going on, but she still didn't like being ignored. She opened her mouth to protest, but Blake rested a hand on her lower back and nudged her forward. The contact sent a jolt of warmth through her and snatched away her objections.

"This is Luci." Even in a few short words, Blake commanded the situation. "She had the distinct pleasure of running into Morrigan, so no, I didn't make it in time. Did we know there were other pantheons involved with her name?" He looked at Luci. "And this is my brother, Eli, and his fiancée, Marley."

Fiancée. The single word soothed Luci more than she thought possible, especially given the last hour or so of insanity. What the hell was wrong with her? She'd known this guy for a few hours, he'd already threatened to uproot her life, and she was crushing on him? She stuffed any further reactions deep down inside, focused on being calm and logical, and smiled at Marley and Eli.

"Fuck." Eli drummed his fingers against his legs. "You still have the copies of the Celtic myths surrounding Morrigan, correct?"

Something resembling a growl rumbled from Blake's chest. "What do you think? And why are you in my house? A phone call wouldn't do?"

"We're here because the old filing cabinets that had the documents with your name are here." Marley looked at Luci. "Goddess in your apartment? You have my sympathy. Are you all right?"

No one seemed to have any issues with this entire bizarre conversation besides Luci. "I'm really fucking confused, and someone promised me an explanation."

Marley reached for Luci's hand and squeezed her fingers. "Don't blame them. They've had centuries to deal with it."

Blake sighed.

Eli wrapped an arm around Marley's waist and pointed her toward the front door. "We'll catch up soon."

Luci's head spun, as silence engulfed her and Blake again. He finally spoke. "Do you want something to drink?"

"I want answers." She hated to sound like a broken record, but the last of her restraint was slowly slipping away, leaving in its place a panic she couldn't define and didn't think she could contain.

He nudged her to the right, toward an open room. It was the embodiment of the term *sitting room* brought to life. A fireplace dominated the far wall, and leather sofas and chairs were arranged to face each other. Blake took a spot on one of the two couches and waved for her to join him.

She couldn't sit. Too much energy thrummed through her. She folded her arms, to keep herself from shaking apart. "I'm waiting."

Chapter Five

Blake was done searching for the best way to phrase things. At this point there was no reason to try and break the news gently, or ease Luci into things. He hated the worry lines around her eyes, and the way she chewed the inside of her cheek, but something told him meting out information wouldn't ease her expression.

Besides, as gods they didn't keep their immortality and power secret because of things like concern for their safety. Once upon a time, they'd worn the label proudly. It was just that these days, no one believed them anyway. The numbers of people who kept the faith were so small, a god wearing his birthright like a badge didn't make any sense.

Luci stopped her pacing, and started at him. "Well?"

He sucked in a deep breath. Might as well start at the beginning. "Morrigan, the woman in your apartment, is a god. She's not the only one. Eli and I are as well. Marley wasn't, but she is now, and..." He trailed off when Luci's brow furrowed and confusion settled onto her face.

"And at least one of you wants me dead. I get

that. But why?" she asked.

"I'll back up." He patted the couch next to him. "Sit. It's going to take a while."

She shifted her weight from one foot to the other, and then dropped into the chair across from him. She drew her mouth into a straight line and watched him, eyes wide in expectation.

"Every pantheon... you would call them mythologies"—he hated that term, but he needed to make her understand this was real, not a children's story about imaginary creatures—"has their own curses, fates, and texts surrounding the end of the world."

She held up her index finger. "Stop. I'm not super up to date on my mythology, but I'm pretty sure there are no gods named Blake. Or Eli."

He resisted the urge to roll his eyes, not at her but at destiny. "It's not our fate for people to know our names."

"Really." Her tone was flat.

"I'm not just saying that," he said. "The text around us specifically says only our brother will be famous. But you're right. Eli's full name is Byleist, and mine is Helblindi."

"I guess I can see why you don't go around calling yourself that."

He scowled. "Thanks. Anyway, besides stripping away our notoriety, our legends say a lot of gods will die, and others will take their place during and after the rebirth of the world as we know it. As you can imagine, not everyone's so keen on seeing that happen. Especially those gods who aren't supposed to survive. None of us took it seriously until a few months ago, when the poems and rhymes we'd recited for centuries started coming true."

"Let's say I believed you." She wrung her fingers together. "Why do any of them care about me?

And how did—" She clenched her jaw and shook her head. "Why me?"

He wanted to push her question, find out what else was in her head, but something told him that wouldn't get him anywhere right now. "That's what Eli and Marley are trying to figure out. It's why..." He let out a slow breath. "It's why I'm looking for contractors. All of this information is written down in so many random places, we need to pull it all together. Digitize it."

"But it's not like you can tell someone what you're working on, without them thinking you're insane. So you're having it built in separate modules." She filled in the rest of the thought for him.

"Exactly. Apparently there's a reference to you in one. We'd have known that if we already had the system online."

She flopped back in the chair and turned her gaze to the ceiling. "And it's completely a coincidence that I showed up on your interview list."

The way she said it made the entire thing sound so... conspiratorial. "It is. We still would have found you, but not like this."

"Wow. That makes me feel so much better about the entire thing." Sarcasm dripped from her voice. She dropped her chin to her chest and locked her gaze on Blake. "When can I go home?"

"I don't know."

She rubbed her face, and a tiny whimper escaped from her throat. Her frame shuddered. She dragged the back of her wrist across her cheeks, and looked at him again. "What now?"

"We keep you safe until we have answers and a plan."

"That's swell"—she was on her feet again, pacing—"but it's not going to work for me. I have a life. Things to do. And that doesn't involve sitting around in the middle of—where are we, anyway?—just waiting for the other shoe to drop."

"We're in Nevada. About ten miles outside of Las Vegas." He didn't understand why, but it tore at him to see her so upset. It knotted his muscles and coiled his instinct, making him search for a target he wouldn't find. He stood and stepped in her path. She huffed. When she tried to step around him, he rested his hands on her shoulders and forced her to look him in the eye. He kept his voice low and calm. "It sucks. I get that."

She let out a snorting laugh. "How could you? If this is true, you have no idea how I feel."

"You're right, I can only guess. But I can still tell it sucks. I've had my home, my life, and the people I love ripped from me enough times..." He clenched his jaw at the surge of memories. Grace, in nineteen-twenties' New York. Sayuri, with the flowing dark hair and kimono. Elizabeth, in the silk Victorian dress. An ache throbbed in his chest. "You don't have to just sit down and surrender, but we do need a plan, and we need information first."

"Then let me help."

A compulsion sped through him, and he brushed a thumb over her cheek. The direct contact added another wash of color to the images vying for his mind's attention, blurring her face with others and morphing them together. Except instead of drawing his attention from her, the memories honed his senses in on her presence. On top of it all was heat and desire and the need to protect Luci. "I will. But right now, if we dive into a random spot and start digging, we'll be spinning our wheels. Once Eli has more information, he'll let me know.

She nodded and covered his hand with hers.

Lust jolted through him. She licked her lips. "What do we do until then?"

Find out if Luci tasted as delicious as she looked. "I'd still love to buy you a drink," he said.

Some of the lines on her face faded, and the corner of her mouth pulled up. "The last thing I need right now is to be drunk. Though, trust me, it's tempting."

The slightest twist of his hand, and he could wrap his fingers in her hair. A dip of his head, and he could claim her mouth. Ancestors, she was wreaking havoc on his thoughts. "I'll buy you dinner, then." Or make her the main course. Trace his tongue down her chest. Dip between her breasts.

"Dinner. Crap." She frowned and stepped out of his grip. "I completely forgot I ordered pizza before my reality imploded. The poor driver is going to be pissed. I need to call them and apologize."

Desire still skittered over Blake's skin. He clenched his fist, to bring his racing pulse under control, and tried to ignore the strain of his cock against his slacks. He was disappointed at the lost moment, but something about how flustered she looked over a forgotten dinner delivery was still enticing. Flushed cheeks, wide eyes. He laced his fingers through hers. "Calling them will wait."

She caught her bottom lip between her teeth. Did she have any idea how seductive that was? "I feel bad," she said.

He could think of a couple very specific ways to distract her into feeling something else, but the moment was gone. "I don't suspect they'll hold a grudge. If you're that worried about pizza, I can have something more authentic delivered."

"Authentic pizza. In the middle of Nevada. How do you define authentic?"

He knew the perfect place in Naples. Italy. And the goddess who ran the place just happened to be a close friend. "Trust me."

Luci's smile slid back in place. "Oddly enough, I do."

Chapter Six

Luci struggled to wrap her brain around the entire situation. Gods. Myths. Fate. There was no way any of it existed, let alone that she played any part in it. Her logic said it would be just as stupid of her to ignore what was right in front of her as it was to believe it. That included the way Blake kept looking at her. The way his gaze dipped over every inch of her. The flashes of unfamiliar but sharply sensual images every time he touched her. It should be the last thing on her mind, but it consumed most of her remaining mental resources.

She was certain of some things. The pizza he'd ordered had been almost heavenly—hand tossed crust, brick-oven crisp, and like nothing she'd ever tasted before. And she was sure that when she said she trusted him, she meant it. The idea of giving her faith to someone she barely knew terrified her. Now that it was clear what he'd been hiding that morning, the lingering uneasiness vanished. Whatever else happened, she believed him when he said they were working to find answers and keep her safe.

She settled back onto one of the couches after they finished eating, a permanent smile on her face from the conversation that had drifted from one topic to the next with ease. "You really got the pizza from Italy?"

He took the seat next to her, and his thigh brushed hers before he turned to face her. "You meet people when you've been alive as long as I have."

Part of her wanted to know how long that was. Numbers ticked through her head. Five hundred years? One thousand? Her mind twitched at the logic of someone actually living that long. She could only handle so much reality in an evening. "I bet you've seen some amazing things."

He furrowed his brow for a second, but his smile returned so quickly she thought she'd imagined the change. "I have. There are a lot of pluses to being immortal. It gets a little lonely at times, though."

"But you saw so much as it happened. The moon landing, right? Were you there for that?"

"On the moon? No." He winked. "But yes, I remember that. And hearing about the Wright Brothers taking their first flight. And watching large portions of Europe sail to the new world..." He trailed off. "But it all blurs together after a while. There are so many new and amazing things that new and amazing becomes passé." He shook his head, as if to clear away a fog.

The new world. He really was that old. She struggled to place herself in that frame of mind. "It does sound like a lot, but I still bet it was awe inspiring. The world doesn't do incredible things anymore."

"Sure it does." He slid his fingers under hers, where they rested on her knee. "It's not a matter of scope; it's what you remember. The day you graduated high school. Or college. You remember those?"

Should she pull away? No. This was comfortable. Reassuring. But she did wish it wasn't all focused on her. "Of course. But those aren't the kind of things that change the world."

"They change someone's world. Yours, and that's important. Mine, since it's part of what makes you who you are now. You remember your first kiss, right? The anticipation. The buildup. The nervousness?"

His smooth voice glided under her skin and summoned every sensation he described, until her pulse sped through her veins and her lips twitched from the suggestion. "How awkward it was."

He dipped his head in, until his mouth hovered millimeters from her neck, close enough his breath shifted across her skin with every word. "But you had to start somewhere, right?"

Her chest constricted as he traced a line up to her jaw, never making contact. He rested his hand at the back of her neck. Tiny sparks danced through her entire body at the barely-there caress of his lips brushing hers, and she whimpered. He pulled back, but his gaze still lingered on her face, desire darkening his eyes. "It's not about the big things. It's about enjoying those things that are significant to you." His tone was low. Hypnotic.

She wanted more. She licked her lips and tried to make her vocal chords work. "Like meeting a stranger in a coffee shop, who turns my entire world upside down?"

His grin was sinful and hungry. He traced tiny circles along the base of her neck with his thumb. "Exactly. Like that the most gorgeous woman who was in that room is sitting on my couch now."

The compliment nudged a corner of her mind she was trying to keep locked, and her insecurities flooded back in. "You don't have to say that." Damn it, she hadn't meant to let that slip out.

"Say what?"

"That I'm gorgeous." Negative thoughts clawed their way to the surface. She wasn't pretty. She was pudgy and clumsy and plain. Sexy guys like him—he was a god, for hell's sake—didn't look twice at women like her. His gaze said he meant the words, and his touch lit her nerve endings on fire, but her stupid self-doubt screamed in her skull.

"You are." He glided his hand from her neck, to trail a finger down her cheek, gaze never leaving her. He traced her bottom lip. "Every inch of you is stunning." He sounded sincere. He looked genuine.

But her mind still refused to accept it. "I bet that's one of those things you don't forget—the beautiful women you've loved in your lifetime." Why had she said that? There was something wired wrong in her head. Maybe it would take the focus off her, though. Give her a chance to rebuild her walls and stash her uncertainty again.

He intertwined his fingers with hers. "I'm no more likely to tell you that, than you are to tell me about your past love life."

Now he was keeping secrets from her. It was an irrational reaction, but knowing that didn't stop her from feeling it. Her own insecurity was sabotaging an amazing conversation, and she couldn't make herself stop. "I'll tell you about my past loves. I was engaged once. To a handsome, smooth-talking, well-dressed guy, who turned every head when he walked in a room." Shut up, shut up, shut up. It was too late. Blake's frown told her that.

"And madly in love with him, I assume." His seductive tone was gone, replaced with something unreadable. "I suspect a guy would have to be pretty spectacular, to catch your attention like that."

He was making fun of her, wasn't he? Except despite his flat words, there was no malice in his gaze.

Not that she was any good at recognizing things like that. "He talked a good game. Even convinced me to go into business with him. Let me handle the accounting. Brought in huge sales." She swallowed the growing lump in her throat at the swell of unpleasant memories. It was good she'd dredged this up. A painful but appropriate reminder she knew better than to lose herself in someone's attention. "Until he skipped town, and I was brought up on money laundering charges." That had been painful, humiliating, and incredibly difficult to clear her name of. If they were talking about moments burned in their memories, the day she testified against her ex was one of the most bittersweet of her life.

"Fuck, Luci." His expression softened. "You didn't deserve to go through that."

"It was my own fault. I let myself be sweet-talked into oblivion and ignored some really obvious signs. I know better now than to trust too-good-to-be-true, all-encompassing lines like 'you're gorgeous.'" A new ache joined her discomfort when Blake frowned. She shouldn't have said that. Her subconscious seemed to know better than her, though. Even if she took the words back, she wouldn't sound genuine.

Blake cupped her chin and forced her to look him in the eye. His voice was firm but calm. "I'm not him. And I mean what I say."

She wanted to believe him, but the mental floodgate was open, and she couldn't convince herself he was sincere. Then again, she also couldn't make herself pull away. "I spilled my guts. Now it's your turn. You must have someone who's left an impact on you. Some stunning beauty from the centuries of your life."

He clenched his jaw and stood. "And if you weren't using it as an excuse to sour the conversation, I

528

might tell you about one of them."

One of them... Of course he'd had eons of lovers. A guy like him, living for as long as he had. She clenched her hand hard enough her fingernails dug into her palm. "That's fine. You have your past, it doesn't impact me. I don't have to know the details, as long as I remember it doesn't have anything to do with me."

"It doesn't." All emotion had vanished from his face and voice.

Chapter Seven

Luci lay in the unfamiliar bed, staring at the ceiling. Once she'd derailed the conversation with Blake, it was over. He'd backed off, shown her where a guest room was, and handed her a T-shirt to sleep in, if she wanted.

That had to have been at least an hour ago. Sleep eluded her, though. Everything around her smelled like Blake, seeping into her senses and taunting her with whispers of almost-kisses. She hated herself for derailing the conversation the way she had, but at the same time, it was for the best. As long as she kept repeating that, it would sink in, and she'd believe it. He and his brother would figure out why someone wanted to kill her, and they'd send her home, and life would go on.

She rolled onto her side, so she could see out the window. They were too close to the city for there to be anything besides black and the faintest smattering of dots. Light pollution bled into the bottom of the sky. She pulled her knees to her chest and tried to block out her onslaught of swirling thoughts. Life would definitely go on, and she'd be better for the experience once she came out the other side.

****

The sound of a knock on Elizabeth's bedroom door sent her steadily beating heart pattering at a gallop. She lit the candle on the stand beside her, climbed from her bed—not that she had been able to sleep in this unfamiliar house—and crept to answer.

Henry nudged his way into the room as soon as she cracked the door, and toed it shut behind him. Her tall, blond, strapping Henry. "My beautiful Beth." He placed his hands on her hips and drew her close. He trailed his fingers under her nightgown and over her birthmark. The one shaped like a crow, that he loved to kiss. "Finally, I have you all to myself."

She rested her hands on his chest, intensely aware she wore nothing but the thin shift she slept in. The heat from his palms seared through the fabric and left traces of longing on her skin. "Dinner did seem to wear on for a bit, didn't it?"

He kissed her forehead, then her nose, and finally brushed his lips over hers. "It does not matter. It's over now"—he guided her backward—"and you look stunning." He spun before they reached the bed, dropped onto the feather mattress, and pulled her between his legs.

"What if someone hears us?" Even though they weren't married yet, they'd been together several times, but he had so many guests staying at his home now. All in anticipation of their wedding in a few days.

"Then they will be jealous I've got the privilege of making the most gorgeous woman in the house scream in ecstasy." He kissed her stomach through her nightgown, and her breasts tightened with need.

"My parents won't be impressed."

531

"Your father has already granted me your hand. No one but you may revoke that honor now."

"I won't scream with so many people here."

In a single fluid gesture, he stripped her clothing off. The cool air brushed her flaming skin and caressed the dampness between her legs. "That sounds like a challenge."

"It isn't," she squeaked out.

He cupped her bottom and drew her close. Her stomach fluttered in anticipation, as he tilted his head in and drew a nipple into his mouth. When he flicked his tongue back and forth over the sensitive nub she groaned and dug her fingers into his shoulders. He worked his hands forward, until he brushed her wet desire.

She gasped at the sensation. Damn being overheard. She leaned in enough to reach the laces on his breeches and fumbled until they were loose. When she worked him free, her fingers wrapped around his hard length, he let out a low groan that penetrated every inch of her.

He grabbed her wrists. "I want to watch you on top of me." He lay back and tugged her with him.

He was so vocal. The words and desire throbbed inside her. She knelt on the bed and positioned herself above his erection. In a single thrust, he pushed inside her, and a cry tore from her throat.

"That's my beautiful Beth." His gaze traveled over her, as they built to a frantic rhythm. He slid his hands up her stomach, to her breasts. Each caress was a feather-light buzz through her body.

She groaned as the soft touches melted into hungry pinches and tugs. He rolled her swollen nipples between his fingers. Pleasure built inside her, dancing along the different sensations of Henry's attentions. Each time with him was more spectacular than the last.

Would it be like this forever?

When he dropped one hand between her legs and pressed against a sensitive button, another cry tore from her throat. That was new. And incredible. Her breathing turned into short pants for air, as he rubbed the new spot and thrust himself inside her. Her thoughts fluttered away, lost in a haze of bliss. Each push from Henry stole more of her reason. Waves of revelry splashed over her, and she ground against him, riding the intensity.

His grip on her breast tightened, and his grunts became staccato. She recognized the sound of him drawing close to finish. He drove up, filling her.

Luci's eyes flew open, and she gasped. She'd had dreams like that before, where she was someone in the past, but they'd never been so vivid. Her lover had never had a name, now he had two. Henry from her dreams was Blake. The man whose guest bedroom she lay in.

The intensity of the vision still flooded her senses, mingling with faint scent of Blake on everything surrounding her. Need throbbed between her legs, and her nipples ached for attention. She didn't know where the sleeping vision had come from, or why her subconscious had given her the name Elizabeth and placed her in Victorian England. At least, despite all the random unknown variables, her mind had been sadistic enough to still give her that damned birthmark on her hip she hated so much.

Right now, she didn't care. The memory of Blake-as-Henry flowed over every inch of her, obliterating her sense and filling her with an insatiable desire. Still half-lost in the fantasy, she moved her hands to her chest and whimpered at the first brush against her sensitive skin. She squeezed, drawing back the images of his hands on her skin. The pinch of pain and pleasure.

She glided one palm down her stomach, to the pleading need between her thighs. How could a dream be so intense and feel so real, as if she'd lived it? She pushed her panties aside and dipped her fingers between her wet folds. Her clit blossomed in delight when she sought it out.

She rubbed frantic circles, hips pumping against her hand. Climax tore through her, and she had to bite the inside of her cheek to keep from crying out. In her head, she still felt the visions mingling with the present, as if Blake had been buried inside her, stroking her until she came.

Her orgasm ebbed, and she eased off and slumped back against the mattress. Reality slunk its way back in, as the buzz faded, reminding her where she was—what had happened. Pointing out there were voices drifting up from somewhere in the house.

Wait. Voices?

*

After Luci went to bed, Blake tried to work. He didn't need sleep unless he'd exhausted his power on something, and tonight he wasn't interested in indulging the habit. Instead, he spent a few hours staring at the wall, trying to figure out how the conversation that evening had gone so completely off track.

He hated to see Luci's insecurities rear their head, and that was what he was dealing with. On the other hand, he refused to indulge them. He could only tell her he was being honest so many times, before it wasn't worth the effort anymore.

Except he couldn't make himself believe he'd been right to stop trying when he'd done so. At least sending her upstairs and putting some distance between them had helped him banish the flashes of his past that had haunted him all day.

The past. Something was there... The notion floated just out of his conscious reach. What was it? He closed his eyes, to block out as much external distraction as possible, and honed in on his thoughts. Something about Beth. Grace. This morning.

Morrigan. Of course. Seeing her had never been a good sign. Millennia ago, he and she had dated. When she'd killed Sayuri, he'd assumed it was jealousy. When she obliterated Elizabeth, he suspected it ran deeper than resentment and insanity. And when she went after Grace as well, he knew there was more there.

The words of the legend floated to mind. Words he'd memorized after Grace, hoping he could make sense of them.

The woman who bears her mark will undertake a battle of overthrowing.

He'd never figured it out. It seemed obvious on the surface, given they'd all had the same birthmark, except he had no idea why his past loves would be play a part in overthrowing Morrigan. There certainly hadn't been any battles involved. It had always ended in an instant. He cringed at the vivid memories.

But the women Morrigan had gone after before had been Blake's lovers. Wives. Luci certainly made his pulse race, and he enjoyed her company, but the relationship wasn't the same. Luci wasn't the same as the rest. Then again, there was that sense of déjà vu every time they touched. That flash of memory. That feeling he knew Luci on a deeper level than was possible after such a short amount of time.

And he was reading too much into the situation. Never a good idea.

A soft knock interrupted his painful journey into

the past, and he padded to the front door. Surprise and concern filled him when he saw Marley. He stepped aside. "The phone was too difficult to pick up?" What was meant to sound teasing came out as a bark. He gave her a weak smile. "Sorry. Long day."

She didn't seem to take offence. "Tell me about it." She stepped inside and handed him a manila folder. "How's your guest?"

"As well as can be expected, I suppose."

Marley rested a hand on his arm. "You don't know this, but it's not easy being where she is. You just turned her entire world upside down. At least you filled her in quickly and didn't drag it out for several months. But she has to cope."

He didn't miss the hint of irritation that crept into Marley's voice. Even though she said she understood Eli's reasons for keeping his identity secret for so long, Blake knew it still bothered her on some level. She'd gotten immortality out of the entire affair. Was that what waited for Luci?

For some reason the thought left a foul taste in his mouth. Marley seemed to enjoy the newfound power that came with godhood, but Blake wouldn't wish immortality on anyone. Not unless they got to walk into it eyes wide open.

He shook the thought away and held up the folder. "What's this?"

"Can we talk in your office?"

He held out an arm in that direction. "After you."

Seconds later, she closed the door, shutting them off from the rest of the house. "Look inside."

"Just tell me what it is." He opened the folder anyway. His stomach lurched at the contents. Photocopies of documents he'd buried long ago.

"You recognize them, then." Marley's tone was

soft.

He should. They were marriage certificates—or at least their historical equivalent. One from feudal Japan, one from Victorian England, and the last from here in the U.S. almost a century ago.

Chapter Eight

"And?" It took effort for Blake to form the single word.

"Look at the birth dates on them." Marley prompted.

Nothing stood out, except that they'd all been born during harvest season. A whisper of memory tickled his thoughts. A notion from decades ago tensed through his muscles and throbbed in his head. There was a reason he'd shoved that bit of his past aside, though he couldn't recall what that reason was. He didn't have the patience for this. If his past insisted on haunting him so completely, he'd like to know why sooner rather than later. "Just tell me what I'm supposed to be seeing."

She twisted her mouth and raised her brows. "Fine. They were all born on their calendar's fall solstice. They've got other similarities. They were born in foreign countries—to their parents anyway—but raised back home. They were all still single, disgracefully so I'd assume, when they turned thirty. And they all had birthmarks on their hips. Apparently at one point you or someone you knew thought that was relevant, because since Grace, you've been keeping a list of everyone who met those specific criteria."

"It sounds vaguely familiar." It sounded intensely familiar. A ghost he'd chased almost a century ago. An obsession he'd forced himself to abandon, when he realized he could spend the rest of eternity chasing the phantom, and it still wouldn't change the past. A grief-induced dream he'd walked away from, in order to carry on. "But we gave that up."

"You may have, but someone kept searching." Marley's voice dropped in volume. "Look at the last document in there."

He flipped to the photocopy of a more recent birth certificate. From Canada.

Lucinda Beth Tansey.

Born September 23, 1985.

Distinguishing marks: oddly shaped birthmark on the left hip.

He looked back at Marley.

"That's why her name is on a list," Marley said. "And she's the only person in almost seventy years."

Fuck. Damn it. "Fuck it all to Hel". He didn't know how to process the information, but that didn't stop dread and undirected fury from spilling through him.

"There's more." Marley pulled her phone from her back pocket and swiped the screen to unlock it. A paused video waited, and she clicked it to start it playing.

Blake watched, rage growing, as images of Luci's apartment burning played behind a reporter's head. The man droned on about how an explosion had rocked the building early that evening, and while the police weren't releasing any information at this time, there were rumors of a terrorist attack. He said their sources inside the Salt Lake Sheriff's department were certain nothing but a bomb could have caused that level of destruction.

A bomb or a pissed off god. The thought bounced in Blake's head.

The office door creaked open, and Marley's spun on her toe at the same time Blake's head shot up. Luci stood in the doorway, his shirt hanging halfway down her thighs, over her ripped jeans. She looked gorgeous and concerned and so very fragile. How was he going to explain this?

*

Luci hovered outside the door. From the tour Blake gave her earlier, she knew it led to his office. Two voices floated out—she assumed the two she'd heard through the vents upstairs. Blake, and if she was hearing right, Marley. There was also a muffled noise she couldn't make out, like conversation coming through a tiny speaker.

"That's why her name is on a list. And she's the only person in almost seventy years."

"Fuck it all to hell." That would be Blake. Even muffled, his voice was distinct.

Should she knock? Walk away? She definitely shouldn't eavesdrop.

"There's more," Marley said.

And then silence. Awkward curiosity trickled through Luci, until she couldn't sit still anymore. She knocked, but there was no answer. She turned the knob and pushed gently.

Blake and Marley both twisted toward her, tearing their attention from a phone in Marley's hand. Marley turned her gaze to the carpet, and a scowl marred Blake's expression.

"Did I miss something?" Luci asked. What was

meant to be a light-hearted question, came out as a soft, cautious squeak.

Marley looked at her, brow furrowed and eyes turned down at the corners. "I'm sorry."

"We should do this somewhere else." Blake stepped around her and rested a hand at Luci's elbow.

Luci stepped away from his touch, hating her body for betraying her by reacting to the gentle warmth. "Where?"

"The den."

She followed him down the hall to a room at the back of the house. Unlike the sitting room, which felt sterile and ancient, this entire place radiated Blake's presence. A single recliner sat near the doorway, remotes on the table next to it, and a large screen TV covered most of the far wall. "Have a seat," he said.

She crossed her arms and leaned against the wall. "I'm fine here." If she didn't feel the cold, she was afraid the heat from her dream might consume her. That, and despite her brain's attempts to sabotage her, she wasn't forgetting why she needed to keep her distance from Blake. Secrets. She wouldn't live with secrets.

"Suit yourself." The strain in his voice defied the casual words. He grabbed a remote, and seconds later the TV flickered on. Channels surfed past, until he landed on a news station. The video to the side of the anchorman showed her apartment building, burning bright and spewing smoke into the night sky.

Acid surged in her throat, as the man on TV rambled on about what little they knew. She hugged herself tighter, and her legs wobbled before she gave up trying to support herself and sank to the ground.

"Luci?" Blake's concern barely nudged the edges of her clouded nausea.

"Why is this happening?" She heard her own

voice, though she didn't remember saying the words.

Blake crouched in front of her, his face distinct despite the disorientation jumbling her thoughts. His expression conveyed concern, and his tone was sympathetic. "I think a better question is, who are you?"

Chapter Nine

"I'm nobody." Luci's voice barely reached her own ears. She didn't mean it in a self-effacing way. She honestly didn't understand why any of these people— creatures?—were interested in her at all. "I'm just a computer programmer, who needs work." In the background, the newscaster droned on about how the blast had been localized but the fire spread quickly. Some tenants were successfully evacuated, but they didn't have a death count yet.

Death count. People had lost their lives because of her? She was going to be sick. She swallowed back the bile and tried to breathe deeply. It didn't work. Her pulse hammered in her chest. What if she'd been there still? At least she wouldn't have to deal with this guilt. What if they—whoever they were—came after her here or wherever she went next? Was this the rest of her life? She gasped, unable to get enough oxygen. She didn't know what to do.

"Luci, stop." Blake's firm words shattered her welling panic. He rested a hand on her arm. "This isn't your fault."

"Bullshit, it's not," she said. He didn't know

what he was talking about. He was one of them, and when someone had immortality, how could they care for a human life? The thought added more guilt to the pile growing inside her. That wasn't fair, and thinking it didn't help her feel any better, but she wanted it to.

Marley knelt next to her and draped an arm around her shoulders. "Hey. What can I do?"

"Bring them back. Make that not happen." Luci nodded at the TV. "You're a god, right? Give those people their lives back."

"I'm sorry, that's not something I can do. I'm one now. I wasn't a year ago." The gentleness in Marley's tone overlapped the concern on Blake's face, as he watched, silent. "So I know what you're going through."

She had no idea what Luci was going through, unless she'd watched random people die because of her. Luci swallowed the bitter retort. Reason was slinking past the grief, and pointing this out wasn't going to accomplish anything. "Then no. There's nothing you can do."

"If you're sure…"

Blake stood and offered Marley a hand up. "Thanks for the information. I've got the rest handled."

Marley stepped from the room but returned seconds later. She handed Luci a piece of paper with a phone number on it. "If you need someone to talk to, who understands what it's like to be mortal"—Marley cast a glare at Blake—"call me. Wake me up. I don't care when it is."

"Thank you." Luci forced a smile onto her lips.

*

Blake didn't like Marley's implication he was incapable of understanding, but he knew why she'd

544

thought it. He let her see herself to the door, knowing she wouldn't be offended. His priority right now was Luci. Except, as with so many times in the last twenty-four hours, he wasn't sure what to say. Luci's grief combined with Marley's revelation—the reminder of what he'd discovered almost a century ago.

When he met Grace, things were too similar to this. Too many pieces clicked into place. He'd figured out before Morrigan got to her that she was a reincarnation of Sayuri, just as Elizabeth had been. His knowledge hadn't been enough to save her, though. When he'd lost Grace, the spiral he slid into almost destroyed him. He'd forced himself to lock away the notion of ever seeing her in another body again, mostly so he could move on with eternity.

This couldn't be her, though. Fate wouldn't give him back the woman he loved a fourth time. He'd lost his chance a little more each time he tried to protect her. Even only knowing Luci for a day, he couldn't imagine giving her up, despite the past, or the logic he tried to force on himself.

So he was either looking at destiny again, or his obsession had reached new, insane levels. Not reassuring, either way.

Luci met his gaze, and her laugh sounded forced. "Do I have something on my face?"

Maybe he shouldn't have stared so long. "No." He helped her to her feet. "Just grief." If it was her, how was he supposed to tell her? And what if he told her, and it wasn't true—or worse, she decided she was done with this insanity and left? That might be for the best. At least she could get out before she lost her life again. "Come on." He guided her toward the recliner, sat in the chair, and tugged her to him.

She hesitated for the briefest moment, then slid into his lap and buried her head in his chest. "This doesn't change *anything*." Her words were muffled by his shirt.

"I know." He wrapped his arms around her and held her. Silence settled in, and they sat like that as the minutes ticked toward an hour. Her weight, her warmth—it all felt so right. "You wanted to know about my past. About the women I've loved before."

Her bitter chuckle shook her entire frame, but she didn't pull away. "I'm responsible for an entire apartment building of people being exploded. They don't even have a body count yet. That happened because of me, and you think telling me about your ex-girlfriends is the best way to take this conversation?"

She had a point, but he was running on instinct, and that rarely failed him. "First of all, what happened to your apartment isn't because of you. You couldn't have predicted or prevented it. Someone else made that decision. Don't let the guilt destroy you. And second, they're not ex-girlfriends; they're wives."

Her entire body froze in his arms. "Excuse me?"

If he overthought this, he'd talk himself out of it. Very little coming out of his mouth sounded rational, but he knew it was the right way to go. "I was married to each of them."

"Oh, of course. That makes it all better. Awesome." She sat up and shifted her weight.

He grabbed her wrist before she could leave, loosely enough she could break free if she wanted, but he hoped with enough force to convince her to stay. "I have a past. Everyone does. Pretending it doesn't exist won't make it go away." She might just be proof of that. He didn't want to hope, but couldn't help himself. "Besides, you wanted to know who I am and who I've loved."

She clenched her jaw and started at the floor, but she didn't stand.

"You don't have to listen," he said. "But you should know, even though I remember them, they're in my past." Mostly. Was he stretching the truth too thin? "I'm here now, not there."

She finally met his gaze. Red rimmed her eyes, though she hadn't been crying, and dark circles lingered underneath. "What were their names? It had to hurt, watching them grow old and die. Except you didn't. Did you?"

Was she guessing or...? "All three of them died within weeks of marrying me." He didn't talk about this with anyone. Even giving her the vaguest information unlocked more of himself than he liked to acknowledged. "Sayuri, Elizabeth, and Grace."

"Beth," she whispered. "That's what you called her."

A jolt ran through him. "Yes." He summoned his restraint and pushed down the surging reaction. It could be a lucky guess. "Beth died because of me—they all did—so I know how you feel right now." That was enough sharing. He needed to close the door on those thoughts before they consumed him with guilt and hope.

"How do you deal with it?" she asked.

Not very well. "I change the subject a lot."

She leaned into him, head on his shoulder and fingers splayed over his heart. "In that case, tell me how Marley ascended. You've both said more than once she used to be human."

He could do that. It might give him the segue he needed to tell her his theory about who she was. It might not, but it was a starting point and a distraction. "I told you there are all sorts of poems out there about the future of the world and the gods' place in it. There's one about my brothers and me, as well."

"What does it say?"

"Eli's stanza comes last, since he's the youngest, but it played out first." He recited the lines with little thought. "As you are, for all of time, to taste neither love nor death. When you find the one worth more than life, she'll draw her last mortal breath."

Luci shivered in his arms. "Creepy."

"Not as much as it sounds, apparently. Marley died and then ascended. She's immortal now. One of the first of the new gods."

"You said brothers. How many of you are there?"

"Three." And he really didn't want to talk about the other one. At times it seemed as if saying Loki's name summoned the asshole, and that was the last thing they needed. What were the odds she'd just gloss over it?

She traced lines over his chest, touch so light he barely felt it. "When do I get to meet the third?"

"I'm sure he'll find a way to introduce himself."

Chapter Ten

Luci knew the entire conversation was an excuse to distract her, and she couldn't summon a reason to complain. It was a struggle to push aside how many people had died tonight, even just enough to keep herself sane. Blake's behavior was sweet and comforting and exactly what she needed. He tensed under her when she asked about his other brother. No reason to sour the mood by going down that path. "What about your bit in all of this?"

He trailed his fingers through her hair. "It's a little vague, the way fate tends to be. The world is yours, as you search for your soul. No lover shall bind you to the land. The one you discover, who quiets your might, will bring your journey to an end." His voice had taken on an almost musical tone, laced with melancholy. Each time he spoke, his chest vibrated against her ear and cheek.

"It's pretty." She wasn't sure what else to say.

"I suppose. I've always just seen it as being there."

"It must be disconcerting, though"—she tried to choose her words carefully, as to not derail the calm—

"having your future laid out for you like that, from the moment you're born. Or created or whatever."

He paused his hand's attentions on her hair, and then resumed again. "'Born' is as appropriate as anything. And it's not as if it's my entire life—just one portion of it."

"One of the more important portions." Why had she said that? After her past, she'd convinced herself falling in love was a luxury she could live without. Traces of her dream rushed back. Not just the physical sensations it left, but the love Beth had felt when she saw Henry. A pure and complete adoration that still lingered in Luci's chest.

"Maybe." He shifted beneath her, and wrapped an arm around her waist. "Since you're letting me air my thoughts, I meant what I said earlier."

Her entire day was more emotion than detail. "You'll have to be more specific."

"You're beautiful. Not because I'm trying to trick you or manipulate you, but because you are."

Embarrassment heated her face. "Thanks." An empty pit still lingered. A bottomless gaping hole lined with despair. But having Blake there, regardless of the words exchanged, helped her step around it. She couldn't figure out why someone she barely knew was so comforting, but despite the mess that had been her day, sitting with him like this felt familiar and right.

Neither of them spoke. She wasn't sure what else to say, and he seemed to have run out of confessions. She wanted to spend all night talking to him, but at the same time exhaustion was staking its claim.

"Hey." He nudged her gently. "It's so late it's early. You need more sleep."

"I guess." She stumbled, as he helped her to her feet and stood next to her.

He wrapped an arm around her waist again and guided her toward the stairs. She was conscious enough to walk straight. His grip was too tempting to refuse, though. He stopped in front of the guest room he'd set her up in. "Get some rest."

She intertwined her fingers with his. "Stay, please?" It was a selfish, childish request she didn't want to take back. She wasn't ready to surrender that sense of safety yet.

He hesitated, and for a moment she was afraid he'd tell her no. Instead, he guided her toward the bed. "All right."

Still dressed, she lay on her side, and he took the spot behind her. He drew the blanket over both of them, and then rested a hand on her hip. Even through her clothing, she knew he traced circles over the spot where her birthmark sat. The same one Beth had in her dream.

The thought vied for her attention, but she was too tired to grasp and decipher it. With his chest pressed to her back, their breathing falling into sync, sleep took her quickly.

****

Grace giggled in delight when Blaine swept her off her feet, one arm under her knees and the other at her back. She encircled his neck and pressed her lips to his. Kissing him still felt new. Exciting. She hoped it always would. He stepped into the hotel room, still holding her, and kicked the door shut behind them.

He took a few steps before setting her on the ground, back to him. "Ancestors, you're gorgeous, Grace." He dropped a row of kisses along her neck. Each new touch sent pleasant shivers running through her, and anticipation pooled in her gut.

He dragged down the zipper of her wedding

dress, and the fabric loosened around her torso. Nervous excitement joined her jumble of emotions. She'd wanted to wait until their wedding night to be with him. She knew it had been tough on him, but he'd respected her wishes. Now that it was finally happening—they were married and she was his—a sharp longing ached between her thighs.

"We'll take this slow." He drew her close and rested a hand on her hip. Her skin hummed from the gentle caresses. The soft, teasing touches. He traced her pelvis with his finger, on top of a birthmark she'd always hated. She knew he wouldn't mind when he discovered it. There was no doubt in her mind he loved her as much as she did him.

His breath flowed over her skin, hot and enticing. "I've looked for you for ages. I'm not letting you go again."

Luci's eyes flew open, but the dream didn't leave her. She gasped as it continued to skip forward in her head. That was Blake. Again. And...

Grace lay in the hotel bed, enjoying the breeze on her bare skin. They'd have to return to real life soon, but the honeymoon had been amazing. Blaine stood next to her, gorgeous and naked. Blond, tall, muscular. All hers. He climbed on the mattress and pressed his lips to hers. He sought out her breast and squeezed lightly.

Each new sensation in the dream—memory?— flushed Luci's skin. She struggled to push it away. She saw Blake's guest room, registered the familiar ceiling, and smelled his scent on the sheets, but it overlapped with something else. Visions that were hers but not. She struggled to move. To pull away from the man behind her, though she didn't know why.

A crash shattered the playful mood, as the door exploded from its frame and clattered into the room.

"There you are." A woman stood in the doorway. Her pale blue gaze locked on Grace's, satisfaction and death burning in her irises. "You did a good job hiding her this time."

Morrigan. The name passed through Grace's mind at the same time Blaine said it.

"You remember me." Morrigan's smile radiated destruction.

No. The word repeated over and over in Luci's head. She didn't want this. It needed to go away, whatever this vivid vision was that felt as much a part of her past as waiting in line for coffee yesterday morning. A whimper rose inside, but she couldn't force it out.

There was no way Grace remembered this madwoman. She'd never seen her before. Morrigan raised her hand, thumb and forefinger together, as if to snap. Blaine cleared the short distance between them faster than Grace could blink, and slammed Morrigan into a far wall. He growled. "Never again." A glow radiated out from him, engulfing both bodies.

Morrigan looked over Blake's shoulder, smirked at Grace, and snapped her fingers.

Agony shredded through Grace, as if she were yanked apart in a million different directions. She tried to scream, but her vocal chords didn't work.

"Luci." Blake's concern cut through the foul memory. She focused on him leaning over her, concern painting his face.

Her entire body still screamed in agony, though part of her knew she was fine. She struggled to draw in another breath.

"Love? Are you with me?" He brushed a strand of hair from her face.

She sucked in another desperate gulp of air, more grateful than she should be that it was an option.

Reality displaced the memory and left confusion in its wake. "I was..." She didn't know. What was that?

"It's okay." He helped her sit, shifting so he could support her. "You're here, not somewhere else. It was just a dream."

Except it wasn't. She looked at him and saw the face of a man who had worn four different names. But they were all him. She dropped her hand to her hip. "You knew." Her voice rasped out past dry lips.

He furrowed his brow and studied her. "Knew what?"

That was a good question. If those men were all him, and what she'd dreamed was real, how did she know it as though she'd lived it? And why was she so convinced it wasn't just a waking nightmare? A voice whispered in her head. An insistence she not write this off like she always had in the past. That meant she *was* those women. She always figured it out too late. Just as Morrigan killed her. But that didn't make any sense.

No more sense than the fact she was sitting in a god's guest bedroom, wondering how much he'd kept from her. She wrenched away from him and stood. "You knew who I was."

"No." Even the single word had a waver to it. He held her gaze. "I didn't."

Except he did, because he knew what she was talking about. Rage and betrayal roared inside, carried on the lingering agony of remembering her own death three times over. "You did. And you lied to me about it."

Chapter Eleven

Blake didn't know what Luci had seen, but for several minutes it hadn't been him. He'd awoken to her whimpering and shivering, but couldn't shake her from her glass-eyed gaze. Whatever had been in her head, she knew something now. He could feign innocence and try to draw the details out of her, but he had a pretty good idea what she was talking about. "I didn't know until tonight. And even then, I wasn't certain. It's what Marley came to tell me."

Luci stepped back from the bed, fury and confusion warring for dominance of her features. "It's true, then. I'm the living embodiment of those women you were married to."

How much did she know? He wanted to sit and talk it through with her. Find out what she'd seen. That probably needed to wait. "Maybe. Probably. Apparently. I wasn't sure, even after Marley showed me. I wanted to find out before I said anything to you. You're already dealing with enough discovery."

"Maybe it should be my decision what is and isn't enough. You sat there and prodded me. Feeding me names. Nudging me, to see how I'd respond to stories about your past."

"That's not what I was doing." Or maybe it had been. "I wanted you to know who I was. And if it's true, if you're them, I need to figure out how to stop this from happening again." He kept his voice firm.

"I'm not *them*." She clenched her fists. "I'm me! I refuse to be a walking memory, so you have something to cling to rather than move on with life. So your fucked up associates have another ghost to hunt down. You want to know how to keep me safe? Stay away from me. Maybe they'd have lived to see forty if you'd done that."

"You have the birthmark, don't you?"

She rolled her eyes, jerked up the hem of her shirt, and tugged down the waistband of her jeans. A splotch of a crow glared back at him, distinct against her pale skin. "Really? That's what you care about right now? Do you even like me, or do you just see shadows of your past every time you look at me?"

"That's not a fair statement." Now probably also wasn't the time to argue the logistics of reincarnation with her and point out she was them, even if she had a different face, name, and childhood. "I was attracted to you before I knew. While you were a stranger in a coffee shop, not a mysterious link to the gods."

She didn't want to hear reason. "I'm done with this bullshit." She backed toward the door. "With hiding and whimpering and waiting for you to find a way for me to be safe. Seems to me the safest place I can be is where you're not."

The words burrowed deep, slicing at his core. She had a good point. "I shouldn't have brought you here, but you can't go home. It's not safe."

"I don't have a home, remember?" Hysteria surged into her question. "Some psychopathic bitch who thinks I'm part of an ancient prophecy blew it up."

Right. "I mean you can't just go wandering out into the streets."

"I won't. I'm calling a cab and checking myself into a hotel long enough to figure out where to go next, but with any luck, not long enough for any of them to get hurt because I'm there. I need to be anywhere that's not near you. Someplace *they* can't find me until they realize I'm not a part of this."

Was it really that simple? He hated to think so, but if she wasn't a part of his life, his fate wouldn't impact her. "You're right."

Her shoulders slumped, though fury still spilled from her. "Of course I am."

He nodded toward the door, hating what he was about to say. It was the best way to do this, though. He hadn't known with Sayuri or Elizabeth, but he'd been selfish with Grace, thinking he could hide the truth from her and keep her to himself. Letting Luci leave was the only solution. "I won't look for you. We'll do whatever we can to keep Morrigan away from you. Go live your life."

She worked her jaw up and down, shook her head, and spun away. Seconds later his front door slammed shut, rattling the entire house.

He dropped back onto the bed with a grunt. Every inch of him ached over watching her walk out. From her perspective, he barely knew her, but that wasn't true. He'd already lived three lifetimes for Luci.

This was the best solution, though. The only way to keep it from happening again. He lay there, replaying everything in his head, as the sun crept into the sky and light spread across the room. Empty longing grew inside. Emotions he'd locked away ages ago and never intended to let free again played on an endless loop in his head.

He bolted straight up. Fuck, he shouldn't have

let her leave. Morrigan already went after her once, and that was before Blake had any idea who Luci was. Even if Luci never forgave him, he wasn't going to let this happen again. He'd move heaven and earth to save her. He sprinted to his study and grabbed his phone.

"What's up?" Eli picked up the other end.

"How long to tell me if Luci's used her credit card to check into a local hotel today?"

"Ten minutes, tops. You let her leave?"

"'Let' is a strong word. Call me back when you have an address."

Blake paced. A million solutions jockeyed for his attention, each discarded as quickly as it formed. He needed to get to Luci now.

*

Luci sat at the desk in her hotel room, staring at the wall. Take a flight back to Utah or rent a car? Either way, she would be paying for this unexpected trip for a few months. She'd better find work as soon as she got back. And a new place to live. The deposit on another apartment wouldn't be cheap either.

She used her irritation with Blake to suppress an onslaught of memories that weren't hers, but her resolve grew weaker with each new image that slipped through the cracks. She wanted to hate Blake for lying to her, but she understood his reasons. 'Hey, you might be the fourth reincarnation of my dead wife,' wasn't exactly casual conversation.

Or she was just getting sucked into someone else's life too quickly, and was guilty of the same thing she'd accused him of—seeing his past instead of her present. The longer she thought about it, though, the more she realized it wasn't that simple. Grace, Sayuri, and Elizabeth weren't separate people; they were all her. They knew things about Blake, and now she did too. They'd fallen for him, and she could see why.

A pit echoed inside her and resonated with a painful combination of longing and realization. She'd loved him, more than once. It pinged in her chest and twitched in her fingers and filled her thoughts. And she wanted to find that again. Was it possible? Marley had gained immortality. Maybe all Luci needed to do was stay alive long enough for that to happen. Death obviously wasn't the right course in her case, but survival might be.

She should call Blake. Or maybe she should wait until she was back in Utah. The distance would give them time to know each other.

"Boo," a female voice said in her ear.

Luci jumped to her feet and whirled, heart hammering in her chest. Her pulse increased several more notches when she saw Morrigan standing in front of her, a smirk on her face.

"How'd you shake the bodyguard?" Morrigan asked.

Luci tried to swallow past her fear and couldn't. "I left." She finally managed to speak. If she could convince Morrigan she didn't care about Blake, would the goddess leave her alone?

"Aww..." Morrigan gave her an exaggerated pout. "Lovers' spat?"

"We're not lovers." Luci dredged up more resolve. "We're not anything."

"See, that's where you're wrong. You may have convinced yourself of that, but your heart knows otherwise."

"How do you know?"

Morrigan stepped closer, mouth hovering near Luci's ear. "A goddess can tell." She pulled away again and studied Luci. "The question is, what's it going to take to keep you from coming back again?"

"Not killing me?" Luci needed a weapon. She didn't know if it would do her any good, but trying to figure out what she could grab made her feel better. "Let me life a long, fruitful life away from all of you, and destiny will be done with me forever?"

"No. I don't think that's the answer." Morrigan's smirk grew, until she showed teeth. "Nice try, though. I'm looking for something a little more immediately permanent."

Chapter Twelve

Morrigan never turned her attention completely from Luci, as she wandered the room. "How long do you think it will take Helblindi to get here?" The goddess's voice was sing-songy, set to a rhythm Luci couldn't hear.

"Blake's not coming for me." Even as she said it, Luci realized exactly how true it was. Why did she walk away from what little security she had?

Because this wasn't supposed to happen if she left.

"Oh, Lovely... That's what he calls you, right? Lovely Luci? He's coming." Morrigan picked the remote from the nightstand, turned it over in her hands, then whirled and threw it.

It flew at high-velocity toward Luci's head, and Luci ducked just in time to hear it whistle past her ear. This was worse than being killed instantly. Or maybe it wasn't. This was different from every time in the past—she remembered that. Morrigan had never talked before. Was this how she kept Luci from ever coming back? Maybe Morrigan intended to talk her to death this time.

"He'll always come for you, Lovely." Morrigan picked through the far end of the room, ruffling her fingers over the curtains and glancing out the window. "That's why I need to figure out how to stop you from coming back. You're his obsession. As long as you keep showing up, he'll keep pursuing you. Even the first time, he mourned you for over a century."

The idea warmed Luci more than she wanted it to. "Why do you care?"

"Hmm..." Morrigan tapped her chin. "Because I don't like him. That's strictly personal."

"So you keep killing me?" Luci's fingers brushed something smooth and cold. The phone. Would clocking this madwoman in the head buy Luci even a few seconds? She was willing to find out. She inched her fingers over the device, a few millimeters more every time Morrigan turned away.

"Oh, that. No. I keep killing you *in front of him* because I don't like him. That's why you're still alive right now. But you're in more than one fate, Lovely. You're destined to be my downfall, and the idea anyone is capable of replacing me is a load of horseshit. I'm not going anywhere, but you are until you stay dead."

"It must suck to be you." Luci meant the bold words to be a distracting taunt, but something about them rang deeper. What would it be like to spend an eternity always looking over her shoulder, wondering when her life would end? Maybe she didn't want immortality after all.

"It doesn't." Morrigan wiggled her fingers in the air, and the phone was wrenched from Luci's hand. It slammed into the far wall with a sickening clang and left a dent in the plaster. Pieces of plastic clattered to the ground.

Luci stretched her fingers, panic surging back again. Morrigan had to be wrong. Blake didn't know where she was and wasn't coming for her. That meant she was safe until Morrigan got bored and offed her anyway. Instinct told her that was a very imminent possibility. Luci gripped the back of the chair next to her. Could she use that as a club?

Morrigan's mouth stretched into an exaggerated yawn. "The problem with waiting for someone who can't move quickly is not knowing if he's on his way and just slow or if we're going to be here all afternoon."

"You can leave. I won't mind." Luci tried to keep her tone light, but terror gripped more of her thoughts every minute. She remembered what it was like to be torn apart by Morrigan's magic and wanted very much for it to not happen again. Her heart hammered in her chest, and her stomach turned in on itself.

"Nah." Morrigan perched on the edge of the bed and crossed her legs at the knee. "We'll give him thirty more minutes, and then I'll just obliterate every last inch of you. Or maybe only ten. I have other things to accomplish this year."

Luci tightened her grip on the chair, forced all her strength into her arms, and swung. The furniture shattered before it reached Morrigan. Splinters bigger than Luci's forearm flew at Luci, some slicing her skin, and others slamming into her bones and bruising.

"Or we'll do it now." Morrigan stood, brushed invisible dust from her clothing, and stalked toward Luci.

Shit. Panic, fear, and the distinct desire to live at least a few more years spilled through Luci. She threw a wild punch, and Morrigan knocked her hand aside. Luci stepped back, but the desk was in the way. What was she supposed to do now?

"I never figured out what he likes about you." Morrigan's sing-song voice returned. She drew a line in

563

the air, following the curve of Luci's neck. Though Morrigan never made contact, Luci felt the skin slice and warm blood trickle down. "You've always been odd." Morrigan continued a downward path, and a tear split Luci's shirt above her right breast. This time she saw the ugly red gash appear. "You're fat. You're boring. You're whiny." She dragged her nail past the waistband of Luci's jeans and over her hip.

Luci couldn't hold back her scream, as the cut sliced through denim and her birthmark. Her legs threatened to give out from the pain.

"And you're not suited to wear my mark," Morrigan said, "let alone take my place."

*

Blake heard Luci scream halfway down the hall, and his sprint turned into a flat run. He slammed through the hotel door in time to see her drop to her knees, red splattered around her.

Morrigan spun with a smirk. "You took yo—" Her taunt ended in a gurgle when Blake pinned her to wall by the throat. He summoned his power from within and forced it out. His gift was unique among gods. No one else but Marley had the ability to stop another immortal from accessing their power, and unlike in the past, he had enough warning and experience to keep Morrigan incapacitated. As long as he held her in place, she couldn't do anything.

The problem was, neither could he. She wasn't mortal like this, just powerless.

"You're here." Morrigan's voice held too much glee.

Blake wanted to check on Luci. To see if she was all right and to figure out how to stop the bleeding. But if he let his attention shift for even a moment, he and Luci were both fucked.

"Stalemate," Morrigan said, her tone taunting. "What are you going to do now?"

Chapter Thirteen

Blake lifted Morrigan off the ground by the throat, hoping to find enough leverage to cut off her air and stop her babbling. She didn't need oxygen to survive, but she did need it to talk. He couldn't squeeze her windpipe tighter, though. Her energy pushed against his. Mentally, he shoved back. He was vaguely aware of Luci climbing to her feet, but he didn't dare give her more than the barest recognition.

He summoned more from within, pushing harder against Morrigan. This wouldn't happen again. He wouldn't let it. Out of the corner of his eye, he saw Luci stumble toward the bed.

A surge slammed into him and threw him back from Morrigan. The goddess dropped softly to her toes, grin sliding back onto her face. The expression vanished when Luci brought a framed print down on her head. Glass shattered, dropping in shards around Morrigan. She snarled, whirled toward Luci, and flung her into a far wall. Luci landed with a loud slap. A crack rent the air, and she screamed as her arm snapped to an unnatural angle. The cuts on Morrigan's scalp were already healing.

Blake reached inside and grabbed everything he had. He pushed it all toward Morrigan in a single burst, building a bubble of helplessness around her. He dragged up the last bits of what he had and then scraped further for more. He poured every bit of power he'd ever known into keeping Morrigan from accessing her own.

Her smugness vanished, and she dropped to her knees. The cuts in her head re-opened, and blood flowed freely. Still he pushed harder. He wouldn't let Luci die. He refused to. Pain seared his veins, burning through his muscles, ravaging his joints, and he forced out more energy.

The edges of his vision blurred and then grew black. Spots danced in front of his eyes. He was vaguely aware of someone screaming. His name maybe. He wasn't sure. Morrigan collapsed on the floor, and the persistent glow of her aura vanished.

Blake's world went dark.

*

Luci cradled her arm to her side and bit the inside of her cheek to keep from screaming. Blake and Morrigan both lay on the floor, unmoving. The cuts on Morrigan's scalp had reopened, and blood matted her hair. They needed to leave before the goddess woke up, but Luci had trouble standing. There was no way she could drag Blake out of there. She pulled herself onto the bed, doing her best to avoid broken glass and wood, grabbed her phone, and dialed Marley's number.

"Hello?" a tentative voice answered.

"We need help." At least talking didn't hurt. She gave a brief rundown of what had happened.

"Shit. We'll be right there," Marley said.

Luci slumped back against the wall, exhaustion

flowing through her. Every movement hurt, and she didn't dare take her eyes off the bodies on the floor. It felt like an eternity before her doorknob rattled, but was only a few minutes according to her phone. Seconds later, a jolt bounced off her eardrums and the door swung open. When Marley and Eli rushed into the room, Luci let out a breath she didn't know she held, and let the pain muddy the edges of her vision.

The scene around her passed in a blur. Eli was on the phone, barking orders for cleanup and containment. Marley knelt next to Blake and then was by Luci's side. Someone else appeared in the middle of the room and vanished just as quickly, taking Morrigan with them.

"Hey." Marley nudged her leg. "Look at me."

Luci forced herself to focus on the other woman's face. "Is he...?" Dead wasn't the right word. Gods didn't die. Except he'd said they could. That was part of the legends.

"Mortal." The syllables rolled off Marley's tongue, but they didn't make sense.

Blake groaned, and Eli helped him sit.

"I... What?" Luci stared at Marley, looking for some indication this was a joke.

"Let me see your arm." Eli rested his palm on her shoulder.

A frantic dance of sparks raced through the limb, until she thought her head might burst in a tower of sparks. The pain amplified and then vanished. She gasped at the contrasting sensations.

Blake rubbed his face and wobbled to his feet.

"Better?" Eli asked.

Luci nodded. She wanted to ask what he'd done, but she needed to know something else first. She looked at Marley. "Go back to what you said."

Blake joined them on the bed, despite how

crowded it had grown, and flopped onto his back next to Luci. "She said mortal."

"Take it from someone who knows," Marley said. "Never think you can guess what the legends actually mean, until they play out."

Luci wasn't sure if she wanted to laugh or cry.

"Hey." Blake reached up and laced his fingers through hers. A smile played on his face, instead of the negativity Luci expected. His voice was calm, and soothing, despite the fact he sounded exhausted. "It's all okay. I'm all right, and so are you."

****

Hot water sluiced over Luci's head and down her back. She leaned forward in the shower and pressed her forehead to the cool tile. She couldn't help but smile. She'd only been here at Blake's for a week, and especially if she ignored the insanity that had been their first twenty-four hours together, it had been an incredible week. She was still adjusting to the memories of three other lifetimes, but she knew now they were all hers. Not overlapping time lines or conflicting ideas, but experiences she'd lived in another time and place.

The shower door slid open, and the cool air chased steam around her before vanishing again. Blake rested his hands on her hips, pressed his chest into her bare back, and traced his lips up her neck. "Good morning, *Elskede.*"

The word filled her. He'd told her it meant beloved. Despite the jumble of past lives, it was hers and hers alone. She leaned against him. "I'm pretty sure you already showered."

His hard length pressed into her ass. He traced along the scar on her hip. Eli had been able to heal the slash through her birthmark, but not hide the wound. She didn't mind. It felt right that the symbol was scarred over now. "But I'm feeling dirty again," Blake said.

"I know a solution for that." She plucked the shower gel from the shelf in front of her and handed it over her shoulder. After the incident with Morrigan, they'd determined Blake had exhausted his power and completely neutralized the goddess's, leaving them both mortal. They'd stuck Morrigan with local police, amid protests that she was a goddess and threats that she'd make everyone pay.

Luci heard a squirt, and seconds later, something cold hit her stomach. She squealed at the sudden jolt.

"Sorry." Blake sounded anything but. His touch warmed quickly, as he soaped his palms up her torso. Her giggles faded into a moan when he brushed the underside of her breasts. His tight grip, combined with the slick surface, sent shudders of pleasure through her.

She squirmed under his touch. "Do you really want to do this in here?"

"Here. The bedroom. Anywhere I can have you." He dipped a hand between her legs. His touch was light at first, caressing her outer lips and teasing the wetness from her.

She ground against his erection. "Anywhere?"

"Pressed against the glass, moaning in pleasure. Bent over the dining room table." He parted her folds and sought out her clit. "Anywhere."

Water cascaded over them. The soap rinsed and pooled at their feet before vanishing down the drain.

He rubbed her aching button. "I have a lot of catching up to do."

Anticipation built inside as he stroked. Her senses soared. Her gasps became short pants for breath.

He dug his teeth into her shoulder, and she sucked in sharply through her teeth. He eased off and then pressed harder. Her head threatened to float away, as blood rushed downward, toward her swollen bud. The sharp scents of citrus soap and Blake filled her nostrils. Luci swam through all of it—the heat of the water, his skilled touch, the sound of his grunts. It all crashed over her when she came, carrying her on a wave and drawing her through ecstasy.

She pushed against his hand, until she couldn't take anymore and shuddered away.

"See?" His deep voice drilled into her thoughts, and he nipped at her earlobe. "Now, we take this into the other room."

Chapter Fourteen

Luci reached for a towel, and Blake grabbed her wrist to stop her.

She struggled halfheartedly. "We'll get water everywhere."

"Oh, no." He traced his nose up the side of her neck. "Then everywhere might have to dry out. Besides, I'm impatient." He steered her away from the shower and toward the bedroom. He'd be the first to sing the praises of mortality. It had been centuries since the world around him was so intensely vivid, and part of it was seeing things through Luci's eyes. Everything felt and tasted and smelled more distinct now, as if a filter had been removed from his senses.

She hesitated at the foot of the bed, and he propelled her forward, urging her to lie on her back. He crawled toward her, visually drinking in every curve and nuance of her body as he moved. "They're sheets. Water won't kill them." He kissed her navel and followed a path up her chest, until he claimed her mouth. She tasted like toothpaste and smelled of oranges and felt like satin sliding against him.

His fingers slid easily between her folds, and

she groaned. The teasing in the shower had been fun, but his cock ached for attention. Especially after the way she'd ground her generous ass against him. He'd been tempted to bend her over then and there, and thrust inside her.

He wanted to see the expression on her face when she came. Another thing he didn't think he'd ever get tired of. He rolled onto his back and tugged her on top of him.

She smirked and hovered inches from his dick. The heat of her pussy taunted him, warm and tempting and just out of reach. "If you can tease me, I can tease you." Her velvet voice tickled his senses.

She reached between her legs and grabbed his shaft. A guttural groan tore from his chest. Her damp opening met the swollen purple head, and he thrust up with a grunt. "Ancestors, you're tight."

She rose up almost to the tip, then dropped down against him again. The slow build-up raised the friction between them. He wanted to memorize every touch. Every whimper that drifted from her throat. He gripped her thighs, digging in his fingers, and increased the speed. When she closed her eyes and leaned back, driving him deeper inside, he knew he'd hit the right spot.

"Fuck, *Elskede.*" He liked the way the endearment rolled off his tongue almost as much as he liked the way she squirmed when he licked her to orgasm. He drove one hand up her chest, pinched a nipple, and rolled it between his fingers. She gasped and pushed harder against him.

His balls tightened at the feeling of her squeezing him, but he wasn't ready to come yet. He wanted to draw this out as long as possible. See the flush flood her body. Watch the tiny circles her full mouth formed as she drew close to climax.

He dug his fingers into her thigh, as their pace grew more frantic. Her lips parted, gasps blurring together. He found her clit, swollen and peeking from its hood, and drew tight circles around it.

She leaned back with a cry, and she raked his legs with her nails. Her gorgeous, full chest heaved when she came. Her pussy clenched around him, milking him. Breaking down his resistance. Ancestors, she was incredible. He couldn't hold back any longer. He spilled inside her, hot and frantic, thrusting until he was spent.

They both struggled to catch their breath, as they slowed to a stop. She shuddered, smile never leaving her face, when he pulled out of her. He tugged her forward, so her head rested on his chest, and trailed his fingers up her spine.

"Are you going to miss eternity?" Her question was muffled by his chest.

He'd wondered when she was going to ask about that. So far, she'd danced around the issue, inquiring in the vaguest terms if he was all right but never mentioning it directly. As if she was terrified he might change his mind. "No. Even if I had a choice. If someone came to me right now and told me I could have godhood back, I'd tell them no."

"Are you sure?"

"The only other thing I've ever been as certain of is how much I love you." He lifted her head so he could look her in the eye. "And if I can have you by my side for the rest of my life—no matter how short or long it is—that's all I care about."

She dropped her head back onto his chest, but not before he caught a glimpse of her smile. "I love you too." Her words were distinct this time.

From here on out, he was happy to help his kin with their fate however he could, but he was never going back to that life. This was his fate, and he couldn't have asked for a better one.

The End

A Very Wolfie Christmas, A Snowdania

Wolves Novella, by Sofia Grey

A Companion Story to A Handful of Wolf (Snowdonia Wolves 2)

It's their first Christmas together, and Sasha wants to make it memorable for his Mate, Megan. However, it looks as though she has some surprises for him too.

Sasha's homesick for the snow of the Welsh mountains, but the New Zealand sun and Santas in board shorts are worth it, if he gets to spend the holiday with his Mate, Megan. Besides, he's got a surprise planned for their first Christmas together.

When he discovers he's not the only one keeping secrets, his plans threaten to crumble. Can he make this a holiday they'll never forget, for all the right reasons?

Chapter One

It just wasn't right. Sasha stared at the brass band from behind his sunglasses, and wondered for possibly the millionth time if he'd ever get used to this. The musicians played on, barely drawing breath as they segued from *Silent Night* to *Oh Little Town of Bethlehem.*

Shoppers surged past him, some dropping coins into the collecting buckets, others just dodging around the musicians. Nobody paid him any attention. Standing there in his T-shirt, denim shorts reaching past his knees, and flip flops on his feet, he blended easily with the crowd, especially since he also carried a number of brightly coloured shopping bags. Christmas presents. Even if it didn't feel like Christmas.

It was the twenty-fourth of December, and yet the sun blazed down, and the temperature nudged twenty-seven degrees. He should be wrapped up in a quilted jacket, ankle deep in snow, not sweltering in the middle of summer.

With a sigh, he turned and set off toward the bookshop. One more thing to buy, and then he could call it a day and go home. Well, his current home, not his real one.

He loved Megan and couldn't begin to imagine a life without her, but he missed Snowdonia. The dull ache of homesickness surged, and for a moment he felt lost. If he could do anything at all right now, he'd grab Megan by the hand and take her back to the Welsh mountains he came from. He'd shift into his wolf form and run, bounding through the snow to circle back to his Mate. He imagined her throwing snowballs, while he chased after them, playful as a pup.

Maybe one day. He'd agreed to live here in New Zealand for another year, possibly two, and he didn't break his promises. Not only did it make Megan happy to stay close to her family, but Sasha had taken on an important role with the resident wolf pack, and his pride demanded he see it through.

Thinking of Megan, he dug a hand into his pocket, and touched the little box that sat there. Would she like it, or would she think it too soon for such a commitment? Not for the first time, he wished he'd paid better attention to his cousin Jake's courtship of a non-shifter.

He paused again, bemused by a sparkling window display. A row of Santas wearing board shorts and sunglasses? Shaking his head, he moved on.

****

Sasha hauled the shopping bags up the steps to his front door, and let himself into the house. The first thing he saw was the Christmas tree, and he felt another wave of homesickness. He knew it made sense to have an artificial tree in this heat—after all, a real tree would be dead in a few days, to say nothing of the insects that would infest it—but it was just something else that was wrong.

A Very Wolfie Christmas by Sofia Grey

Back home, his parents always squeezed a monster fir tree into their lounge, its top scraping the ceiling. That was how Christmas trees were supposed to be, every branch creaking under the weight of baubles and lights and ornaments. And chocolate coins wrapped in gold foil. Man, he loved those, but they were impossible here. They'd melt within hours.

He stashed his parcels underneath the small neat tree, and thought about Megan. Would she like his presents? This was their first Christmas together, and he had no idea what she expected. What her traditions were like. Back home, they'd swap one present each at midnight on Christmas Eve, then open the rest after a fun and relaxed breakfast the next morning. Sasha always shared breakfast making with his twin sister, Tammy, to give their mum a break.

Dinner would be a giant roast with a mountain of vegetables, and his mum's special homemade gravy. A dense, fragrant Christmas pudding would follow, and then after they'd cleared away all the dishes, they'd go and run in the snow. He'd missed the traditions last year, while exploring New Zealand, but he'd fully expected to be home by now.

He'd never imagined finding his Mate. Was there any chance of spending Christmas Day alone with Megan? Their first together,

When in Rome, he reminded himself. They'd have to visit her family, and he'd behave, play nicely with her over-protective brothers, and be polite to her father and stepmother. Although the barriers were slowly dropping, they were all still wary of him, and he hoped he didn't have to spend too much time with them.

What the hell was wrong with him? He never used to be like this. Mopey and introspective. He had a Mate now, the woman he loved more than life itself, and he would do anything to make her happy. Even be friendly to her brothers.

He heard a car engine outside, and then doors banging, and he hurried to the window. Megan was home. His mood soared. He trotted down the steps, met her on the street, and swept her off her feet with his embrace.

"Cariad." He nuzzled her throat, and just like that, his wolf settled. With his Mate in his arms, her caramel-spice scent swirling around him, he couldn't fail to be happy.

"Hey, babe." She squeezed him back. "Give me a hand with the shopping?"

"Always." He dropped a tender kiss on her lips, and then turned his attention to her bags. There weren't many, only two garish plastic bags of groceries and one from the city's premier department store. "Is this everything?" She'd told him she was picking up the groceries on her way home, and for a normal week, there'd be six or seven bags. For a holiday period, when they'd both be at home—and hoped to entertain friends—this didn't look right.

Megan grabbed the glossy paper bag, and he dutifully picked up the food, after a quick peek at the contents. Milk, eggs and bacon. A loaf of bread. Some apples. A bottle of maple syrup. He was carrying the makings of a good brunch, but not much else.

His heart sank. This could mean only one thing. They weren't spending much of Christmas at home.

With the groceries dumped on the kitchen table, and his hands now free, Sasha took the opportunity to hold his Mate. Her thick, dark hair was soft beneath his fingers, and her luscious curves were enough to make his mouth water. "Why don't we start celebrating early?" he murmured in her ear. "You can get out of your work clothes, and into something more comfortable. Or stay naked—that works for me." His wolf yipped in agreement, and Megan giggled.

"Tempting, but we don't have time right now." She wrapped her arms around his neck, her breasts pressing against his chest, and it took every ounce of his self-restraint to hold back from peeling her right out of her work suit.

He had to make do with sliding his hands up the back of her skirt, and palming her delectable ass. If he were a poet, he'd write sonnets about her ass. He hadn't stroked her skin since this morning, and he could think of little else. Wait. What did she say? "We don't have time, because…?" he asked.

Megan sighed. "We're due at my dad's. Don't tell me you forgot the plan."

Sasha racked his brains to remember what the plan had been, and came up empty. He'd told Megan that he was happy to go along with whatever she liked. He'd hoped it meant spending most of the holiday in each other's arms. Maybe not. "Wanna tell me what we're doing?" He tried to sound enthusiastic.

"Well"—she blew out a breath, and his heart plummeted even further—"there's a barbecue this evening, and Dad wants me there early. There's some crisis or other."

Okay. He could manage that. Megan's father was a high-ranking politician, and always on the move, fixing a multitude of problems, while shaking hands and smiling for the media. It meant Megan and her brothers came under the spotlight more than Sasha was comfortable with, but he was learning to deal with it.

"Sure. You got time to shower first? I think you might need some help scrubbing your back."

"Sasha." Her voice was firm, but her curving lips showed her amusement. "Do you only think about sex?"

A Very Wolfie Christmas by Sofia Grey

"Hey, who mentioned sex? I was just offering to scrub your back." He ran his fingers up her spine, and enjoyed the way she trembled. "If you can't keep your hands off me while we're there, it's not my fault."

"Really, babe, we don't have time. I had to stay late at work, and then the supermarket was packed, and the traffic was horrendous. We're already late."

Sasha's wolf whined inside him, but he pasted on a smile. "Come on, then. The sooner we go, the sooner we're back."

Megan's gaze skittered away to the window and the brilliant sunshine outside.

Uh oh.

"Do you mind if we stay overnight? Come back Boxing Day?" she asked.

He was on the verge of pointing out that was two nights, but the anxious furrow in her brow made him pause. This had to be important to her. His last daydream of a quiet and secluded Christmas evaporated.

Chapter Two

Sasha had never seen so many cars at Megan's home. The gravelled forecourt held at least a dozen, with more abandoned along the driveway. "Wow. How many people have been invited?"

She glanced at him, the anxious lines creasing her forehead again. "This is normal for Christmas Eve drinks. It'll be fun, Sasha."

She didn't sound convinced, and doubt settled in the pit of his stomach. His wolf whined some more, and scratched at him. His animal didn't want to be here either. Feeling like a lamb led to slaughter, he followed her into the house, their hands tightly linked.

Megan had changed into a tantalisingly short denim skirt that showed miles of golden leg, and Sasha cheered himself up by imagining what he'd do later. It involved kissing from her ankles to her thighs, and then—when she asked him nicely—devouring her pussy and making her come. Repeatedly.

Lost in thought, he glanced up to see her older brothers, Alex and Hugh. Or Hellspawn, as he still thought of them. They greeted Megan with enthusiasm, and then nodded politely to Sasha. No baiting comments this evening. Odd. Maybe they called a truce for the holiday season.

It wasn't that he disliked her siblings. On the contrary, he respected the hell out of them for being so protective of Megan, but at the same time, they could be giant pains in the ass.

"Hey, Sasha." Alex stood from his perch on a chiller box. "Want a cold one?"

"Sure. Thanks." Sasha accepted the beer, popped the top, and took a swig. Yeah, had to be a temporary ceasefire.

Megan slid her arm around his waist, and then snagged a glass of wine from a passing waitress. "I need to go mingle for a little while. Will you be okay here?"

"We'll be fine," said Alex, an innocent smile on his face. "Dad was looking for you, anyway."

"I won't be long." She gave Sasha a swift peck on the lips, and then hurried away. Mesmerised, he watched her swaying hips, as she crossed the vast expanse of wooden deck toward her father.

"She's amazing with his constituents." Alex gestured at Megan with his beer bottle, and Sasha noted the care with which the other man spoke. As though he was slightly drunk already. Alex and Hugh had spent several evenings trying to drink Sasha under the table, and failed miserably every time. It wasn't a fair contest, but he'd never admit to that. His shifter metabolism was better at processing alcohol. That was all.

"We're planning a night out," announced Hugh. "Meggie thinks we should drink more. Uh, *do* more. As a group, y'know. So we're going clubbing. Next weekend."

Sasha was only half listening, his focus on Megan, who shook hands with a well-dressed elderly couple. The Hellspawn were right. She could charm the birds from the trees, and that was just one of the things he loved about her. He had to make more of an effort to fit into her life. Stop moping over the Welsh mountains he missed so badly, and turn himself into the guy she needed by her side. The guy her father would be proud to have as a future son-in-law.

"Mighty Mike's. Yeah"

Sasha snapped his attention back to Hugh. "Mighty Mike's?" It was a shifter club in the city, and not somewhere he'd ever expect Megan's brothers to go.

"Oops." Hugh's expression was comical, and Alex jabbed his brother in the ribs.

"Dickwad," he hissed. "You weren't supposed to tell him."

"What's going on?" Sasha asked.

"Nothing." The Hellspawn spoke together, but Sasha didn't believe them for a second. He took a sip of his beer, and stared at them. He knew he'd get nowhere, if he pushed them. He'd have to be smart. "You...uh...into rock music?"

"That's *it*." Hugh sat up straighter in his garden chair. "Your mate's playing, and he invited us."

Sasha's bonded Mate was Megan, but her brothers had zero idea of his shifter nature, and that was how it'd stay. "My mate?" The penny dropped. "You mean Dion? And his band?"

"Yes." Hugh was an enthusiastic as a drowning man clutching at a thin straw.

Sasha was about to call bullshit, when a familiar caramel-spice fragrance tickled his nose, and he turned to see Megan returning.

"Sorry, babe." She caught his hand, and squeezed his fingers. "Dad wants me to stay with him, while he talks to his voters. I could be a while."

Sasha made a lightning-quick decision. He

could lurk on the fringes of the party, or he could step up to his new life, and take his place by his Mate's side. "Why don't I come with you?"

Her eyebrows shot into the tumble of hair that fell over her forehead. "Shaking hands and making small talk with businessmen? Even Hugh and Alex balk at that." At her words, her brothers grinned and held up their drinks.

She didn't think he was up to it? Sasha loved a challenge.

He smiled at her, loving the flustered look in her eyes. "Lead on, *Cariad*."

*

Sasha lost count of the number of people he greeted, the middle-aged women he flashed cheeky smiles at, and the amount of times he repeated the same stock phrases:

I'm Megan's boyfriend. I'm a civil engineer.

Yes, I'm from Wales. Have you been there?

No, Sasha is a Russian name. My grandmother was from Siberia.

With every passing minute, Megan's smile grew warmer, and the cramps in his hand were almost worth it. When things wound down, her father turned to Sasha and clapped him on the shoulder. For the first time in the ten months he was dating Megan, he saw approval in the older man's eyes.

"Good job, Sasha, I think they liked you. If you ever consider a career in politics, let me know." George de Salis bent to whisper in his daughter's ear. "Take your boy, and go enjoy yourselves now. I'll let you know when it's ready."

Sasha pretended not to listen, but his superior hearing meant he heard everything. He puzzled briefly over the words. When *what* was ready? Not dinner, as that was a continuously served barbecue selection. Had to be something work related. Now he and Megan were free, he had other priorities, and kissing her was top of his list.

He grabbed her hand, and led her round the back, to the rose garden. The sweet floral perfume filled the air from yards away, and to his delight, they were the only people there.

"Thank you, Sasha. You were awesome."

His wolf rolled over in delight at the love in Megan's eyes. His beast longed for her to run her fingers through his fur, and the man wanted much the same. He framed her face with his hands, and dropped his head to brush his lips across hers. God, she tasted incredible. He needed more.

Digging one hand into her thick hair, he tilted her into the perfect angle to take his kiss, and then turned up the heat. The little hitch in her breath ramped him up more, even before her hands slid around his back and under his T-shirt. Her cool fingers brushed over the hot skin low on his spine, and his cock leapt to attention.

His wolf urged him on. *Take her. Now. Here.* Common sense nagged at him, though. They stood in a very public section of the garden—her father's garden. He and her stepmother could appear at any minute. Anyone could.

"I need to be inside you, *Cariad*." He murmured the words against her throat, and then flicked his tongue over the pulse, enjoying the way it raced at his touch. He thought fleetingly of the gift buried in his pocket. Was this the right time to ask her?

"Not here." Megan giggled. "But we could go back to my room for an hour. If you wanted to."

Sasha lifted his head, and gazed into her warm

eyes. With her cheeks flushed and lips swollen, she looked as close to perfect as he could imagine. With an effort, he dragged his thoughts back to her words. "Only an hour?"

"We still have family stuff to do." Her eyes flickered to the ground and back up again. "Traditional stuff. You know."

She was fibbing, he knew instantly, but judging by the mischievous grin that was fighting to escape her, it was nothing for him to worry about. He stole a kiss as he thought again about the ring burning a hole in his pocket. He wanted her full attention for that. Best to wait.

"Talking of family stuff, your brothers tell me we're going clubbing with them."

"What?" Shock flashed across her expressive face, followed by an annoyed frown. "Did they say anything else?"

Sasha slid his hands down her sides to curl around her hips, and pulled her into his body. "Mighty Mike's."

"The idiots. I'll kill them. I really will. It was *supposed* to be a surprise." Megan looked woebegone. "How much do you know?"

"Dion's playing."

Was it his imagination, or did she look relieved? "Yes, he is."

"When is it?"

"New Year's Eve. It's going to be a private party."

"You've organised a party for me?" He was touched. Spending more time with her brothers wasn't his preferred idea for a night out, but since he was trying to fit into her life, he'd do it. "I know a good way to say thank you." He stroked her bottom, caressing her through the denim skirt. "A *really* good way," he murmured.

"Hmm. Does it involve getting naked?" Megan leaned against him, her amazing breasts rubbing over his chest.

His wolf panted, eager for more. "Let me see." He pretended to think. "It might do, yes."

"One hour."

"*Cariad*, we can do a *lot* in an hour."

Chapter Three

With their hands tangled together, they snuck into the house and managed to avoid everyone, as they hurried to Megan's bedroom. At last the door was closed, and Sasha tugged down the window blinds, to block out the bright evening sunshine and give Megan and him some privacy. They tumbled onto the bed together, in a tangle of limbs and hot kisses. Now he finally had her attention, he wanted to make the most of it.

Her shirt went first. Up and over her head, and dropped on the floor to reveal a lace-edged, coffee-coloured bra.

"Gorgeous," murmured Sasha, pausing to cup his hands around her full breasts. Her nipples firmed beautifully when he brushed them with his thumbs, and he did it again, harder. The way she trembled at his touch threatened to unhinge him.

They'd been together almost a year, but sex with Megan was still the best part of every day. He didn't think he'd ever tire of her. Of *this*. She was so responsive. So completely into him. The scent of her arousal drove his wolf wild, and he needed to taste her.

To hear her moan. To make her come.

The close-fitting denim was hot, but what lay beneath was better. With clumsy fingers, he tried to unzip the skirt and tug it down her legs, only to give up. "Fuck it," he growled, and shoved it up to her hips instead.

Megan's delighted laugh made him smile, and he gave her stomach a playful nip. Remembering his earlier daydream, he took a short breath, and then a longer one, and tried to put the brakes on his libido. His cock was hard enough to hammer nails, but he could wait a few minutes.

On his knees, he moved further down the bed, and caught one smooth, golden ankle in his hand. Her skin was like satin, soft to his lips, and delicious. Her surprised giggle faded, when he trailed a series of kisses up her calf, circled her knee, and then continued up the inside of her creamy thigh.

Reaching his goal, he paused only to blow a breath across her visibly damp lacy panties, before continuing his trek down her other leg.

"Sasha"—Megan dug her fingers into his hair—"you're teasing."

He slowed when he reached her other ankle, and gently tickled the side of her foot. She squeaked and tried to jerk it away, but he held firm and nipped at her heel. "No, *Cariad. That's* teasing." Like all wolves, he loved to play, and who better to play with, than his Mate?

"Sasha." Megan tugged gently at his hair, but he ignored her and continued to kiss a slow trail up her leg. "Babe. There's something I need to tell you."

He paused, her words sinking in. Shit. That didn't sound good. Lifting his head, he gazed at her flushed cheeks. "What's up?"

Her eyes widened. "Nothing. This is—umm—

an early Christmas present." She looked adorably nervous, and the anxious knot in his stomach eased. "Come here. Let me kiss you."

He complied, unable to resist her. He kneeled over, braced his forearms on the pillow to cage her in his embrace, and then leaned down to claim her lips. "Talk to me, *Cariad*," he whispered.

She wrapped her arms around his neck, holding him close, her breath a warm puff against his throat. "Remember we talked ages ago about ditching the condoms?"

He nuzzled her cheek. "Mmm hmm. You were thinking about going on the pill."

"Well I did. I *have*. And we're safe now." *Huh?* "You have to wait four weeks, but I waited six to be sure. So now we can. If you still want to." Megan only ever babbled when she was nervous, and that was rare enough.

Sasha replayed her words in his head. Did that mean... "I can go bareback?"

Her cheeks coloured even more. "Yes."

"Oh." For once, Sasha was at a loss for words. He gazed at Megan awestruck, and must have been quiet too long.

She cleared her throat. "We don't have to...you know, if you've changed your mind. I'm happy either way."

He broke into her awkward words. "Whoa. I'm just"—he hesitated, his voice rough to his ears—"I'm blown away by you. I know we talked about this, but yeah." He gazed down at her, a lump forming in his throat. This was a huge measure of trust on her part. God, how he loved her. Even his wolf sat dumb inside him.

It was as though his mind and body suddenly figured what she was saying. His lust, already inflamed, exploded in a dizzying cascade of heat, desire igniting in his veins. Christ. If he didn't get out of his jeans immediately, the zip would be embedded in his cock forever. So hard now, his dick ached for release, and Sasha felt light-headed.

"I need you." He spoke slowly, carefully, as though he was drunk. The wolf inside him was going crazy, and he gave in to his beast. Slow and teasing was now a thing of the past. "On your knees, baby." His voice came out as a growl.

Megan scrambled into position, and then peeked at him over her shoulder. She gave him the sweetest, most beautiful smile, her entire face lighting up, and little sparkles dancing in her eyes. "Please don't rip my panties, Sasha. I like these ones."

It took immense restraint, but he tugged her panties down far enough to get access, and then pushed two fingers inside her. She moaned, and ground onto his hand. Christ, she was soaked already, the musk of her arousal tying him in knots.

Sasha knew he wouldn't last long when he finally got free from his jeans. He never had a hair trigger on his cock before, but he'd never had sex without a condom, and with Megan especially... Kneeling behind his Mate, he stroked her gorgeous ass, and then pumped some more with his fingers.

His cock begged him to move. The ache in his balls made his teeth hurt, but he'd make sure Megan was satisfied before he went any further.

The moment he slid his fingers over her clit, she tensed and cried out, her orgasm squeezing his fingers. "Sasha. Please." She sucked in a ragged-sounding breath. "I need you, baby."

It was too late to worry about disgracing himself. He knew he'd not last long when he got inside her. Taking care to unzip his jeans, he sighed with relief his cock springing free, and ready for action. He shoved the denim far enough down to be out of the way, and then positioned himself behind Megan, one hand on her hip, the other grasping his cock.

So beautiful. This was the most perfect sight in the world.

His knees trembled with the effort of holding back, so he gave in to his instincts. One surge, and he drove in to the hilt. Little white stars danced before his eyes. Jesus. Everything was magnified. Every nerve ending. Her heat. Slippery.

His brain could only think one word at a time.

Love.

Need.

Mine.

Megan's breath hitched, and she arched her spine, throwing her head back. He was close, probably only seconds away from imminent detonation, and he needed to mark her. His wolf totally in control, Sasha dug his teeth into the delicate skin at the base of her neck.

Her cry as she came again was drowned out by the roaring in his ears at his own climax. His wolf's triumphant howl was one of possession, devotion and everything that was good between Sasha and his Mate.

They collapsed into a trembling heap on Megan's bed, and it felt like hours before Sasha had gathered his wits enough to speak. "*Cariad*, that was"—he groped for the right word. Failed—"in-fuckin'-credible." His heart continued to race. The most amazing rush ever.

Megan twitched beneath him, a muffled giggle coming from the pillows. "I came twice, and I'm still wearing most of my clothes." She craned her neck and flashed him an innocent smile. "Thank you for sparing my panties."

A Very Wolfie Christmas by Sofia Grey

With an effort, Sasha pulled out of Megan, and then rolled to his side, taking her with him. "Any time. Although you do look even better without them."

She snuggled into his embrace, and pressed tiny kisses along his jaw. "I'm all sticky now. And I have cum dribbling down my thigh. This is going to take some getting used to." She didn't sound concerned.

He stole a kiss. "You're telling me. I'm going to try for a full thirty seconds next time. If we practice really hard, I might last for two minutes by the end of the week."

"Uh huh. Just as well we have some time off work." Megan yawned, her eyelids drooping. She wasn't far from going to sleep, and Sasha wondered if *this* was the right time. She'd just given him a present to remember, and maybe he could do the same? He pondered some more. She'd draped her arm over his leg, covering the pocket he needed access to.

Before he could move, Megan lifted her head and gazed at him, bleary-eyed. "I'm starving. Let's get some food, before it all goes."

Never mind food. The moment was gone.

Chapter Four

Megan was inevitably sidetracked when they emerged onto the sprawling deck area again. "Family friends," she muttered, as people approached. "This is going to take a while." Sasha filled up plates with steak, bread, and salads, and went back to rescue her. After just a few bites of dinner, more partygoers wanted her attention, and soon there was a continuous stream of them.

It was only until Boxing Day. Then he'd claim her all to himself.

Megan was keen to introduce him every time, but after a few curious looks his way, the guests chatted with his Mate, leaving him standing by her side. Despite his best efforts, Sasha was bored, and he strolled over to the pool, pretending to watch the partygoers splashing around. In his head, he saw snow covered mountains.

Thoughts of home tugged at his heart. His beloved twin, Tammy. His parents. His friend, cousin, and pack Alpha, Jake and his darling Mate, Lillian. Sasha snickered as he remembered telling Megan that Jake had Mated with the world famous singer everyone knew as Ella Hart, and Megan's disbelief at his story. She'd thought him to be delusional.

He'd wait a few hours, and then he'd call them. He didn't have any news, hadn't told anyone about the ring he'd picked for Megan, but he longed to hear their voices. Christmas was a time for family. The old cliché was true, especially when they were on the other side of the world. And much as he loved his Mate, this wasn't *his* family. Jesus. Could he manage up to two more years here?

"Sasha." Megan slipped her hand in his, and tangled their fingers together. Glancing down at her, he knew if it took ten years before they left, he'd put up with it, to have her by his side. To hell with waiting. He wanted to give her the ring now. No more delays.

"*Cariad*, I just-"

She squeezed his fingers, and pressed a kiss on his lips. Her eyes sparkled, and she fought a smile. "We have to be somewhere."

This time, Sasha stood his ground. "I need a few minutes with you. Alone."

"Same. Come with me." Her smile burst free. "Please, babe. This is important."

As long as he had her full attention.

He followed her hasty steps to the back of the house, to one of the several guest lodges dotted around the property. Her father had built the cosy wooden cottages to give his frequent guests some privacy from his family.

Megan pulled him to the door of the largest unit, and released his hand so she could open the lock. Sasha used the moment to dig into his pocket, and close his fingers around the velvet-covered box.

Now. As soon as they were inside. He had to make sure Megan knew how he felt about her. About *them*. His wolf yipped agreement, and Sasha stepped forward into the hallway of the cottage, focused on one thing only.

It was cool inside, shaded from the brilliant sunshine. Perfect.

"Wait," he said, and caught Megan by the hand again. Ignoring her stifled gasp, he dropped to his knees in front of her, held up the box, and flipped it open to show the ring.

"Megan, *Cariad*, I never asked you properly, so I'm asking you now. I want you to marry me, to be my wife and my Mate, and for us to spend the rest of our lives together." He'd rehearsed the words, but they still felt awkward and rushed. He shivered. Not only cool in here, it was cold, and if *he* felt the cold then Megan had to be freezing.

"I love you, Megan."

"Oh." She stood there, hands pressed to her mouth, and for one heart-stopping moment, he thought he'd made a hideous mistake. "Yes, yes, *yes*, please." She dropped to her knees too, and threw her arms around him. "God, I love you so much. *Yes*."

Their lips met, hungry and needy, and filled with as much love as Sasha could ever wish for. Relief burst out of his chest, making him feel dizzy, and he held her close. "Why is it so cold in here? Is the A/C broken?"

Her delighted laugh was a sound he adored. "No, it's actually working perfectly." She shivered, and he felt goose bumps on her bare arms. "There's something you need to see, babe, but I want to put on this beautiful ring first. Oh, my God, it's so gorgeous. It's perfect. Absolutely perfect."

With care, he slipped the ring free from its satin nest, and holding her hand, eased the slim band onto her finger. It fit like a dream, and he pressed a kiss over her palm. He'd spent ages searching for the right design, and had finally stumbled on this. Tiny obsidian chips and shards of diamond, set in a highly polished silver band. It was unusual—*unique*—and he hoped Megan would love it.

After deliberating all day, he couldn't quite believe he'd finally done it. She'd said yes. He felt humbled by how lucky he was. Some wolves never found their true Mate, never got to experience the depth of love that could be shared between Mates.

Megan shivered again, and Sasha pushed to his feet. "Let's go somewhere warmer."

"No. This is for you." Huh? She scrambled to her feet too, and grabbed the handle for the inside door. "Merry Christmas, Sasha."

An icy blast of air hit Sasha in the face, as soon as they entered the open-plan living area. What the hell? It was also dark, with heavy blinds pulled down over all the windows. His keen night-sight and sharp sense of smell identified a huge pine tree in one corner, and the scent of freshly chopped logs.

A second later, Megan flicked a switch, and a fully decorated Christmas tree burst to life. Laden with flashing lights, baubles, tinsel and—*yes*—little bags of chocolate coins, it looked almost like the festive trees back home. The fresh logs in the fireplace were ready to be lit. It felt like winter in here.

He spun to face Megan, and caught her hands. "You've made it a wintery Christmas? For me?"

She nodded, her eyes sparkling and a huge smile lighting up her face. "I got Dad to reset the A/C down to the absolute minimum, and kept it cold in here all day." She shivered, but then reached to a shelf and picked up a box of matches. "Would you like to light the fire? Get it nice and warm?"

"Well, yes." He laughed in delight, still confused by what she'd done. "Why did you do this?"

A Very Wolfie Christmas by Sofia Grey

"Why?" Megan slid her arms around his neck, and stretched up for a kiss. "Because I know you're homesick. Because I love you. Because I want our first Christmas together to be memorable." Her cheeks pinked. "And did I say, I love you?" Another swift kiss. "Now light the fire, before we both freeze."

For the second time in as many hours, she'd reduced Sasha to dumbness. While he groped for something to say, Megan shrugged with a beautifully feline-like grace. "We have the lodge to ourselves, right up to Boxing Day."

Sasha pulled his wits together. What was he supposed to be doing? Lighting the fire. Yes. He fumbled with the box of matches, dropped most of them onto the tiled hearth, and bit back a curse at his sudden clumsiness. It felt like an age later that the fire burst into life, the room immediately warming.

Megan busied herself in the kitchenette, and then came back with a bottle of champagne and two glasses, which she placed carefully on the coffee table. "You know, I planned for us to drink to our first Christmas together, but now we can celebrate even more." She extended her left hand, her attention focused on the ring, and then looked up to meet his gaze. Her eyes were damp, but her smile was huge. "What did I do to deserve you, babe?"

Funny, Sasha often asked himself the same thing. Megan was the best thing to ever happen to him. "Well"—he pretended to consider her question—"I'm not sure. Maybe you need to come a bit closer. If we sit on the sofa for a while, we might figure it out."

"I feel like Little Red Riding Hood, when you look at me like that, Wolf Boy. Are you going to bite me?"

He snapped his teeth, and then held out his arms. "Only if you're very good…"

Epilogue

New Year's Eve

After four days of chilling out by the sea, in the cottage Megan borrowed from her gran, Sasha and Megan had to head back into the city.

Megan fizzled with nervous energy, and he wondered what she was up to now. They had the not-such-a-surprise party later, but even so. From the way she kept checking her cell phone and replying to texts, he knew there was more going on.

He'd not seen Dion or any of his other friends this week, and looked forward to catching up with them tonight and telling them Megan wore his ring. Yeah. His wolf strutted every time he thought about that. He was one lucky wolf. He'd phoned his parents and Tammy, and then Jake and Lillian. Megan's family had taken it well, and it was probably just his imagination, but the Hellspawn were no longer being such assholes. Alex had asked about his hometown in Wales, and seemed genuinely interested in knowing about it. Weird.

They didn't leave for Mighty Mike's until almost nine, by which time Megan acted as though she'd burst with excitement. Sasha watched the wiggle of her delicious ass, leading him up the stairs to the top floor club. The muffled boom of rock music assaulted his sensitive eardrums, but the enormous bouncer at the door slipped him a pair of foam earplugs, and the noise muted to an enjoyable level.

Sasha got a real buzz from Mighty Mike's, Non-shifters came here too. Some commented on the strange vibe, but many felt uneasy. Not Megan though. He'd figured out she most likely had some shifter blood in her heritage, many generations back. It made sense for his wolf to recognise that, and for her to accept him so well.

They arrived just as the first band was finishing. Lost in thought, he was startled when one familiar face after another greeted them in the club. Dion bounded over to greet him, and they fist-bumped. "Just in time, man. We're on next." Dion bounced on the balls of his feet as his spoke, his attention darting all over the place. "Dude, it's going to be an awesome gig tonight." He clapped Sasha on the shoulder. "Best one yet."

Maybe there was a talent scout in the audience? The prospect of a record deal was the only thing that could make Dion so hyper. Time to do some fishing. "Special guest in the crowd tonight, eh?"

"What?" Dion froze. "Who told you?"

Sasha jerked his chin at the Hellspawn. "Alex. Or it might have been Hugh."

"Holy fuck. Megan is going to seriously kick their asses." Dion shook his head and leaned closer. "Pretend it's a surprise. She's put a fuck-load of effort into this."

"Yeah, of course." Before he could wheedle anything more from his friend, Dion was called away, and went to take his place on the stage.

What was Sasha's Mate up to? He turned to

look for Megan, and found her instinctively in the press of people gathered around the bar. As though recognizing his gaze, she glanced over her shoulder and flashed him a smile. They probably only had a few minutes before Dion's band started up, and this time Sasha meant to get some answers.

He strode toward the bar, only to be sidetracked by a hand on his arm. "Hey, Crasher."

Crasher? Only one person called him that. He spun around to see Tammy, his twin sister. "Tamster?" He'd spoken to her a few days ago. She'd been at home. In Wales. Thousands of miles away.

"Don't I get a hug, bro?" She smiled, and the next moment was hugging him, squeezing him tight. Sasha's heart felt as though it would burst. *This* was what his Mate had been planning.

"When… How did you get here?" It was a dumb question, but Tam didn't laugh. She just ruffled his hair, and kissed his cheek.

"We're all here. Megan worked out the details with Lillian." All here? Sasha could have been beaten around the head with a baseball bat, for all the sense his brain was making. He followed his twin's outstretched hand, and saw his parents, Jake, and Lillian. Damn, if his vision didn't go blurry for just a second. He didn't know what to do first. Greet his family—here, when he thought they were on the other side of the world—or kiss the fuck out of his wonderful, thoughtful, amazingly fuckin' brilliant Mate.

Several things became clear over the next hour. Lillian planned to guest with Dion's band, as well as performing after midnight. No wonder Dion had been so excited. Alex and Hugh were both awestruck at meeting Lillian, and now treated Sasha with something close to reverence. Tam and the others would be staying in Wellington for a week, and so he'd have plenty of time to catch up with them.

And Megan had, without a doubt, made this the most memorable Christmas ever.

The End

About Allyson Lindt

Allyson Lindt is a full-time geek and a fuller-time contemporary romance author. She prefers that her geeky heroes come with the alpha expansion pack and adores a heroine who can hold her own in a boardroom. She loves a sexy happily-ever-after and helping deserving cubicle dwellers find their futures together.

~*~

About Sofia Grey

Romance author Sofia Grey spends her days managing projects in the corporate world and her nights hanging out with wolf shifters and alpha males. She devours pretty much anything in the fiction line, but she prefers her romances to be hot, and her heroes to have hidden depths. When writing, she enjoys peeling back the layers to expose her characters' flaws and always makes them work hard for their happy endings.

~*~

About Sotia Lazu

Sotia's making do with Greek reality, while writing and mostly thinking in English.

She loves romances with a twist and urban fantasy novels, always with vivid erotic elements. Her favorite characters to write are not conventional hero-material at first glance, and she enjoys making them fight for their happiness.

Sotia shares her life and living quarters with her husband, their son, and two rescue dogs, one of which may be part-pony. Sappy movies make her bawl like a baby, and she wishes she could take in all the stray dogs in the world.

Also, she hates mornings!

www.ingramcontent.com/pod-product-compliance
Lightning Source LLC
Chambersburg PA
CBHW052341020726
47503CB00001B/57